WRATH-BEARING
TREE

JAMES ENGE

WRATH-BEARING TREE

A TOURNAMENT OF SHADOWS | BOOK TWO

an imprint of **Prometheus Books**
Amherst, NY

Published 2013 by Pyr®, an imprint of Prometheus Books

Cover illustration © Steve Stone
Map by Rhys Davies
Cover design by Jacqueline Nasso Cooke

Inquiries should be addressed to
Pyr
59 John Glenn Drive
Amherst, New York 14228–2119
VOICE: 716–691–0133
FAX: 716–691–0137
WWW.PYRSF.COM

17 16 15 14 13   5 4 3 2 1

Library of Congress Cataloging-in-Publication Data

Enge, James, 1960-
    Wrath-bearing tree : a Tournament of Shadows, book two / by James Enge.
        pages cm
    ISBN 978-1-61614-781-5 (paperback)
    ISBN 978-1-61614-782-2 (ebook)
    I. Title.

PS3605.N43W73 2013
813'.6—dc23

2013012125

Printed in the United States of America

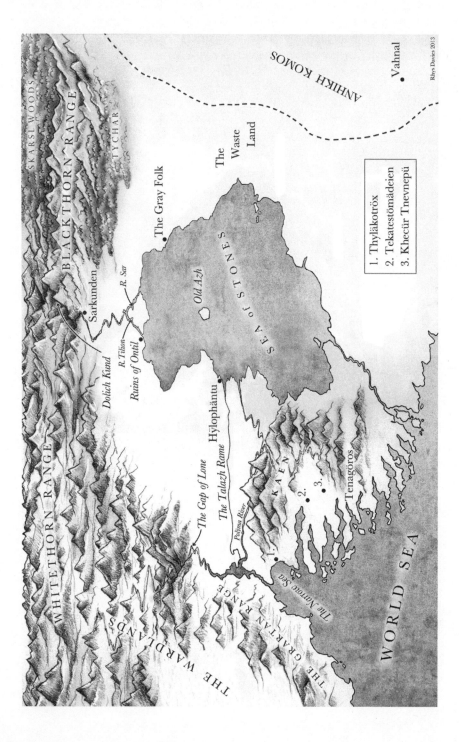

For Diana
"Set me as a seal upon thine heart,
as a seal upon thine arm:
for love *is* as strong as death."

ACKNOWLEDGMENTS

I'm not sure what the canons say about thanking your editor in public, but thanks are surely due Lou Anders for giving me a chance to tell the story that's been trying to gnaw its way out of my head for a generation or so.

I also want to mention three people who will never read these words or this book. My father, Lawrence Pfundstein, died of cancer in October 2012. He was the polar opposite in temperament of the Merlin in this book (and elsewhere in the Morlock novels)—there was never a better father or a better man. Chris Ales was one of my closest friends growing up, though we had drifted apart over the decades. He also died in 2012, of an illness as destructive as cancer. And Andre Levi died of cancer in September 2012. She was my high school sweetheart and taught me a lot of what I needed to know to be a writer and also to be something approximating a human being. Certainly this would be a very different book if we had never met.

The patience and helpfulness of my wife, Diana DePasquale, also deserves some mention. When the plot required me to address matters anatomical and social that were completely out of my range of experience, she was always there to listen and comment as I proposed increasingly bizarre, "What do you think would happen if . . .?" scenarios. This book is hers, and much else besides.

CONTENTS

WRATH-BEARING TREE

History has many cunning passages, contrived corridors
And issues, deceives with whispering ambitions,
Guides us by vanities. Think now
She gives when our attention is distracted
And what she gives, gives with such supple confusions
That the giving famishes the craving. Gives too late
What's not believed in, or if still believed,
In memory only, reconsidered passion. Gives too soon
Into weak hands, what's thought can be dispensed with
Till the refusal propagates a fear. Think
Neither fear nor courage saves us. Unnatural vices
Are fathered by our heroism. Virtues
Are forced upon us by our impudent crimes.
These tears are shaken from the wrath-bearing tree.

—T. S. Eliot, "Gerontion"

PART ONE

DRAMATIS PERSONAE

Act first, this Earth, a stage so gloom'd with woe
You all but sicken at the shifting scenes.
And yet be patient. Our Playwright may show
In some fifth Act what this wild Drama means.
—Tennyson, "The Play"

CHAPTER ONE

The Balancer, Balked

With hands that were not hands the man that was not a man made a machine that was not a machine. All the while he muttered words that were not words with his mouth that was no mouth: "Keep me clean. Keep me clean. Keep me clean."

But he knew it was too late. He was stained with memories, with hopes, with life. He would never be clean again. He said "me" and meant it. He was infected with the idea of self.

There was a way out of this hell that was not hell. If he could cleanse this world of life and make the way clear for the ever-strangers who waited beyond the Soul Bridge, beyond the end of the world, if he could do that he could also be cleansed of life and return to the selfless being he was meant to be, that he should have remained forever.

He made his machine that was not a machine and laughed. He would sweep them all away, everything that lived. He would make them pay for making him care about them, about himself, about everything.

Chapter Two

The Necromancer Leaves Home

Merlin Ambrosius was in his basement workshop when he heard the god breaking into his attic. The event was far away, and the house well-proofed against sounds, but Merlin had no doubt what he was hearing. There is something about the footfall of a god that, once heard, is not easily forgotten.

"I knew I should have gotten around to insulating that attic!" he berated himself. "Now I'm in for it."

His watch-beast remarked, "There is a god in the attic, apparently without permission." A pause and the beast continued, "But have you considered the peace of emptiness that you might receive from union with the Illimitable Cloyn, Arbiter of the Infinite? If I had a soul—"

Merlin reached out with his long clever fingers and snapped both the necks of the watch-beast. The dreamy light in its seven eyes faded. Merlin was disinclined to be evangelized by his own automata, particularly on behalf of a puny god like the Illimitable Cloyn, Arbiter of the Infinite. (It was always the little gods that grasped at those big-sounding names.)

Still, he was in some danger. The puniest god might be deadly to the mightiest mortal, and Merlin did not feel particularly mighty this morning.

Against the lesser gods the best weapon was outright unbelief. Unfortunately, Merlin was old and wise; his cynicism had been battered by centuries of experience. The purer forms of unbelief were increasingly difficult for him.

Fortunately, he had foreseen the risk and armed himself in advance.

He broke open a glass jar near at hand and removed the dried but still living brain of a fervent atheist. He grabbed a pair of boots lying nearby with his left hand and, holding the dusty brain out in front of him like a dagger, he leapt up the basement stairs two at a time. Old he was. Feeble he was not.

Cloyn was already descending from the upper floor, wrapped in a cloud of metaphysical comforts that slid like fog down the spiral staircase.

"Back, you!" Merlin shouted, and brandished the dried brain wildly.

Cloyn retreated semi-visibly. Merlin and his weapon had the god's complete attention: nothing fascinates a god like an atheist. Cloyn raised up a shield of apologetics and a long pointed blade of theology. The god was readying for a battle.

Merlin couldn't risk a prolonged conflict. His atheist had been harvested while still young and uncontaminated by experience, but the brain was very dry and brittle by now. Already he could feel the god pressuring it with golden gifts of emptiness and surrender.

He threw the atheist brain down at the god's feet and it shattered. He could feel the waves of agony emanating from the dying atheist. The god became wholly absorbed in comforting and healing the atheist's death.

It was Merlin's chance. He ran out of the house and sat down on the door-step to pull on his boots. Although he heard the footfall of the god behind him, he took the precious seconds required to tie his bootlaces. He had tripped once wearing seven-league boots and had no desire to repeat the experience.

Cloyn was almost on him when he leapt to his feet and took a single stride.

The dense thickets of the Lost Wood sank below him, dark green in the morning light. He felt the ecstasy of flight and sternly repressed it: the feeling was akin to religion, and he wanted to leave no trail for the god pursuing him.

He landed lightly on his right foot in a mountain meadow, seven thousand paces from his god-violated house. He swung out with his left foot and took to the air again.

He had not many strides left before the boots became exhausted and reverted to their mundane selves. It took a fearful amount of impulse energy to charge them even for a single stride. But he would take a few more at least. The Illimitable Cloyn might not be the only god who was after him.

Merlin Ambrosius meditated as his boots carried him across the long flat curve of the world. Who, among his many enemies, was powerful enough to command gods as hunting dogs? He could not tell, and it was vital for him to know.

The enemy might strike at his children, too. Yes, that was quite likely. He wondered what he might do about that to turn it to his own advantage. His daughters, if he remembered correctly, were not too far distant, on one of their ridiculous rescue missions to the Vale of Vraid.

CHAPTER THREE

Vesper's Prey

You are what you eat, and Vesper had mostly been eating monsters. He had drained a werewolf, south of Wuruyaaria—a little hard to digest, but full of silver-edged shadows, very sustaining. The Kembley's serpent he had consumed in the Ketchpur valley was also very tasty, bristling with venomous shadows. Best of all, among recent meals, was the mandrake he had devoured in the Blackthorn Mountains.

Ah, the mandrake! The mandrake! Never had Vesper known, or even suspected, such joy.

He had been slithering along the ground in the shadowy semblance of the Kembley's serpent. (He had no shape of his own, so it was easiest to assume the form of the entity he had most recently devoured.) Suddenly he stumbled across the tail of a dead dragon. The vast corpse was going to pieces like a fallen tree in a forest, no shred of life left there, nothing for him. But nonetheless his shadow-pulses quickened with excitement.

As Vesper knew, dragons don't reproduce as most animals do; it was rare, at any rate, for a dragon to possess genitalia unwithered by venom and fire. But, once a dragon was dead, its teeth would hatch like eggs and little mandrakes would emerge, to plant themselves in a nearby stretch of favorable soil. Eventually, when they matured, they would uproot themselves and begin walking about, as manlike chrysalides from which dragons would eventually emerge.

How this final transformation occurred, Vesper neither knew nor cared. But, if he was lucky, some of the mandrakes who had been born from this dead dragon might still be somewhere nearby. Vesper scuttled around to the front of the rotting dragon, pausing briefly in the shadow of the ruined, pockmarked jawbones, bereft of teeth.

As it turned out, he was almost too late. Of all the rows of mandrakes who had been there (with his shadowy eyes, Vesper followed a long triple-trail of empty holes), only one was left. And even as Vesper approached, the last mandrake was struggling to uproot itself from the ground. It was fully grown, with toothlike protrusions already prominent on its upper arms, its head and its lashing lizard-like tail.

Vesper moved quickly. Luckily for him, it was evening, and there were many long useful shadows in the mountain valley. (As a shadow-being, he could not safely bear complete darkness or direct sunlight.) When he was near enough, he extended shadow-tendrils toward the mandrake and made contact.

At first the mandrake had no idea what was happening. (They never do, Vesper thought.) When it realized it was being attacked, it started lashing about with its powerful scaly arms, but it was already too late. Vesper had implanted his shadowy tendrils and began to feed. He drained its ability to move its own limbs, and it stood, quiescent, while he continued to feed.

Beings which live and move and take action have two natures: bright essence and dark matter. The light of their unfettered essence would destroy Vesper, and the dark heaviness of their matter was too crude to be useful for Vesper's light airy body. But the essence and matter of material beings mingled in a shadowy substance on which Vesper could feed. It contained memories, and hopes, and fears, and many other things; and once it was gone, the animal was dead—that is, its bright essence was permanently severed from its dark matter. But Vesper was sustained, and that was what counted.

This is how it was with the mandrake. Vesper planted his tendrils and drained it dry of shadows, leaving the monstrous fang-armored body dead, half-buried in the ground.

But the shadows themselves . . . The essence of dragons, it seemed, was dark as well as bright. And the gross matter was luminous with fire, as well as dark with flesh. The torrent of red-hearted shadows was scalding, illuminating, terrifying, satisfying. Vesper was sad when there was no more.

But that was the nature of things. Nothing lasted forever . . . except Vesper himself, of course.

Vesper now assumed the form of the mandrake, and moved swiftly through the shadows of evening. He would go north, he thought: to the Skarsl Woods north of the Blackthorn Range. Complete darkness would slay him even more surely than direct sunlight, but, night and day, there were always shadows in the Skarsl Woods and no lack of interesting prey.

>≈≈

At sunset, Ambrosia Viviana sealed her focus with the rune of the Open Fist. She was planning a long walk through the Skarsl Woods, north of the Blackthorn Range. Only a fool would walk there during the day, because of the daymares and solstroms and other sunlit dangers of that evil wood. Ambrosia was brave enough to get by in a dangerous world, but she wasn't a fool: she would travel by night.

But the night had its own dangers, and Ambrosia thought a focus full of sunlight might come in handy during her journey. She had set the focus on a pinnacle of unshadowed rock to absorb sunlight throughout the day. Now, with the sun red on the horizon behind her, she wrapped the spherelike focus in *vekka*-cloth and stashed it in her wallet by her mirror and writing tablet.

Ambrosia Viviana: with the crooked shoulders and aquiline nose she inherited from her father, Merlin Ambrosius. Her dark red hair and gray eyes were more like her mother. Her build was that of a girl on the verge of womanhood, but her expression was harsh with a wisdom many grew old and died without ever achieving. She had many skills, sorcerous and mundane, that made her dangerous. With these was one weakness; she spoke of it to no one, but she was always aware of it, as it could overcome her at any time, despite all her abilities.

Ambrosia waited until the sun had wholly left the sky, and then imbued her bright gray eyes with the Bitter Glance. This spell would cause her eyes to emit beams of light for the next half-day. The light was dim enough, even in the gray evening air. But it would be handy in the dark places of the wood.

All three moons were up, and if someone else had been there to see, they might have said that the moonlight was playing strange tricks: as if the one woman had two shadows. There was no one there but Ambrosia, though, and she ignored the double shadow from long habit. Plunging into the woods, she began her long walk eastward.

She had not been walking long before she began to feel sleepy. This was very bad. It was the worst of all possible events, as far as Ambrosia was concerned. She had slept all day, preparing for tonight, so she knew it was not the weariness of her body speaking. It was the onset of her weakness, the flaw she could not defend.

She swore briefly and sat down to scribble a note on the writing tablet from her wallet. She had hardly finished when unconsciousness swept over her in a dark tide and her awareness drowned in it.

⊁⊰

Vesper crept north into the Skarsl Woods, flitting (in the veil of the mandrake's form) from shadow to moonlit shadow. There was much animal life around him, but nothing he thought fit to take as his prey. Vesper was becoming rather choosy about what sort of life he would consume. He thought of himself as a dim garland of monsters, and not everything that walked the night was fit to join that shadowy company. Even now he regretted some of the choices he had made earlier in his career, lives he had eaten merely to stay alive.

As he lingered thoughtfully at the margin of a moonlit clearing, he saw something rather strange. It was a pair of dim lights, just bluer than moonlight, passing to the north of him, going from west to east. Intrigued, he pursued it.

At first, as he closed with the moving lights, he was disappointed. It was just a woman, her eyes enchanted to help her see as she travelled the dark woods. She had red hair and a hawklike nose, and the general air of one of those-who-know, the confraternity of sorcerous knowledge. This made her dangerous: one of those few who were likely to understand what Vesper was and how to stop him. There was something else odd about her, though, so Vesper (for lack of anything better to do) followed her for a while, keeping what he hoped was a safe distance.

She began to stumble and waver as she loped along. Perhaps she was drunk, Vesper thought. (He'd never been drunk himself, but he had often eaten the unprotected lives of drunken men and women.) Or she might be sick. Once he had eaten the delirium-laden life of a fevered child; it had been an interesting experience.

Eventually she sat right down in the yttern-track she had been following. She unhitched the wallet swinging from her belt and scrabbled for something in it. As Vesper watched warily, she brought forth a wax tablet and a stylus. She tapped the stylus on the wooden frame of the tablet, and its tip began to glow. She hastily scribbled some words onto the waxy surface; they glowed slightly in the darkness.

Eventually the stylus and the tablet fell from her slack fingers. The light in her eyes died, and she fell over as if she'd been struck with a hammer.

What was happening now? At first it looked as if the woman were melting, like snow in sunlight. Then he saw that a new form was being imposed on the woman. Now she was much taller, her body thicker in some places, thinner in others, her hair paler. And there was another change, something he could just catch with his fugitive shadow senses: a different flavor, a different scent.

The truth hit him then. This woman was a pair of twins, sharing a single body. He knew, better than anyone, that what most call substance is merely the unstable form given by the shadow that is true life. When one sister dominated, her shadow gave form to the body's substance.

He had heard a rumor of a creature like this, in the mind of someone he had eaten. The tale said that the Two Powers who ruled in Tychar would give a great bounty for something so trivial as a vial of this one's blood.

Vesper was charmed. How lucky he had been to find her (or them)! What an addition they would make to the pandemonium of monstrous shadows he was collecting! What a complex and interesting shadow-life there would be, with two spiritual essences competing for the control of one body! He could hardly wait to taste it. And if he could please entities as powerful as the Two Powers with the remains, so much the better.

He would not wait: now, when she was still disoriented from the change, was the best time to strike.

He approached her tentatively through the shadows. These were deep and dark enough to be dangerous to him, so he picked his way carefully among them. His shadow-tendrils were fully extended to grip and feed.

⊰⊱

Hope Nimuelle awoke from infinite darkness to a darkness that was slightly less intense. Blinking, she took in the night-deep shadows, edged with moonlight, the dark shapes of the trees.

Ambrosia! she groaned within. *Where have you dragged me to now?*

There was, of course, no answer. Ambrosia was as thoroughly eclipsed now as Hope had been until a few moments ago.

Hope glanced around. Ambrosia wasn't the best of all possible sisters, but she did try to leave Hope a clue or two as to where she found herself on awakening. (Hope naturally did the same for her, when she could.)

Almost immediately she found the note on the wax tablet, its letters still glowing in the shadows. The note said:

> *Hope,*
>
> *I'm sorry to say that you find yourself about an hour's run into the western edge of the Skarsl Woods. I've been travelling to the Vale of Vraid in the center of the woods, if you know where that is. You should be able to reach it by morning, if you hurry. If you are in any doubt, head back to the western edge of the forest. In any case, get out of the forest by dawn.*
>
> *I have filled a focus with sunlight and stashed it in the wallet. Make use of it as you see fit. The focus is sealed with the rune of the Open Fist.*
>
> *Your sister,*
>
> *Ambrosia Viviana*
>
> *P.S.*
>
> *Situations like this might be avoided if you would show up at regular intervals!*
>
> *A. V.*

Hope was genuinely dismayed. The Skarsl Woods were a bad place to be, by night or day, and she was nothing like the warrior and witch that her sister was. She was tempted to run back westward, as her sister had hinted that she should do, as fast as possible. Still, Ambrosia must have had some reason for wanting to get to the Vale of Vraid, and Hope had been there before. Perhaps she should risk going forward. If worst came to worst, she could probably find a cave to hide in during the day: there were a good many of them in the rolling hills over which the forest had grown up.

She was also genuinely annoyed. She had often appealed to her sister (via notes) to set up some regular schedule, by which they could both share their single life on an equitable basis. Ambrosia had always refused. She repressed Hope until her strength to do so failed, and that was why Hope displaced her at irregular intervals. Hope was inclined to write her a stinging note to this effect on the wax tablet, then decided it could wait.

The decision saved her life. She angrily shoved the tablet and the stylus into the wallet. This pushed aside the *vekka*-cloth covering the focus, which winked at her with a dark gleam. She lifted it out and held it in her hand speculatively. Perhaps she should test the focus, to make sure she could release light from the thing.

Standing, she held the spherelike focus of power in front of her and spoke the rune of the Open Fist. The rune glowed briefly in the center of the sphere; she found herself in rapport with the power of the focus and, yes, it was hot with unshed light. She experimented with it, releasing a faint reddish sunset glow from the focus.

She was shocked to see a gray shadowy form like a mandrake standing before her. Like a mandrake . . . but from its chest extended half a dozen shadowy tendrils ending in toothless maws. Their function seemed tolerably obvious. And they were pointed at her.

She had only a moment to choose. She meditated drawing the short stabbing sword that Ambrosia favored . . . but she doubted a material weapon would do any good. This creature seemed no more substantial than a shadow as it stood there, agonized in the light.

No. Not *in* the light. *From* the light.

Hope raised the focus over her head with both hands and cried aloud, renewing the rune of the Open Fist. She felt it burn in both her eyes as a day's worth of sunlight was released in a single moment from the focus. She directed the searing wave of light at the creature's chest, blasting its tendrils and throwing it back screaming soundlessly in agony.

A dead tree behind it burst into flame, and it fled into the red shadows, its mandrake form ragged with damage.

Hope scooped up the wallet from the ground and hitched it to her belt. She ran along the yttern-track, often stumbling in the dark, heedless of other dangers, thinking only of escape from the shadow beast.

Had she killed it? Certainly not outright; it had been moving under its own power as it disappeared into the fiery shadows. Perhaps it was mortally wounded; she had no idea what that would mean for this sort of creature . . . or even if it was mortal. Ambrosia would know, but she didn't. Ambrosia might know how to fight the thing if it returned, but she didn't.

Hope stopped short. She had only one weapon to wield against the shadow-thing: her sister Ambrosia. She hated to relinquish awareness: even this deadly danger was preferable to oblivion, and she knew that if Ambrosia ever found a way, she would suppress her forever. But Hope couldn't let that stop her from doing what was right for both of them.

She sat with her back to a tree and pulled out the glowing stylus and wax tablet. Wiping off Ambrosia's message, she wrote:

Dear Ambrosia—

It is the same night as it was. As I tested the light in the focus, I found I was being stalked by some sort of shadow-demon in the form of a mandrake. I released all the light and damaged it greatly, but I fear it is not dead. This task is clearly yours to do, but I am sorry to thrust it on you.

Love,

Hope Nimuelle

P.S. I think I made a mistake in throwing all the light at it. It seemed to be immobilized by the first faint light I sent out. Only after the great wave of light passed did it seem able to move again. If you can summon up more light, perhaps you can trap it again.

H.N.

Hope gripped the message in her hand and threw herself into oblivion, summoning up her sister.

⊰⊱

Sun-colored chaos! Destruction! Death! They swept over Vesper, immobilized by the red sunset light of the woman's focus. Much of what he had been was blown into nothingness by that deadly light, and he feared it was the end. For the first time in his long hungry existence, he *feared*.

Then the terrible light had passed and he could move of his own will again. He staggered back and dissolved into the fluttering red shadows about the burning tree. Safe! Safe!

He greedily ate the shadows of all the animal life around him: the rats, startled from sleep by the wave of light, owls and bats, stunned by the noon-bright blast, crooked dryad-beasts, dwelling within their tree-shells, serpents cowering in their lairs.

As his strength returned, his fear faded. In its place came another new emotion, the converse of fear: anger. That woman had hurt him, scattering his monstrous dreams and blowing him in pieces. But he was still alive, and he would make her pay. Yes: she would pay!

Now he turned again to attack: with the shambling gate of a dryad beast, the needle-toothed maws of a thousand rats and snakes, the dark wings of owls and bats, the myriad staring eyes of nocturnal beasts. He was a legion of the night. He would find the woman. He would eat her shadows. He would kill her. He would kill both of her. This woman who could not understand that she was Vesper's prey would know it at last.

He found her running through the thickest part of the woods, the yttern-track long abandoned. She had changed, again, to the red-haired sister with glowing eyes. That was good: it made her easier to track through the dark woods.

But some of those woods were very dark! Vesper paused, concerned. He could move easily through shadow, but direct light or full darkness were both dangerous to him.

Still, both of the major moons were high overhead; there was some tracery of shadow on nearly every part of the forest floor tonight. And the woman seemed to be headed south, toward the foothills where the forest petered out. He would risk following her. He would risk anything rather than let this prey go unpunished. And she had already passed out of sight.

Vesper oozed his chimera form along a silver track of shadows. He could not take the straight reckless path into the dark the woman had taken, but he could move more quickly than she could, and he expected her to come back into sight soon.

She didn't, though. He saw no sign of her anywhere.

Vesper went toward the darkest part of the wood, guessing she was hiding from him there. It was a good guess, but he could still find no trace of her. He exerted all the sharp shadowy senses of his verminous selves, circling slowly among the deeper shadows.

Suddenly, he caught a flash of dim blue light: the woman's eyes. There!

The gleam of blue shone out clearly from the depths of a cave whose entrance was shadowed by a stand of trees.

Several of his shadowy ratlike heads nodded in rueful appreciation. In the whole forest, perhaps, there was no place to him as dangerous as this, at least while night lasted. Inside the cave was darkness as complete as could be found outside a buried coffin.

Except for her eyes. Their light was too dim to do him harm, but they did give enough light to create a faint path of shadow he could safely travel. He could leap down it and plant his tendrils in her before she was aware of it.

Of course, if he killed her there, her eyes would close and he would die in the cave's darkness. But he thought he could drain her of volition without killing her, and then compel her body to walk out of the cave. Then he could finish feeding on her in safety.

It was risky. But he was willing to take any risk in order to capture and kill this elusive, infuriating prey.

His amorphous twisted body followed his thought and leapt into the cave mouth, charging down the dim path of bluish shadow.

He was well into the cave, several lengths of his body, when he slammed into a barrier. The eyes still seemed to be many feet away. Yet they weren't . . . they peered glassily at him from the barrier. As he leaned toward them, his own shadowy form impinged painfully on their light.

Slowly, too slowly, Vesper understood. The barrier was the wet earthy wall of the cave itself. And the eyes . . . were just reflections of eyes in a mirror, set in the cave-wall.

Vesper turned and saw the woman standing, watching him, several yards before the cave-mouth. She was just a darkness in the darkness, except for her luminous eyes. He leapt toward her, but as soon as he began to move she shut her eyes. The darkness of the lightless cave fell down on him like a ton of black stones.

The last thing he heard was the woman's laughter, darker than the darkness that was killing him.

Ambrosia Viviana kept her eyes clenched shut, waiting for the monster to die. If her guess was right, total darkness would be as deadly to its shadowy frame as direct light. Eventually she heard a slight sigh as the subtle body of the shadow beast dissolved into the surrounding darkness. She kept her eyes shut for a long time afterward: in case it was a trick; in case it was a trap. There were so many traps in the world, and she had to face them all alone. She was almost used to it, now.

Presently she turned away and resumed walking eastward, with the one person she could trust trapped by the oblivion within her.

CHAPTER FOUR

Fire, Water, and Thorns

A dark narrow ship—*Sammark*, out of the Wardlands—was sailing up the Kaenish coast when fiery stones fell out of the night to batter it. Sailors threw water on the flames, which splashed back at them, burning, and they ran away, screaming, and plunged over the rails and sank into the dark cold sea, still burning.

Morlock Ambrosius (turned out of his cabin by the noise) ran forward groggily, against the tide of burning sailors. He was hoping to quench the flames in some other way: he knew something about the magic of fire. But by then the hungry flames had gnawed deep into the vitals of the ship: it broke in half and sank. The shock of the craft's death threw Morlock clear, and by the time he managed to get his spluttering head above water the broken *Sammark* could be seen, burning in several parts, deep beneath the surface of the sea.

Chance had saved Morlock, rather than any skill in swimming. He managed to keep afloat and keep moving and was therefore lucky enough to find himself, at dawn, crawling on his hands and knees along the rocky coast of Kaen, vomiting up an astonishing amount of seawater.

Of course, this was the upside (dead men do not vomit). But on the downside, there he was in Kaen: friendless, armorless, weaponless, shoeless (he had kicked off his early in the nocturnal swim). Kaen, where men and women of Morlock's nation were routinely killed for sport in the arena. Kaen, land of dark magics where evil subterranean gods protected the people and demanded a fearful price in return. Kaen, where cruelty was a religion and intrafamilial murder was considered the highest form of art.

"Eh. I wonder what their shoes are like?" Morlock muttered. The downside would not have seemed so very depressing if he'd had some shoes: the ragged coast of Kaen was carpeted with bitterly sharp rocks. In the end, he took off his shirt, soaked it in seawater and tore it into strips to bind his feet with them like bandages. It wasn't enough: blood was soaking through the makeshift pads as he walked. The blood caused the wet cloth to seethe with steam, a minor discomfort he was used to. His blood was dense with latent fire: that was part of the heritage of Ambrosius.

It was safer for him on the coast. Except for certain religious purposes, any use of the sea was illegal in Kaen. But, "I'll never make it home this way," Morlock observed to his bloody feet (who were telling him the same thing without words). He took one last hungry look at the western horizon. There lay the blue spiky line of the Grartan Mountains, the eastern edge of the Wardlands: home, for Morlock. But he couldn't get there from here; he'd have to take the long way overland, northward through the Gap of Lone. And his feet could not stand any more of these stones. He turned his back on the west, the sea, the bitter black rocks and home, and walked into the hateful land of Kaen.

He found a track of smoothed stones that soon turned into a full-fledged road. There he came across something he had been expecting: a bloodstained shrine for one of the Kaenish gods. What he had not expected was that it would be desecrated: the ratlike face was split more or less in half so that one of its eyes stared up into the sky while another peered down at the earth, and the broken bloodstained mouth wore a crooked loser's grin.

"Hah!" said Morlock, who had no love for any of the brutal blood-drinking gods of Kaen. It looked as if something had overturned their cruel worship in these parts. Morlock walked along more cheerfully, in spite of his wounded feet.

After a while Morlock came upon a woman walking along the road in the opposite direction. Sort of walking: she stumbled along blithely to the side of the road, tripped over that, laughed politely (as at a joke she didn't understand), and stumbled away to the other side of the road where she did the same. The general trend of her walking was toward Morlock, though. When she was quite close, she saw him.

"You!" she cried in Kaenish. "You! You! You! You are happy, happy and bright?"

Kaenish was one of the seven languages which Morlock's foster-father had made him learn, and he knew it pretty well. But he could hardly understand this woman's slurring speech; she seemed to have something wrong with her mouth. And perhaps something wrong with her mind as well: her feverish eyes focused on him intently, as if it were a matter of life and death that he was happy, happy and bright.

Morlock had been shipwrecked, spent a large portion of the night swallowing seawater and a chunk of the morning vomiting it back up. His feet were lacerated sores bound in bloody rags, and if the Kaenish sun beat down on his pale shoulders much longer they would soon be bright indeed, but not happy.

"I'm well," he said gruffly. "And you?"

"Well?" she said doubtfully. "Not happy? Not pretty? Not bright?"

"I'm as pretty as I'll ever be," Morlock replied (which was perfectly true, and nothing to brag about).

"You come with me," she said, suddenly decisive. "Be happy. Be pretty and bright."

Morlock was a young man. The woman was strangely attractive, if possibly insane, and she was offering him happiness, prettiness, and brightness. It seemed unlikely he would have a better offer that day.

"Then," he said, and gestured at the road. When she didn't seem to understand him he said, "I'll come with you."

"Oh!" she said, very excited. "Oh happy! Oh bright! Oh pretty pretty!" and reached out to touch him.

"Thanks," he said, avoiding the touch of her hand and its curving clawlike nails. He had just realized why she talked so strangely—or at least why her speech was slurred. When she opened her mouth to cry *oh* he saw that there were thornlike protrusions growing from her tongue. It must have been agony for her to speak.

She took him to a nearby town. It was walled as most Kaenish towns were. (Civil war was also an art to the decadent Kaenish.) But the gates were wide open and the brutal images of the local god had been thrown down and smashed in the road. Above the open gateway was written, in the cuneiform that the Kaenish used, the name of the town and its fallen god: Thyläkotröx.

"No gate?" he asked, falling into her childish pattern of speech. "No god?"

"Bad god!" she said, scowling. "Not pretty or happy."

"Or bright, I suppose."

"No! And gate . . . why should not all be happy?"

"Eh," said Morlock, who had always hoped that happiness was overrated.

They entered Thyläkotröx. The city showed signs of recent war: burned buildings, sections of the paved streets torn up, many dark brown patches on the pale street stones where blood had pooled. Whatever had overthrown the local god had not triumphed without a struggle: the citizens of Thyläkotröx (or some of them at least) had resisted. But peace had come to Thyläkotröx: stacks of notched weapons, axes especially, lay disused in the streets, dust settling down on them. People wandered the town, even more bemused than his guide. No shops were open; no business seemed to be taking place. The bitter internal war had been followed by an endless holiday in which everyone was happy and bright . . . if not exactly pretty. The smugly vacant look on their faces repelled Morlock.

The woman led Morlock to a public square where many people were milling about. A large branch was growing up out of a pale mound of shattered paving stones. The branch ended in a nimbus of long greenish-black thorns. People with anxious, troubled looks shouldered their way through the crowd and pressed their faces against the thorns. They stiffened suddenly and wandered off into the sunlit square, a dazed smile on their faces, no longer troubled but happy and bright.

The woman with thorns in her mouth smiled and gestured and made several sounds that might have been words. Morlock cautiously approached one of the thorns growing from the branch. The end was hollow and dripping some dark fluid. Morlock leaned in to examine the fluid, and a sharper needle-like thorn appeared in the hollow opening. Morlock leapt back just before it sprayed a cloud of dark mist at him.

"Happy now?" the woman behind him asked.

Morlock turned around and faced her. "As happy as I want to be," he said soberly. If he hadn't leapt back in time that muck might be running through his veins now.

The woman with the thorns in her mouth sighed, and Morlock thought she was about to say something about *happy* or *bright*. Instead, in seven syllables, she offered him his choice of three different sex acts, and she let him know it was a matter of some urgency.

Morlock was a young man, and he had been partnerless for some time; but as soon as he found himself considering the idea he reminded himself that her other orifices were also likely cluttered with thorns. He told her no, and continued telling her no until she wandered off, her face twisted with frustration. Her feelings were urgent, but she had no ability to concentrate. A few moments later he saw her asking a statue if it was happy and bright.

He walked back through the square, sightseeing in Thyläkotröx.

It was interesting, in a way. Clearly the local god had failed to protect its people. Perhaps something had come out of the sea, some plant that lived as a parasite on people. There were strange things in the ocean at the edge of the sky, swept in from the Sea of Worlds when the sun passed through the gate in the west each day. Or perhaps this plant parasite was the aftereffect of some disastrously miscalculated Kaenish magic, or a new form of Kaenish art, like killing your neighbor's baby.

Morlock felt bad for the infected people. But they were, after all, Kaenish. If they were living their ordinary lives they would probably be engaged in plots to kill each other in various ostensibly esthetically pleasing ways, or planning raids on the east coast of the Wardlands, or just sitting around being Kaenish, which (in Morlock's somewhat biased view) was bad enough. In any case, it was not his problem.

His first thought was to steal a shirt from someone too happy and bright to care. But then he realized that the clothing, perhaps the very air of the city, might be infected with spores of the parasite plants. Best to get out of town as quickly as he could, Morlock decided, and keep a close eye on his orifices for thornlike growths.

He was headed out of town at a brisk pace when he heard a buzzing voice call his name.

"Hey! You're the one called Morlock, aren't you? The vocate?"

Morlock halted and looked around. It was true he was a vocate, a full member of the Graith of Guardians who watched over the border of the Wardlands. It was also true that the Graith were hated in Kaen like nothing else. Fortunately the people standing near him seemed especially happy and bright, and also the voice had addressed him in the speech of the Wardlands, which the locals would be unlikely to understand. But he couldn't see the speaker.

"Here I am. In front of you. Don't you know me? I'm Zoyev. I was on board the *Sammark* with you."

In front of Morlock was something he had taken for a badly trimmed ornamental thornbush. Looking closer, he saw that it was a man. Thorns were sprouting from all over his skin, and he appeared to be rooted to the ground. The final state of a man preyed on by the parasite plants?

"Zoyev," Morlock replied, "if that's who you are—"

"Why do you doubt it?"

"Your body is imprisoned by thorns, and there appears to be an abandoned wasp's nest on your shoulder. These things did not happen overnight."

The buzzing voice was silent for a while, and then it said, "I don't know what body you mean. I seem to have many bodies. I—Oh, God Avenger, it must not have been a nightmare. It must have been true."

"What?"

"I dreamed . . . I thought it was a dream. After the shipwreck . . . did the ship really burn underwater?"

"Yes. The Kaenish seem to have some sort of stuff which burns even when immersed."

"Then it was true. It must have all been true. Morlock, when the ship broke up and sank, I was almost dragged down with it. Many of us were, struggling against the whirlpool pulling us down into the green orange murk. But I fought to the surface and swam away into the dark. I thought I was headed for the coast, but a current took me, dragging me . . . north I think. Up the coast. It was strong. I couldn't fight it. In the end there was an undertow that dragged me under the surface. By the distant light of burning *Sammark* I saw . . . something there on the sea floor. A great mouth or womb with thorny lips. It . . . I think it ate me. And I'm a part of it now, and I see through the eyes of the other bodies it has taken over . . ."

"I would help you if I could, Zoyev," Morlock said quietly.

"You pity me, I see. But I hate you for being alive while I'm dead . . . and I hate myself for being dead while you're alive. I wonder if this is what every ghost feels?"

"Zoyev," Morlock asked, "is there really just one plant in this city . . . one parasite infecting all these people?"

"Yes . . . I think . . . I think it's thinking about me . . . I'm forgetting what I knew, but remembering what the One knows. Yes, we came here, not so long ago. From somewhere else, a long journey in the dark. When we eat enough, we'll expel seed pods. Then we won't be alone. The One will then be the First One—first of many."

Morlock did not like the sound of this. One plant, the size of a city, and not yet full-grown . . .

"I just realized something," the buzzing voice said brightly. "I'm *not* Zoyev. I'm just a part of the One that has some of his undigested memories. Hm. I don't like what I remember about you, Morlock. I think you're a danger to the One."

There was a sound on the street behind Morlock, and he turned. The woman he had met earlier was standing there, her face no longer so happy and bright. Then the woman with the thorns in her mouth bit Morlock on the shoulder and he was happy.

"But *now* you're all right," the buzzing voice remarked brightly.

>=<

The wound glowed with a spectrum of warm greenish pleasures. The greatest pleasure of all was to be free from pain: from his bleeding feet, from weakness and hunger, from the join in his crooked shoulders, from memories he hated and could never escape.

The thorns in the woman's mouth were bright and fuming—burning from the latent fire in his blood—but she seemed to suffer no more from this than from the thorns themselves. She had already torn her clothes off, and she was clawing at the fastening of his trousers with fingers made clumsy by long thornlike nails. He was eyeing her pudenda with interest . . . the sharp thorn-like hair there reminded him of something he had seen or heard of . . . it didn't seem important compared to the happiness he felt . . .

Then he remembered, and it *was* important. The womb or mouth that had eaten Zoyev, the mouth of the One underwater on the coast.

He came back to himself with an effort and knocked the woman's hands away. She shrieked something about happy joy and brightness, her face twisted, unpleasant, marked with pain, smoke drifting from her mouth. He ran away past the thorn-bound man up the street as fast as he could go to the open gate with the broken ratlike god of Thyläkotröx.

"If you'd done your job this never would have happened," Morlock snarled at the smashed idol as he passed.

There was a scrubby wood of black trees with orange-pink leaves off to the side of the road. Remembering how much trouble the thorny woman had had in simply walking down the road, he thought he was safe from the One and its minions in the woods.

Of course, he reflected grimly (the dark ship of his awareness still afloat on the green-gold tide of false euphoria) it was only a matter of time until he was one of those minions himself. He was almost certainly infected, a thornlike parasite taking shape even now in his wounded shoulder.

The thought maddened him: that soon he would be enslaved by the One, the extension of its will. He swore he would make the One pay for the harm it had done (and would do) to him—revenge himself on the thing that had infected him.

Getting word to the Graith was obviously out of the question, and he could think of no way to alert the Kaenish kingdom . . . and wasn't sure the Kaenish rulers would even care. They might decide that the One was an avatar of the Kaenish god of death and incorporate it into the pantheon.

No, it was up to Morlock himself to act. And, as he lay there, dozing in the shade of orange leaves, he realized there was one thing he could do.

➤◄

Fyor-tirgan Shollumech ruled the largest part of the west coast of Kaen, facing the Narrow Sea. Unlike most of the Kaenish nobility, Shollumech took his religious responsibilities seriously, especially the duty of harming the Wardlands whenever possible. He had mounted three different invasions of the Wardlands, each of which had been circumvented by the Graith of Guardians using various ignoble tricks.

Shollumech had then settled on piracy, attacking the ships sailing up the Narrow Sea to Glenport. But the problem with piracy was that it was profitable, and Shollumech was uneasy about that. The Court of Heresiarchs had long forbidden any useful or beneficial activity involving the sea. The gods of Kaen were earthy gods.

When Shollumech's alchemists had invented an agent which would burn in water, the Fyor-tirgan was delighted. He designed a catapult of enormous range and settled down to destroying ships that passed near the Kaenish coast. This was clearly in accord with the religious teachings of the Heresiarchs, as it profited nobody. Also, the burning ships and sailors were pleasing to watch, satisfying Shollumech's impulses as an aesthete.

It was really beneath his dignity as Fyor-tirgan, but Shollumech enjoyed supervising the catapult shots himself. It was exciting to give the orders personally, and the view from the catapult tower was better than that from his own residence (where the windows looked away from the sea, as religion required).

And it was quite safe on the tower, nothing like taking part in a battle (a pleasure denied to one of his high rank). His nearest ally-enemy was the Tirgan of Thyläkotröx City, some distance to the north. Thyläkotröx had no catapults or siege equipment, and Shollumech knew for a fact that his own walls were unscalable. He didn't even bother to have his local gods place a protection on the tower: the human sacrifices required would be prohibitively expensive, and there was obviously no need for it.

Shollumech was quite surprised, therefore, to see a half-naked man climb over the rim of the tower and jump down beside the catapult.

Esthetically speaking, the intruder did not impress. He was shirtless; he had unruly dark hair and gray glaring eyes. There was a great dark wound at the base of his neck, which had bled all over his chest, and his feet were bound in bloody charred bandages. There was something wrong with his shoulders—one was rather higher than the other. So unsightly! Shollumech could not abide anything approaching a hunchback. And the man's fingers (and the blunt toes emerging from the ragged ends of the bandages) were simply covered with mortar dust. Shollumech realized that the man must have clawed handholds for himself in the ancient mortar of the tower walls. Such a grubby way to make one's entrance into a stronghold. Effective, of course, but utility and beauty were never quite the same thing.

The man's behavior was of a piece with his unpleasant appearance. Besides Shollumech himself, there were three soldiers and an alchemist next to the catapult. It was clearly a quasi-battle situation, but the intruder indulged in none of the usual courtesies: introductions, boasts, insults, challenges, etc. He simply reached out with one of his horrible long-fingered hands and broke the neck of the armed man nearest him. He slipped the fallen soldier's sword out of its scabbard as the corpse fell past him and raised the blade to guard.

The alchemist, quite properly, did not engage in any fighting: his caste did not permit it. And Shollumech, too, refrained. Indeed, he almost felt as if he had better leave: it was not customary for anyone higher than the rank of yr-tirgan to be present at a battle.

But while Shollumech pondered this important esthetic question, the battle—if that's what it was—was over. Shollumech's soldiers, with a regrettable lack of propriety, had drawn their swords and attacked the intruder using the barest preliminary of threat-barks. The stranger kicked one of them against the wall, leaving a bloody smoking footprint on the fellow's shining breastplate, and then turned to face the other. The duel was so brief as to not merit the name: there were no flourishes, no ceremonial sidesteps, no drama. The intruder simply put several holes in the soldier until he fell motionless beside his comrade with the broken neck.

By then the last soldier had recovered and charged upon the intruder, who dodged the fellow's rush and turned to stab him in the back of the neck. He fell across his peers and lay there. Three men dead, and to so little esthetic effect! Really, Shollumech was disgusted with the intruder.

Now Shollumech drew his sole weapon: a poison-tipped dagger. It was meant for suicide if the occasion seemed to demand it—as it did, but at the moment he had an even more important task. He threw the dagger into the throat of his alchemist. The fellow looked at him gratefully (at least, Shollumech hoped it was grateful; truth be told, the dying face seemed a little hostile) and slumped with a certain grace to the stones.

Shollumech was engaged in the opening steps of the Dance of Justification when the intruder approached and slapped him on the side of the head with the flat of the bloody sword.

"Stop that prancing," the intruder said in fairly good Kaenish (with a Wardic, almost a Dwarvish, accent).

"My religion requires it," Shollumech replied, with as much dignity as he could muster.

The intruder said something inaesthetic and, as far as Shollumech knew, untrue about the requirements of Kaenish religion. "I want you to tell me about this fire-under-water stuff," the intruder continued. "I don't have a lot of time, and I can't afford to be gentle. Will you tell me?"

"The soldiers might have told you," Shollumech explained. "And the other man was my alchemist; he would have been your property at the end of the battle, so I had to kill him. He would have told you."

"You're not answering my question."

"I do not answer questions. I am the Fyor-tirgan Shollumech Kekklidas and I defy you to the death. Moreover, I have taken an oath by my right hand never to surrender the secret of my fire-in-water agent. May I know your name?"

The intruder stared at him for a few moments with his searing gray eyes and then said, "Why not? I am Morlock Ambrosius, vocate to the Graith of Guardians."

"Ambrosius," Shollumech repeated. "That would account for the . . . the, uh . . ."

Morlock was amused. "Yes, that accounts for my crooked shoulders."

In fact, Shollumech had been warned by his gods to watch out for any of the Ambrosii who passed his way. They had gotten on the wrong side of the Two Powers somehow. If Shollumech were a shrewder, more businesslike man he might have been able to turn this situation to his advantage somehow. But he wasn't sure what the religious implications would be if he did a favor for the Two Powers. They weren't *his* gods . . .

But the intruder was saying something. "You are serious about this oath to your right hand?" he asked.

"No one," Shollumech assured him, "below the rank of heresiarch takes oaths as seriously as I do. They bind me with the powers of the gods I feed."

"All right," said Morlock resignedly, and slashed off Shollumech's right hand.

Shollumech passed out before he could even scream. But he awoke while Morlock was cauterizing the stump of his right wrist in the brazier the dead soldiers had used to light the catapult shots. Then he screamed. He screamed and screamed.

Morlock let him go on for a while, but then he stuck the fuming stump into a bucket of soldier's wine and said, "Listen to me. Look at me."

Shollumech did so. The bloodstained vocate held up Shollumech's severed hand. "I now hold your right hand, and your oath," said Morlock. "You will now tell me what you know about the fire-in-water agent."

Shollumech's mind, never very swift, was now slowed with pain and blood loss. Nonetheless, it seemed to him that Morlock's demand was in accord with the dictates of religion.

"There are bottles of red fluid and bottles of blue fluid," Shollumech said dully. "Next to the catapult in a sort of box. Either is inert by itself; when combined, they burn. In air, the fire will spread normally. In water, the fire will burn whatever it touches until the agent is consumed."

"How is it made?"

"I don't know. The alchemists discovered it. One killed the others to keep the secret for himself, and now I've killed him. He made up the agent, day by day, for my night attacks."

Morlock went over to the catapult and found the bottles arranged in the alchemist's maijarra wood case. He closed it and brought it with him back to Shollumech, sitting sprawled on the tower stones beside his fallen soldiers.

"Listen," said Morlock, tossing the severed hand aside. "I don't want to kill you if I don't have to. Will you take an oath by your head that you won't raise the alarm against me before dawn?"

Shollumech replied in the negative with the most inaesthetic thing he had ever said in his life. He was surprised at himself. Apparently some instincts ran even deeper than the esthetic impulse. He was still pondering the ramifications of this discovery when Morlock stabbed him through the heart.

><=

Morlock armed and clothed himself from the fallen soldiers' relatively unbloodied gear. One of them wore boots that were about his size, so he took those as well. But he tore Shollumech's insignia, a dancing yellow boar, from everything he took. And he cut off Shollumech's head and brought it with him as a passport. As he understood the customs of the country, the death of the Fyor-tirgan would absolve his followers of any obedience or loyalty. It didn't mean that they wouldn't want to kill him for other reasons, but he'd face that contingency when it arose.

In the event, he saw no one. Apparently Shollumech's agonized screams had been enough to set off the frenzied looting of his quarters that was the traditional accompaniment of a Kaenish noble's death. Morlock made it down through the unguarded tower unseen and left Shollumech's head on the threshold for proper burial with the rest of his body.

Morlock's shoulder was beginning to bother him, near where the woman had bitten him on the neck. It might have been his imagination, but he felt as if there was something long and thornlike there, deep under the skin. And his veins screamed in sick longing for the drug the woman's bite had poisoned him with. He didn't think that he had gotten the dose that the citizens of Thyläkotröx got straight from the One. If he had, he might not have been able to resist.

He suspected that the woman with the thorns in her mouth was designed by the One to lure people into the city by infecting them with the drug and making them want more. Or she might (with her alarming sexual urges) be part of the One's peculiar reproductive setup. The two purposes weren't necessarily at odds. In time the One would probably grow shrewder, learn from its mistakes, and make better lures. Morlock hoped it wouldn't have time to do so . . . but he was achingly conscious that it was he who was running out of time.

Morlock walked along the bitter black beach northward from Shollumech's tower. He really only had one line of attack open to him, and because the One knew that as well as he did, they were waiting for him.

Chariot, the major moon, was sullen as it sank toward the east. Horseman, the second moon, was high overhead, with Trumpeter, the third moon, fierce with renewed light as it rose in the west over the Grartan Range. By the combined light of the three moons he clearly saw his antagonists.

They were, or had been, citizens of Thyläkotröx, lining the way from the rocky beach to the city on the heights. But their silhouettes were distorted in the varied moonlight. They looked almost as if they were wearing armor, but on approaching them Morlock saw that their torsos were wrapped in tight cages of black shining branches. Their hands were entirely gone: the arms ended in long bladelike thorns. Clouds of thorns obscured their faces.

They were well protected, and there were many of them. But they walked with awkward stiffness, and Morlock, with a thorn growing in his shoulder, thought he understood why. This was his advantage, then: speed.

He used it. He'd looted two swords from Shollumech's dead soldiers, and he drew them both now. (The *maijarra* box with the fire agent was strapped to his shoulders.) He charged the thorn-soldiers at the end of the line, striking off the hand-blades of the last thorn-soldier with a double stroke, then swung both his swords around to bring them back up without slowing and struck off the thorn-soldier's head. It bounced off Morlock's chest, piercing it at several places, and the body slumped down to the black stones of the beach.

The next soldier in the line was almost upon him. Morlock stabbed his enemy in the open area between the basket of thorns protecting his head and the breastplate of black branches. The man went down coughing up blood . . . of a sort. Blood would have been black in the moonlight; this stuff was transparent, yellowish or green.

He killed a few more, working his way up the line, but then they began to cluster around him, using their numbers to advantage. So he ran northward up the shoreline.

His thinking was this: it was the parasite thorns that slowed the soldiers' movements. They would have been infected at different times. It was reasonable to assume that they would move at different speeds, with different amounts of the thorn-parasite cluttering up their insides.

Morlock looked back as he ran and saw with satisfaction that they were stringing out behind him on the black beach. He spun around without slowing and ran back at the straggling line of thorn-soldiers.

He killed the first one with a stab to the neck; the second he disabled with a leg cut and finished off with a thrust between the slats of the breastplate. From there he was in the thick of it, striking down thorn-soldiers as he went with a savage satisfaction he rarely felt in a fight. He felt he was not killing these men but ending their slavery to the One. The thorn in his shoulder glowed green-gold with pleasure but he was not aware of it.

His satisfaction ended when a long thorn stabbed him in the side from behind. He broke off from the thorn-soldier he had been fighting and put his wounded back to the sea.

There was *another* line of thorn-soldiers shuffling toward him; the nearest held a thorn-blade already afire from his Ambrosial blood. They must have been placed farther to the north. Morlock did not understand why the One had done that, and there was no time to think about it as several thorn-soldiers attacked.

Morlock slashed frantically with both his swords at the thorn-blades stabbing at him. When he could afford to move he ran northward up the beach, splashing sometimes through the shallows as the waves surged up among the rocks.

What had worked in his favor before was working against him now. It was the swiftest of the northern line of soldiers that had attacked him from behind. The other, slower ones were straggling behind northward in a rough line parallel with the water's edge. Morlock was in real danger of being pinned against the water.

This is the end, said a voice in his mind, and the thorn in his shoulder throbbed with sudden agony. Only then did he realize it had been feeding him pleasure as he fought. It had done so for a reason, but he didn't have time to think about it now.

Not normally a cursing man, Morlock damned the thorn—its pleasure, pain, and despair—and cast his eye as he ran, along the ragged column of thorn-soldiers. It had to be ragged; there had to be gaps.

He saw one: a single thorn-soldier shuffling by itself behind a cluster of faster ones and a clot of slower ones. Morlock charged him and struck him down as he passed, heading into the higher land, approaching the town (black on the horizon in Chariot's red light).

Once he had a little height he stopped and turned back. The thorn in his shoulder punished him with a blaze of suffering, so he knew he was doing the right thing. There was something he didn't understand here, and it was important. It was more than just the heat of battle clouding up his mind: something was trying to keep him from understanding, luring him with pleasure to fight the endless parades of thorn-soldiers, missing the real point.

The thornlike pain in his shoulder and neck was growing even more intense. He seemed to hear a blurry voice whispering to him that it was too late, that there was no point, that even if he did understand there was nothing he could do, that what he had to do was run now, far and fast, to save himself.

That was what the voice within him wanted him to do, so he didn't. He planted himself on the slope and looked at the ragged groups of thorn-soldiers shuffling toward him and he thought.

Two lines of soldiers made a certain amount of sense, so the one could reinforce the other, but why so far apart? It had been long minutes before the northern column had staggered down to assist the southern column.

The answer came crashing in on him at last. There was something between the two lines that the One wanted to protect . . . almost certainly the same thing he wanted to attack: its underwater mouth.

Morlock sheathed his swords and unstrapped the *maijarra* box from his back. He knotted the straps into a single long tether and hooked it onto the box. He drew a sword with his free hand and ran down the slope, whirling the box over his head.

The clot of thorn-soldiers in his path seemed to stare for a moment at the whirling box, and then they suddenly separated, shuffling in different directions.

Morlock leapt toward one. As he whirled the box over his head the thorn-soldier did a dance of anxiety (strangely like the dance Shollumech had done when he had killed his alchemist) and ran back into the sea to escape. Morlock followed and, when the soldier was knee deep in the surf, he smashed the *maijarra* wood box on the thorn-soldier's head. Some of the bottles inside broke, and fire agent splashed all over the thorn-soldier, setting him instantly alight. Morlock thrust with his drawn sword through the box as it fell past the thorn-soldier's neck and left the sword in the wound, pinning the box in place. The flailing thorn-soldier gave a buzzing scream and jumped into the deep water to douse the flames. Morlock took a long breath and followed.

The Narrow Sea didn't have the tremendous surging waves of the ocean that faced the edge of the sky. But it did shoal fairly rapidly; they were already deep in the dark water. The thorn-soldier was not flailing any longer; he appeared to be dead. But still he burned, tiger-bright in the night-dark sea, drifting slowly downward.

Then, by the light of the burning thorn-soldier, Morlock saw his target in the green-black gloom of the sea floor: a great pulsating mouth, rimmed with thornlike hair. This was the route that Zoyev had travelled after the *Sammark* was wrecked, the route he meant the burning corpse to follow now. There must be some sort of stalk or throat that ran under the ground to a belly beneath the town. Was the One really a plant, or some sort of animal?

The wounds in Morlock's side and neck were burning from the salt water; the thorn in his shoulder was an agony brighter than the burning corpse he was shepherding downward with his remaining sword. His lungs were straining to hold their air. Perhaps this was not the best time to speculate on the genus of a monster he was trying to kill.

The burning body was drifting down toward the mouth, but too slowly to suit Morlock. He ran it through the chest with the second sword in his hand and left this sword also in the wound.

Then he let the burning corpse fall away and he arrowed upward through the night-dark water to the surface shimmering with the light of the three moons. He broke through the surface and trod water for a while, breathing life back into his lungs.

Presently he poked his head beneath the waves: he thought he saw a gleam of orange swallowed in the gloom below. He hoped that the One could no more refrain from drawing things into its sea-mouth than a tree could refrain from drinking through its roots or a man could refrain from breathing. If so, his little present to the One was well on its way.

It was. The burning corpse entered the thorny sea-mouth and travelled, submerged, down a pulsating tunnel. A trail of fire followed on its wake, down the floor of the pulsating tunnel. It surfaced at last alongside a heap of debris in an underground chamber, also covered with pulsating flesh. This was where the One absorbed the bodies and spirits of the things it swallowed through its sea-mouth. Zoyev's half-consumed body was there, along with others from the *Sammark* and still others from other vessels lost at sea, and dead sea creatures, and other wrack.

The fire began to spread from the burning corpse to the drying matter in the great island of offal in the One's belly. It began to be hot—hot enough to dry the pulsating walls. The pressure increased with the heat as the belly filled with smoke and steam.

In the end, the belly of the One exploded, sending flames shooting far up along its stem, showering them through the city of Thyläkotröx.

Morlock first guessed that his stratagem was working when the thorn in his shoulder burned its way out through the flesh.

He had been playing hide-and-seek with the thorn-soldiers for hours, it seemed, ever since he had waded to land. Annoyingly, they always seemed to know where he was: led by the parasite within him, no doubt.

When the thorn began to grow hot, Morlock first assumed that it was a trick by the One to make him cry out, so naturally he did not. But the pain grew even more intense and seemed to move outward through his flesh. And he heard the thorn-soldiers thrashing about and shrieking with suddenly clear voices down on the sharp-stoned beach. That was when Morlock understood what was happening.

Morlock gritted his teeth and clenched his fists as the thorn emerged, smoking, from his shoulder, burned its way through his shirt, and fell to the ground, wriggling like a snake made of embers on the dark stones.

The agony was intense, but even greater was the relief that it was out of his body. Somehow the sympathy that allowed the One to control this fragment of itself meant that the fragment was compelled to die along with the One.

And the One was dying, perhaps was already dead. Morlock raised his eyes to the dark battlements of Thyläkotröx and saw they were outlined in light: a fountain of fire and sparks rising up into the sky from the city center. Then he knew for certain that the seed of fire he had planted in the sea had flowered into the One's blazing death.

The thorn-soldiers lay silent, bright as live coals scattered over the dark shore. Morlock looked at them and didn't like to think of what it was like in the city now. Many of the people must be dying horrible deaths as the parasite thorns burned their way out of the host bodies. Perhaps some of the citizens would survive, but he doubted they would bless the man who took their happiness away with this deadly brightness.

He watched the fire rising over Thyläkotröx for a while, triumphant at the One's death but still guilty over the suffering he had caused. While the One was alive, he had known exactly what to do: whatever the One opposed. Now he wondered if he had been right to be so single-minded, if his determination to oppose the One hadn't made him into a distorted reflection of the One, the same image painted in more fiery colors. Maybe there had been some third way he could have taken, to oppose the One but save the people it had infected. . . . But, if there was, even now he couldn't see it.

Morlock shrugged his crooked, wounded shoulders and turned away from the burning city, walking northward up the dark shoreline toward the Gap of Lone and home. For a long time, as he walked, his distorted shadow danced before him, outlined in fiery light.

CHAPTER FIVE

Maintaining the Guard

The road along the coast facing the western edge of the world was gray in the light of the three moons; the green of the trees that lined it was black in the same bloodless light. Aloê Oaij was running northward along the road with the long steady stride of a woman who has been travelling much of the night, and is prepared to do the same through the day.

Nonetheless she stopped when she saw a light growing in the sea. It was faintly green-blue, now, beneath the blue-black sky. As she stood beside one of the elms lining the road, she saw the color of the sea lighten and brighten, a blue shot through with gold, brightest at its western edge. The waters began to roil near the shore, their steady lapping against the rocky beach disrupted by new currents. The gate in the west was opened: waters were pouring out through it, others pouring in from the Sea of Worlds that lay beyond the edge of the world.

Aloê began to sing as the sea grew radiant blue, shedding light upward on a brightening sky. She had spent the last year or so among people who believed that the souls of the dead collected in the west during the night, to pass into the Halls of Those-Who-Watch when the sun opened the Westward Gate in the morning. Aloê had no opinion on this, but she thought it a pleasing custom, so she sang for the souls of the dead and their benefactor, the sun. Rain fell about her, though there were no clouds in the sky.

Then the brightness in the west became intolerable to look at; the sea became a darker blue as the sky above grew pale and bright. The sun was up. The waters settled. Aloê concluded her song and ran on northward to find a man and kill him.

Presently she came upon a village, a knot of farmers' houses by the road. If she had not been misled, the man she sought was here. She approached a house and knocked on its door.

There was no answer. This was strange, and had Aloê been raised on a farm she might have thought it stranger that no one was moving about this farming village, though dawn had come and gone. Land-farming was not one of Aloê's talents, though. But she knew by the smoke coming from the chimney that this house was occupied. She pounded again on the door and called out, "Your courtesy, this is the Graith's business. I need not enter, but I must speak with the holder of this house."

"Go away!" a girl's voice screamed within. "You can't fool me! He killed them, and now you'll kill me! *I know you! I know you!*"

"Listen," Aloê said urgently, "who is 'he' and who do you think I am? I am a vocate of the Graith of Guardians. I seek an exile who killed a man at Anglecross Port, southward on the coast."

Silence.

"He is a tall man, white-skinned, red-haired, speaks with an eastern accent," Aloê continued. "He calls himself—"

"That is Clef," the girl within said, with the false calm of weary hysteria. "He killed them. He would have killed me too, but I hid. Then he left, before dawn. That was when you killed him. Now you'll kill me. But I won't let you kill me, Green Man!"

"I'm not a man," Aloê said, somewhat miffed. "And I am a vocate, a member of the Graith of Guardians," she explained, more patiently. "My name is Aloê Oaij. I've come to kill no one, except perhaps the man you call Clef. Look out at me!"

"I didn't say you were a man. You're the Green Man, the one who hunts along the coast before dawn! I won't look at you! No one who sees you lives!"

Aloê threw up her hands in despair and shook her head. If the exile had been here and left she was wasting time. There was a chance he was within, though. She gently pressed against the door, felt the stresses in the old wood, and guessed where the hinges and bolt were.

"I'm sorry," she called out. "It seems I must come in after all. Stand away from the door."

"You won't!" the girl screamed triumphantly. "The Green Man won't break gray wood!"

Aloê braced her left foot and kicked in the door with her right.

She stepped in and found the girl standing, barely, to the right of the doorway. The girl held a hand over her mouth, eyeing Aloê with pale terror. Then she dropped her hand and laughed. She pointed at Aloê's face, and laughed and laughed. "You're not him!" she cried. "You're not green; you're all black and gold!"

It was true that Aloê's skin was darker than the norm in Westhold, and her hair lighter. Farm folk, in particular, seemed to be surprised by her appearance, and she had heard this description of herself often enough to find it annoying. But she said nothing about it. Behind the hysterical girl, two battered bloody forms lay on their backs without moving.

"Your parents?" Aloê asked.

The girls turned, looked, turned back to Aloê. "Yes," she said, almost as if she were unsure. "Clef killed them, then left. Did you really kill him?"

"Not yet," said Aloê, moving to the motionless forms on the floor. By custom and the Graith's own First Decree, she was supposed to expel Clef from the Wardlands, and kill him only if he resisted. But Aloê had already decided that Clef would resist.

The sprawled man Aloê did not bother with—his throat was cut deeply and the wound was already drying out. But the fallen woman's flesh was still warm, and her breath stained with mist the glitterstone hilt of Aloê's knife when she held it before the woman's face.

"Your mother's alive," Aloê said. "Go get help."

"No one will open their doors until the sun's up," the girl said faintly.

"The sun is up. Hurry, girl. You've been brave, but you must do more. Don't you understand? Your mother is not dead, and may live."

><

When the girl's mother had been put to bed, her wounds bandaged and her bones set, Aloê stepped out into the street to find the village's Old Women waiting for her. They introduced themselves, and their chief, Naege, said, "We owe you a debt, Vocate. The thing is bad, but it might have been worse."

"Tell me about Clef, then," Aloê said. "When did he come here?"

"A few days ago. Harl, poor Tarith's father, hired him to help him clear some land. I knew something was wrong when I saw him stealing one of my horses early this morning."

Aloê looked sharply at her.

"I keep a few horses in the stable yonder. Sometimes the others in town hire them; a few times travelers on the road have purchased or traded for them. This morning I heard someone mucking about in the yard, and looked out in time to see Clef ride off on my best stallion."

"And you didn't raise the alarm against him?"

"No one goes out before dawn." There was a murmur of agreement from the other Old Women.

"Because of this Green Man Tarith spoke of."

"You can call it the Green Man, or you can call it God's will. People who travel by themselves on the coast road often disappear. The most dangerous time is at night; even the village street isn't safe then. I'm not going to get myself killed for a stupid horse."

"I'll never catch him on foot. Can I borrow a stupid horse?"

Naege sighed. Clearly she thought it was throwing good horses after bad. But she was chief of the Old Women, not only because she was oldest, and she let Aloê have the horse.

>≈⇐

Aloê did not expect to catch up with the exile especially soon. She was no great horsewoman, and her quarry had a considerable head start. So she was surprised at what awaited her, a little north of the village along the coast road.

A large form lay across the road, underneath a dark-leafed twisted tree. It was the dead body of a black horse; its blood had pooled on the road.

Aloê dismounted and approached the dead thing. She kept her eye on the trees near at hand, looking out for the exile who called himself Clef. She circled around, keeping her eyes and ears open, yet she saw nothing. Still, she felt very strongly that there was someone nearby, watching her.

Her eyes caught a gleam at the foot of the tree. There, in a strangely warm hollow filled with dark grass, she found a steel buckle in a Kaenish design and a handful of coins, all smeared with blood.

Aloê sighed in vexation. It was the buckle that had given Clef away in

Anglecross. Had he abandoned it here to make himself harder to find? But why kill his horse? Perhaps he was trying to make it seem as if he, too, had been killed by a highway robber (this Green Man they spoke of in the village). Why, then, leave the coins? Any robber would have taken those, no matter how much blood they had on them.

She circled around into the line of trees and beyond them. She was a fairly good tracker, and it did not seem to her that anyone had passed that way recently. The ground was soft; her own footprints were clear in spite of the sparse grass and the dead leaves of former years blowing about.

Moving back to the road, she eyed the shore. There was no cover for a man. Still . . .

She went back to the coins in their dark blood-warm hollow beneath the twisted tree. She felt a bit queasy as she crouched down to fish out the coins and the buckle—possibly it was the bleeding horse nearby. She leaned on the old tree and, as she stood up, noticed an odd gooey sort of moss clinging to her hand. She shuddered with disgust and brushed it off on her red cloak. Then she put the coins and buckle in her wallet, mounted her horse, and rode back to the village.

>⋞

She found Naege at the door to her stables, the spring sunlight golden in her gray hair.

"You're back suddenly, Vocate," Naege greeted her wryly. "Found your man?"

"Maybe," Aloê replied, and dismounted. "This Green Man of yours—"

"He's not mine."

"—is he a robber or just a killer?"

"Hm. I could answer that question better if I knew what the skank you were talking about."

Aloê showed her the coins and the buckle she'd found beneath the old tree. "I found your horse—I guess it's yours—up the road a bit, dead. These were lying on the ground nearby, covered with blood."

"That's Clef's belt buckle."

Aloê nodded. "Then Clef was the exile I was looking for. I'm guessing that he ran into your Green Man."

"He's not mine. And you're right—the Green Man never takes money. Just life. He never lets go of someone he's marked. Mal Harl's son got away from him once, but it didn't do any good. The Green Man caught up with him a few months later, and no one's seen Mal since. That was a bad time—the Green Man was in town all the time. Usually he stays on the road."

"What does he look like?"

"I've never seen him."

Aloê bit back the first reply that occurred to her, scratched her golden unkempt hair (it had been days since she'd properly washed it in fresh water), and said finally, in a neutral voice, "Then how do you know he was in town?"

"You handled that nicely, young woman. So I'll tell you. You can feel it when he's around. Kind of a sickening feeling."

Aloê nodded, remembering how she had felt on the road.

"Tell you something else. You can spot someone he's marked. Someone he'll come for, sooner or later, when he can find her alone." Her glance at Aloê was freighted with meaning.

"Are you talking about me?"

"I'm talking about you. I'm sorry to say so. There isn't a skank of a lot I can do for you, young woman. But you can keep the horse, if you'd like, and ride it down to Anglecross. It's crowded there—and you could take a ship far away. Maybe the Green Man wouldn't follow. As far as I know, no one's ever tried it."

Aloê shook her head. "I'm not done here. Clef may have faked an attack by your Green Man—"

"More yours than mine."

"—and may be hiding somewhere nearby. You should watch out for him."

"He's dead. But you're going to look for him along the coast road."

"Yes. Him or the Green Man—one or the other will be able to tell me what happened."

"Uh-huh. The Green Man, they say he doesn't say much. But who knows? Any messages for your kin?"

Aloê smiled gently. She didn't care for her relatives. She shook her head. "But," she said, "if I'm not back in a month or so, you might send a message to Vocate Naevros syr Tol in A Thousand Towers, and let him know what has happened here."

New respect, tinged with fear, entered Naege's eyes. "Naevros, eh? I send my son Easthold-way on business every now and then. I suppose it could be done."

"Thanks." Aloê turned and walked back to the road.

>=<

Aloê nearly missed the place on the road where the dead horse had been. She did pass it, her eyes intent on the trees alongside the road. (There, if anywhere, the Green Man—or Clef—would be waiting.) Then, glancing forward along the road, she noticed that ahead, looming over the trees, was the blue shoulder of a distant hill. She'd already come farther than she had before. She stopped and turned on her heel. This time she kept her eyes on the pavement of the road, with occasional glances to the left and right.

Soon she found the spot: bloodstains, unmistakably fresh, on the dusty road-stones. There was no sign of the horse; there were strange marks in the blood—splashing, as if the horse had been dismembered by blunt force. And then . . . ?

Well, Aloê herself had eaten nastier meat than horseflesh. But she suspected Clef had come to a juster and more gruesome demise than Aloê's oath to the Graith would have permitted.

This Green Man, though . . . clearly he was a greater threat to those under the guard than Clef had ever been. How long had he been here? What was he?

Where he had come from was at least clear. Many things from the Sea of Worlds washed up on the coast, driven there by the dawn storms that opened the western gate of the world. There were strange beasts in the waters that no one dared fish or swim. There was strange flotsam on the beaches from day to day. And it was not utterly unheard-of for something to make it to the coast alive—a traveller, a refugee, a wild animal. Aloê guessed the Green Man was one of these.

She also knew full well that she was a match for Clef, but not necessarily for mysterious Green Men from beyond the world. It might be smart to seek out reinforcements. Illion the Wise, for instance; his home at Three Hills was fortunately not too many days' travel away on this same road.

Aloê turned again and trotted northward at a wolf's pace, long springing strides she could sustain all day, if there was need. Her sense of being watched faded as she ran, was gone by dusk.

⋙⋘

Aloê sat up in the darkness, her eyes gaping for light. There had been a crash— or was that a dream?

No. Something had fallen across her campfire, she saw: a tree, scattering coals across the campsite and killing the flames. In the red light of the last embers she rolled to her feet and drew her knife with the glitterstone hilt.

Light, kindled in the crystalline blade, threw back the curtain of night. Aloê held the magical blade high, so as not to be blinded by its glare, and turned toward the fallen tree. Her stomach twisted within her. The tree had been pushed to the ground: she saw force-marks on the trunk, saw the green living roots that had been torn from the ground. Her stomach twisted again, and then she knew.

"Green Man!" she called. "Show yourself! I feel your presence."

There was no reply. Aloê peered among the trees beyond the fallen tree, but saw no one there. True, she thought she saw someone, for a moment. But that was just an odd shadow cast by one of the older, more twisted trees. It was leafless, and looked likely to fall soon itself. She moved closer, stuck by an odd thought. At the tree's foot there was a dark hollow, filled with something that looked like grass. . . .

Aloê leapt back in the instant before the Green Man struck, lashing out with its leafless twisted limbs. Because she had no other weapon, Aloê struck back with the glow-knife—and thus lost the only weapon she had. It stuck, deep within the wooden flesh of the Green Man. The blade's light grew yellowish, greenish, went out. So much Aloê saw in glances over her shoulders as she fled through the dark.

She ran, but she knew she could not run far. It had been a long road from Anglecross to here, and she was nearly spent. Illion's house at Three Hills was several days' journey north—it might as well be on one of the three moons. To the east, beyond the coastal woods, was the narrow plain of Westhold: a fine place to raise wheat, an unlikely place to discover monster-killing weapons. South was Naege's village, and further south yet Anglecross Port. She could reach neither one without sleep, which meant she would not reach them alive. What did that leave? The empty sea westward, facing the closed iris of the world. . . .

Aloê nodded her head reluctantly. It was a long chance, and even if she succeeded she was likely to be killed along with the Green Man. But it had come from the Sea of Worlds, and to the Sea of Worlds it would return.

※

Aloê crossed the coast road and went down to the rocky beach beyond, to where the black water of the world's last sea licked hungrily at the shore. The three moons were high overhead, giving plenty of light for her to see the Green Man leave the woods behind and creep toward the roadway. The ground seemed to ripple around its base when it moved, as if it were wading through the earth the way a man wades through the water. The road proved a significant obstacle: Aloê waited impatiently while the Green Man inched across the paved stone surface. But it moved rapidly once it reached the other side, and Aloê backed into the dark whitecapped waves until they were surging about her knees.

The Green Man came right up to the edge of the water and stopped. Aloê found herself hoping it had an aversion to water; then she could simply swim her way northward.

But that, of course, would leave the Green Man to prey on those travelling the coast road.

Aloê grimaced, bent down, and grabbed a stone from the sea-floor. She pegged it at the Green Man with annoying, if not deadly accuracy: it bounced off the thing's barklike skin with a woody thump and dropped down into the dark mouthlike hollow at the Green Man's base. After a moment's struggle, the Green Man managed to push the stone out to fall among its fellows on the rocky beach.

Aloê bent down and fetched up another stone from the seafloor. She held it toward the Green Man—she had no idea what the thing used for senses, but it was worth a try—and said distinctly, "Nyaah, nyaah!" She lifted the stone as if to throw it.

Abruptly the Green Man entered the water. Aloê dropped the stone and dove. She swam like a seal toward the dark line in the west where the sky met the sea.

Over her own swift strokes Aloê could hear the even swifter progress of her enemy. She glanced back and saw the Green Man oiling through the hard whitecapped waves even faster than a seal. A seal with oars, perhaps: the leafless branches swung along in fierce circles, propelling the Green Man through the water. Awed, Aloê, who had some interest in ship-building, speculated on the possibility of a ship driven by mechanical oars—perhaps a series of oarblades in a circle, like the blades of a windmill . . .

Then the enemy was upon her, and the invention of the propeller was struck out of her head by one of the Green Man's branches. Aloê retained the presence of mind to dive below the surface. There, she guessed, the Green Man's clublike blows would lose their force, slowed by the medium of water. And this was true enough. But she hadn't bargained on the Green Man's untreelike suppleness in the water. She found the Green Man coiling about her chest like a slimy green snake. When she realized she was being constricted she reached under the body of the Green Man and tried to push herself out through the tightening coil. But the barky skin was too slimy in water; her hands could get no grip. Then her right hand closed on something: the handle of the glow-knife she had left in its hide. It gave her the purchase she needed to push free. As she kicked herself away from the Green Man, toward the seafloor, she winked, through the stinging sea-water, at the knife blade glittering in the hide of her enemy.

Glittering with reflected light. Aloê opened her eyes wider, despite the stinging salt, and saw that the water all around her was alive with blue-green light. The dawn storm was beginning. She dove deeper, down to the ocean floor itself, and held onto the biggest rock she could find.

Looking up, she saw the dark form of the Green Man floating ominously above. Whatever it was, it knew something about the tactics of hunting. Its position was strong: it stood between Aloê and the air she would need. Eventually. But the gills on her neck had already opened; she could breathe the air dissolved in the water for some time before she needed to come up for an ordinary breath. She hoped the Green Man would be gone before then.

Aloê waited. She engaged in the dreamlike thought-exercises with which seers preface Withdrawal, which are supposed to reduce the body's needs. She reflected that her death might be a fair price to pay for the removal of this monster from the Wardlands. She reflected that, on the other hand, if she died and the Green Man was not swept out of the world, she would have died for nothing. It occurred to her that thoughts like these were not nearly as nourishing as air.

And the water grew brighter, green-gold to sun-bright. The gateway in the west was open. The Green Man began to wave its boughs to struggle against the current, but it was swept resistlessly westward.

Aloê would have laughed if she could have spared the air. The counter-current struck her in turn. It was not pulling her westward but pushing her eastward, striking her like a cold watery fist, knocking her loose from her rocky perch.

She fought upward to the air as the cold current carried her to shore. Suddenly she had passed into the upper current, and her body was twisted around, dragged toward the west. But the water was growing dark, the surface above her head dazzlingly bright, broken by a shower of cloudless rain.

Aloê burst into the air spouting like a porpoise. The shore was surprisingly far away, considering how briefly she had been in the westward current. She lay supine on the surface of the water, half-submerged, basking in the morning sun until the sea currents grew quiet.

The Green Man was gone. Somehow she knew it—the same way she had sensed the thing's presence; she knew it was gone into the wilderness of worlds beyond the gateway in the west.

She wished good luck to whoever had to deal with it next. Perhaps it would land in a world too hostile to let it live. In any case, it was no longer a danger to those she had sworn to guard. She rolled over in the water and struck out wearily for shore.

          ⋙⋘

Jacques Le Boeuf and John Lilly were tending the stream by the sawmill of the Great North Lumber Co., and nasty work they found it. Partly because they were doing it together—there was no man in the whole lumber camp that either one detested as much as the other—but mostly because of the odd things that came down the river.

Jacques lost his footing and fell in among the logs. Quickly he heaved himself out again (knowing that the lumber jostling in the stream could crush him, and that he would wait a long time before John Lilly fished him out). He put one hand on one of the logs (an odd, oaklike thing), and his hand sank mushily into the greenish bark.

Jacques hissed in disgust and vaulted out. He stared in horror at the green slime on his hand and smeared it on his shirt. "Some damn weird things come floating down the river after a fog," he said to Lilly. "Look at that damn green oak. It never came from the damn lumber camp: it's still got its damn branches. We should haul it out—it'll jam in the damn flue."

"I think it will pass," said John Lilly stiffly. "If the Lord grants us bounty without labor, shall we refuse? Please do not say 'damn.'"

"Why the hell not?" replied Jacques truculently. He saw, with annoyance, that John Lilly was right and that the green slimy oak passed easily along the flue. "Next you'll be telling me not to take the Devil's name in vain."

"Please don't."

"There's nothing in your English Bible against it. I was reading it last night—"

"I told you not to read my damn Bible!" shouted John Lilly, and he might have continued if at that moment there had not come a high-pitched inhuman scream from inside the sawmill.

"Your damn green oak has bound up the damn buzz saw!" Jacques shouted, with enormous satisfaction, and they ran into the mill to see.

Jacques was right and wrong. The saw was jammed, but not by the oak: it was caught on a knife with a weird glittering hilt. Beneath the buzzsaw they found the remains of the green oak, or so they guessed. But there was little wood, just an envelope of greenish bark—severed by the buzzsaw—and flowing from it quantities of red stinking fluid that looked like blood, but wasn't. And swimming in the fluid were quantities of bone fragments, deeply etched as with acid. This was what they saw, but they could not explain it, then or ever.

>⋹⋹

Meanwhile, in another world, Aloê Oaij took the coast road southward, bringing the news to the frightened town by the sea.

PART TWO

GUARDED AND UNGUARDED LANDS

Life was a fly that faded, and death a drone that stung;
The world was very old indeed when you and I were young.
—G. K. Chesterton

CHAPTER SIX

A Thousand Towers

Tower Ambrose, ancestral home of the Ambrosii in the Wardlands, was struck with lightning seven times in a single night, after a month of increasingly frequent lightning strikes. The next morning, half the remaining workers there quit.

"It's a bad omen," one of them told Deor syr Theorn as he paid her off.

"Personally, I don't believe in omens," said the next one. "I just don't want to get struck by lightning."

"I know what you mean," said the dwarf. "Silver or stones?"

"Stones, thanks."

When they were gone, Deor sadly eyed the household's depleted stock of silver and gemstones and then flipped the strongbox shut. The eye on the lid winked at him and clamped the bolts shut like teeth.

Deor climbed the long winding stairway to the top of the tower where Morlock's workshop was. The lock on the door recognized him as he approached and loosened its brazen fingers from the doorpost, allowing him to enter, which he did cautiously.

Morlock Ambrosius lay in deep visionary withdrawal on the floor of the workroom. The Banestone, the gem whose final making had killed Saijok Mahr, glowed luridly on his chest: Morlock was using it as a focus for his vision these days. Over him a cloud of black-and-white crystalline fragments floated in the air. In their center was about half of a longsword made of the same black-and-white crystal. As Deor watched, one of the fragments settled into place and seemed to grow into the sword.

Deor picked up a long wooden stick he kept by for this purpose and reached out with it to prod Morlock. "Hey!" he shouted. "You! Descend from your vision! We need to talk."

Deor know that Morlock heard him—he was not asleep, after all—but he expected the process to take some time. He sat down on a nearby bench and watched the half-made sword descend into a long lead-lined box, and the crystalline fragments followed it in a steady rain, each one fitting into place on the sword like a piece in a three-dimensional puzzle.

When that was done, some more time passed. Deor thought about what he'd had for breakfast, and what he was going to have for lunch.

Eventually, Morlock's eyes opened and he rolled to his feet. His dark-ringed eyes were bloodshot; his face was paler and thinner than Deor had ever seen it. The dwarf was worried for his *harven* kin, though he hardly knew how to say it, what question to ask.

"Praise the day, Vocate Morlock," the dwarf said. "I suppose you were at that nonsense all night."

"Most of it," Morlock admitted. "Couldn't sleep. How are you?"

"Unhappy. Half the workers quit this morning. I've got some of the dwarves running the impulse wheel, and the cleaning staff has mostly stayed on (thank you, God Sustainer). But there is no one working in the kitchen at all."

Morlock thought of food as fuel and was more or less indifferent to its form. His response in full was, "Eh."

Deor's opinions on food were wholly different, and he gave Morlock a selection of them now. "That won't do, *harven* Morlock. There are people in this tower besides yourself: the workers who braved lightning bolts to stay here deserve something better than dried meat and stale bread. So do I, if it comes to that. What if you have one of your colleagues over for dinner? What are we to offer them?"

"There's a cookshop down the bluff that could cater a meal."

Deor thought for a moment and then said with horror, "You can't mean the Speckles? You understand they got their name from the condition of their produce? When they brag about their fresh meat, they are talking about the things living in their uncooked vegetables. The meat proper is cooked on a biannual basis, and I have it on good report that they harvest it exclusively from swamp rats."

"I ate there all the time when I was a thain."

"I'm sorry to hear it. No, that won't do either, Morlock."

"We'll have to hire new people, then."

"With what? Our stocks of silver and gemstones are very low. You're sure we can't make a little gold? Just a little gold?"

"No."

"It's quite easy."

"Yes. So easy that it would be of no value. Silver passes as currency only because people believe that artificial silver can be detected."

"I bet we can make silver that would pass any test, Morlock."

"Yes. Except the most obvious one. A convenient and indefinite supply of silver with no known source will inevitably raise suspicions."

"So? It'll get us through our present difficulties. And then . . ."

"And then no one will want our money. No, we'll just have to sell some things."

"Sell what? The shelves are bare, Morlock."

"Go to a few markets today; see what people are paying good money for. We'll make it better and sell it for less. I've been drawing templates for a new deck of cards, also. We can run up a few of those; the original packs were pretty well-liked."

"When will we do all this? Your Graith resumes its Station in a few days, if you haven't forgotten."

"There'll be time." Morlock looked at Deor and said, "What's really wrong?"

"I don't like all this lightning," Deor admitted uneasily. "I don't understand what you're doing with *that*." He gestured at the lead-lined box. "It's no kind of making I can understand. Why do you have to use that damn Banestone? Can't you just swing a hammer, like the old days?" He was half joking, half not.

Morlock shrugged his crooked shoulders. For a while, Deor thought that was the only answer he would get. At last Morlock said, "It's the kind of making this work needs. I meditated long over the nature of Gryregaest. When I found it in pieces on the Hill of Storms, I thought it was broken."

"And it wasn't?"

"Not exactly. It was . . . dead. The pieces were once united by a talic bond, like the one uniting soul to flesh. I am . . . reweaving them again, piece by piece. But when it is whole, if I can make it whole, it will not be Gryregaest anymore. I will give it a new name. One to honor Oldfather Tyr, I think."

Deor bowed his head in honor of the late Eldest of Theorn Clan, Morlock's *harven* father. The old dwarf had died recently while Morlock was out in the unguarded lands, and Deor knew his *harven* kin was still in grief. So was Deor, for that matter.

"And the lightning?" he asked presently, thinking Morlock's attention had wandered.

"Deortheorn," Morlock said, without seeming to reply, "have you read Lucretius?"

"No. What is it?"

"A poet from my mother's world. He lived four or five hundred years before she was born. I've been reading a lot of Latin lately."

"No wonder you look sick."

"I look sick?" Morlock seemed dismayed. That dismayed Deor: he had never known Morlock to worry about his appearance. Never.

"Yes. You were telling me about this Latin poet, Lucretius."

"He claimed that everything was made up of invisible particles called atoms."

"God Avenger! What do the superstitious maunderings of a deranged poet have to do with these lightning strikes?"

"When I am deep in my vision, reweaving the blade . . . I seem to see them. The atoms, or . . . or something. They dance in the air like motes of dust. There is a darker kind, implicit with some physical energy that is just subtalic, on the verge of the immaterial. They cluster about like flies as I reweave the blade. They seem to call the lightning to them somehow. Or they are a silence the lightning strives to dispel. I don't know. I don't know. But I am starting to know. I summoned most of those thunderbolts last night; the aether from the lightning was useful in binding the blade."

"You"—Deor hastily revised what he was going to say—"always surprise me, Morlocktheorn. But in the interests of keeping our workers—"

"Do they have relatives?"

"I don't know who you mean," Deor admitted.

"The workers who stayed."

"I don't know. I suppose some of them must have." Deor still didn't see what Morlock was driving at.

"Maybe they are also unafraid of lightning. You might ask if they are interested in working here. I also have friends in the League of Silent Men. You might send a message to them, seeing if any of their people need work." Morlock's bloodshot eyes peered at his *harven* kin. "I'm not giving you too much to do?"

"Not really. Anyway, I'll repay you double when you get back here tonight. I suppose you'll be off on your usual rounds?"

"Yes." Morlock ran one hand through his dark tangled hair, another over his stubble-laden chin. "How do I look?"

"I told you; you look sick. You should stay home and get some rest, but you won't."

"I'm not sick. But I'll wash and shave before I go. Change clothes too, I guess. Is there hot water in the washroom?"

"How would I know, Vocate Morlock? I washed before dawn, with cold water in my closet, as God Creator intended. But the impulse wheel has been running for hours, so I assume the hot water reservoir is full."

"Then." Morlock nodded to his *harven*-kin, punched him gently on the shoulder as he passed, and ran down the stairs.

"Don't forget to eat something!" Deor roared after him, without any hope he would be listened to. Heard, yes; listened to, no. If Morlock was not sick, what in the canyon was wrong with him?

Deor wandered through the workroom, looking for the templates Morlock had talked about. If they were anywhere near complete, he could get some of their kin to start working on them right away: dwarves liked to do things with their hands, even (or especially) when they were running on the impulse wheel.

He found some of the new cards on a drawing table. Deor found them disturbing, but that didn't mean they weren't good. There was one of Tower Ambrose being struck by lightning; a dwarvish figure with a bundle in his arms was seen jumping from the tower. "Watch over us all, Oldfather Tyr," Deor said, smiling, when he recognized the figure, remembered the story.

Next to the sketches was a piece of Latin (Deor could recognize it, if not read it), and on the same page a bunch of scribbling in Morlock's hand. It looked as if he was trying a translation from Latin verse into Wardic. The clearest part ran like this:

But my tongue can't talk;
a slender fire sears me under the skin;
ringing re-echoes in my ears;
my two eyes are touched by twin night.

Was it a medical text? Deor wondered. These sounded like pretty unpleasant symptoms. Something from that Lucretius fellow? Deor didn't like to think about atoms bouncing around inside his nose and ears; it seemed unsanitary. Maybe that's what it was about.

But there were a few other words on the page that stood out clear, among many that were struck out or smeared with ink: "like a god" and "sweetly laughing."

Slowly the pieces of the puzzle came together, like the pieces growing into Morlock's damn sword.

"This is a love poem," Deor said aloud, not quite believing it until he heard his own words. "He's in love."

It all made sense now. Deor had actually seen Morlock comb his hair on five occasions in the preceding month, and he never left the house anymore without putting on fresh clothes, sometimes of rather bizarre cut.

It seemed all too likely to end in disaster. But courtship was rather different for dwarves, and Deor could think of no way he could help.

"Poor Morlock," Deor said. "Poor whoever-she-is, too," he added, equally sincerely.

CHAPTER SEVEN

The Graith

Naevros syr Tol was the greatest swordsman under the guard, perhaps the world, and it had been seventeen years since he had last felt the impact of another's blade, in practice or in a real fight.

Before this morning. The second time he felt the blunted end of his pupil's practice sword graze his left arm, his eyes grew hot, and a broad angry smile spread like burning oil across his dark handsome face.

He brought his pupil's sword into a bind and knocked him off balance, and delivered what would have been a killing blow to the chest, if Naevros had been using a real sword. It must have stung a bit, even so.

The other man's pale hard face hardly twitched. The gray eyes took on a knowing look, though, and Naevros could not even pretend to himself that he had not overreacted out of vanity.

"You hold yourself a little out of true, because of your shoulders," he said to his pupil. "You'll want to watch that. It makes you unstable, as you see."

"I'll remember," said Morlock Ambrosius wryly.

"That's enough for today. My blood is running a little hot, I'm afraid."

Morlock nodded impassively and turned away to put his practice sword in the wall-sheath. He picked up his red cloak and threw it over his forearm; he was still sweating from the practice bouts. His shirt was an unusually stylish one this morning. If Naevros wasn't mistaken, the garment had been run up by his own tailor. But it was the sort of thing one only wore on formal occasions; Naevros himself was wearing a raggedy old thing he usually threw on when he was exercising.

"You've done some real fighting since we last fenced," Naevros said as they walked from the courtyard to the front door of Naevros' modest city house.

"In Kaen," Morlock said, nodding.

"Real fighting makes all the difference somehow. The same sort of decisions appear in a different light when one's life is riding on the outcome. Kaen, eh? Haven't been there for a hundred years. Is it as bad as ever?"

"I only saw part of the coast. Hope I never go back," the crooked man added with a grimace.

Naevros could not cordially like the man, but he refused to dislike him either. For one thing, the fellow was dangerous, and Naevros made it his practice never to dislike someone who was dangerous, even if he had to kill them. It was easier to see someone's strengths and weaknesses without a cloud of dislike in the way. They said that love was blind, but in Naevros' extensive experience it was really hate that kept people from seeing, or understanding what they saw.

"It's lunchtime," he said to Morlock, as they stood in the street. "Come down to the cookshop and we'll split a chicken and a pitcher of wine."

Morlock was about to give one answer when all of a sudden he paused and then gave another. "Sorry. Must go. Thanks lesson. At Illion's?" If the last was a question, as it seemed to be, he ran off without an answer.

Naevros was still decoding this, and pondering a few other matters, when a familiar contralto voice broke into his meditations. "I find you deep in thought, Vocate Naevros. Planning your strategy for the new Station?"

"Nothing is ever decided at Station," he answered reflexively. "Though some things get settled at the parties before and after. A good midday to you, Vocate Aloê. Will you split a chicken and a pitcher of wine down at the Benches cookshop? I am dying of hunger."

"I will not split a chicken," Aloê Oaij replied. "But I might eat part of a chicken someone else has split. They cook it well with peppers down at the Benches. They have good pastries, too. Those puffy glazed things filled with ellberry custard? Glorious."

"You're a glutton, Aloê," said Naevros, smiling as he turned to walk down toward the Benches. "How do you maintain your girlish figure?"

"It's a womanly figure," Aloê said, not walking alongside him, "and I maintain it with frequent exercise. Speaking of which, were you going to change?"

"Change what?" Naevros was surprised. "My clothes? To go down to a cookshop? Are you serious?"

"I've noticed that excessively handsome men are sometimes careless about their appearance. I suppose they think they can afford to be."

"I hadn't noticed that at all."

"That's why I brought it to your attention."

Naevros grumbled a bit, but when he saw that Aloê was serious he went back into his house. Aloê waited downstairs, reading a book, while he took a quick run through the flood room and threw on some decent but not gaudy clothes. He was not rich, and he was saving his gaudy clothes for the social events surrounding the Station. Besides, he had no need to show off in front of Aloê: they were old friends; he was her sometime mentor, now ally. And she thought him excessively handsome. He liked to dwell on that last part especially.

Naevros ran into his housekeeper, a gossipy old queck-bug named Verch, on his way downstairs. "The Vocate Aloê is waiting downstairs!" the house-keeper said eagerly. "Is she staying for lunch?"

"We're going out for lunch, Verch. There's no need to trouble yourself."

Verch pouted a bit. "Are you at least taking her to the Dancing Day at Vocate Illion's?"

"I'll be accompanied by the Honorable Ulvana, as you well know, Verch," Naevros replied, a warning tone in his voice.

Verch's face fell further. "Honorable," he repeated rebelliously under his breath and stood aside to let his employer pass.

Aloê was perched on a chair close enough to the foot of the stair to have heard this whole exchange. She grinned at Naevros as he descended, and then he was sure that she had.

"Verch is still taking good care of you, I see," she remarked when they were safely out of doors.

"Nearly unbearable. But he's cheap, and I'm broke."

"And Noreê says you were saying the same thing two hundred years ago."

"Some truths are eternal." He looked sideways at her. It seemed odd to him that he had not known her two hundred years ago, that he hadn't always known her.

She was worth knowing. She was nearly as tall as Naevros himself; her skin was dark brown; her hair: dark ringlets of gold; her irises: brighter rings of gold; her lips were darkly rosy and full. She had the hard balanced muscularity of a dancer or a wrestler. But to say that she was the most beautiful woman in A Thousand Towers—and many did say it—was hardly to scratch the surface of this remarkable woman. That she was daring and courageous in mortal combat was a fact Naevros had witnessed with his own eyes. That she was deeply learned in the intricacies of Wardic custom he had been assured by those who knew and cared about such things. Most importantly, for Naevros, she had a kind of mental deftness, a feel for situations.

He admired her very much, and from almost their first meeting there had been a rapport between them, an unstated bond of admiration and trust. It had never, somehow, become a sexual relationship. He had many of these (the Honorable Ulvana being merely his latest partner and perhaps not the most notable one), but somehow they never lasted, and none of them had ever mattered like his bond with Aloê.

He dreaded the day when she made a public union with someone. There were many suitors, male and female, in A Thousand Towers and elsewhere, who would have gladly paired with her. But somehow she walked untouched among them all. If she coupled with anyone—he assumed she did—they must not have mattered to her; she never walked with them in the light of day as she was doing with him, now.

He was glad of that. He hoped, knowing it was selfish, that this would never change. But he feared it must: someday she would find someone, and their bond would be transferred to that other . . . and then Naevros would kill him. It would be pointless and horrible, and Naevros knew all that, but somehow he thought he would do it all the same, the way barbarian kings ordered slaves executed at their funerals. His link with Aloê had swiftly become the most important bond in his life; its death might require a barbaric funeral, some sort of sacrifice.

"That mushroom of yours is back in town," he said aloud, to turn the conversation into a safer stream.

"Mushroom. Mushroom," she mused for a moment, and then said, with an indifference that warmed Naevros' heart, "Oh, you mean Morlock. I thought I saw him standing with you, but he ran off so fast I couldn't be sure."

"It was him."

"Back for more lessons? Hasn't he learned all you can teach him yet?"

"Only about swords."

She moved her darkly golden head to indicate her indifference to swords and the people obsessed by them.

"I think he's taking notes on my wardrobe."

Aloê smiled gently.

"No, really," Naevros said. "I'm fairly sure he's consulting my tailor, anyway. He was wearing a wide-sleeved shirt with yellow silk inset, like one I was wearing a few years ago."

"I remember."

"I think he's hoping to make a splash at the Station, or perhaps to catch someone's attention. Poor woman."

"Or man, as the case may be."

"I don't think so. He's sporting a new bite mark at the base of his neck, and I'm pretty sure it was made by a woman's teeth. Although the edges are a little ragged . . . I might be wrong, I suppose."

Aloê shrugged.

"Someone is killing gods in Kaen," Naevros remarked.

"That's— Oh? Really? How do you know?"

"Their embalmers keep writing me for advice. How do you think I know? People travelling in Kaen have said so. A number of cities on the eastern coast of the Narrow Sea have lost their name-gods. Some cities have just gone vacant. Your mushroom was telling me an odd tale of a city taken over by a giant plant. But others say there are cities that have turned to the worship of the Two Powers."

"Has there been an invasion from Anhi?" asked Aloê, naming the confederation of cities far to the east, where worship of the Two Powers was the state religion.

"Not a military one. Hard to say what the number of missionaries may be. The Court of Heresiarchs was encouraging foreign missionaries for a while."

"Yes, I remember hearing they would soak them in pitch and use them as torches for their evening parties."

"Kaen is a brutish place. But there's something to be said for their attitude toward missionaries."

"Have cities in the interior been losing their gods?" Aloê asked.

"Apparently not. Just on the coastline."

"Facing us, across the Narrow Sea."

"Yes."

"That sounds like another invasion attempt, doesn't it?"

"Yes, that's the best opinion among those who've heard the news."

"You always have the best news, Naevros."

"I hear it from my tailor. What do you think the Graith ought to do about it?"

By then they were at the Benches, but they continued to talk about foreign affairs and avoid talking about their own all the way through lunch.

><

A few days later, the Graith assembled at the Station Chamber, just inside the crumbling and disused wall of the city. In a ritual older than the Wardlands themselves, the Summoner of the City called the vocates to stand at the long oval table in the domed chamber in the early light of morning, with the light of the sun filtering through the windows on the western edge of the dome.

After the opening rituals, the day was given over to the news from Kaen. Five vocates and three thains spoke; all had travelled in or near Kaen over the past year, and all had news of some god who had been displaced from its name-city—all of them along the eastern coast of the Narrow Sea. Morlock spoke briefly of his experience over the summer past, but did not join in the discussion that followed.

Neither did Aloê, but most of the vocates present had one or fifteen thousand words to say. Even Naevros spoke at some length, smiling wryly as he caught Aloê's bored eye. Another time Aloê saw Morlock looking—not at her, exactly, but in her direction. He was dressed less splendidly than the previous day (if Naevros hadn't been joking about that), and his face looked a little haggard, as if he weren't sleeping well. The sight made her want to sneak off and take a nap. How they all talked and talked and talked. . . .

Of course, nothing was decided. The sun was setting when Illion asked leave to stand down. His request was granted by acclamation, and the Summoner of the City adjourned the Station until the next day at noon. Many of them had been attending Illion's parties on the opening night of Station for more than three hundred years, and the rest had other plans for the evening.

In the scramble that followed adjournment Aloê met up with Illion and Naevros, who were talking about the government of Anhi.

"Vocates," Aloê said coolly. "You've seen more of these than I have. Is the first day of Station usually so boring?"

"Only if something important is happening, or likely to happen," said white-haired Noreê, coming along behind her. "Then everyone wants to get his oar in the water, so that he can say afterward he helped steer the Graith in its crisis."

"But nothing ever gets done at Station—only talking. So those-who-know tell me," replied Aloê, with a quick glare at Naevros, who grinned unrepentantly back.

"There's some merit in deliberation," suggested Illion.

"Only if it leads to useful action."

Illion the Wise smiled and did not disagree.

"Come away with me, Aloê," Noreê said. "These gentlemen have deliberating to do."

Aloê would have rather stayed sniping and snarking with the men. They amused her; and Noreê, with her bitter scarred face and bitter blue eyes, rather scared her. But she was not inclined to give into her fears, so she took the older vocate's arm and they walked together out of the chamber and into the street. Both places were crowded, but wherever Noreê walked a way opened up before her.

"I won't keep you long, young Aloê," Noreê said. "But I wanted to keep you from sliding into the error that many members of the Graith fall into."

"What is that?"

"They think the Graith is important."

"Oh." Aloê looked at the woman who had slain two of the Dark Seven with weapons, and a third with her bare hands—a woman who had dedicated her life to the defense of the Wardlands, a woman who had worn the red cloak of a vocate for four hundred years. "The Graith is *not* important?"

"Of course not. A pack of silly old fools, full of talk and empty of action, just as you saw it today."

"Then—"

"But the individual Guardians—especially the vocates one by one: *they* matter. Today was just talk. Tomorrow will be just talk. Stations are mostly talk. But talk can spark ideas, and ideas can fire some person, some individual, to action. That is why we do this."

"I think I see."

"Good. Run and play, then. Perhaps I'll see you tomorrow."

The deadly old woman walked away, leaving Aloê stunned by the double blow. Run and play? If she'd patted Aloê on the head, she couldn't have been more patronizing. And: *perhaps* she'd see Aloê tomorrow? Why *perhaps*? Was that a second insult . . . or a piece of veiled advice?

She was still pondering the matter when Jordel walked up to her and asked her why she was standing there in the street like a silly cow.

"To get your attention, of course," she replied. "What else does any woman in A Thousand Towers want to do?"

"I consider that remark a violation of the Treaty of Kirach Starn," Jordel said coolly, referring to the memorable day a few years ago when they had agreed to stop hating each other's guts.

"Then let's have less cow- talk," she replied briskly, and he shrugged and nodded. "What's up?" she continued.

"Baran and Thea and a few of her friends are all getting something to eat and then going over to Illion's."

"I guess I'll chew the cud with you, then."

"Enough with the cows. I'm sick of cows."

"Did another one break your heart, J?"

⊰⊱

Jordel was still obsessing about cows when they arrived at Illion's an hour or two later, so Aloê took the opportunity to sneak away into the already-dense crowds.

It took a lot of people to crowd up Illion's place. It had belonged to Illion's family for some portion of forever, before the city had stretched out this far, and the garden walls rambled over a group of hills that had stayed green and fairly wild as the web of stone streets spun itself on every side. But the family had built a medium-sized house and a rather gigantic dance hall in the center of the hills, and (ever since Illion and his brother had inherited the property) they held a Dancing Day on the first and last days of Station. Practically everyone in the world attended them.

Everyone in the world seemed to already be there. She saw Callion the

Proud and his wife, whatshername; they were bickering, as usual. She gave them a wide berth. She ran into Rild of the Third Stone and talked for a while about herbs. Afterward she met Vocate Vineion and talked for a while about his dogs. Eventually Vineion drifted away in search of a beer. As Aloê wandered on, she came across Morlock Ambrosius shuffling a deck of cards and explaining to a few hangers-on how they worked. Since she was interested in the matter herself, she stood nearby drinking a glass of cool wine.

"How do the archetypes know the future, though?" someone was asking.

Morlock shrugged his crooked shoulders. From the expressions of a few people watching, they would have preferred that he hadn't. Aloê wondered if he had done it because he knew it would bother them, or because he didn't care. Either way: good on him.

"The cards, and their archetypes, don't know anything," Morlock replied, after a pause to choose his words. "A well-made archetype is connected to the future and the past. As the future changes direction, the cards are inclined to fall in different patterns. A good reader reads the patterns."

"The future changes direction?" someone wondered.

Morlock nodded. "Until it becomes the past."

"Well, I don't know. I'm not really interested in the future."

"You can also use them to play games," Morlock replied. "Patientia, or Púca, for instance."

"Púca? What's that?"

"I'll show you." Morlock, with a deadpan expression, shuffled the deck and began to deal out cards on a nearby table.

"The man is a shameless whore," a voice remarked quietly from near her elbow.

"*Ath, rokhlan,*" she said, raising her glass, when she recognized the speaker as Deor syr Theorn. She didn't know exactly what *ath* meant, but she knew it was a polite greeting for a dwarf who could claim the rank of dragonkiller (*rokhlan*).

The dwarf's dark gray eyes moved in slightly different directions, an oddly lizardlike behavior that she had learned to associate with dwarvish embarrassment when she was in the north a few years ago.

"*Ath,*" he replied. "*Ath, rokhlan, sael.*" He raised the mug of beer in his fist.

"I hadn't realized that whoring was among your *harven*-kinsman's talents,"

Aloê remarked easily. She knew about fifteen words of Dwarvish and liked to trot them out whenever she had the chance, which wasn't too often in A Thousand Towers.

"Neither had I," Deor replied. "But poverty brings out new sides of people, it seems."

"Poverty? God Sustainer: I thought the Ambrosii were as rich as filth."

"I'm not sure what that means, *rokhlan*, but I am sure that Morlock is poor as a fish."

Aloê wasn't completely sure what *that* meant, but she nodded and gestured with the wineglass to continue.

"I mean, if he's going to keep striking the tower with lightning, how can he expect to keep workers?"

"Um. I'm not sure." In fact, she was not sure what the metaphor *striking the tower with lightning* meant; it sounded vaguely salacious.

"The old workers have to be paid off; the new workers have to be hired; it all costs money. And a little goldmaking would solve all our problems."

"Don't do that," she said reflexively. "No one will do business with you anymore. Not that lots of people don't do a little goldmaking now and then," she admitted. "But the trick is to do it when you don't seem to need money. Uh. So I've heard."

"And so I've heard. So we have to sell things, right? Morlock is a master of makers, perhaps the greatest of all since, well, you know."

She didn't, but nodded anyway.

"So Morlock is teaching these rubes to play Púca so that they'll all want packs of cards. Which we happen to have stacks of in Tower Ambrose; we spent the last couple days inking them."

"Hey, I got a regal velox!" someone at the card table was shouting.

"Remarkable," Morlock said coolly. "A very rare hand."

"Where can I get some of these?"

"Take the pack away with you. I have more at home."

"Thanks, Crookback! Who's in for the next hand?"

Morlock's left hand clenched as he turned away to look straight into the pale scarred face of Vocate Noreê.

"Good fortune, Vocate," he said politely.

"It'll be good when you and all your kind are dead," remarked the terrible old woman, loudly enough to be heard by Aloê and a number of other people in the crowd nearby, who turned to look pointedly at the exchange.

Morlock shrugged. "Then. Bad fortune to you, I suppose."

The crowd laughed and turned away, judging Morlock the victor in the exchange.

Aloê herself thought that he'd handled it well: his calm indifference to Noreê's naked hate seemed especially wounding to the old vocate.

"Morlock's pretty good at backchat," Deor conceded grudgingly. "If he says only one word in a conversation, it'll be the last one. What in the canyon is wrong with him now?"

Morlock had turned away from Noreê's hate-filled gaze and taken one long haggard look in the direction of Deor and Aloê. Now he turned again and walked away into the crowd.

"Noreê must have stung him pretty deeply," Aloê guessed, grabbing a fresh glass of wine and another mug of beer from a passing steward. "Here." She handed the beer to Deor.

"Thanks!" the dwarf said. "I always have trouble getting their attention, for some reason." Now he had two mugs: his full and his empty.

Aloê had left her empty glass on the steward's tray, but the man hadn't waited for Deor's mug. "Steward!" she called out, and the man came back as if she'd grabbed him by the ear.

"Take my friend's empty also, please," she said.

The steward looked at her, gazed vacantly about, finally saw Deor waving the empty mug, and lowered his tray to accommodate the dwarf. He stole one last glance at Aloê and walked away into the crowd.

"I like how you did that," the dwarf said approvingly. "I usually have to whack them on their belt buckles to get them to notice me. But I don't think it's your height. There are lots of people here taller than you. You didn't scream at him, either. It was as if he had a reason to listen whenever you talked to him. I—oh. Uh-oh. Oh, God Avenger."

"What is it?" Aloê said with some concern.

"Nothing too important. A question has been bothering me the last few days, and I think I just figured it out. You—um, you're not looking especially well tonight, Vocate Aloê, are you? You always look pretty much like this, don't you?"

"You're not flirting with me, are you, Deor?"

"Eh? God Creator: no. Our relations are much better regulated than the conniptions you of the Other Ilk twist yourselves into. For instance, I just got a note from the gynarch of my clan, indicating whom I am to mate with and when, subject to the Eldest's approval and my consent. It won't be too much trouble, and I'm looking forward to raising a few younglings. No, I was just asking a factual question."

"All right. In that spirit: no. I think I must look as I usually do. My tunic isn't especially new; it's one of the three I wear regularly. Why do you ask?"

"Just a kind of . . . a kind of esthetic interest, I guess. What do you think of this Kaenish mess?"

They talked for a while about the dying gods of Kaen, and then the currents of the crowd carried them apart.

Later she found herself sitting with Thea on a stone bench by a fountain outside of the entrance hall. Thea was fending off questions from a woman who wanted her to do something Thea had no interest in doing.

"But if those statues aren't wrong, nothing is wrong!" the strange woman was insisting. "There they are, naked, doing things no one should do in public! Someone should do something about it! But the Graith has refused my plea many a time!"

"I don't say it's right," Thea replied. "I just say it's none of my business. I don't judge; I defend. Those statues are not a threat to the Wardlands."

"They are a threat to the Wardlands' morality and ethical fiber. What is more important than that?"

"Them," Aloê corrected absently. "Those are two things."

"Look," said Thea patiently, "if you think the statues are so dangerous, why don't you take them down yourself?"

"But they're on his property!"

"Why do you assume we can do what you can't do? Why assume you can't do what we can do?"

"But . . . but . . . you're the Graith."

"'A pack of silly old fools, full of talk and empty of action,'" Aloê quoted dreamily.

The strange woman glanced with horror at Aloê, still wearing her bloodred vocate's cloak, and seemed to be about to say something.

"We have no more rights than you in the matter, madam," Thea intervened. "The Graith is a voluntary association with a specific purpose—like the Arbiters of the Peace or the Road-mender's Union. But we are not a government. We're just people who are responsible for what they do—like you."

"But I had to send my children to school by a different route!"

"That seems like the best solution, all around."

"But I want a better one!"

"Maybe you'll find one. But, God Avenger witness my words, I hope it does not involve the Graith, or me. And now, if you'll excuse us, madam, my friend and I are going to go in and dance."

They left the woman sputtering behind them and re-entered the entrance hall.

"I'm not sure if I'm dancing tonight," Aloê said.

"I'm sure that I'm not," Thea replied. "A horse stepped on my foot at Baran's place a halfmonth ago, and it's still giving me trouble. But I was tired of explaining to that woman that she did not live in a monarchy."

"I was at dinner at Earno's the other day—"

"Namedropper."

"—and someone . . . it was Thynê, the chronicler, as a matter of fact, if it's names you want. Anyway, she was saying that monarchy is a natural instinct, that people want to follow a leader like sheep want to follow a shepherd, that the Wardlands is destined to fall back into a monarchy someday."

"What do you think?" Thea asked.

"I don't know. There are lots of people who are afraid to take responsibility for their own lives, like that woman back there. But there are just as many people, some of them the same people, who are afraid of having their lives interfered with. So. I don't know. What do you think?"

"I don't think anything's inevitable. Except my next drink."

There was a stewards' table near at hand, and Thea tapped on the red-cloaked crooked shoulders of the man standing in front of it.

"Order us a drink, won't you, Morlock?" Thea said cheerily.

"Eh," said Morlock, and stood aside.

"I guess that will be more efficient," Thea agreed, and they stepped forward. Thea had a mug of beer and Aloê a glass of gently steaming tea. Morlock sipped one of his own and eyed them gloomily over its rim. He still hadn't recovered from his encounter with Noreê, apparently. Anyway, whenever he met Aloê's eye his face seemed haggard, his expression wounded.

"You're not saying much today, Morlock," Thea said, after a pull or two at her beer. "What do you think of this Kaenish mess?"

Morlock shrugged. "If the Kaenish gods are dying: what's killing them? I don't care about the Kaeniar—"

"It's not nice to say so."

"—but a threat to them might be a threat to us. That's all."

"Well, that's our business, isn't it?" Thea reached out and touched the scar at the base of Morlock's neck. "What's that? Any threat to the Guard there?"

"Woman bit me."

"Did she have reason?"

"She thought so."

"Business or pleasure?"

Morlock's face took on a remembering expression. "Both."

"Oho. I didn't think you were the type to pay for it, Morlock."

"I do not. I did not. You will excuse me." He brushed past them and walked into the crowd.

"Will we excuse him?" Thea wondered. "I'm not so sure. I thought he was a little terse when we were fighting dragons together up north, but he was positively chatty compared to the way he's been lately. What the rip is wrong with him?"

"Noreê's getting at him, I think. They had words, earlier."

"Oh. Yes. She does hate all the Ambrosii. That's nothing new, though. I mean, she tried to kill him on the day he was born."

"What? You're joking."

"What's the punchline, then? No, I think it's true. The dwarves stopped it somehow; I heard about it from them when we were up north. They don't care for her much up there."

"Ick."

"Well, I used more syllables when I heard, but yes. Come on; let's mingle. Maybe we'll see Morlock and Noreê mix it up. Maybe we'll see some pretty fellows dancing. Maybe Naevros will show up without that vile whore he's been squiring around town. The night is full of possibilities, and beer."

"I hate beer."

"Then try the possibilities."

>€

Morlock was walking through the crowd, as blind as a stone, when he heard someone say quietly, *"Hwaet, Morlocktheorn."*

In that crowd, there was only one person that could be. It was against dwarvish custom to speak a language that those nearby didn't share—unless what was being said was none of their business, as this obviously was.

"Hey, Morlock-my-kin," Deor was saying in Dwarvish. "Did you talk to her?"

"Thea?" Morlock replied. "A little."

"No, thump-head. Did you talk to *her*? Please don't pretend you don't know who I'm talking about."

"What would be the point?" Morlock said, opening his hands concessively.

"The point of talking to her? Those-who-watch, guide my steps. How in Helgrind's stone jaws should I know what the point is? If you of the Other Ilk had sensible arrangements like us, the question wouldn't even arise. But I tell you something, my *harven*-kin— No, you will *not* turn away; you will *listen* to me."

"I am Other Ilk. To you. To her. To everyone here. To everything that lives."

"What? No, don't try to explain it. Listen, I said, and listen I meant. You don't have anyone to arrange a mating with her. Stop writhing; that's what you are thinking about, I take it?"

"It's not *thinking*," Morlock said miserably.

"All right. Whatever you call it. No one can set you up. You will have to do it yourself."

"I've seen others talk to her. She sends them all away. It's no good. Nothing would be any good."

"Is she mated with Naevros? Is that it? I've heard some people say so."

"No," Morlock said thoughtfully. "I don't think so."

"Then I don't see what you have to lose. If you are waiting for her to be attracted by your air of mystery and make the first advance, I'm afraid your strategy doesn't seem to be working. Just talk to her. About the Graith. About Kaen. About that sword you are making. About cards. About anything. Give something a chance to happen."

"I can't."

"Are you . . . are you afraid?" The notion seemed so bizarre that Deor hesitated to even suggest it.

Morlock reflected for a moment, then said, "Possibly. But I mean I *can't*. When I see her—when I am near her . . . I can no longer see her nor anything else. A golden haze hangs in front of everything and my tongue turns to stone. I don't know what's happening. I can't speak. I have been afraid; I have been insane with anger; I have been ashamed, exultant, forgetful, remembering. None of it was like this. Yet it was all like this."

"Um." Deor thought of the poem he had read in Morlock's workshop. "Sounds like love, I guess."

Morlock shook his head, not as if he disagreed, but in bewilderment. "I loved Oldfather Tyr. I love you, my *harven*-brothers, Trua Old, and my other friends. I love my work. I love the mountains of Northhold. This is not like that."

"It may be the wrong word. Your mating, the mating of your *ruthen* kin I mean, isn't just a necessary thing, like eating, but something wrapped with emotion, delight, and pain. They call that 'love' around here. But maybe there's a better word."

"I have mated with women before. It was not like this."

"You have?" Deor hadn't known this. "Well, you are full of surprises, Morlocktheorn. Perhaps you should seek out one of those women again to relieve your—er—whatever it is you're feeling?"

"Another woman?" Morlock muttered. "Besides *her*?"

"Precisely. Precisely that. Do you think it would work?"

"No. I've no better notion, though."

"Then."

Morlock nodded solemnly, punched him gently on the shoulder and walked away into the crowd.

Thea and Aloê had joined up with Jordel and Baran again. After a quick raid on the refectory, they drifted on the currents of the crowd. These carried them finally into the great octagonal dancing hall at the center of the honeycomb of smaller rooms.

"What is that music?" Thea asked, as their ears were assaulted by a barrage of drums, lightened by the harsh bright voices of bells.

"Dancing drum-choir," Jordel said, with feigned reluctance. "You get them in Westhold. I guess we're for it, Baran."

"Speak for yourself," Baran replied. "You're the one who likes to kick his heels up."

"The people demand it. Who am I to deny them what they want?"

"I want you to take a vow of silence."

Jordel held a finger in front of his mouth and silently offered Thea his hand. They spun away onto the dance floor—in spite of Thea's foot, in spite of Jordel's cruelty in the past, in spite of everything. Aloê looked at the transfigured expression on Thea's face, looked away, and shook her head. She wondered what it was like to feel that way about someone. The drummers and bell-ringers of the choir were all skipping about in unpredictably coiling patterns; the other dancers dashed between them whenever they found an opening. It seemed to be half dance, half competition.

"There's your friend Morlock," Baran pointed out.

Aloê followed Baran's gesture and saw Morlock whirling through the tangled lines of the drum-choir. Wrapped in his arms, and vice versa, was a tall cold-faced dark-haired woman.

"Why do you call him my friend?"

Baran was surprised. "He is often with Naevros and you. Or so I thought."

"With Naevros, but not me."

Baran shrugged. His eyes were still on the dancers. Morlock and his partner—whatshername, that frosty woman, the Arbiter of the Peace up in that horrible little town by the Hill of Storms—anyway, the two of them were plunging back and forth through the choir, who were laughing and trying to block them. But whenever a gap in the line closed, another opened up, and the deft-footed couple spun through.

"He's good," the big man said reluctantly.

"She leads as often as he does," Aloê disagreed.

"That's part of being good—letting your partner lead when she knows what to do."

"Then why don't you say, 'She's good'?"

"She is."

"B," Aloê laughed, "you're trying to get me to dance."

Baran blushed a little and admitted, "I do kind of like it. But the girl is supposed to ask. Woman, I mean."

"I'll never figure you Westholders out. Baran, will you dance with me? I am not good, and have no idea what I'm going to do out there."

"I'll clue you," said Baran eagerly, and took her outstretched hand.

It was something just short of a disaster. Their first time through the drum-choir, Aloê knocked a bell right out of the ringer's hand by smacking it with her elbow. The next time she inadvertently stomped on some poor drummer's toes.

But her feet soon learned the rhythm that the drummers were making, and she also learned to trust Baran's gentle guidance. He was surprisingly light on his feet for such a big man, and quick in his mind if not quick with words. On the one occasion when she saw a collision coming (and he apparently didn't), he responded immediately to her alarmed look and her increased grip on his arms. He swung them both into a clear patch of floor and then back into the whirl.

"You're good!" she shouted, over the drums, over the bells, not really sure he would hear her. But he smiled down on her and nodded agreeably.

He didn't appeal to her eye particularly (his fistlike bumpy face was repulsive to her), but he was a remarkable man in many ways. Unfortunately, he didn't like girls, except as dancing partners.

After a few more numbers the drummer's choir retired and pair of citharodes began singing a slow ballad. Aloê and Baran dropped out by mutual agreement and retreated to the edge of the room where there were steward-tables set up. Aloê took a glass of water, and Baran grabbed a mug of dark tea that smelled like tar.

"Ick," she said cheerily, gesturing at his beverage.

He grunted absentmindedly, gazing off into the crowd, and downed the boiling hot mugful in a single gulp. "Ow," he said then, still somewhat absentmindedly.

"*What* are you looking at so intently, B?"

"Not what. Who. That boy Zalion is here. That young man. I. He. Well."

"You should go talk to him," Aloê urged him.

"Talk. Huh." He looked at her with tortured eyes.

"Dance with him, then. B, you talk better with your feet than most people do with their mouth."

"Boy isn't supposed to ask. The man, I mean."

"When it's two boys, someone's got to. I don't know what rules are bothering you, B, but you're not in Westhold anymore. No one is going to be shocked if you ask Zalion to dance."

"Uh. See you." He handed her his mug and walked off toward his heart's desire.

Silently wishing them both luck, she sniffed the dregs left in his mug, shuddered, and set it aside on the steward's table. Each to their own.

She ran into Callion and his wife, who had passed the bickering point of the evening and were in a more convivial mood. She talked with them for a while about the news from Kaen, and Callion had some interesting things to say about how one actually killed a god. He was so handsome and so impassive that one sometimes forgot there was a mind under that marbly surface.

Joyous shouts broke out behind them, and they all three turned to see the triumphant and calculatedly late arrival of Naevros syr Tol and his woman-of-the-hour, the Honorable Ulvana.

Naevros was looking well, she had to admit. He was wearing a tight-fitting suit of dark red with a plenitude of dark shining buttons—tight enough to display the taut lines of his remarkably fit body, but loose enough that he could move with his natural grace.

As for the Honorable Ulvana . . . Her dressmaker had run out of dresses, it seemed, and had settled for covering the minimal amount of her client's pasty skin with semitransparent gold bandages. That skin. It always reminded Aloê of various types of stinking cheese with the mold just scraped off: quivering, pale, and full. Ulvana had decorated herself with gobs of makeup like dabs of jam amongst the cheese. But the chief thing you noticed about Ulvana was her voice.

When Aloê was a girl she'd had a speckled hunting brach who had a bad habit of yowling through the night. Her yowl was particularly harsh on the ear, demanding attention, comfort, company, food. Ulvana's voice always reminded Aloê of that desperate lonely bitch.

"God Creator," muttered Callion's wife. "How can he stand that intolerable woman?"

"Oh, I don't know," said Callion.

Aloê turned away with a muttered excuse. She did not want to be present if their mood turned to barking again, nor did she want to have to make polite conversation with Naevros and Ulvana.

Unfortunately the currents of the crowd brought her face-to-face with Naevros before too long. He was standing at a steward's table with some sort of chocolatey confection in his hand and a quiet smile on his face. Fortunately his abominable cheese-woman was somewhere else at the moment.

They greeted each other by name and stood in silence for a while, listening to the music. It had turned more lively again: a band of horn-players, string-pluckers and bell-ringers was playing a sprightly tune with a simple rhythm.

He knew exactly how she felt, of course. His smile said it all. And he would not let her feelings change his behavior one jot; he would not apologize for his mate-of-the-moment. And, really, it was none of her business; she felt that strongly—as strongly as she felt repelled by the whole business.

They might have reached some sort of peace, standing there, listening to the music, letting their rapport speak for them. But the crowd parted like waves, and from them stepped forth the technically honorable but certainly deplorable Ulvana. She held a glass of some milky fluid in her hand and a vacantly cheery expression on her face.

"Oooh!" She gave her raspy, whine-edged wail. "Naevy-dear, you have one of those yummy treats. Gimme."

She dropped her head down and ate from his hand like an animal. He let her, his quiet smile lengthening a little as he looked down on her, giving him a fierce predatory look. Her busy tongue was licking the last traces of chocolate from Naevros' palm, a long milk-white thread of phlegm connecting tongue and hand.

Aloê turned, her throat knotting with revulsion, and walked away into the crowd.

"*Veuath, rokhlan!*" came a cheery greeting from a gap in the crowd ahead of her.

"Rokhlan Deor," she said, nodding.

"Hey, you haven't, um, you haven't seen—"

Aloê wondered desperately if there was something in the drinks that was robbing males of the ability to speak.

"—haven't seen my *harven*-kin around here anywhere, have you? Sorry for asking."

Aloê had no idea why he was apologizing but said, "I don't think I've seen him since the drum-choir retired."

"Excellent. Excellent."

"Um." Now she was doing it! "Why do you say that, if may ask? Are you trying to avoid him?"

"No. No. Maybe I shouldn't say it, but I was hoping he would slip out of the party with an old friend of his. If you know what I mean."

"Oh. Well, that's why some people come to these things—to leave with the right person. Or any person at all," she added grimly, batting away the thought of Naevros and his trull. "Things a little tense around Tower Ambrose these days?" she added.

"You have no idea. Really, you don't. I'm sorry to rush off, but I'm slated to play in the next set."

"I'll walk with you," Aloê said.

"Thanks," said the dwarf. "I won't have to stomp on so many feet that way."

They forged their way through the crowd to the dais where the band was playing. As they approached, the band wound up their tune and stepped down to general if unenthusiastic applause from the crowd.

There was a crowd of dwarves standing nearby, and they leapt up on the dais and started setting up their instruments. Two of them were putting together a great wooden wheel studded with extrusions like wineglasses tinted in the whole spectrum of colors, a glass rainbow running around the edge of the wheel.

Deor took his place in front of the wheel and made a few adjustments. There were pedals that turned or slowed the wheel, and he wanted them set exactly right. Then he worked a pedal to bring the wheel up to speed: the glass bells shone like colored lightning, reflecting the cold lights of the dancing hall. Deor took up two strikers, each with two business ends. The one he held in his right hand terminated in a flange of silvery metal on one side, with a thumblike wooden end on the other. The one he held in his left hand had a cloth-muffled end and an end like a long-haired metallic brush.

With casual skill, Deor spun both strikers in his hands. The other dwarvish musicians took up their instruments: recorders and drums and some odd stringed instruments played with some kind of stick or bow. All their eyes were on Deor.

Deor began to play, and the other dwarves joined in.

Aloê was spellbound by the glass wheel, and Deor's skill in playing it. He would let the brushes trail continually over the bells, issuing a long unearthly bloodless stream of sound, while he struck the bells swinging by on the other side of the wheel with a hard striker to rap out bright bitter exclamations of sound. The wooden end made a slightly different sound than the metal one, and Aloê was amazed at Deor's deftness. Either he was hitting those bells with exactly the right strength, to issue a maximum of volume without so much force as to break the glass, or else the bells were made with something stronger than ordinary glass. But the music was more wonderful than the instrument that made it.

Soon she realized that she knew the tune. It was a country round from Westhold. She had even danced it a few times, while staying at Three Hills, where Illion and his brother lived. Her feet itched to join in. She danced a little by herself, unable to refrain.

A hand touched her elbow. She turned to face a man she didn't know. His face was red as a beet, but it was split by a bright agreeable smile. He nodded toward the dance in progress.

"Yes!" she shouted, and leapt after him into the coil of dancers.

She didn't actually kick or maim anyone, and her partner was as enthusiastic but not necessarily more skilled than she was. She stayed with him for a second dance, since she recognized that tune as well.

But it wasn't long before she realized the second dance was a mistake. Naevros and Ulvana were also on the dance floor, and this round required all the dancers to swing past each other, hand-to-hand, at one point or another.

She pondered stepping out of the line and walking away. But she thought she could at least pass by them in a round-dance without undue pain.

As they came nearer to her, though, and she weaved through the dancers hand-to-hand, plunging toward them, she became more and more repelled. And when she saw Naevros' hand actually extended toward her she suddenly remembered how she had last seen it, his palm slick with Ulvana's milky phlegm, and she knocked it furiously aside. She stepped out of the line and walked away.

"Aloê!" She heard Naevros' voice behind her, rising over the music, tense with anger. She turned to face him, to shout at him that . . . that . . . she didn't know what. But she welcomed the confrontation.

But Ulvana came out from behind Naevros, like a pale moon from behind a storm cloud. She shook a long white fleshy finger at Aloê and shrieked, "You can't stand it! You jealous thing, you can't bear it that Naevy and I love each other!"

"Love," Aloê repeated incredulously. "Love! *You silly trull, can't you see how he hates you?*"

She screamed the words at the shocked cheesy-faced woman. They rang out like bells in the suddenly silent dancing hall. The musicians had stopped playing. The dancers had stopped dancing. Everyone was turned toward them now, attending to this vile domestic comedy. Everyone was looking at her.

She turned on her heel and walked away through the crowd. It parted like mist before her. By sheer luck she found herself headed toward an exit. She plunged through it and into the sheltering night.

Outside, still laboring in the dark, were the men laboring at the impulse wheel that gave light to the dancing hall and heat to the kitchens.

"Is everything all right, Vocate?" one of them asked as she passed, and (unable to speak) she laughed unsteadily in answer.

Aloê's fury left her with the light of the room. She thought ironically of the position she had left Naevros in, and shrugged. It would not faze him. Nothing that happened in a crowded room could faze him.

She leapt up the slope toward the ridge that stood over Illion's dancing hall. She saw someone coming toward her down the slope. God Avenger, would she *never* be alone with her thoughts? But the person coming toward her showed no inclination to speak to her—in fact, gave her a wide berth as they passed each other. Aloê recognized her as the frosty mushroom who was one of the Arbiters of the Peace for the Rangan settlements up north. The woman had a bitter unsatisfied look on her frosty face. Aloê wondered idly what had annoyed her. Some man, no doubt: they were everywhere underfoot these days, like spiders in summer or snakes in spring.

She mounted to the top of the ridge and breathed out a sigh of relief before she realized that she still wasn't alone: she could see the other's crooked shape against the starlit horizon. She smiled to herself. She had thought about turning aside, but she would not now. She had come out to be alone and cool her overheated mind, but this was an opportunity she would not refuse.

"Stand fast there, Vocate!" she called out, as she saw the crooked outline start to move away. "I've something to say to you."

She dashed up the last few paces and stood, facing the other on the height.

"Then," the other remarked laconically.

"I think you've been avoiding me, Morlock," she said, locking gazes with him. His face was split into halves: coldly in the starlight on one side, warm on the other in the light from the bright windows of the house.

He met her eye. "Of course."

She raised one eyebrow. "'Of course'? Why, 'of course'? Do I annoy you so?"

"No," he said slowly, "I should not say 'annoy.'"

She would have thought he was flirting with her, if his voice were not so flat, so searchingly precise.

"What is it, then?" she demanded, challenging him. "Are you afraid?"

"I fear your presence," he acknowledged, after considering the question carefully.

She was astonished, then annoyed in her own right. He was having her on, of course, in his fishlike Northern way. "I would have thought a dragonkiller wouldn't be afraid of anything."

He again considered carefully before replying at last, "You are a *rokhlan*, as I am; you earned that honor in the North, as I did. Yet you fled the house, as I did."

A denial was hot on her lips—but she could not utter it. At last, she laughed and said, "I see your point, I suppose. God Sustainer, I've been rude to you! I'm sorry, Morlock."

"*Hurs krakna!*" muttered Morlock.

"I don't know what that means," she said gently. "I've never known, Morlock."

"It means . . . in this particular case . . . it means that I have taken no offense. I have welcomed this conversation," he added stiffly.

"So that is what it means."

"Yes."

"Well, you have faced your fear boldly, my fellow-*rokhlan*. I suppose I should go and do the same. Good night."

Morlock bowed wordlessly over his arm, exactly like a courtly hero in an old painting. She turned away swiftly and ran down the slope, covering her mouth with her hands to hold in the laughter. When she entered the open window she was sober, but smiling broadly.

The first person she saw was Illion, and she greeted him gladly. "Ah, Illion, I was just coming to talk to you."

Illion bowed wordlessly over his arm.

She glared at him for a moment, then laughed. "Ah, you know it all, as usual, Illion. Well, Morlock has just been telling me I ought to leave. He says if I am going to run around raging like a banefire and insulting all your guests that I ought to go home, where people have the option of being rude back to me. So I'm leaving."

"Hm," said Illion thoughtfully, "I must go out and break Morlock's jaw for him."

"Too late! The word is spoken, and a true word, too, my friend. Oh, besides, you daren't go outside now, you know. He's running about, pounding on his chest, boasting of slaying dragons with his bare hands. Really, I was frightened, so I had to come back in."

"Yes, I saw your grimace of terror as you came down the slope. Well, we're sorry to lose you. Your misstep is more entertaining than another's perfectly trod pavane."

"Missteps always are, but how loathsome you are to mention it. Oh, Jordel, Illion's throwing me out—says he can't have me insulting his guests right and left. Walk me home and get me drunk, will you?"

"Walking!" protested the fair-haired vocate, who had just wandered by. "Not really?"

"Oh, it's only three streets up and a couple more over. It'll give us a chance to talk."

"Walking!"

"Come along, you pampered youth," said Aloê grimly.

His heart pounding, Morlock stood on the ridge staring into the darkness, drinking in the night air. The golden veil that always seemed to descend before his vision when *she* was there had faded into the shadows. His hands were trembling. He could not remember what he had said, or why. He remembered, with stinging clarity, seeing her laugh as she ran off. . . .

His hands were trembling as he raised them to wipe off his sweaty forehead. He was exultant (*he had seen her, talked with her, stood with her*) but in despair. (She was laughing as she ran off. God Creator, what a fool he had been. What had he said?)

He had to leave the city. He was weary of this obsession, weary of avoiding her, weary of being destroyed by exaltation and despair when he failed to avoid her. . . . God Creator knew how long it would last, whether it would ever go away.

It had not always been like this. When they had first met she seemed beautiful to him—the way a precious stone is beautiful. When he saw her again in the Northhold, she had troubled him deeply. And now whenever he saw her, heard her voice in the chamber of the Graith, heard someone mention her name, he went blind, paralyzed by longing; the bright world faded to the luster of her dark golden hair. . . .

He had to leave the city. Right away, before the Station was over. If anything would help, being away would help. He strode down the slope, consciously following her, and entered the house.

As he searched the crowded hall for Illion, he felt someone touch his sleeve. Turning, he saw his white-mantled senior in the Graith of Guardians, Summoner Earno.

"Morlock, my friend," said the stocky red-bearded summoner, when they had greeted each other, "have you had enough of the entertainment?"

"I was just seeking Illion to say good-bye."

"He's upstairs, waiting to talk with us both. Come with me, if you will."

Morlock would and did. They went together to the broad stone stair leading upward; Earno led him to a small room overlooking the street. Within were Illion and the other two Summoners: Lernaion, Summoner of the City, and Bleys, Summoner of the Outer Lands.

"Is this a meeting of the High Council?" Morlock said, a little sharply, naming the graith-within-the-Graith that was the Three Summoners.

"You are a stickler for formalities, Morlock Ambrosius," Lernaion remarked. (He was a Southholder as *she* was; his skin was dark as varnished wood, in stark contrast with the white mantle of his rank.) "That's well: if your father had been more that way he might still be among us. But this is nothing so formal. Nor are any of us trying to woo you for their respective factions—Illion's presence is proof of that, I hope."

Bleys' mouth issued a warm musical hum of distaste. His hairless wrinkled head, oddly like a turtle's against the high hump the white mantle made on his bent uneven shoulders, turned to Morlock. "You want to know why you're here, I guess. Well, it's your own damned fault—you and your father's. I disagree with my peer, by the way. Merlin was born with a penchant for trouble, and no power in the worlds could have kept him in the Graith longer than he was. You seem to have inherited that penchant for trouble, young Ambrosius, and we intend to use it and you, as we use everything, to maintain the safety of the Wardlands."

"Eh." Morlock glanced at Illion, then Earno. "I have no objection to being used," he said slowly, "for that purpose. But I, of course, will be the user."

"Formalities," muttered the oldest Summoner, and drew his head back among the folds of his mantle.

"Facts, rather," Earno said. "Morlock, we brought you here not to browbeat you, but to ask you a favor. For the safety of the Wardlands, as Bleys correctly has said."

"What favor?" Morlock demanded bluntly.

"We want you to leave the city—soon, before the Station ends. What was that?"

"Nothing. Go on."

"It is the Two Powers. You remember . . ."

And that was just it: Morlock did remember. He saw at once why the Summoners had turned to him. A few years past, during the invasion of dragons in the Northhold, Morlock had briefly come into rapport with his natural father, Merlin—and had somehow acquired a memory of Merlin's about a confrontation with the Two Powers in Tychar.

" . . . the dragon invasion was a gambit of the Two Powers," Earno was saying. "That, now, is clear. We cannot suppose that, having failed in their first attempt, they will leave our realm in peace. The missionaries they are sending to displace the gods of Kaen may be the advance force for a new attack against us."

Morlock grunted. "I'll just dash out and destroy them, shall I?"

"Calm down, boy," Bleys snapped. "We just want you to go to Anhi and ask a few questions. If we intended anything like a confrontation with the Two Powers we would send a serious challenger—Noreê or Illion himself. Killing a stray dragon is no particular—"

"Then Illion and Noreê will not go," Morlock interrupted. He looked at Illion, whose grin told him his guess was correct.

"They both refused to go," Lernaion acknowledged. "We respect their reasons."

"No doubt we would, if we knew what they were," Bleys remarked drily. "But it's no great matter. You, young Ambrosius, can do the job. It's only a mission to ask a few questions in Anhi, to learn more of the Two Powers than we now know. You are just insolent, bad-tempered, and childish enough for that. Further, whoever goes will have to deal with your father; that's in the cards, as the modern slang expression is. He may be favorably disposed to the mission or not. If not, you have as much a chance against him as anyone in the Graith, though I don't envy you those particular odds."

"Why won't you go, Illion?" Morlock asked the older vocate.

"I think it's your job, Morlock," the other replied. "If you will not go—and only you can judge the rightness of that—I would appeal to Bleys himself. Whoever goes will go sooner or later between the paws of the Two Powers. Only one person we know has done so and escaped: Merlin. So we need to send someone as much like Merlin as possible."

"That's poor reasoning. I am both like and unlike Merlin. I am my mother's son as well—and my *harven* father's."

"Yet you cannot see yourself. I say my reasoning is sound. The choice is yours, though."

"But what am I choosing? What do you ask me to do?"

"*Find out what they want!*" shouted Bleys. "We sit here, across the Narrow Sea and behind our hedge of mountains, and bother no one. Yet the Powers have sent their agents across the world to destroy us, and may be about to do so again. Why? It makes no *sense.*"

"It may never make sense," Lernaion said quietly. "Evil exists; malice exists. Yet the truth is, we know very little of the Powers, compared to deadly enemies we have faced in the past. We need to know more before we can act. Morlock, go; find out what you can; and come back."

Morlock raised his eyes to find Earno's on him. "I have gone on such a mission before," he said to the summoner frankly.

Earno flushed, but did not flinch. "All the more reason to send you now."

"I will go," Morlock remarked thoughtfully. "I should leave tomorrow if—"

They protested with one voice, telling him that "the ship" would not be ready tomorrow.

"What ship?" he asked suspiciously.

"The ship that will carry you to Kaen, to the Anhikh marches, to the Sea of Stones on the borders of Tychar if need be," said Lernaion. "You were not thinking of walking, were you?"

Morlock *was* thinking about walking. He always had bad luck when travelling by sea, and anyway was prone to seasickness. He shrugged, rather than say any of this.

"And while you circumnavigate the world on foot," Bleys remarked cheerily, "the Two Powers will rip the Wardlands open like a bag of oranges and suck them dry."

Morlock sullenly acknowledged the advisability of sea travel.

"We've a fair ship and a decent crew of seagoing thains," Lernaion remarked. "But we're still provisioning, and looking for a vocate competent to command at sea. Now that we have your answer, we will approach Baran or Jordel, again: they have both travelled as shipmasters to the wilderness of worlds."

Morlock grunted. The prospect of being shipmates for an indefinite time with Jordel, who loathed him, was not attractive. But he could at least hope that the converse prospect would make Jordel reluctant to join the cruise. In any case, he would not withdraw his word now.

He stood. "Then."

"When our chosen captain tells us the ship is ready, we will send you word," Earno said.

Illion rose as well. "Summoners, stay as long as you like. But I'm a shameful host, and should attend to my remaining guests." He and Morlock left together.

Jordel was not one of the world's great listeners, but he was listening tonight with great interest. His friend Aloê, sitting cross-legged on his refectory table, was raging with great detail, at high volume, and with a striking command of vulgar rhetoric against their mutual friend Naevros. That sort of thing is always interesting. Moreover, he had once had romantic designs on Aloê but had been balked by what seemed to be a relationship with Naevros. Yet, apparently, they were not in a relationship. Still, somehow they were. The matter perplexed him, and he welcomed the chance to understand it further (though he had long since given up the idea of Aloê as even a temporary bed-partner).

Still, although he enjoyed the vivid and brutal word-portraits she painted of Naevros' last fifteen lovers, somehow when she ran out of steam and started to take a few pauses to pull at her drink, he still didn't understand the situation any better than before. Did she herself want Naevros or not? If not, what did it matter to her what he did with his penis? If she did, why didn't she reach out, grab him by his well-tailored collar, and drag him off to the nearest patch of shrubbery? It was clear to Jordel, anyway, that she could do so any time she chose.

Jordel swirled his drink thoughtfully. Maybe she didn't choose to be a member of any parade that consisted of such lovelights as the Honorable Ulvana (who was not really so bad, Jordel felt, when she wasn't trying so hard). There was something to that. And maybe that was part of it. But it wasn't all of it.

In the several years Jordel had known Aloê, as thain and now as vocate, Jordel had never seen her with anyone who could be described as her lover—not even in the hand-holding, eye-gazing, poetry-writing sense. She walked alone. She had friends; she had colleagues; she had this thing, whatever it was, with Naevros. That was all. Maybe there was someone waiting for her back home in the Southhold, but Jordel doubted it. She never went there—rarely even spoke of her family.

This thing with Naevros. If it was not the center of the matter, it was close. It was what was hurting her now. Jordel had no great reputation for wisdom, but he could see things as they were, and he saw that she could neither bear to put down this torch she was carrying for Naevros nor stand to carry it any longer. He wished he could do something for her. There wasn't much he could do but listen to her, so listen he did, although he was not one of the world's great listeners.

Eventually, after a somber sip of Lyrmlok (the sweetest, clearest, bubbliest wine in Jordel's none-too-extensive cellar), she said, "I should just get out. Out of the city. Out of the Wardlands. I'm no good here. How can I even stand at Station tomorrow with all those people looking at me and snickering about me?"

"It's Naevros and his bimbo they'll be snickering about. Or ought to be."

"People never do what they ought to do. Do you, J?"

"No. But I am unique."

"Everyone is. That's what makes them all the same. No, I need out."

Jordel listened with decreasing interest to Aloê's various plans for escaping from the city until the Station was concluded.

"Listen," he said reluctantly, when she had run through three of these. "I was offered a job by the Summoners. I was going to take it: it sounds interesting, which is more than I can say for the opinions of my fellow guardians at this Station. Still, if you want to get out of the city, maybe you should take it instead. You'd be commanding a ship bound for the unguarded lands . . ."

➤◄

Bleys sat alone in an otherwise empty room on the third floor of Illion's city house. He was waiting for the party to die away before he departed. For certain reasons, he did not choose to be seen in public these days. Eventually the scandal would die down, but for the time being he lived a solitary life—which he was inclined to prefer in any case.

Now, though, his pleasing solitude was punctured by Noreê, who appeared, a white shadow in a dark doorway, to glare silently at him.

"What is it you want, my dear?" he said as warmly as he could, although he disliked her and knew full well what she wanted.

"Is he going?" the pale bitter vocate demanded.

"Of course he is, my dear. We had only to appeal to his selflessness and prod his ego. The young are so pitiably malleable. The Guardians who go with him, of course, really deserve our pity, but that's their lookout. If they wanted to avoid danger they should not have joined the Graith."

"Jordel is the choice of a captain, I think. I will miss him."

"I will not."

"You are very happy with the night's work, are you, Bleys?"

"So should you be, my dear. We want the same thing."

"But we don't want it for the same reason."

"If you ever reach my advanced age, my dear, you will have learned to accept results and let motives look after themselves."

She turned and left without a word.

That night she sent a message to the Two Powers by magical means.

In part it said, *We are sending Ambrosius out of the Wards to you. Destroy him, if you like, and leave the Wardlands in peace.*

She had little hope that the Two Powers would leave the Wardlands alone. But she did very much hope that they would dispose of the Ambrosii, once and for all.

And then, at last, she slept. It had been a long day, but a good one. She hoped tomorrow would be as good.

CHAPTER EIGHT

Under Weigh

On a gray misty morning, before the rising sun had cleared the ragged high horizon to the west, Morlock went down the bluff from Tower Ambrose to the edge of the River Ruleijn: the Banestone on a chain around his neck, a bag in one hand, and a long silvery throwing spear in the other.

A flatboat was waiting for him there on the water, a movable wooden bridge running from the bank to the boat. He walked along it with cautious speed, so it seemed to him.

The opinion was not shared by others. "Can't you hurry up?" one of the oarsman called. "We're in a hurry! We have to get this vocate to her ship while the current runs true in the Narrow Sea!"

"The ship won't be going anywhere without me," Morlock replied.

"True enough!" called one of the boat's passengers. "This gentleman is also a vocate and *rokhlan* of renown."

Morlock glared through the gloaming shadows at the cheerful speaker. "I thought you were still asleep, Deor."

"And miss the chance to say farewell to my *harven*-kin Morlock and my new-friend Aloê? By no means. I'd lose years of sleep rather than miss this chance."

Aloê was sitting beside Deor on the passenger bench in the middle of the boat. She looked at him with more than a little puzzlement. She clearly didn't understand why the dwarf was so amused. Morlock, who understood full well, chose to ignore him. He muttered, "Good day, Vocate," sat down on the deck with his back against the deck shack, and closed his eyes.

It was not exactly a pose. True, he had practiced saying those three words to say to her—practiced them over and over until he could say them without thinking, as if it were no great matter. He had planned on pretending to nap if his nerve failed him when he saw her eyes (as it had). But he was indeed tired—unbelievably tired, bone tired. He did not really sleep, but his mind wandered far away as he sat on the deck and listened to their voices, the slap of the oars on the water, the morning birds calling through the mist on the waterside.

Presently he felt a tentative touch on his elbow. He opened his eyes to see Deor crouching beside him in the light of rising day. "Sun's rising," the dwarf said, and then looked at Morlock uncertainly.

It was the custom of Morlock's *harven*-kin to praise the day at the rising of the sun. Morlock rarely did so these days. But he was not going to stand aside from *harven* Deor while the dwarf prayed in the presence of Other Ilk.

He stood, stretched, and nodded at Deor. As one they turned westward and, facing the bright light rising over the crooked high horizon, sang the most common Praising of Day.

> *Heolor charn vehernam choran harwellanclef;*
> *wull wyrma daelu herial hatathclef;*
> *feng fernanclef modblind vemarthal morwe;*
> *Rokh Rokhlanclef hull veheoloral morwe.*
> *Dal sar drangan an immryrend ek aplam,*
> *dal sar deoran an kyrrend knylloram.*
> *Varthendunidh onkwel varthal veroldme ankwellandh;*
> *Hurranidhclef Haldanidhclef Heorridhclef awlim hendonnin.*[1]

Morlock felt Aloê's eyes on him as he sang, but he didn't look toward her. This was a ritual: he could get through it because he had done so countless times before. He would find other ways to do what he had to do in her presence. The golden veil threatened to descend, but he ignored it.

A few of the boatmen seemed to think it was an entertainment and stomped their feet in applause. Others looked thoughtful, others bored. Aloê's golden eyes held a cool measuring look as Morlock incautiously met them.

The golden veil descended before his vision; blood roared in his ears. He knew she was saying something, but couldn't be sure what it was. He bowed his head in acknowledgement when she seemed to be done, but was unable to respond because he hadn't heard what she'd said. That made him angry—not at her, but himself. How useless it was to stand here, like a lump on one of the boards of this badly made deck, and say nothing.

"We should talk about our mission," he said abruptly. It was one of the things he knew he would have to say to her, so he had practiced saying it also. He could say it. He had said it. He felt a disproportionate sense of triumph at the tiny victory, like a man who was learning to walk again after a long illness.

". . . talk about that here?" she was saying, when he belatedly attended to her response. He had surprised her by saying something unexpected. Somehow this was a cooling, calming thought.

"Not if you don't want to," he said. "But we must talk soon about our course, and it seems unlikely anyone will report our words to the Two Powers."

Aloê shrugged . . . and he saw it. He could see her, look right at her without dismay. Another victory! His eyes rested with fierce satisfaction on the notch in her collarbone, the coppery twist of a talisman resting there, hanging from a thin chain around her neck.

"The towns that have lost their gods are all near the south coast of Kaen," she was saying. "I thought we might run down the Narrow Sea and land somewhere to gather word."

"Or we could pass by Kaen entirely and go to Anhi."

She did not respond immediately. He realized he was staring at her—glaring at her, it may have seemed. He opened his hands and looked over her shoulder. He looked at the wrinkled eastern horizon, the blue sky above, the dark gold of her curling hair reflecting and challenging the light rising in the west.

"Very well," she said eventually. "You know something I don't. What is it?"

"Know?" he said, startled.

"Know. It is an action one does with the brain. Or the mind. Know."

"All I know is that I hate Kaen," Morlock admitted. "My feet bleed whenever I think about that coastline."

"Is that metaphor some charming Northerner slang with which I am unfamiliar?"

Morlock sat down on the deck and pulled off the shoe and footpads from his right foot. He solemnly held it up for her inspection. "From my last trip along the Kaenish coast," he explained gruffly, since she seemed to be equal parts amused and bemused.

"I don't exactly— Are those *scars?*" she asked, interrupting herself and pointing at the sole of his foot.

"From the rocks on the shore."

"Hm. I like a rocky coast myself. But the rocks there must be like blades!"

Morlock grunted and put his footgear back on.

"The people are almost equally hospitable," Deor said impishly. "You should ask him how he got the scar on his neck."

Morlock was moments away from strangling his *harven*-kin and closest friend when Aloê gave the dwarf a golden glance and said casually, "He mentioned it to me on another occasion." If Morlock was not misreading her, she understood that Deor was teasing him and declined to be a part of it.

"Gleh." Deor seemed disconcerted. "All right. Maybe I'm putting too much wear on you both. My apologies."

Morlock kicked him companionably and sat back against the deckhouse, and the three remained in silence for a while.

They came at last to Sandport on the southeast coast of the Wardlands. Now the boat was riding down the Long Canal that ran alongside the blue-gray Grartan Mountains. At notch in their southern foothills lay Sandport, a sleepy town on a silt-filled, rock-rimmed harbor.

There the ship awaited: *Flayer*, a galley with three ranks of oars. The crew was already assembled: it turned out that Aloê had already been down to tend to the ship a number of times.

Also awaiting were two Guardians in red cloaks: bitter white Noreê and tall fair-haired Jordel.

"You probably thought you'd seen the last of me," Jordel started saying, shouting across the water at Aloê before the boat had tied up at the riverside dock, "and I hope you're not seeing the last of me now. I had a bad dream last night, so I thought I'd come down to see you off. You, too, Morlock, of course."

"I want to hear all about your dreams, Jordel," Aloê called back, as the boatmen snickered, "but why don't you wait until we're all on solid ground?"

"That's just it. I—"

"*Wait!*"

Jordel waited, shifting uneasily from foot to foot. Noreê, standing next to him, was still as a stone.

Once the boat was alongside the dock, Aloê leapt lightly off the boat down beside the two waiting Guardians. Morlock followed her, less gracefully but with even more enthusiasm. Deor waited until the boatmen threw down the walkbridge, but he watched and listened to the Guardians' conversation with open amusement.

"So I had this dream—"

"Do you really want to talk about this here and now, Jordel?" Aloê said.

"Why not? We're under the Guard. There can't be agents of the Two Powers listening. So I had this dream about you—"

"Is this going to be excessively intimate or personal, Jordel? We don't want to shock the stevedores."

"*I had this dream and I'm not the only one.* You were in a prison without walls. The Two Powers had changed you into sand of different colors, and they were sifting it into different piles with a sieve made of mist."

"Oh." Aloê became serious. "That sounds bad. Others had this dream?"

"Another friend of yours saw you being dissected by a knife with two blades. Different dream; same omen. That's what Illion says. And Illion himself—"

Morlock interrupted, speaking to Noreê: "Have you collated these dreams?"

She replied without looking at him. "There has not been time. And only one has been caught in a dream glass."

"Would you suggest that we delay our departure until you have time to collate the dreams and meditate on them?"

"No. We can always send a message after you if it seems needful."

Morlock grunted and walked away, just as Deor joined the group. The dwarf looked at them, looked at his *harven*-kinsman, and then followed him away, calling out, "Wait a moment, Morlock. Wait a moment. Canyon keep you, slow down!"

Jordel looked after them, an unusually solemn expression in his hazel eyes. "I'm afraid that fellow thinks I dislike him. It's too bad, really."

"Why would he think that, Jordel?" Aloê wondered.

"Well, I sort of told him I couldn't stand him, once. But that was before I really knew him. You have to admit he's not easy to know."

"Do you know him now, Jordel?"

"No, but now I know that I don't, and that—Listen, who cares? It's you

I'm worried about. Noreê seems to disagree, but I don't think you should go on this mission."

"I don't disagree," said Noreê, surprising Jordel very much (to judge from the height he jumped).

"You just said we shouldn't delay sailing," Aloê pointed out.

"But there's no need for you to sail with the ship," Noreê replied.

"I'm not in the business of avoiding danger."

"*If* there is need to face it. There is no such need here. You have value to the Graith, to the Wardlands. The danger seems to fall on you specifically."

"Then, if I don't go, the danger may fall on someone else. Specifically."

"You're not doing a good job of selling this," Jordel said to Noreê anxiously. "Can't you just shut up and look foreboding while I talk?"

"It doesn't matter what either of you say," Aloê replied. "Jordel. I'm glad you're worrying about me, but I'm sorry to be a worry to you. I gave my word and I'm going."

"I hoped to change your mind," Noreê said, "but I didn't expect to. Good luck to you, Vocate. Come and see me when you return."

"Maybe we should go along?" Jordel suggested.

"Four vocates on shipboard with a crew of thains?" Aloê said, with real dismay. "No. I'll sail with Morlock, because he won't try to share command. Apparently he doesn't like sea travel."

"Ha ha ha. You'll find out."

"But I won't have any doubt about who's in charge at sea. It's not safe, Jordel. There isn't time for debate in the middle of a storm."

"You're right, of course. So I'm back to asking you not to go at all."

Noreê threw up her hands and walked away.

"Finally," Jordel muttered. "I wondered if I was going to have to talk all day to drive her off. Sometimes I think—"

"Did you want to say something to me in private, Jordel?"

"Give you something." He handed her a woolen cylinder. "Message sock. Only me and Illion can use it from this end; only you can use it from that end."

She deftly tucked the sock into her wallet and said, "Thanks. Why?"

"You might need it. And there's something weird going on. Maybe we can see all of the elephant if we look at it from different angles."

"What is an elephant?"

"Legendary beast."

"I thought that was you, J." She hugged him good-bye and ran off to catch her ship.

Morlock was already on board, having said farewell to his *harven*-kin. His pale face was paler than ever, and covered with a slight sheen of sweat.

"Don't mind it, Vocate," she said, pounding him companionably on his lower shoulder. "The ship does bounce around a bit at anchor, but she'll glide along like a seabird once we get under way."

His wretched deep-sunk eyes glared a little, but she didn't let it bother her. Seasick people tended to be touchy, she knew (although she wasn't sure why, never having been in the state herself).

"Thain Koijal," she called out to her second. "Are the oar-thains in place?" She could she they were.

"In place and ready to row, Vocate," Koijal replied.

"Cast off. Port-siders push off from the dock. Starboard-siders, five strokes in reverse. Get us out of here, Thain. I want a fish caught in the middle of the Narrow Sea for my supper."

"I hear you, Vocate," Koijal said formally, and gave his orders to his thirds-in-command at the sides.

Aloê glanced at Morlock; she assumed she would find him stealing a last look at dry land. Instead he was eying the maneuvers of the oar-thains.

It was something to see: the long white oars swinging in unison through the air, dipping as one into the green-blue water and out the other side, each oar leaving a trail of foam behind, scarring the dark shining surface. Not just once but time after time—a bit like a seabird, perhaps, but really like nothing else. As a maker, Morlock was no doubt impressed.

"Just wait," she said. "We'll put up the sail in a bit: we can usually catch a breeze off the Grartans. That'll be something to see."

"Inefficient," he replied curtly.

The truth dawned on her. That sour expression wasn't just from an unhappy belly. He was seeing the same thing she saw, but he didn't like it.

"Are you saying the ship is badly designed?" she asked. But what she meant was: *Are you saying* my ship *is badly designed?*

"Half the crew," Morlock said. "Put them to work on an impulse wheel. Go faster. Less weight, less provisions."

"And use mechanisms to drive the oars? That would waste the crew's energy, Morlock. These things have been discussed before—"

She was going to favor him with a brief course in ship design when he interrupted her. "No oars. Take the oar blades. Put them on a wheel. Put the wheel on the outside of your ship, under the water. The impulses drive the wheel of oar blades. You could have more than one—steer that way, more stable than a single propeller."

"Propeller?"

"A wheel with little oar blades on it." He sketched it briefly in the air.

"Brilliant!" she said. "I thought of something like that once. But, I, I guess I forgot it when a monster bonked me on the head this one time."

As soon as she said this she was worried that it sounded like boasting—not a probable story, on its face.

But he didn't seem skeptical, just nodded acceptingly and said nothing.

Which was for the best: she didn't want to hear anything more just now. What he'd said already was sweeping through her like a wildfire on the prairie. *Propellers* to drive the ships. No sails needed—or maybe wind power could add to muscle power, giving strength to the impulse wheel. Ships could be redesigned. Ship routes could be redrawn. Would propellers work in the Sea of Worlds? What if . . . ?

She looked up and saw a day bristling with undreamed-of possibilities, a world that was utterly changed, that could never be the same.

The man who had changed it was bent over the taffrail, spattering the side of the ship with his vomit, to the amusement and disgust of the thains nearby.

Aloê sighed. This would be a strange trip. That much was clear.

NOTE

1. *Blindly Death takes hold of the timid and the brave;*
   vermin devour the evil and good alike;
   maker and miner sleep in the same silence;
   Dragon and Dragonkiller fall under the same fell.
   There is one darkness that ends all dreaming,
   one light in which all living will awake.
   Those-Who-Watch beyond death wait for the world's waking;
   Creator, Keeper, King stand at every milestone.

CHAPTER NINE

Encounter off Tenagöros

Aloê was feverishly sketching out designs for propeller-driven craft in the main cabin of *Flayer*. She didn't want to discuss them with Morlock—not yet, not until they were ready for his cold judgemental eye. Morlock was in fact near at hand, but unlikely to notice her work. He was wrapped up in a hammock, with a bandage over his eyes, cotton stuffed in his ears, and he was snoring slightly. Seasickness had kept him from sleeping well, but he was sleeping now and seemed likely to sleep all day, which was fine with her. The less they interacted, the better she liked him.

She had a number of sketches complete, from the wildly unlikely to the fairly conservative. But there was one in the middle range that she thought even above Morlock's criticism, and she was using it as a basis to plan out a whole new ship. She called it the *New Flayer*, as a sort of apology to her current command, the ship Morlock had taught her to despise.

She had been neglecting her duties a bit, as captain. She could not look at *Flayer* the same way anymore. The trireme was still a beautiful thing, with a wonderfully trained crew, but it was a thing of the past for her now, nothing so real as the ships that sailed without sails in her dreams. She let her thain-lieutenant do most of the ship-running, lest her attitude somehow become known to the crew. But she worked with her ears alert for anything that might be happening on deck, so she caught the first shout of, "Smoke in the sky! East and north, east and north, halfway to zenith! Smoke in the sky!"

It was the most dreaded cry in a shipmaster's lexicon: a dragon sighting. Dragons preyed heavily on the commerce of the world, especially attacking cargo ships in shallow waters, where they could destroy a ship and hope to fish the remains of its valuables out of the pale bitter water along the coast. And

Flayer was just passing through the famously shallow seas off the southern coast of Kaen, near the Tirganate of Tenagöros.

She should have been expecting this, Aloê realized, as she ran out to the main deck between the upper rank of oar-thains. That told her what face to present: this was a danger, but not a crisis—definitely not a shock. She must look as if she *had* been expecting this.

She stepped out into a muggy, cloud-covered day whose very silence spoke of thunder. One cool breeze would release the rain in those heavy clouds. It had taken a keen eye to spot the trail of the dragon's smoke in that sullen sky; she made mental note to commend the watch-thain who had sung out— Ekylen, she thought.

Aware of all the anxious eyes on her, Aloê glanced idly at the darker smear of smoke in the dead-gray sky, remarked casually to Koijal, "Doesn't seem to be headed for us. Still: a good chance for some drill. Have the offcrew of the upper rank deploy the fire-nets. Have the offcrew of the middle rank stand by the missile weapons and prepare to engage if the dragon approaches. Have the offcrew of the lower rank stand by for firefighting. Maintain course and speed."

"Yes, Vocate," said Koijal gratefully, and began barking orders to his under-thains. She wondered if her title as dragonkiller was helping calm his nerves. She wished it would have the same effect on hers, but hypocrisy itself gave a certain comfort. She knew what she should pretend to feel, and that gave her something to do.

She watched the dragon's flight at intervals between giving orders to Koijal and encouragement to the underthains actually doing the work. She tried to be especially encouraging to the thains constructing a ballista on the platform above the main walkway. She feared it would do little good against the dragon if it attacked, but it was the only weapon they had other than handheld spears. And if it came to that, many of her underthains would die. So she cheered them on as heartily as they could.

The dragon grew nearer, but not much nearer. It soon proved that the predator was circling them in the sky, well out of the range of their ballista or any other weapon. The dragon had spotted them, was interested in them, but was waiting for something. What? The rest of his guile? Some sign of wealth onboard? What did a dragon think worth waiting for?

"Take us south of here, Koijal," she said calmly to her second in command. "I want deep water under our keel."

"Vocate, I obey," said Koijal—so readily, that Aloê suspected he had been itching to give the order himself. Maybe she should tell him to make suggestions . . . but a command deck should not be like a Station of the Graith, with everyone weighing in on the debate. She smiled quietly at her second and nodded.

The dragon had completed a second long smoky circle in the hot sullen sky when Morlock emerged from the cabin, a plug of cotton still adorning one ear, his hair wildly disordered from sleep, and muttered, "*Hurs krakna!*"

"*Ath, rokhlan!*" Aloê replied, as if she knew what he meant, and to remind her crew that there were two dragonkillers aboard. (Everybody knew that much Dwarvish these days.) "We have a visitor, you see."

It was one of Morlock's few admirable traits as a conversationalist that he never said anything when he had nothing to say. He watched the dragon circle in the sky for a time. Then he eyed the ship's feeble protections: the nets latent with fire-quell magic, the ballista bolted to the platform over the main walkway, the long steel spears in the trembling hands of the deck-crew.

"Vocate Aloê, a word," he said presently.

"Speak it."

"A word in private."

"Koijal, join me," she said, glaring defiantly at this green-faced landsman with cotton absurdly sprouting from his ear.

The three Guardians stepped back into the cabin.

"Things could not be worse," Morlock began.

Koijal exploded in a fury that surely masked a measure of fear. "You lie like a cowardly landgrubber! We have our defenses! We have our fire-nets and our spear-thrower, if the beast chooses to approach! There is no guile, only a single dragon! Soon we will be in deep water, where the dragon does not dare attack us!"

"A dragon's tail could smash this ship to splinters," Morlock said drily. "What use your fire-quell magic then? Dragons don't fear water. And your spear-thrower might be useful if the target were nailed to some convenient quarter of the sky. Since everything you say is untrue, I ask you not to waste our time. I will have a word with your senior, my colleague. Be silent while we speak."

Koijal was silent, largely because he was speechless with fury, and Aloê said quickly, "What's your thought, Morlock?"

"I will go out in a small boat and challenge the dragon to a single combat."

The plug of cotton was still protruding raggedly from his left ear as he spoke. His hair was sticking out like that of a strawman made to scare crows. His eyes stared out from dark holes in the greenish pasty surface of his face.

"I don't see that as the best possible option," she said diplomatically.

"Name a better," he said.

"I could go."

"You are the captain of this ship. I'm just a passenger with a red cloak."

"I'm a Guardian of the Wardlands and so is every member of this crew. If we need to die, we can die together—at least make the dragon pay for his fun."

"No. Aloê. Think."

"Think of what? You were eloquent enough in quelling my second-in-command. Say what you damn well mean."

"Is it a coincidence we were attacked within a day of leaving the Wards?"

"You say no."

"I say no. Someone was warned we were coming. That, in itself, is news the Graith must know. Even if my fight with the dragon only buys the ship a little time, you must use it to bring the ship nearer home."

"God Avenger scorch your stupid guts!" shouted Aloê, because she knew he was right.

"I'm sorry," said the man they both knew was going to his death.

Morlock took the long spear that lay wrapped underneath his hammock and shook it free from its covering. It gleamed silver even in the dull light of the cabin. Also under the hammock was the Banestone, the baleful jewel that had killed Saijok Mahr. He put its chain about his neck and walked out of the cabin. Aloê and Koijal, following him out, watched him step to the edge of the deck nearest the circling dragon and spin the silver spear in his fingers. Even in the dim humid day, the silver spear glittered notably, and the dragon seemed to take note, or perhaps it was the Banestone the dragon noticed. He dropped below the horizon, settling down on the surface of the sea, enfolding his wings about him, until he was like a volcanic isle, sending up a column of smoke and steam as it drifted on the steel-gray waves.

"How can he do that?" Koijal wondered in a subdued tone. "I held a dragon's vertebra once—it was heavier than bronze. Do they get heavier after death?"

Morlock shrugged. "I don't know. I'd like to know." (*I would have liked to know,* Aloê translated.)

"I'll need a little boat," he said to Aloê. "Or do you call it a ship, too?"

"Boat!" she snapped. "See to it, Koijal."

They put the odd pale man in the boat, swung it over the rail and lowered it into the sea. Then, as he unhandily began to row toward the waiting dragon, Aloê stonily gave the orders to bring the ship about and strike for home.

≫≪

It was a wretched day to die, and Morlock was in no mood for it. He had to stop rowing twice to vomit on the way to parley with the dragon, and the thin bitter bile (which was all his belly had left to give up) burned in his mouth even after he rinsed it clear with salt water.

But he was glad to see *Flayer* running westward with all its oars swinging. Even better, the dragon didn't seem to be pursuing it. He took no trouble to hurry toward the rendezvous, therefore. The longer this took, the longer she had to get away.

Morlock wondered if there was some way to row a boat facing forward. He disliked the sensation of approaching a dragon with his back turned. But at least he did not have to meet the dragon's eye (malefic? amused? something of both?) after retching over the little boat's side, as he did several times on the short journey across the rough gray water. It was hard for him to gauge his progress in paces or boat lengths. But he could feel the regard of the dragon on his neck. A sensation of heat, like sunlight on this cloudy day, grew on his shoulders. Eventually he could hear the hiss of water becoming steam from contact with the dragon's fire-hot skin. He smelled the smoke and venom of the dragon's breath. He had come far enough, he guessed. He pulled the oars inboard and let their handles fall down in the bilge.

He cleared his throat, spat out some dark mucus. Standing up, he turned to face the dragon.

The enemy looked on Morlock with a long lupine grin that was not a smile. The dragon's scales were black and green, like Saijok Mahr's. He floated

on the gray waves, Koijal's mystery, with his wings folded about him like an
island. A volcanic island: the smoke of the dragon's breath drifted upward in
a long column in the stagnant air of the hot cloudy day.

So you are the sacrifice, the dragon rumbled in Wardic. His red-gold eyes gazed
with naked greed at the Banestone hanging from Morlock's neck. That was one
reason Morlock had brought it along: to give the dragon a reason to fight.

"I am Morlock Ambrosius, also known as syr Theorn," Morlock replied
in Dwarvish. "It was I who slew Saijok Mahr and broke the guile of masters."

You are the one I seek, then, rumbled the dragon, still in Wardic. *I am Rulgân
the Outlier, also known as Rulgân the Kinslayer and Rulgân the Thief.*

"Eh," said Morlock.

You are not one of the wordy Ambrosii, I see, the dragon reflected. *Nor does my
dragonspell seem to be effective on you.*

"Then?"

*Then let us get down to business, Ambrosius. I can earn a great gift of strength and
wisdom from the Two Powers. All I need give them is you, or the proof of your death.*

Morlock stooped and lifted up his spear from the bilge of the boat. "You
find me ready."

Morlock's defiance was rewarded with a moment or two of silence.

We can fight, Rulgân at last, *and we will if you choose. But it occurs to me that
we each have something to buy that the other can sell.*

"I have my life. What is it you have?"

*The life of that ship. You rowed yourself out here in that pitiful fragment of wood so
that the trireme might have a chance to get away. If you surrender to me, I will spare it.*

"I don't believe you."

I will self-bind myself in oath. Of course, I would expect the same from you.

Morlock briefly considered it. A self-binding oath, with anchor's in the
swearer's own tal, was a powerful instrument. Breaching the oath made the
swearer susceptible to external control, even death. But there had to be some
person free to activate the terms of the oath. If Morlock surrendered his free
will to the dragon's he doubted he could enforce the oath, and no one on *Flayer*
would be party to the terms.

"No."

Rulgân eyed him curiously, as if waiting for more words. When no more
were forthcoming he said with slow emphasis, *Then we fight.*

"You find me ready," Morlock repeated.

Why are you unreasonable? the dragon wondered. *I can offer you a clear gain, at very little cost. You cannot withstand my attack, but if you surrender yourself I will spare the ship and its crew. Is that not what you came out here to achieve?*

"I came out here to challenge you to a duel, Rulgân the Outlier. It is long months since I killed a dragon, and I need the practice."

The dragon was amused. *Why should I engage in anything so formal when I could be tasting your heart's reddest blood in mere moments?*

"You could swear in a self-binding oath that you slew in single combat the man who killed Saijok Mahr. Even an outlier with no guile to lead must find it useful to boast now and again."

The dragon laughed lazily. *A guile to lead! What an idea! Every guile master that ever lived was a slave to his servants. To be a master in their eyes, he sold his freedom. That I will never do. No, I follow after my own thinking and my own desires. It so happens that your life, or proof of your death, will buy me what I desire, from those well able to give it.*

"Then," Morlock said, and tapped the point of his spear on the frame of his boat. The spear was long enough to reach a dragon's brain through its eye or the roof of its mouth—long enough to pierce a draconic heart within its lizardlike chest. The dragon knew it: Morlock saw that. The red-gold slotted eyes half-closed in contemplation.

Single combat, Rulgân said lazily. *Like a song from the Longest War. Why is it, Ambrosius, that people like you and me, who should be making the future, are forever fighting the battles of the past?*

"I will make the future after I am done killing you."

You badly wish to provoke me, I see. You will not find it easy to do, my two-legged friend with the voice of a Softclaw. If you succeed, you will wish you had not.

Morlock opened his free hand and turned it face down, an insulting gesture in Dwarvish that he hoped the dragon would understand.

If Rulgân did, he gave no sign of it. He did not speak for seven long smoky breaths. Then he said, *Here is what I propose. You will take your little boat to whatever quarter of the sea, within sight, that you choose. I will take five runs at you. If you are still alive after the fifth, I will self-bind to let you live.*

"I reject your terms. I challenge you to the death."

But I live on my terms, not yours, replied the dragon coolly in words licked by flame. He leapt straight up into the air and spun upward in a long lazy spiral.

Morlock sat down on the bench and tossed his spear back into the bilge. He picked up the oars and slowly began to row the boat away toward the shore.

It had gone as well as it could have. But it had not gone very well. His enemy was unreachable by shame, or pride, or anger. What other weapons did Morlock have, except a pointed stick and the willingness to risk death?

As *Flayer* moved steadily westward through the choppy seas, Aloê glumly watched the dragon leap silent from the surface of the water. She had watched the conversation without hearing any of the words, but its import was fairly clear. The dragon was taking flight in a long spiral, and Morlock began to row toward the shore. Had he specified the place of the duel to give *Flayer* a better chance of escape? She had no doubt of it. That hateful son of a bitch's brach.

Aloê was not used to running away from a danger someone else was facing. She had to admit Morlock's point that the Graith needed to know what they knew. But she didn't have to like it . . . and, anyway, who should she tell?

Then she remembered the message sock Jordel had given her.

Cursing herself, she ran into the deck cabin. It was in one of the pigeon-holes in the table she'd been working at. . . .

She found it. She also found all her sketches and plans carefully stacked to one side. One lay by itself—the oddest, strangest, most knifelike design. She had loved it, but put it aside as too strange.

On it lay a note in Morlock's tall tangled script: *Not the others. This.*

He had looked at her designs. He had judged them, the cold-eyed unblinking bastard. And he had approved the one she had loved too much to approve, her secret dream that no one else was meant to see.

She swore violently and incoherently. She took the pencil and scribbled a quick note to Jordel and Illion on the back of the knifelike design. She stuffed it into the message-sock and twisted the fabric to send the message.

She ran out onto the deck, and almost knocked down Koijal, who was coming after her, apparently.

She shouldered off her red cloak. "Koijal," she said, "I'm leaving you to carry my cloak. If you bring this ship and its crew back to the Wardlands more or less intact, I'll see that you get a red cloak of your own. If I can. Tell everything you saw and heard to the Vocates Jordel or Illion and no one else."

"But—"

"I'm going to stand by Vocate Morlock. Good luck, K. I hope you don't need it."

"But—"

She kicked off her shoes and dove over the rail, past the long white oars toiling in the sea, into the bitter gray water.

><

Morlock rowed as far into the Shallows as he dared. Rulgân was patrolling in the dark skies overhead, occasionally eclipsed by low-lying clouds.

Morlock decided he had stalled as long as he could. He dragged the oars inboard of the boat and stood, wobbling a little, in the bilge. His hands were actually trembling as he bent down to pick up the spear, twin to the one that had carried death to Saijok Mahr. He wondered dimly if it was fear or sickness making him tremble. The latter, he thought. He should make sure of his aim before he threw away his only weapon. But underneath his trembling, underneath his caution, was the rock-solid certainty of striking his target.

He waved the spear in the air and stood waiting for the battle to begin.

Slowly, lazily, the bat-winged form of his enemy turned in the charcoal sky and began a long, twisting attack-run.

Flayer still labored in the waves in the middle distance. He had bought them some time—probably not enough. But Aloê was on board, a *rokhlan* in her own right. She would think of something.

Rulgân flickered in the air as he approached: lifting, falling, swerving left and right, sketching a serpentine twisting route through the hot gray sky. He was luring Morlock to throw his spear. Morlock knew it, knew that his enemy was waiting for the throw, and he watched patiently for the chance to strike at his enemy in truth. Part of the game Rulgân was playing involved giving Morlock a real chance for a killing blow—as long as he saw it in time, as long as he was able to make use of it.

The dragon was just within the range of a longish spear-cast when he stalled in midair and roared fire down on Morlock and his boat and the surrounding water.

Morlock's Ambrosian blood would protect him from the fire, but he clenched his eyes shut against the venom and smoke and kept them shut: they'd be of little use in the fog. But he heard the shriek of the dragon's wings on the air, and he guessed his enemy's next move: to swamp the boat. Following the sounds of the dragon in the air, he jumped to one end of the boat and stabbed out wildly with the spear.

His advantage was that he had spent long years under the earth, often without light: the absence of sight did not frighten him. His disadvantage was that he wasn't used to his ground sliding away under his feet as he fought.

His spear blade bit something, and there was a fierce satisfaction in that. But his foot caught on a bench in the boat, and he fell facefirst into the bilge.

He struggled to his feet, spitting bilgewater, blood, and steam. If the dragon had spun about and struck him it all would have been over. But Rulgân was already more than a spear-cast away to the east. He resumed his leisurely patrol, fire-bright eyes ever peering at Morlock through the heavy murk of cloudy hot day.

Whatever Morlock had caught with his spear blade, he hadn't drawn blood. The dragon hadn't fled. Rulgân wasn't afraid. He was . . .

He was the cat and Morlock was the mouse. The cool-headed dragon was amusing himself at Morlock's expense.

Morlock tried to remember that this was good. He tried to remember why he was doing this: to give Aloê a chance to get away. He tried to be glad that Rulgân was mocking him, like a cat with its paws on a mouse's tail, watching with interest as it struggled to get away. . . .

Morlock clenched his teeth and watched with fury as the dragon idly cruised the sky, turned as if to attack, resumed his patrol.

When Rulgân dropped into another attack run, Morlock was ready for him. He kept his eyes on the dragon's wings until he felt their beat like the rhythm of his own heart. He watched the twists and turns that Rulgân took in the air, and he thought he had a sense of how long it took the dragon to turn in the air.

This time, this time he would draw blood. He knew it. He would show Rulgân the Outlier what it was to mock Morlock Saijok's-Bane.

The moment came. The attack was a feint; Morlock knew from the lines he was drawing in the sky, his judgement of the dragon's speed and momentum and path. But Morlock attacked in earnest, throwing his spear straight through the window of opportunity his eye had sketched in the air.

The wound might indeed have been fatal if Morlock had thrown the spear at his target. But his hands were still trembling and, in the act of releasing his weapon from his hand he felt, like an iron bell, the unintended tap of his thumb against the shaft of the spear, sending it wildly off course. He watched in mute disbelief as it fell into the rough gray water and disappeared. The dragon passed like a storm, but still he stood staring at the empty air and water to the west.

He had thrown and missed.

He still had a long knife in his belt, not nearly long enough for this fight, and the Banestone as his focus of power, if he could think of some way to wield the Sight or the Strength as a weapon through it. But he . . .

He had thrown. And he had missed.

It was so long since that had happened that Morlock didn't remember how it felt. Even as a child, tossing pebbles at cups during the games of Cymbalfeast, even then he hit his targets.

He had told himself that he had come out to face death, and he had known that defeat was the likeliest outcome of his challenge.

But he hadn't expected this. This was the true defeat, the true mockery.

He had thrown and missed.

Rulgân took a single half-circuit of the sky and dropped down into an attack run again. And this was no twist-filled feint. He was headed straight for Morlock, jaws open, front claws extended. He was coming in for the kill.

Morlock grimly drew his dagger and thought about his options. There didn't seem to be any. He hoped he could at least leave a mark on the beast.

His lost spear rose up in front of him, gleaming from the water.

"Take it!" Aloê's voice snarled as he stood there gaping.

He seized the shaft and brandished the spear.

Rulgân saw. He spun aside and drove upward. He was well out of throwing range as he passed overhead.

"*Khul, gyrmar!*" Morlock shouted in fierce satisfaction to the dragon flying eastward. The veil of mockery was torn open, at last. The dragon feared a spear in Morlock's hands, as well he might.

The satisfaction passed almost as quickly as the storm-swift dragon. Morlock turned his head downward to watch bemusedly as Aloê Oaij climbed into the little boat.

He was racked with shame: she had seen him fail. And fear: God Avenger, hadn't he done this so that she would have a chance at life? And here she was standing in the path of the dragon.

Gleaming from the water that was native to her, so alien to him, she was glorious indeed, but he was wounded by something deeper than her beauty. He saw it in her golden eyes, in her defiant stance. She couldn't stand to see someone in danger and not stand beside him.

He feared for her danger as he did not for his own, but he felt a strange warmth also. He had faced death so many times, almost always alone. He could not share his life with her, but he could share this—this moment of danger, even death.

"Thanks," he said presently.

"Don't worry about it," she replied curtly, which he took as a refusal. "Do you think you can hit him with that next time?"

"Doubt it. You should get out of here."

"Fuck yourself."

After a few moments' consideration, Morlock took that for a refusal also. He felt a real chill then, as of approaching death.

Or was that what it was?

"Is the breeze cooler?" he asked.

"Hard to say," she said, rolling her eyes at him. "I've been underwater for a while. But . . . you know, at least there *is* a breeze now."

He turned away from her, an odd idea growing in his head. If the weather was breaking . . . if the clouds had grown tall enough to press against the vault of the sky . . . then some aether would seep through.

Then lightning would fall. It would fall . . .

He snapped the chain around his neck with three fingers and bound his focus, the bane-jewel that Rulgân had coveted, to the shaft of the spear.

"Is that smart?" Aloê asked. "You'll probably lose both."

"I expect to," Morlock said.

Rulgân was dropping down into another attack run. Morlock held the spear up as high as he could, knowing the dragon could see it, baiting him with it as the dragon had baited Morlock with his own life, waiting for the enemy's approach. . . .

When the dragon was still well in front of him, Morlock threw back his body and hurled the spear—and its cargo of gem—straight into the sky.

Rulgân could not resist. He did not resist. He plucked the spear out of the air like a hawk taking a sparrow and flew westward with it.

Morlock saw a flicker of light, silver among the leaden clouds.

"I'm going to go deep into the rapture of vision," he said, turning to Aloê. "Why?"

Morlock glanced at the sky, measured the dragon's course.

"No time to explain," he said. "If you won't go—"

"I won't."

"—I guess you could hold me up. I don't want him to think I'm cowering in front of him."

"You seem to value his opinion very much."

Morlock wondered if that were true, then shrugged. "Suit yourself." He planted his feet as firmly as he could in the bilge, closed his eyes, and summoned the dream of ur-shapes that always enfolded him.

>=<

Aloê had studied the arts of Sight with Noreê and the sages of New Moorhope, but she had never seen anyone scale the heights of visionary rapture as swiftly as Morlock did. Maybe he was always a little bit in the visionary realm. That might account for his lack of conversation, now that she thought of it: it was notoriously difficult to use words while in rapture.

She was prepared to do as he asked and hold him up, but it seemed unnecessary: his body was relaxed, but somehow did not fall, or even slump over. His irises glowed slightly, shining through the thin skin of his eyelids: that was not uncommon in deep vision.

The clouds seemed darker, the breeze distinctly colder and stronger. Was Morlock able to master the winds? Could he strike at the dragon with them, protect them somehow?

It seemed unlikely, and now the enemy was even nearer. She saw the beast still greedily clutching the spear and the gem bound to it.

Now was the time to dive for safety, if ever. She shook the thought loose with a shudder of disgust: she hadn't come here for that. She calculated, as coldly as she could, the chances of catching hold of the dragon's foreleg and wresting the spear from its claws. She might at least manage to do some damage to the beast before it killed her. . . .

Morlock's slack form lifted up from the little boat, drifting in the air. His back bent like an ill-made bow. His arms lifted out from his body, his fingers spread wide.

In all the world there was only the sound of the onrushing dragon's wings. The breeze had stopped, as if the sky were holding its breath.

Then the sky spoke: two bright bitter words. Lightning flared, from east to west, from north to south, long ragged shrieks of light that crossed in the sky just where the dragon flew.

Morlock's body fell down into the boat, sprawling over the side like a marionette whose strings had been cut.

The dragon's body tumbled in the sky overhead, wrapped in flame and smoke, its eyes lifeless and dark as coals, its right foreleg burning bright silver where lightning had melted the spear.

The dragon struck the water just beyond their boat. The wave capsized the little craft, and the world became a chaos of water, fog, and smoke. Aloê managed to grab Morlock's body as it bobbed next to the overturned boat and dragged it away toward the shore.

He came out of his trance halfway there. His eyes went dark, then opened; his mouth gasped and filled with water; he began to sink, floundering in the water.

"Can't you swim?" she shouted.

He snarled something—she thought maybe it was Dwarvish—and began something like swimming. It reminded her of a time when one of her cousins had tossed a cat from a boat. The little beast had crawled desperately through the water toward land—not about to give the water the satisfaction of killing it.

Eventually they crawled up onto the sharp rocks of the Kaenish coast.

Aloê liked a stony beach, but she immediately hated this one. She had hardly taken a step on it when her feet were pierced by the evil edges of the dark rocks littered everywhere.

She turned to make a remark to her companion, saw that Morlock was snorting out water from his nose, and turned away to contemplate the dragon drifting motionless, flameless, steam-wreathed, half-sunk in the shallow waters. She turned back to the man who had struck it from the sky with lightning, and watched in some dismay as he blew snot and saltwater from his nose into his red cloak of office.

"I suppose we can wash it," she said pointedly.

"Bury it," he said. "A little way inland. No one wears a red cloak in Kaen."

"Why not?"

"Because we wear them."

Aloê nodded, remembering. They hunted Guardians like unicorns in Kaen, it was said.

Morlock looked at last out to sea, at the drifting form of his fallen enemy. "Wonder if he's dead."

"Can you do the thing with the lightning again?"

"Not without a focus. Also, lightning doesn't like to fall in the same place twice."

"Then we'll want to be a long way away from here when he wakes up. If he does."

They turned and walked northward, into the rough red lands of Kaen. By then the rain had begun to fall steadily, and more thunder shouted behind them over the long gray waves.

CHAPTER TEN

The Wreck of the *Flayer*

Koijal awoke from dreams of lightning to a day shrouded in fog.

"It's like we slipped through the gate in the west," he remarked to his second-in-command, a dour Eastholder named Stellben. "Like we're sailing off-course through the Sea of Worlds."

"That's water under our keel," said Stellben, who understood the wind and waves of the world-ocean as well as any woman alive, but whose grasp of simile and metaphor was less masterful. "We're not so far out from Sandport," she added. "Passed by the Iljhut Rocks around dawn."

"Home today, you think, then?"

"Tonight at the latest. Is that," asked his literal-minded navigator, "a god on the foredeck?"

Koijal looked at the foredeck: a black-on-white presence was standing there—and a white-on-black entity that was somehow the same but opposite.

"Two," he said, and issued his last order as commander of the *Flayer*. "Abandon ship."

Stellben looked wonderingly at him rather than passing along the order, and then the stillness came upon them.

When Koijal saw the oar-thains grow still, saw the sudden stiffness in Stellben's face, felt the weight on his own limbs, he had one moment left to speak. He wanted to express his frustration and anger for *almost* returning home, his shame and his grief for the crew of his first command, his fury at the forces that were killing him. He got as far as, "Why—?" and then the stillness fell on his throat and lungs.

"No word will pass from this ship to the Graith."

"My decree from before time forbids it."

"My silence, stretching back from after time's end, has swallowed it."

"Natural law, the conflict of our wills, informs us—"

"The meaningless pattern of meanings that means whatever I will—"

"The Graith stands as a wall between Time and Time's end."

"The Graith has been infected with my Chaos."

"It has been wounded by my ceaseless sword of Fate."

"The infection must spread."

"Liar. It's a wound, not an infection. The wound must bleed the lies of Chaos away."

"You're the liar. But the Graith must not know any truths that will heal your lies, lest they also cure the infection of my empty truth."

"No, it's the other way around."

As the gods bickered, the fog surrounding the trireme thickened and brightened. It worked its way into the oars and the hull, splitting them into fragments, and the fragments into fragments.

Now *Flayer* was gone; Koijal and his crew were now adrift in the dense dissolving mist. It wormed its way into them, dividing them into segments of themselves, and the segments into segments, until there was nothing left that could feel pain anymore and death was a convenient door to shut against the snarling of the gods.

PART THREE

THE GODS OF KAEN

You've set out on a long journey. And it's expected that you'll slip, and bump into something, and fall, and get tired, and shout, "I wish I were dead!"—in other words, you'll lie. You'll pick up a companion in one place, bury him in another, and you'll know fear in still another. These sufferings are the milestones on this broken road.

—Seneca, *Letters*

CHAPTER ELEVEN

The Purple Patriarchy

The rain fell hard but didn't last long. The rocky hollows of the bitter shore soon ran over with brackish, barely drinkable water that they drank without hesitation. It was a relief to have the salt water rinsed from her skin and her tunic. Aloê would have liked to skin off her underwear and rinse it out, but somehow was reluctant to do so in Morlock's presence. The charm around her neck seemed to have come through seawater and rain without harm, so she did not fiddle with it. She didn't want to do that in Morlock's presence either.

She had to admit that, if Morlock was more or less useless at sea, he was a capable companion on land. When he noticed that Aloê was tracking blood behind her—the sharp rocks of the shoreline had pierced her feet—he had her sit down and made a pair of sandals for her, using knotted cloth torn from his own clothing and the thin tough-stemmed grasses that were the only thing growing this near the coast.

She set about bandaging her wounds herself: her companion was no medic, or so she guessed from the ugly scars on his neck and elsewhere. But she gratefully put on the footgear Morlock had conjured up out of nothing.

"Thanks!" she said, and might have said more, but he just shrugged and opened his hands. Either he thought it no great matter, or her gratitude was not important to him. She found him an odd man, hard to read.

There were chew-marks on some of the grasses nearby. From the size and shape of the toothmarks she guessed there was some sort of rabbit. She followed a trail of chewed grass until she found a couple of plump furry creatures gnawing on the tough grassy stalks.

She crept close to them before they noticed her. One of them looked up in alarm, unfolded two long hairless legs, like a crane, and ran swiftly away through the grass.

The other was a tad slower. She knocked it over and broke its neck.

"Sorry, fellow," she said to the dead beast. "But we can't live on grass." She brought it back to Morlock.

"What is it?" he said, looking curiously at the odd carcass.

"Supper. Let's walk until we find some brush and make camp. We need to talk"—she stressed the word gently but firmly—"about our next move."

He nodded in agreement, apparently saving up words for later.

They came fairly soon to a stand of trees with peach-colored leaves and black flowers. Morlock took some of the deadwood, leaves, and a stone (the ground was still very rocky) and somehow made a fire, in spite of the fact that everything was still damp from the recent rain. Aloê skinned and split up the two-legged bunny with a sharp rock, spitted the meat on a few sticks, and roasted it.

She was worried that Morlock would be squeamish about eating the meat. In her months in the north, she had never so much as seen fresh meat, and she had come to wonder if dwarves ever ate anything except hideous dry sausage-cakes and flatbread. But whether they did or not, Morlock ate his share of the meal without flinching. In fact, he spent much of the meal fiddling with bones from the extendable legs of the dead creature, which Aloê found a bit morbid.

"What next, do you think?" she said, when they had washed down the last of their meal with a refreshing draft of muddy water from a rocky hole.

"Nearest town." Morlock was rubbing the bones with hot sand from the base of the fire. "How's your Kaenish?"

"*Jhüsh fnöja wäkkleh,*" she replied, which meant roughly *I speak it better than you do.*

It was mere boasting (she had learned the tongue in deep trance only a couple of days ago), but he nodded solemnly. "Yes, I think you do. I can't make vowels sound like that."

"You could, but you won't."

He shrugged.

"You've been to Kaen before, though? You were here last summer?"

He nodded.

"Was it this bad?"

Morlock winced. "Worse," he said, but did not explain. She remembered the scars (on his feet and neck) and didn't ask more about that. They had more pressing issues.

"You're a font of information, Vocate," she said wryly. "So, what do you think? Do you remember the map of Kaen well enough to find the nearest town?"

He shook his head. "Let's walk that way." He gestured with his left hand, seeming to indicate a line parallel with the shore.

"But there won't be any cities on the coast, right?" she said. "Kaenish religion forbids it."

He nodded. "But rivers run down to the sea."

"And people build cities by rivers," she said. "Right. We'll walk near the coast until we find some running water and then follow it upstream. Is that what you suggest?"

He nodded again and took off his shoes. He undid something, some leather-stringy knotty thing, and the soles fell apart. Inside there were a few thin, clipped silver coins. He handed them to her.

"Kaenish issue," he said.

It was enough to live on for a while—longer, if they could live off the land. She'd have asked Morlock about it, but he probably only would have grunted or made some odd gesture with his hands.

His hands, in fact, were a lot more eloquent than the rest of him put together. As she watched, he refastened the soles of his shoes and stood, slipping the bones into an odd pocket in the side of his shirt.

Aloê was puzzled by that. She had heard that dwarves were acquisitive (although she hadn't noticed that in dwarves she actually knew, like Deor). Maybe Morlock had picked up some of their habits? It's true they didn't have much in the way of possessions; the bones were not nothing. In the same spirit she held onto the stone she had skinned the creature with, although she had no pocket to put it in. And her other hand held their meager store of silver coins, which Morlock had carelessly handed her. (So much for dwarvish greed.)

Without her having to say anything, he noticed that her hands were full and ripped another strip from his shirt. He worked it with his fingers a bit and then handed it to her. She took it, as wordless as he, and knotted the coins and the stone into it one by one, so that they wouldn't jingle. Then she wrapped the makeshift money belt around her left arm.

If Morlock on dry land was a more capable entity than Morlock at sea, Morlock in the unguarded lands was a rather more sinister presence than Morlock in A Thousand Towers. Without his vocate's cloak his shoulders seemed even crookeder. And he watched the track and the land on either side of it constantly, as if it were a sleeping animal that might wake up and bite him.

Well. He had been here before, and it *had* bitten him. Aloê tried to look at it the same way.

It was on odd-looking place, certainly. Plants were scarce thereabouts, and green ones a rarity: even the weeds had an odd peachy color that blended in with the rusty sand and red protruding stones.

They came to a small river that was undrinkably filthy. Aloê wouldn't have wanted to cross it even in a boat. She met Morlock's cool eyes and nodded with satisfaction: there was a city upstream.

They turned right and began to walk along the bank of the river. Now they were following something that might charitably be described as a dirt road. Others had passed this way, fairly often. She found that cheering, although she noticed that Morlock did not.

The land by the river was more farmable, and soon they came on an actual farm. The fields were enclosed by fences, and the fences were adorned with many a protective idol whose protruding teeth and claws and phalluses obviously threatened anyone thinking of an intrusion.

The air was smoky, and as they rounded a hill, they saw why. In an open field was a great fire, and the farmers were dancing around it, throwing things on the flames.

"Are those people burning food?" Aloê asked Morlock.

He shrugged unhappily and walked on without looking back. "Possibly. Mostly trash, I guess. But it is a tenet of Kaenish religion to burn part of every crop."

"Why?"

"The religion began in an age of many famines. That's what the books say. Only the strong and cruel could survive. So now they say they must stay hungry, so that they can stay cruel. Prosperity leads to weakness. So they destroy wealth."

"That's crazy."

"It is pretense, I think. Most of the farmer's crops are in a barn some-where; some is burnt for show. That fire is mostly trash, by the reek."

"I saw something moving as someone tossed it into the fire."

Morlock shrugged. "The poverty is pretense. The cruelty is real."

"You hate Kaen."

"People are trapped here. I decided once . . . No, I don't hate the people. But I hate the trap."

Aloê mulled this over as they walked on. The column of smoke was black against the blue sky; she guessed there was a good deal of fat and bone feeding those flames. Probably Morlock considered offal from a butcher shed as "trash" too. But Aloê couldn't forget the wriggling thing she'd seen tossed into the flames. How much of that offal had been alive before it abruptly found itself fuel for the bonfire? Was it that much different than what she had done, killing an animal and eating it? She felt there was a difference, but couldn't say exactly why.

Morlock stopped walking, and she looked up to see why. He was pon-dering an odd brick-colored idol atop a pillar inscribed with Kaenish runes. The idol bristled with large hooked extrusions that looked something like phalluses. The side of each phallus bore a deep long rift bristling with teeth—like a carnivore's mouth, or a toothy nightmare of a vagina.

"Khecür Tnevnepü," she read. "The Maroon Father-of-Many? Or maybe: the Purple Patriarch? What does it mean?"

"It's the name of the city," Morlock said. "And its god. The gates are not far off. Or this god's power extends deep into the countryside."

"One can see why. Universal appeal."

Morlock shrugged and turned away. They trudged onward.

Around the red shoulder of the next hill, they came to the gates of Khecür Tnevnepü. Sleepy guards were leaning on their spears outside the arch. They watched with a complete lack of interest as Aloê and Morlock approached.

"What's your business?" said one of the guards, not as if he cared.

"Passing through," Aloê replied.

"Why? The Festival of Changes?"

This was awkward. As far as Aloê knew, freedom of movement between the Kaenish cities was one of the few edicts enforced by the national government. On the other hand, she could hardly insist on her rights as a Kaenish citizen, since she was not one. But she didn't want to commit them to anything they might want to avoid. And a Kaenish religious festival was definitely something they might want to avoid.

"You're at the wrong gate for that," the other guard said.

"We're just on the way from one place to another," Aloê said stubbornly.

The first guard shifted the weight on his feet and dropped his open hand to about waist level. It was pretty clear he was looking for a bribe. But they couldn't really afford to be buying guards with their slender stock of coins.

Something stretched past Aloê, tapped the open-mouthed guard's empty palm, and retracted.

Aloê turned and looked at Morlock. He had the bones in his hand—the ones from the long-legged bunny-beast. But they had been woven into some kind of stretchy grabber-thing.

"What's that?" shouted the startled guard.

"Something I made," Morlock said. He extended it and retracted it a couple more times. There were claws at the end that could pick up small stones, as Morlock demonstrated. The two guards were fascinated, obviously. Morlock looked at Aloê and raised his eyebrows.

"Look, I'll lay it on the line," Aloê said candidly. "We don't have any cash to speak of. But if you'd like this little dingus, we'd be glad to give it to you, as a token of appreciation for letting us pass."

"Hm," said the bribe-seeker. "Oh, all right, then. Hand it over and you can pass."

A purple-cloaked figure wearing a floppy-crowned hat emerged from the shadows of the gate.

"Stop! In the name of the Purple Patriarch, stop!" the newcomer cried in a gluey resonant voice.

"Told you," smugly said the other guard, the one who hadn't asked for a bribe.

"Shut it," hissed the bribe-seeker.

The newcomer's hat was almost brimless. With a shock, Aloê realized that it was the image in cloth of the odd flanged-phallus they'd seen sprouting from the image of Khecür Tnevnepü. It even had a toothy mouth or vagina stitched into its side, the fangs picked out in golden fabric.

"I'll take that," said the newcomer, seizing the dingus from the slack fingers of the bribable guard. "And I must apologize to our new friends. This was a dismal way to acquaint yourself with the protection of the Patriarchy! Welcome to Khecür Tnevnepü. All are welcome here. I am Ynenck, priest of the seventh mystery of Khecür Tnevnepü, whose foot rests equally on all our faces."

"Thanks," Aloê said. "I'm glad to meet you"—she used the masculine form of the pronoun, hoping she wasn't making an error—the priest's appearance and voice were strikingly androgynous—"and so is my—" She turned to Morlock for guidance.

"—cousin-by-oath," he completed.

"Excellent, excellent. Your secret names you will choose to retain for now, and your old use-names belong to the god of your home-city. Have you use-names that have been accepted by the Patriarchate?" the priest asked.

"No," Aloê said, fairly sure that she was right about this.

"Then I shall dub you Bükwilöt and Pebbexäk! I shall pray for you in those names to the Patriarch in my evening devotions, keeping this little trinket as an offering to the god."

"Uh. Thank you. They're beautiful names."

"Not at all, not at all. This gadget should be useful around the temple, and whenever I use it I will think with pleasure of how I humiliated this scut-gargling piece of motherskin." The priest joyously kicked the bribe-seeking guard with one of his large purple boots.

"Thank you, Your Sanctity," the guard mumbled gloomily.

"Well, come with me, Bükwilöt and Pebbexäk, and I shall introduce you to the greatest city in the greatest country in the world! In *any* world!"

Bükwilöt (Aloê) and Pebbexäk (Morlock) followed the purple priest through the gate into the city of the Purple Patriarch.

"If you have not come for the Festival," said Ynenck the priest, "may I ask what brings you to our city? Not that you need any reason other than the greatness of the city itself, of course."

The greatness of Khecür Tnevnepü was not much in evidence from where they were walking. The inside of the city walls had been painted purple many a year ago, but the color was now dingy where it had not flaked away entirely. There were a number of hovels that might have been shops near the gate, but they were closed, their doors nailed shut.

"We are in flight from our city," Aloê said. "It was taken over by new gods whose reign we could not accept."

"What city?" Ynenck asked swiftly. "Tekatestömädeien or Gröxengrefzäkrura?"

Aloê was uncertain how to respond to this, but Morlock offered, "We dare not say. We don't want our former god to hear and be angry at us."

"Naturally, naturally," Ynenck concurred. "Of course, if you subject yourselves to the boot of the Purple Patriarch, his kicks will protect you from all others."

"Yes, but we're not sure that there is room under the boot for those such as us," Aloê said. "We may need to move onward, sooner rather than later."

"The right to move freely from city to city is one reason Kaen is the greatest country in the world—in all the worlds," Ynenck made haste to add. "Nevertheless, I'm sure that if you stay with Khecür Tnevnepü for even a single night, you will never wish to leave. Multitudes of Kaeniar have done the same, adding their footfalls to the mighty march though time that is Khecür Tnevnepü, the god and the city."

The multitudes marching along with Khecür Tnevnepü were not very evident to Aloê, although there were a few other inhabitants in the street now. She noticed that there were never men and women together. At least, if a woman was walking down the street she might be accompanied by someone or something—but it couldn't have been a human being; it appeared to be walking on all fours. Some men also led purple-cloaked creatures. But there were never men and women together.

"It will soon be night, and you will need a place to stay," Ynenck was saying. "I take it you can pay, in coin or in services? The Purple Patriarch is a cruel and greedy god, and of course we imitate him."

"We have some coin, and we don't mind work," Aloê said. "But we don't need much for the night, perhaps just a single room."

Ynenck swung about and glared at them both, his soft face twisting with disdain and rage, like an angry pudding. "A man and woman sleeping in a single room, like filthy animals in a barn? Is that how they lived in your old city? No wonder the Masked Powers triumphed there. We have a stronger, crueller, purer way here in Khecür Tnevnepü."

Hoping that she had correctly assessed the local etiquette, Aloê knocked the priest's hat off his head, revealing a complicated spiky spiral of hair rising from the crown of his head. The purple hat fell into the gutter, where Morlock stepped aside to grind it into the muddy filth with his right shoe.

Several people, male and female, stopped to watch with interest, but no one moved to interfere. In Khecür Tnevnepü (in Kaen, generally, from what Aloê had heard), victimization was a spectator sport, and the victims were on their own.

"We may fear the gods," Aloê said to the astonished priest, who was holding his soft white hands to the sky, his round mouth open in a red O of surprise. "But we don't fear you. We can also be cruel."

"I understand," the priest said humbly. "May I have my hat back? It is a shame to me to have my hair exposed on the street."

"Buy it," Morlock said tersely.

"Yes," Aloê said. "Give us that grabby-dingus back. You can offer the god its equivalent in coin." She would have rather had the money, but she expected that the priest would cheat them if he could—cheating and lying were the cruelty of the powerless, and through them he might be able to covertly reclaim some status.

Reluctantly, Ynenck surrendered the bone instrument to Aloê, and Morlock picked up the hat from the gutter and handed it to him. "Don't brush it off," Morlock said, as the priest was about to do just that. Reluctantly, Ynenck put the mud-stained purple phallus-hat back on his head.

"Inn," Aloê reminded him.

"Yes," the priest said, and shrugged gracefully. "Yes. But there really is no place where you could stay together. The most I can do is bring you to a place with two wings, one for holes and one for poles."

Aloê eyed him closely to see if the priest was engaged in some fresh, but more subtle, act of contempt. But his face was bland, still somewhat ashamed, but not defensive or sly. If "poles" and "holes" were the vulgar sexual slang they seemed, she guessed they must be in common use locally.

"All right," Aloê said. The thought of being able to lie down in a bed and sleep almost made her dizzy: it had been a very long day.

Wordlessly the priest led them to a large rambling structure. Music and harsh laughter was leaking from the open windows on the first floor. The windows on the second floor were all shuttered and silent. The narrow stone steps led up to a porch where a doorman waited.

The priest stopped at the foot of the stairs, and Morlock and Aloê walked side by side up them to the porch. The doorman wore a wide-brimmed hat, its low crown embroidered with the odd phallus/vagina of the Purple Patriarch.

"A klenth each," the doorman said. "Covers sleep room only. Food and amusements extra. Pay in advance."

Aloê had no idea what a klenth was or whether the price was reasonable, but she made a hiss of disdain and started to turn away.

"All right!" the doorman said. "A klenth for you both, and the first drink is free."

"The first drink is always free," Aloê guessed. "Half-klenth for both of us, and that's just because my feet hurt."

"Yes. Yes, I suppose," the doorman said grumpily.

Aloê undid the money belt from her wrist and handed it to Morlock. He passed the doorman a coin that was probably a half-klenth; the doorman eyed it dubiously in the dim light but then shrugged and pocketed it.

"You're there," the doorman said to Aloê. "Holes are over there," he added to Morlock, pointing at the other side of the porch.

Evidently Aloê had misunderstood the local slang. She was relieved. The prospect of separating from her companion was less pleasant. She could see he felt the same, from his gloomy expression, so she laughed at him. "Come get me if you need me," she said.

He smiled, shrugged, nodded, turned away. She just turned away.

><

The door to the women's side of the lodge opened by itself as she approached; there was no visible doorman. Inside a priest of the Purple Patriarch—strongly resembling Ynenck but with his (her?) face heavily rouged and powdered— welcomed her effusively.

"Sleep rooms are assigned at midnight," the priest said.

Aloê nearly fainted. Then she was on the verge of swearing by God Avenger. At the last minute she changed the curse to a question: "Is there anywhere I can rest? I badly want to get off my feet."

"I know what you mean, dark stranger!" the priest carolled. "I know exactly what you mean. The playroom is through there. You can rest to your heart's content in there—although, of course, entertainment is extra."

"Bleh," she said, and walked through the swinging door to the playroom.

She was hoping for couches, but all she saw at first were chairs. That was enough. They loomed before her like ugly pink trees. She strode toward the nearest one that was vacant and sat down in it.

The relief was epic, as if all the pain in the world had stopped hurting. She basked in sheer relief for a moment. Then she glanced around, taking note of her surroundings.

She didn't much like what she saw, not being fond of pink. The walls were painted a fresh grapey purple, but there was fluffy bunting hanging everywhere, pale pink in color. The tables were enamelled in a pink-and-purple checker design, and the floor was covered with hot pink carpet. The room was lit by oil-lamps with pink shades. Sweet musky perfumes and incense made the air dense . . . but, heavy as they were, Aloê could still smell grosser, fleshier odors: sweat, the stench of unwashed vaginas, and, unless she was very much mistaken, the gluey reek of fresh semen. The dense air was thick with noise, too: giggling, and moaning, and muttered conversation.

"Travelling here for the festival?" said a woman sitting next to her.

Aloê turned to reply, but the stink nearly blocked her throat. "Passing through," she managed to gasp.

"Well, you've arrived at a good time," the other said amiably. She was coming into focus for Aloê: a middle-aged, motherly woman with graying brown hair and pale skin that was darker and more wrinkly around the eyes. "What's your use-name?"

"Bükwilöt," Aloê said.

"Oh, really? That's . . . it's so . . . I'm called Lÿrfü."

Lÿrfü's reaction confirmed Aloê's suspicion that Ynenck had burdened them with ridiculous use-names. A sneaky act of cruelty? Or was that a test they had failed to pass? Both? Maybe she should tell Morlock. But, of course, she wouldn't see him until morning.

"Urm," Aloê said, desperately trying to keep up her side of the conversation.

"Exactly!" Lÿrfü agreed enthusiastically. "I've said the same thing a thousand times!"

Aloê looked a little closer at Lÿrfü and decided the older woman was drunk. She picked out two more scents from the dense cloudy air: poppy smoke and beer.

"Going for a ride?" asked Lÿrfü, gesturing with her left hand at the far side of the room, where most of the noise was emanating from. Her right hand gripped a boozing can that was more than half-empty.

"Too tired," Aloê said. She wasn't sure what Lÿrfü meant, but she knew she was too tired for anything but sitting there.

"Yes! Exactly! Much too early!" Lÿrfü agreed. "As I get older I almost feel I prefer to watch you young things ride than take my own turn. But you're not drinking!"

"No money!" Aloê shouted.

"Doesn't matter! First one is free! I've been here an hour and this is still my first one," Lÿrfü said, and waved her booze-can.

"Hey, minster!" Lÿrfü shouted into the bright pinkish murk. "A gage of beer for my friend, B—for my good friend here."

"Really, I'm not—"

"Look, youngster, if you don't want it you can give it to a pole—or me. It won't go to waste, anyway."

Aloê felt more at ease suddenly: she could understand now why Lÿrfü had befriended her. There was a free drink in the offing.

She let Lÿrfü run on without bothering to say much in reply—not that Lÿrfü seemed to be much concerned about what she did manage to say. The room was not pleasant, but it was out of the night air, and she was sitting down. Some sort of dance or scrimmage or something seemed to be happening on the far side of the room: Aloê promised herself she would stay far away from that. She'd sit here, nursing her drink, until the stars swung around to midnight. Then she'd have her room or she'd get her damn half-klenth back and get out of here.

Something warm touched her hand. She glanced down to see that one of the pink-and-purple tables was right next to her. Except—it wasn't a table. It was some kind of animal. The purple checks were tattooed on.

It was a hideous thing—some kind of ape, she thought. But it walked on all fours like a crab, with its face up. A sort of face, anyway. The upper surface of its head was a vast toothless maw; it had disturbingly human brown eyes, one each on the side of its odd head, and no discernible nose. It was male, and its red phallus was ridiculously erect.

"Ooooh," Lÿrfü crooned at it. "Has some bad boy run away from the riding wall? He's a very bad boy, naughty-waughty widdle boy. Does he want a little drink? A little drinky-winky from Auntie Lÿrfü?"

The creature shied away when it heard Lÿrfü's voice (although Aloê couldn't tell how it heard: it had no ears that she could see). It seemed to cower, so that Aloê was between it and Lÿrfü.

"Oh," the older woman said to Aloê, "that's cute. He likes you. Here's your drink. You should give him a sip and maybe he'll let you ride him. They do that when they like somebody."

It was a priest who bore Aloê's drink—like enough to Ynenck and the priest at the door to be their sister (or brother). The priest handed the drink to Aloê and smiled. Lÿrfü looked at her and smiled. Even the creature who cowered beside her seemed to be smiling with its odd wide panting mouth.

Ride him. That was what they were doing over by the far wall, she saw now through the smoky perfumed air. There were women mounted on these crab-ape things, on their phalluses, and plunging up and down.

Sex with animals? But: what kind of animal?

She looked at the thing crouching before her. It hadn't been born that way. Someone had *made* it that way: there were the bold purplish marks of scars on its shoulders, knees, face—partially obscured by the tattoos, but clear enough now that she looked for them. The hands and feet were human, not apelike.

This thing was a man. Anyway, it had been a man. They had changed it into this thing.

And they did expect her to have sex with it. She turned to look at the faces nearby. A few were openly aroused (like Lÿrfü and the priest). A few were tittering in embarrassment or amusement as they watched and waited. Others were breathing heavily, sickened expressions on their faces—their eyes averted, but stealing the occasional glance, as if to refresh their disgust.

Aloê would have liked to pass the matter off with a joke, or a polite refusal. She'd been in many an odd situation—many more obviously dangerous than this one was. But she found that horror was strangling her, making speech impossible. It was the smell of semen rising from the beast next to her—oppressive, summoning memories that were distant yet all-too familiar, nightmarish.

She shoved her booze-can into Lÿrfü's not-unwilling hand, stood up, kicked the cringing beast out of the way, and walked toward the door.

"Off to see the Festival, are we?" the priest at the door said brightly. "Well, I'll see you later."

"I'll see you in hell; not before," she told the shocked priest. She looked back before she walked out into the night. Lÿrfü was blissfully at peace, eyes closed, slack in her chair with a booze-can on the floor under either hand.

She turned away and stepped out into the clean air of the night. She breathed it in gratefully without thinking. Then: she thought. Her reaction had some degree of panic in it, that was clear. But she sensed something wrong here. Unless she was much mistaken, they needed to get away. Now.

She turned to the doorman, "I need to speak to . . . to Pebbexäk, my cousin-by-oath."

"Can't go in the men's side," the doorman said. "Only men and holes there."

Holes. The subhuman equivalent of the poles she had already seen. She grimaced.

"I don't want to go in," she said candidly. "Can you send him a message?"

"Can't," the doorman said. "Can't leave my place."

"Send a message or I'm going in. Choose."

"Can't—"

She kicked him in one knee, and he tumbled off the porch to the muddy street. She walked past and stepped into the men's side of the nameless hostelry.

"Where's the bar?" she said to the shocked purple priest within. "Or playroom. Whatever you call it."

"You can't be here!" he gasped.

"I won't be long. I'd ask you to carry a message to someone, but you wouldn't."

"Of course I wouldn't!"

"Screw you, then."

She walked past him into the men's side.

It was like and unlike the women's side. The decor was all purple, and the smoke was less perfumy, but still dense with the reek of poppy and beer. There were men riding holes, the hideous parody of women, on every side. There seemed to be many more men than holes, and each one was surrounded by a crowd of hooting spectators.

As she watched, one man dismounted a naked capering hole and another

leapt forward to grab his chance. He kicked another aspirant out of the way
(to the delight of the crowd), but the hole skittered away and wouldn't let him
climb aboard.

He had a tankard of beer in his hands, though, and he poured some of it
into the vast pink maw that was the only thing the hole had for a face. The
maw filled with foaming beer to the thing's rimlike lips. The beer gurgled
out of sight down into the thing's gullet; the lips smacked with satisfaction;
and finally the hole allowed the half-naked man to mount. When he did so he
roared as if he had won a great victory, and the beast bucked under him. The
crowd of men standing near applauded——some already stripped from the waist
down to seize their own chance when it came.

No one saw her at first, and that was good, because it took her a while to
search out Morlock in the wide murky room. But she saw him at last, seated
at a long table, listening with amused patience to some tale being told by a
man wearing a wide-brimmed black hat.

She walked through the room to reach him. Eventually men began to
notice her. Most seemed more frightened than angry, though there was something of both in their reactions.

One pudding-faced man with no pants on grabbed his genitals as if she
were going to steal them. "You can't be here!" he hissed at her as she passed.

"I won't be long," she replied coolly, "much like yourself," and gestured
significantly. He turned away, his pale formless face blushing a savage shame-
filled purple. Apparently just being here was bad enough; she made it worse
by talking. She was glad of that. She resolved to talk to anyone who talked
to her or stood in her way . . . but nobody did, and at last she stood next to
Morlock.

". . . and so we have a barbarian-warrior, a priest-healer, a gnome-thief—,"
the man in the black hat was saying, gesturing at the people sitting at the
table as he named them.

"A gnome?" Morlock asked, nodding at the red-eyed dwarf sitting next to
the man with the black hat.

"Well, a dwarf. Same thing."

"No."

"It is to us."

"You're wrong about that, but it's no skin off my walrus."

"It—what does that mean?"

"Don't let it worry you. Go on."

"Well, we need a mage and a rogue before we start on our quest. I was pretty sure you were one or the other. We were supposed to all meet here at the tavern."

"What's a mage?"

"Someone who does magic."

"What's magic?"

"Magic is . . . It's . . . Well. It's something amazing."

"Eh. Different people are amazed by different things. I amazed someone earlier today with this." Without seeming to move, Morlock triggered the grabby-thing he had made from bones, reached out across the table with it, tapped the rather drunken barbarian on the other side of the table (who proceeded to fall off his bench), and retracted it.

"That *is* amazing!" shouted the man in the black hat. The barbarian raised himself from the floor and made some noises suggestive of agreement.

Morlock shrugged and rolled his eyes. "Anyone who knew how to make it could have made it. Are you sure that's magic?"

"Of course I'm sure!"

The barbarian made some sounds suggestive of disagreement. The man in the black hat turned toward him to make some sort of theological point. Morlock cast his eyes about in desperation, and so caught sight of Aloê.

He raised his mug agreeably to her and smiled, so she learned at last that he could do that. In fact, he seemed more relaxed than she had ever seen him—suspiciously so. Morlock was strangely unmoved by the filth and stench of his surroundings. Maybe these things were different for men.

"How much money have you spent on those?" she asked, gesturing at the mug.

"None," he replied. "First one's free."

"What about the next one?"

Morlock looked surprised. "Why would I want more than one?"

"People do. Never mind; I'm glad it's not a problem. Listen, we have to get out of here."

The man in the black hat was staring at Aloê in amazement. "You can't be here!" he whispered. "You're a—a—a—"

"—a woman, yes," Aloê said. "But your rules don't matter to me."

"Rogue!" muttered the man in the black hat to the person sitting next to him on the bench, the dwarf—so red-eyed and serpentine in appearance that Aloê half expected to see smoke trailing from his nostrils.

"Yuh!" said the dwarf, and smoke did follow his word in the air. He was holding a bowl of some burning herb in his hands; perhaps he had just inhaled some of it. Or perhaps he was near the dragon-change, as his appearance suggested, and only held the smoking bowl to hide that fact.

"She's not a rogue any more than I'm a mage," Morlock said. "She's—"

Aloê was worried that Morlock was going to say "a Guardian" (maybe even in Wardic—he looked more relaxed than anyone under a death sentence had a right to be). So she broke in, "I'm his cousin-by-oath. And we're leaving."

Aloê dreaded the veiled explanations she'd have to make to her partner. She hardly knew herself why they had to leave—she was just sure it was wise.

But, as it turned out, none were needed. Morlock looked sharply at her, then set down his half-empty mug and stood up.

"Good-bye, venturers!" he said. "Good luck with your quest."

"But you can't go now!" the man in the black hat shouted. "A mage *and* a rogue—right in the tavern, where the magister said you'd be!"

But they could go and they did go, leaving the man baffled behind them.

The priest was gone from his station inside the door. As the Guardians approached the doorway to the porch they heard men shouting in the street.

"—strangers from Tekatestömädeien," one man was screaming, "come to preach the false consolation of the Two Powers, to kill our god and destroy our sacred culture and heritage!"

"Maybe we should wait until they finish lynching those poor bastards," Aloê whispered. "We don't want to walk into a riot."

Morlock nodded and drew to a halt—a little unsteady on his feet, Aloê was alarmed to notice.

"—and the brazen whore walked past me, into the men's side, as if she were a man or a hole!" one man was shouting. "That's not my culture and heritage! Is it yours?" Aloê thought she recognized the voice of the doorkeeper she had kicked.

As the crowd outside shouted various flavors of "No!" Aloê met Morlock's eye. No word was needed; both realized that they were the intended guests at this lynching party.

Morlock tilted his head toward the other side of the inn.

Aloê nodded. Time to make a discreet exit through the back door and run like madfolk for the gate. Any gate.

They turned as one and plowed through the crowd in the room, now quieter yet more menacing than before. Clearly some of the men had heard at least some of the shouting in the street.

The inn was as thin as a child's excuse: there was no kitchen or backroom behind the tavern. As soon as they burst through the back door they were in another street. Both ends were crowded with people listening to the ranters on the far side of the narrow house.

High overhead, Chariot the major moon glared whitely down on them from a clear cold sky, and Trumpeter burned bright blue in the west.

As the two vocates hesitated as to their next move, someone shouted, "There they are!" and the mob started to boil toward them from either side of the street.

Aloê wondered desperately how they had been recognized—and then she knew. No woman of this town would be seen with a man, or vice versa.

Morlock looked one way, then the other, and started to run on rather wobbly feet toward the nearer end of the street.

The crowd did seem a little thinner there. She grabbed the thin pole holding up the awning and followed him into the fray.

Drunk or sober, the crooked man could fight. She watched with admiration as he plunged into the crowd, weaponless. With his left hand Morlock grabbed the wrist of a man waving a long knife and twisted. Aloê distinctly heard the wet crack of breaking bone. Then Morlock had the knife—and his right hand wielded a club he had harvested from some other hapless rioter.

Now Aloê was in the thick of it, too, spinning her staff to force back the crowd, and lashing out to strike those who lingered too near.

But surprise and momentum only got them deep into the rioters. Soon they were surrounded and forced to stand back-to-back to protect each other.

It wasn't looking good, with more of the crowd running over from the far end of the street. Mere pressure of numbers was forcing people closer to the two vocates.

Aloê felt a certain fierce satisfaction, though. Everyone had to die some-time, and it was good to be fighting back-to-back with someone who fought as hard as Morlock.

"Time for another lightning bolt!" she shouted, although she knew he could not possibly summon lightning from a clear sky, even if he could have gone into rapture.

She thought she heard him snickering and was pleased.

But nerve wouldn't push them through a crowd as dense as this, and she started to plan for when their weapons got knocked out of their hands, or when her companion was struck down.

Then help arrived. The man in the black hat, waving a long ill-balanced sword, laid with joyous fury into the circle of citizens surrounding Aloê and Morlock. "Venturers! To me!" he shouted pompously, and slashed and stabbed and confused the crowd.

Meanwhile the snaky dwarf wriggled in among the crowd and started cutting their pockets openly. Many who had turned with courage to face their fresh attacker turned again and backed away to save their wallets.

And now the big half-naked barbarian arrived, broadsword in both hands, and he went down into the crowd like a reaper into a field, swinging his weapon with grim and businesslike determination.

The wall of people around the two Guardians was now full of gaps. Aloê and Morlock turned together and ran through a rift in the crowd, past confused rioters, up a nearby alley, running without thought of a goal except to get away from the melee.

For a few breathless moments Aloê hoped that the crowd would let them go. Unfortunately, the self-styled venturers followed, the man in the black hat shouting again and again, "To me! Venturers to me!"

And the crowd, or part of it, began to trail up the dark winding street.

Aloê glanced at Morlock; his eyes were unreadable in the shadows, but he was already turning back. She did the same, and they sprinted together back to face their pursuers.

A mob is strongest when it has no face, when it is so numerous that it acts on its members as powerfully as on anything it confronts. This was just a wispy tendril of a greater mob, the faces clearly distinguishable in the moons' light, like petals on the black branch of the street.

Aloê lashed out at one big-nosed balding man: right on his nose. She felt it give under the blow, all the way up the staff. He turned away wailing, his face dripping blood that was black in the moons' bluish light.

Morlock, meanwhile, passed his sword (where had he gotten a sword?) through one mobster's soft protruding belly while stabbing the eye of a gaping onlooker with the knife in his other hand. Both staggered off screaming down curses on him in the name of their purple god.

The mob, or moblet, changed its mind and started withdrawing from the sidestreet before more of its members were hurt.

Morlock seemed almost inclined to chase after them, so Aloê pounded on his higher shoulder and gestured at the invitingly empty darkness at the other end of the street. He nodded and turned away with her.

Aloê realized that the man in the black hat was no longer shouting. Looking back, she saw why: he was lying wounded on the ground, his black blood staining the dusty street. Near him crouched the priest-healer, muttering some words—a healing spell, perhaps, or a prayer for the dead. On the other side of the body crouched another figure: the dwarf-thief efficiently rifling through the fallen man's pockets, his red eyes aglow with greed, his breath smoking in the cool night air.

This much in a single long glance she saw; then she turned away. The advent of the venturers might well have saved her and Morlock's lives. But if they were to keep them, they had to get out of this town; that was obvious.

They ran on until the street emptied into a square with several exits. Aloê paused there, wondering which way to take.

"Feel groggy," Morlock said.

Aloê was irritated by this remark, which seemed to her quite pointless. Of course he was groggy. She was groggy, too—half-dead on her aching feet.

Then it occurred to her that Morlock didn't make idle conversation. She looked more closely at him. He was standing unsteadily, as if the firm-packed ground under his feet were shifting swampland. His eyes were half-shut. There was the gleam of sweat or drool on the side of his face.

How much had he drunk? Less than half a mug, if he wasn't lying.

Suddenly Aloê remembered looking back from the exit of the women's tavern, and seeing Lÿrfü asleep in her chair . . . after drinking the ale she had ordered for Aloê.

"The first drink is free," Aloê muttered furiously. "Listen, Morlock: you're not drunk; you've been drugged."

"Telling *you*," he said thickly, and perhaps a little sullenly.

"Can you vomit anything up?" she asked. "Might save you from the worst of it."

He glared at her and muttered, "Guess so."

Did he not want to puke in front of her? Aloê found men baffling. He hadn't been ashamed to be seen drinking in that tavern, even though it stank of beer and semen and faceless inhuman whores. But he didn't want to perform a simple bodily function while she watched, even though it might help save both their lives.

Well, come to think of it, she had no interest in watching, either. She pointedly turned away and stared back up the way they'd come.

From the shadows of the narrow street emerged a block of shadow, vaguely man-shaped.

She lifted her staff—ready to attack—but the newcomer held out hands empty of weapons.

"Oh!" she said. "You're one of the Venturers. The barbarian, I think?"

"I am a barbarian," agreed the Venturer. "My mother was a priestess of Iänglu-Thërôn, and my father a bookbinder in the same city. But in my heart I am a barbarian. I reject civilized ways and follow the savage urges of my own heart. I chose the name Kremp to signify all this."

Aloê wondered if this would have sounded more poetic if Morlock were not gagging and retching in the background.

"All right," she said. "What's it to us? Why are you following us?"

"You survived," Kremp pointed out. "You are the strongest. You follow your own self-will and ignore the false cries of mercy and loyalty."

"No, we don't."

In the moonslight of the open square, the self-made barbarian could be seen to smile.

"Anyway, I'd bet that thieving dwarf survived to follow his own self-will."

"You'd be wrong," Kremp replied. "The crowd cut him down. He dropped some of his loot and stopped to collect it. That was his undoing."

"Oh." That sounded likely, in fact. "What do you want with us, though?"

"You are strongest," the barbarian said. "I follow you."

"That's a mistake," Aloê said. "We have an—an oath-sworn loyalty to each other, my companion and I. We can't afford to extend that to you."

"You will betray me if it seems advantageous to you. I understand, and assure you of the same." He went on to talk at some length of the betrayal of others as a necessary loyalty to oneself.

That wasn't what Aloê had meant at all, but the admission from Kremp was useful, in a way. She was wondering whether it was worth it to dispose of Kremp right now, before he became a problem, when she heard something— over the unmusical sound of Morlock's retching, over the careful exposition by Kremp of his barbarian philosophy. The mob was coming.

"Morlock!" she hissed. "Company."

Morlock spat, then gasped, "Hear them. Where to?"

That was the question. There were rioters in more than one street leading toward the little square. There was noise from the streets on the opposite side too—but it was more musical, like singing, or chanting. This Festival of Changes the guards had talked about? A festival crowd would a great place to get lost in.

"This way," she said, tugging his sleeve as she ran past.

He lumbered along next to her. Behind she heard, just barely, the catlike tread of Kremp the barbarian following them away.

The tangled path they took through the streets toward the festival and away from the mob at their heels brought them past a city gate. It was shut and barred, and dark-helmed guards stood before it with their blades drawn. No exit that way, clearly.

The buildings began to thin out as they ran up a street parallel to the city wall. Ahead was an open space—a great market or a temple plaza. It was densely crowded with purple-robed women who were singing or screaming in a rhythm set by loud but unseen drums. Many of them waved torches, and there was a great bonfire, large but not bright, wreathed with dark stinking smoke like the offal fire they had seen that afternoon.

Aloê paused at the edge of the crowd to assess the situation. There were few if any males here—she couldn't see one, except for the two that were with her. This might not, after all, be such a good place to hide.

Beyond the crowd, built up onto the side of the city wall, was a great slope of marble—something like the curve of a seashell, but vastly larger, the home of a mollusk bigger than a house. There were rickety wooden flights of stairs running up either side of it, and low on the marbly slope were two wrinkled holes, again one on each side. They were steaming in the cool night air. A fence divided the plaza into two sides. On one side were the women. On the other side was a sort of sheepfold, and in it animals of some sort milled about, bleating.

And, as the crowd chanted and as Aloê w :hed in mounting horrr , the left orifice emitted a spray of dark fluid anc nuck, squirting it onto the bonfire, which became even darker and smokier.

The crowd of robed women screamed and applauded.

From the opposite orifice, a naked gleaming animal was thrust and fell squeaking to the ground. It was taken by purple-hatted priests and herded over with the other . . . the other things.

The other *holes*, she saw. Inside the shell was something, a machine or a monster, that made women into holes. Maybe men were changed into poles on another night or another time. But that didn't matter. What did matter was that she and Morlock had to get out of there. She, in particular, had to get out of there.

Suddenly, she was seized by either elbow, her staff knocked out of her hands. Two purple-robed guards with spiky mask-helmets had a grip on her; she couldn't tell if they were male or female, but they were extraordinarily strong. They lifted her straight off the ground and deftly evaded her kicks as they hustled her away.

Aloê looked back and saw with dismay that Morlock was looking vaguely at the chanting crowd, seemingly unaware of her absence. Kremp was speaking in his ear, one hand on his arm, drawing him away.

Morlock stared abruptly at Kremp and looked wildly about. He saw Aloê's staff lying on the ground. He shouted inarticulately—anyway, Aloê couldn't understand any words.

She tried to shout out, *Hey, I'm over here!* but all she managed was a long, drawn-out wavering, "Hey-ey-ey-ey . . ."

It was enough. Morlock shook loose from Kremp and, when the self-styled barbarian tried to grab hold of his arm again, he grabbed Kremp's hand and twisted it. Kremp fell to one knee, his face distorted with pain, and Morlock ran on wobbling feet up the narrow walkway.

By now Aloê and her captors were nearly at the stairs. The women just beyond the fence were screaming and cheering as they watched her get dragged to the hateful stairway. All were excited. One was weeping and naked, massaging her genitals fiercely with both hands.

Were they here only to watch? Or would they themselves go up the stairs to lose their humanity and become mere holes?

Morlock was with them, now. He had lost his knife somewhere, but he was waving the notched sword in his right hand. Aloê suddenly remembered that he was drugged and wondered if maybe he would prove an unsafe savior. But his first stroke slashed through the wrist of one of her captors: the aim was too good to be accidental. The hand still clung to her, horribly, but the arm pulled away.

The one captor who still held her tried to continue up the stairway. But now she had her feet firmly on the ground, and she used their combined weight to push the enemy off balance.

Face-to-face with her captor, she saw that it was not wearing a mask. The blades had been inserted into, or were growing out of, the skull itself, which was bare in places, like bedrock showing through a field where the topsoil was sandy and thin.

Well: that meant no face-punches, anyway. She toppled the thing over onto the stairs and stomped on it. There was an audible crunch under her foot, and her enemy spasmed, so she kept stomping until it stopped moving and the purple robe was sodden with some fluid that was not blood—not by the smell, anyway.

She turned to see that Morlock had finished dismembering his opponent and was moving back up the walkway, gesturing for her to follow.

Aloê looked past him to see the self-styled barbarian, Kremp (whose friendship was at best conditional) and beyond him a cloud of purple-robed enemies: floppy-hatted priests of the patriarch and with them spiky faced ministers of the festival. They might get past them, but what then?

"No!" she said, seizing Morlock by one arm. He stared at her as if she had punched him. "Up the stairs!" she said. "Over the wall!" She tried to mime the actions with her hands.

Light went on behind Morlock's eyes, and they ran together to and up the rickety wooden stair.

The crowd began to cheer and scream again, misconstruing their intentions. But, underneath their noise, underneath Morlock's and her own feet, she heard another noise, a lower steadier sound, like breathing. She saw that the surface of the shell, that she had taken for marble, was expanding and contracting slightly along with the sound.

Machine? Monster? Or god? Were they passing over the Purple Patriarch himself?

At the top of the stair she got her answer. There was a hole there, like a trapdoor, and as they stood at the edge and peered down inside she saw the god of the city. It looked like a gigantic octopus or squid, but each one of its limbs was a phallus with a many-toothed vulvic mouth opening in its side. It looked upward with the single glowing eye in the center of its shapeless body, and each one of its bloody mouths opened and sang sweetly and sadly, like doves mourning.

The top of the city wall was tantalizingly near, but they would have to jump for it. She looked at Morlock without words, and he nodded back groggily. He tossed the sword as far as he could, and it vanished on the far side of the wall.

Aloê jumped, feeling the hopeful eye of the patriarch on her every second. The crowd screamed with disappointment when she found herself standing on the crumbling rim of the city wall.

"Come on!" she shouted at Morlock. She saw with dismay that the big barbarian was at the top of the stairs, looming just behind him.

Morlock jumped as Kremp grabbed at him; he passed over the empty space watched by the eye of the patriarch, and landed on the weathered stones of the city wall. The crowd again shouted its disappointment, but the god was silent.

Kremp stumbled at the verge after he failed to catch Morlock and was forced to jump without using both feet.

He barely reached the far side of the gap, reaching out with his right hand to clutch at the edge of the wall.

His wrist was swollen and visibly dark, even in the dim torchy light. That was the hand Morlock had twisted, Aloê realized. As they watched, Kremp lost his grip, and the barbarian fell into the pit with the god. His shocked scream soon changed to a strange cooing sound (did the god drug its victims?) that was drowned out by the rising chant of the crowd.

Aloê was relieved to see that there was a shell-like protrusion on this side as well. She didn't like the idea of climbing down the city wall without gear in the dark. She slid down and put her feet on the shell. Its surface was distressingly blood-warm, and moved up and down slowly, as if it were alive. But it was strong enough to hold her weight, and the surface coarse enough that she wouldn't slide down it. She moved as fast as she could, and kept her eyes open for gaps in the shell, but there were none.

She turned once to see how Morlock was faring. At first she didn't find him at all, and began to worry he'd fallen back down the wrong side of the wall. Then she saw, in the moonslight, someone crawling down the outside of the wall like a four-legged spider. She shook her head and continued down her own way.

When she was near enough to the ground she leapt off the beastlike breathing shell with great relief and ran over to Morlock, who was now on his hands and knees groping around on the ground.

"Sword around here somewhere," he muttered when she ran up.

"No, we're getting out of here," she said. "Unless you want to end up inside that thing with Kremp."

Morlock grunted. "He said we should leave you. Said it didn't matter; there were other women. Other women!" He continued in Dwarvish—so she guessed: anyway, it was a long string of hard crunching syllables that she didn't understand. But he got up and followed her away.

They went over open fields as far as they could, covering their trail as best they could, in case they were followed. But, in the end, they had to sleep—and Morlock's drugged state was something deeper than weariness: he kept on muttering in languages she didn't know.

She found a stand of trees in sandy soil. She dug a pit and filled it with dry leaves. Then she rolled the groggy muttering Morlock into it and climbed on top on him.

Hazily reviewing the day's events, she laughed a little. "I'm glad it was you with me, you crazy crooked bastard," she said.

She scraped some more leaves over herself and went to sleep.

The last thing she remembered was Morlock uttering something between a snore and a curse as the moons looked down with unblinking interest.

CHAPTER TWELVE

Many Mouths

Aloê was dreaming of her pet fish-hound Fnarklo, who used to sleep with her every night back when she was five years old. It was the best dream ever, and when she realized she was dreaming she held onto it as long as she could, and sighed when it left her.

Good old Fnarklo! They'd found him in the woods on Breakfront Isle with his neck sliced open, that sad summer of her sixth year. No one else ever figured out who had done it—but Aloê had known, of course, and of course they hadn't listened to her when she told them, because they never did listen.

She carefully pried open eyes cemented shut by a combination of skin oil, tears, dirt and leaf fragments. She tried to do it with cunning stealth so as not to wake Morlock, but it was all for nothing because the first thing she saw when she opened her eyes were his luminous gray ones looking straight at her.

"Good morning," she said, embarrassed. "I see you've recovered from, er, whatever it was."

"Praise the day," he replied laconically.

"Um. Sorry for piling on top of you last night. We didn't have any blankets, and it gets so cold at night on this deserty ground. I thought it best."

"Agreed."

"I hope it wasn't too uncomfortable for you. I'm not exactly a faint wisp of a thing, as my grandmother observes whenever I see her, which is one of four or five reasons I never do that anymore."

"Am fine."

"Well. I suppose I'll just get up now. I was hoping there was water near here when I saw the trees last night. I could use a wash."

Morlock nodded civilly, and then inclined his head to the left. Now that she listened, she could hear the running water whose sound had been drowned by her running mouth.

"All right, then!" she said, and rolled off his chest. She scrambled to her feet and wandered off toward the water.

An awkward conversation, made all the more awkward by her realization, early on, that Morlock was sporting a sizable erection. She understood this happened to men in the morning and there was probably nothing personal about it—and even if there was, who had flopped down atop whom without an invitation last night? She could not blame him for a perfectly natural response. So she told herself sternly as she buried her hysterical snickering—first in her hands, then in the water of the nearby stream.

The streambed was wide and deep enough (and the water was clean enough) for her to lie down within it, and after scrubbing herself with wet sand, that is exactly what she did, wholly under the water, breathing through her gills. She wanted her blood completely cooled, and her laughter stilled, before she had to meet Morlock's icy eye again.

As she lay there (naked, except for the talisman she never took off), letting the water cool and cleanse her, fish began to swim by. She let quite a lot of them pass. But presently there was a school of fat crested fish that looked like some sort of freshwater salmon. Choosing her moment, she plucked two of them from the water and tossed them on the bank. She managed to flip up a third beside them, using her feet.

She broke their necks and brought them back in triumph to the ersatz campsite, where Morlock had already started a fire and was amusing himself by sorting leaves into various piles.

"I got breakfast!" she said, holding up her catch.

"Hoped you would," he said, grinning back at her. "A moment while I wash."

She used one of their elderly clipped coins to split the fish, fillet them, and was arranging them for roasting on some greenish sticks when Morlock came back, soaked to the skin: he had apparently washed his clothes as well as his person.

She put the fish up over the bed of coals and remarked to Morlock (who was eyeing the remnants of fish skin, blood, and bones), "What will you make from the bones this time?"

He looked at her in surprise, then smiled. "Needles," he answered.

"Needles?"

Morlock had one of the peach-colored leaves in his hand. He pulled at it gently, and a threadlet came loose.

"Aha!" she said.

"Aha," he agreed.

He had a robe of leaves half-sewn before the fish was cooked. The robe was finished before they stood up to bury the campfire.

"It may not last long," he warned. "It depends on how brittle the leaves become as they dry."

"Anything's better than nothing," she assured him. She was tired of walking around in what was the equivalent of underwear back where she grew up.

Morlock was an ugly son-of-a-bitch, but he was pretty useful to have around—a good companion, if not much of a talker.

With a gulp, Aloê realized why she had dreamed of Fnarklo.

Oh, well. Maybe she could keep this friend from having his throat cut. At least, she was grown enough to avenge him as he deserved, if the need arose.

⫸⫷

Discussing their next move over breakfast, they agreed that their next stop should be one of the cities that had been affected by the Anhikh missionaries—Tekatestömädeien or Gröxengrefzäkrura. That day on the road, they learned from a travelling *rünkh*-salesman that Tekatestömädeien was the nearest, three day's walk away on the road they were travelling, so they headed for that.

Aloê also learned that *rünkh* was a popular beverage in Kaen that smelled as bad as the name sounded, although Morlock claimed it didn't taste as bad as it smelled.

"How could it?" she snapped, and he replied with his usual shrug. Not a talker, this one, but she already knew that.

They arrived in Tekatestömädeien much better equipped than when they had fled Khecür Tnevnepü. While Aloê felt a certain honest pride in finding them everything that they ate from day to day—Morlock hunted about as well as he made light conversation—she was in awe of her companion's ability to make wealth out of practically nothing.

As they walked, for instance, he whittled with a sharpened coin on some hollow sticks he gathered from the side of the road. When they arrived at a farmstead that evening, they paid for their lodging with a pocket full of wooden flutes. (The farmer had many children. He may have regretted the flutes before too long; God Avenger knew that Aloê did, trying to sleep in the barn as the children of the house ran around in the dark, tootling like demented geese, as Morlock snored in the haystack next to her.

The farmer had a small forge, and Aloê persuaded the farmer to let Morlock use it for part of a morning.

Morlock melted sand from a nearby sandpit into glass, then hammered a semi-molten piece of glass into a sword and quenched it in a bath of well water.

"It's pretty," Aloê said doubtfully from a distance. (She hated fire.) "But will it be any use in a fight?"

Morlock took the blade and whacked it against the forge. The iron rang like a bell and was visibly notched. "Won't take much of an edge, though," he said regretfully. "If I had more time . . ."

"Are you making one for me? I prefer a staff."

"Right," Morlock said, with a remembering look.

The staff took longer. He braided much of the molten glass with his bare fingers (a process Aloê could neither bear to watch nor look completely away from). And for a larger part of an hour he simply sat with his hands folded and looked at it. She suspected he was in a visionary trance for some of that time.

When he arose and handed it to her he said, "Be careful. It has an impulse well at either end."

"You mean impulse wheel?"

"Well. It stores physical impulses. Spin it around and hit something with it."

Bemused, Aloê went out into the farmyard. She spun the staff like a baton in her fingers, and she knew there was some kind of power in it from the feel alone. She stilled the staff and brought one end down on a stone in the ground. The glass staff shuddered, and the gray stone shattered like glass.

"Champion—!" she shouted, almost adding *Morlock* before she remembered that might be an error. Some people might have heard of Merlin's son.

The farmer, watching all this in wonder, tried to persuade Morlock to make some weapons for him. Morlock was reluctant, but in the end agreed to make shoes for the farmer's animals.

When they left the farm, the farmer was contentedly shoeing his beasts of burden with glass. Aloê and Morlock had considerable silver jingling in their pockets and weapons at their sides.

Maybe he wasn't so pretty, but her companion was indeed useful to have around.

>=<

They reached Tekatestömädeien in the early morning of the fourth day. The left side of the gate was festooned with stone mouths, in honor of the city's god: Tekätestu, the Many-mouthed Rememberer. (So the inscriptions said.) The right side of the gate showed deep scars in the stone, as if other images and inscriptions had been there, but were now removed.

Had this been a city with more than one god? Was there an internal war between the gods, with the defeated one cast out? Was there some other explanation?

They might have asked the guards there about it, but there were no guards or anyone else at the gate at all.

"This looks weird," Aloê said quietly in Wardic to Morlock.

He shrugged his crooked shoulders.

She continued, "You'd expect to find someone on duty here to collect tolls—sound the alarm in case of attack—answer questions . . ."

Morlock nodded. "Open city?"

"Odd. Odd for the Kaen I've come to know."

"The Two Powers at work, maybe."

She nodded and their eyes met. They needed to be careful. But they needed to go in. She drew her staff and used it as a walking stick; he rested his hand on the glassy hilt of his sword. They walked side by side through the wide gaping gate.

The first people they met within the unguarded walls were a youngish woman and a young boy walking hand-in-hand.

"Tell them, Rydhböku!" the woman whispered to the little boy.

The boy looked away, his fair-skinned chubby face red with embarrassment.

"This isn't my son, if that's what you're thinking," the woman said to Aloê confidingly. "I found him in the street and I'll abandon him there later. But he's such a wonderful liar! Such a devotee of the Rememberer, and still so young! Go ahead, Rydhböku! Lie to the nice people!"

"I have twelve mouths!" the boy squeaked nervously, glancing at Aloê and Morlock with dark empty eyes.

"Oh," Aloê said. "Um. Hello, Rydhböku. I'm called Gÿnzne and my cousin-by-oath here is named Znabnu."

They had taken some care in choosing their pseudonyms, and had tried them out on several travellers and farm-people they had passed on the road.

The boy, however, seemed displeased by them. "No you're not!" he said truculently, and stormed away into an alley, dragging the woman with him. Her indulgent laugh could be heard long after the odd pair had disappeared.

"Sometimes I think I'm going crazy," Aloê said out of the side of her mouth to Morlock. "Then I remember we're walking through Kaen."

"The local god is honored by lies, I guess," Morlock said. "That will make it difficult to find out any fact for certain."

"Yes," she said, pleased that she could out-laconicize him for once. Then she realized she could have just grunted concessively at him . . . when he grunted concessively back at her.

"Canyon keep you!" she snarled, and punched him on the arm.

He laughed, and they walked together deeper into the city of lies.

➤❮

They were walking down an empty street looking for the marketplace when they met a young man—almost a boy—whose shaven head was painted in tones of yellow and pink. He was leaping out of a tenement stairway and nearly ran them down.

"Your fault!" he said apologetically, as Morlock fended him off with one arm. "Entirely your fault!"

"Eh," said Morlock, with his usual conversational brilliance.

"Listen, youngster," said Aloê. "We're looking for the marketplace. Can you tell us where it is?"

"Down that way, past Twelve-Tongue Square," replied the young man heedlessly, pointing at a street leading eastward. "And then you—" He stopped short and after a moment said, "Oh, damn! Damn! Damn! Damn! I insincerely-and-only-for-rhetorical-purposes wish I were flayed alive and the skin sold to cobblers!"

"We wish that, too," Aloê said, just to be polite.

"I'm afraid I've incautiously told you the truth about something, and I am already several days behind in my Obligatory Deceptions. I don't suppose you would care to look down this way for the Market?" he said, pointing down the street they were travelling. "I can guide you there and give you other helpful advice as we go?"

"Good luck to you," Aloê said. She and Morlock exchanged glances and walked across the way toward the street the particolored youth had first indicated. They stopped as soon as they were out of sight of the youth and exchanged glances. As soon as the young man was going on his way, Aloê and Morlock stealthily followed him. He had turned up yet a third street.

The sounds and noises ahead soon declared the presence of the city's main market. As soon as the young man with the two-colored scalp-painting entered the market he ran over to a man wearing a saffron robe and high-crowned hat. It was much like the garb of the priests of the Purple Patriarch, but this priest's clothing was embroidered in red thread with the likeness of mouths—a cacophony of gaping mouths all over his garments.

"Master Förndhyl!" he shouted. "Master Förndhyl! I scored two more major deceptions on my way here! A pair of out-of-towners were asking about the market, so I feigned sincerity and pretended to cover up with the False Alternative, creating an unsolvable False Dilemma! By now they are on their way to the eastern wall, or down in the river docks! I'll swear a self-binding oath to the particulars! Do I win the prize for this market-cycle?"

Aloê and Morlock were following him closely, and both the priest and many in the crowd eyed them with some amusement.

Aloê reached out with her staff to tap on the youth's shoulder.

He spun around and gaped at them as the crowd behind him roared with laughter.

"Thanks for your help," Aloê remarked under cover of noise. "Finding the place was easy, thanks to you."

"Thrynglu," Master Förndhyl said in a reedy voice, as the laughter began to subside, "I assign you two points of merit for your intention to deceive these strangers. I assign you fifty points of demerit for your egregious failure. Better luck on the next market-cycle. But you must remember that a dupe is as intelligent as he is—not as stupid as you would like him to be. I attest to the truth of the foregoing statements by my self-binding oath to truthfully relate matters of the great god, the many-mouthed rememberer, Tekätestu. And let me add a few words of personal advice—"

Morlock was already turning away from the crestfallen youth's humiliation, and Aloê followed suit.

Near at hand, a grim-faced man was selling sausages from a cart. Aloê didn't read Kaenish as well as she spoke it, but she thought the sausages were advertised as basted with the nectar of heaven and costing fifty thousand silver coins each.

They might not be nectar-basted, but they smelled wonderful. Three locals were standing and waiting for sausages.

There was an unobtrusive sign attached to the cart. Morlock inspected it and said, "The seller self-binds his food and drink to be non-toxic and non-intoxicating and made solely of healthful meats, spices and condiments." He held the sign between his thumb and forefinger, closing his eyes for a moment. "The oath is valid," he said, opening his eyes.

"All right, then," Aloê said, trying not to hate him for his very useful visionary prowess. "If we can talk him down in price, let's get something. I'm dying to eat something I didn't kill personally."

"I hate sausages," Morlock remarked, almost conversationally, but stepped into line to oblige her. She decided she didn't hate him after all, in spite of his dangerously unsound attitude toward sausages.

The locals were paying a couple of copper coins per sausage, so that's what Aloê gave the sausage seller, too. And she spotted a slab of roasted meat that looked like it came from some sort of bird, along with some brown bread, on a wooden plate near at hand. She bargained with the sausage-seller for that. It was the man's own lunch—it turned out that he shared Morlock's aversion for sausages—but half a silver coin convinced him to surrender it to Morlock.

She stepped aside to relish her savory sausages skewered on convenient spikes of wood.

Morlock eyed the bread and bird-meat, then deftly tore the loaf in half with two fingers, inserted the meat between them, and proceeded to eat without any obvious pleasure or displeasure.

Aloê, unaware that she was present at the invention of the sandwich, was unimpressed with Morlock's attitude toward food. It was just stuff to keep him going—timber for the fire within, but nothing more. For a man with powerful esthetic impulses toward things made of wood, or stone, or metal, or glass, he seemed to have little interest in either food or sex. He had expressed no inclination for her own person, for instance—apart from that embarrassing morning when she woke up atop him, and she wasn't so vain as to take that personally.

She wondered if his ugliness forced this attitude on him: a blindness that protected him from seeking out or sensing rejection.

Of course, in spite of his ugliness, some people might be attracted to him. Ugly women, for instance. And, in spite of his awkwardly made frame, he could move with remarkable deftness. He was certainly stronger than Naevros physically, for instance, and there were bound to be women shallow enough to find that kind of animal power arousing. Not Aloê, of course, but others. She'd known the type. The Honorable Ulvana, for instance. Ick.

Morlock made eye contact with her for a moment, then raised his eyebrows slightly. She realized she'd been staring at him as she ate, and blushed fiercely. It was possible that he couldn't see it—many a pale-skinned northerner could not—and he certainly didn't comment on it. He just inclined his head and said, "Odd."

She listened, and in the middle distance, over the rumbling of the market crowd, she heard someone shouting, "Stinking fish! Stinking rotten fish for sale!"

Swallowing the last ambrosial chunk of sausage she said, "All right; let's go see. But let's stand upwind."

They wandered toward the voice through the milling crowd. They came presently on a woman dressed in a black robe with white sashes inset, sitting in front of an indisputable basket of stinking fish. Her face and hands were terribly scarred. Her voice was already weary, but determined.

"Stinking fish!" she shouted. "Stinking fish for sale!"

Few stopped to listen; none bought. Most hurried past without looking at the woman, expressions of distaste or even fear plastered across their faces.

"How much?" Aloê asked the woman, after they had stood there for a while.

"Whatever you want to pay to haul them away," the woman said frankly. "Not too many people wanted them when they were fresh, which was several days ago. I went to catch them only because the false gods of Kaen said that I should not. But I could and I did. And here they are."

"I don't want any, either," Aloê admitted.

"Well, no one does."

"I just ate," Aloê apologized.

"That may be factually accurate, but you imply that this is the reason you don't want the fish. That's a lie. But there's no need to lie. Tekätestu the liar is a false god who will be driven from his city, as Mädeio and Thyläkotröx and Gröxengrefzäkrura were before him."

Morlock twitched a little at this remark; Aloê wasn't sure why. Maybe because he realized what she had already guessed: this was a missionary of the Two Powers.

"If Tekätestu is a false god, who is the real god?"

"There is no real god," came the inexorable reply. "That is a logical absurdity. All things that are real (and only two things are real) summon into being their eternal opposites. You cannot have fire without ice, light without dark, good without evil, fate without chaos. All is duality. The god-power is dual: both fateful and chaotic, itself and other, until time ends."

"What happens then?"

"As it was in the beginning, the one true god will defeat or be defeated by his enemy, and time will stop as there will be oneness, impossible as time runs."

"And which of the gods is the one true god?"

"There is no one true god. But there was, and there will be again."

She glanced aside at Morlock . . . only to find he was no longer at her side. He had retreated into the crowd, well away from her. He leaned against a booth with a shuttered front, that looked rather like a puppet theater, and gestured to her to go on.

She shrugged and turned back to the fish-hawker, who had resumed her weary relentless cry of "Stinking fish! Stinking rotten fish!"

"Do you mind if I ask . . . ?" Aloê ventured.

"Go ahead," the fish-hawker replied.

"Where did you hear about the masked gods of Fate and Chaos? Are you yourself from Anhi? I understand they are worshipped there."

"God Torlan, power of Fate, be praised: I am not an Anhikh!" The fish-hawker raised her scarred hands above her head. "I am a Kaenish woman by my birth and death! I was a citizen of Thyläkotröx and a worshipper of that foul rat-god until . . . until the One came, from beyond the Sea of Worlds. He came, and with his soft sharp tendrils of joy and his deep strong roots of death, he defeated the god Thyläkotröx and banished him from his own city! Then we all belonged to the One, and he planted his seeds in us, and they grew and ate us from within, even as the drug of his thorns kept us happy and content. It was a joyous dark time. I have never been so happy. I have never been so afraid. I have never been so lost.

"Then *he* came. Agent of chaos or minister of fate, he came: the crooked man, the destroyer with bloody burning feet. The One attempted to defeat him, attempted to devour him, but he slew the One: with fire, with cunning, with the One's own hunger to devour all.

"The One died in fire, and when it died the roots of the One planted within us also burned, crawling out of us like fiery worms. The terror of it, the pain of it: you cannot understand, all you who were fated to be elsewhere in that terrible bright hour. Many died. Many lived. But those who lived were free at last, and the missionaries from Anhi came to us with kindly cruelty and healed us and taught us the Two-fold Truth, the consolation of the Two Powers."

Now Aloê knew, or guessed, why Morlock had sneaked his crooked self away from this woman. Apparently Morlock had enjoyed a more interesting summer than he had let on, at least during the Station.

She also knew, or guessed, that Thyläkotröx City was the place they needed to go next. If there had been missionaries from Kaen there before, maybe there still were. Anyway, she and Morlock would go and see.

Aloê thanked the fish-hawker for her news, and she promised (at the other woman's urging) to ponder the lie in the world that revealed the Two-Fold Truth, and she managed to avoid promising to come to the next meeting of Torlanists in the city, and she promised not to be taken in by the lies of the Zahkaarians, who told the truth in an unscrupulous way that was not in accord with the dictates of Fate, and finally had to pluck the other woman's stinking scarred hands from her leafy sleeve so that she could get away and rejoin her companion.

Morlock was leaning against the puppet theater, ruefully contemplating Aloê's conversation with the scarred woman (who must be from Thyläkotröx) when he heard someone whisper his name—his real name.

"Hey! Morlock!"

The whisper came from behind the puppet theater.

Morlock shrugged his crooked shoulders and stepped behind the theater. He'd have preferred to signal to Aloê, so that she would know where he was going: this looked like an attempt to separate the two vocates. But anyone in Kaen who knew his name was someone he should talk to.

It was the little boy they had first met on coming into town—Rydhböku. He was standing in the puppeteer's entrance to the theater. His features, veiled by the shadows of the shuttered theater, seemed less petulant, more mature, and more sinister than before. Behind him, deeper in the shadows, stood the woman who had been walking with him earlier. She stood with a slack lifelessness, like a marionette dangling from a nail. The young boy still gripped her hand in his.

"You see," the boy said slyly, "I knew your name wasn't Znabnu."

"I see," Morlock replied. "But you lied to us, too, Tekätestu. You told us your name was Rydhböku."

"That is the name of this avatar," the boy said coolly. "I have many bodies, as well as many mouths. I know how to tell the truth, or tell lies that seem like truth, or truths that seem like lies."

He released the hand of the woman standing behind him; she collapsed nerveless into the puppeteer's pit. The boy showed Morlock the red-lipped, needle-toothed mouth on the palm of his left hand, and then the gray-lipped toothless mouth in the palm of his right hand. "I do have many mouths, as you see," the mouths on the boy's hands said in unison, while the mouth in the boy's face laughed.

"Will you worship me, Morlock?" the mouths on the hands asked in concert. "I am a god, and I know your secret name. I could compel you."

Morlock shook his head. "I feel your attempt to do so. It resembles a simple binding spell. Such magic is only effective on people who have them-selves used binding spells."

The red mouth asked, "And you have never done so? You have never self-bound in an oath?"

"No. I say yes if I mean yes, and no if I mean no. So my father taught me."

"Merlin taught you well then."

"I didn't mean him."

The gray mouth said, "Oh? How interesting. My visualization excludes most of your life, which is of no real value to me. Almost as little as mine is to you, it seems. I must say you are very self-possessed. Have you met many gods before?"

"I don't know," Morlock said, after reflection.

"*I* didn't know," said the woman lying in the puppeteer's pit. "He isn't my son. I met him when I was out walking. I didn't know then . . . I didn't know. I didn't know."

"Be quiet," the boy's face said imperiously, and she never spoke again.

"Morlock," said the gray mouth, "you please me. You treat words as if they have meaning. Neither my truths nor my lies can have any effect without that belief. I live in accordance with my nature; thus is my tal sustained. If there are things you would know, I will tell them to you, and I self-bind myself to pass them to you without creating any obligation on your part."

As the gray mouth spoke, the red one whispered the oath. Morlock didn't hear the words, but he felt the talic impact without even summoning the lowest level of visionary awareness.

"I was wondering . . . ," Morlock admitted.

"Ask."

"Why do you tolerate the presence of Anhikh missionaries in the city? Don't you feel they are a threat to you?"

"They are not Anhikh, you know," the red mouth said. "They are as Kaenish as I am, as Kaenish as you are not. The national gods have decreed that all the Kaeniar must be free to move from one city to another, to lend their worship to the city god who pleases them best. Thus a city god may become a national god, as their worship spreads from city to city. Thus a city god may be demoted to a country god, or a household god, or may . . ."

May die? Morlock wondered. But he preferred not to wonder aloud.

"Besides," the gray mouth said, "the missionaries are no threat to me. My people don't want the truth any more than they want that stinking fish. The truth has to be decorated with many lies before people will accept it. That is why I am a great god. I slew Mädeio with my words like stone daggers, and when the time comes I will destroy the missionaries, too."

"Besides," said the boy's face brightly, "I couldn't really keep them out, anyway. The tirgan of my city left with all his warrior-priests for greener pastures some time ago, and the Court of Heresiarchs have yet to assign me a new one."

Morlock nodded as if he understood this.

"The fyor-tirgan of the southwestern coast died recently," the gray mouth remarked. "Shollumech was his name."

The red mouth added, "I don't know if he introduced himself to you before you killed him, Morlock."

"He did," Morlock said stiffly.

"Well," the boy's face continued, "my late tirgan thought he could improve his station by seizing Shollumech's lands and abasing himself before Shollumech's gods. I think he has already learned what a terrible mistake he made, but that won't save him from my vengeance when my hour strikes, as it soon will."

Morlock nodded thoughtfully.

"You're quite wrong in what you're thinking," the gray mouth said sharply. "The region is more dangerous to you, not less, because the fyor-tirgan is weak. Where the ruler is weak, the gods are strong. And Shollumech's gods were strangely fond of him. They are watching for you, Morlock. You must avoid the coast if you plan to go north with your mate."

"I have no mate," Morlock said automatically.

"What?" said the boy's face, startled. "Are you sure?"

"My visualization can't be so far afield," the gray mouth muttered.

"Who is the woman approaching the booth?" the red mouth demanded. "She has golden hair and skin darker than yours."

"My partner, not my mate."

"Oh, my god," the god's three mouths groaned in unison. The boy's eyes looked with disdain at Morlock. Tekätestu seemed to think Morlock was quibbling.

Morlock felt Aloê's presence, and he turned to meet her quizzical golden eyes. "Why are you standing here, and who were you talking to?"

Morlock turned back to the theater, but its back door was now closed, and the door itself was sealed with brittle dusty wax, as if it had not been opened in some time.

"A god, I think," he said, turning back to Aloê.

"Well, well. Saint Morlock, apostle to the Kaeniar."

He snarled at her, and she grinned back. "Well," she continued, "we need to get you out of here before those missionaries from Thyläkotröx City recognize you. I'll need that whole story, by the way. We should head there next; there are Anhikh emissaries in the city, and maybe we can get useful news of the Two Powers from them."

Morlock said, "Eh," thoughtfully.

"A little more detail please, partner."

Had she heard him call her that? He wondered what she thought of it. "We can't go along the coast," he said. "That was what Tekätestu's avatar told me, anyway. The gods there hate me."

"Well, in their defense, you can be a little irritating sometimes."

≲≳

Tekätestu did not need to watch the vocates go with eyes of flesh: he saw them in the most certain range of his visualization-of-the-all. The farther the visualization got from the center of his own city, the less certain it was, and even some of the city was dark to him: for instance, the parts that had been devoted to Mädeio, and those that were now were densely populated with worshippers of the Two Powers.

He had lied to Morlock, or course: that was part of his nature, and he drew strength from it. He blamed Morlock in part for his current troubles, and would be glad to see him suffer for that. But he had lied to him with the truth: Shollumech's gods were indeed on the watch for young Ambrosius. So were the missionaries of the Two Powers. (May they all destroy each other, Tekätestu wished-not-merely-for-rhetoric.) If he could frustrate his enemies and harm Morlock by helping him, deceiving him with truths, he would fulfill his nature and gain in talic strength. Tekätestu pondered the unseen stars in the sky, the season of the world in which he only partly lived, and his memories as a new-shaven priest in the mountains a long age of the world ago. If he had owned a face that was truly his own, he would have smiled. Instead, his avatar nestled its hand with the gray-lipped mouth into the hand of the woman who lay next to it in the darkness of the puppet theater. The woman moaned slightly, pleasingly, and the god fed on her devotion.

CHAPTER THIRTEEN

The Sheep and the Goat

"What we need," Aloê said, "is a map. Or a guide."

"In a city where lies are prayers?" Morlock asked. "No."

"I see what you mean," Aloê conceded. "What do you suggest?"

"Go west into the mountains. Take the first path leading north or northeast."

"Mountains," Aloê said uncertainly. She'd spent some time among them in recent years, but never really got to like them. Morlock, on the other hand, had grown up in them, and under them. "You're sure?"

"We'll get there."

"All right. You get to steer for this part of the journey, then. I hope you're right."

In the event, he wasn't.

Klÿgnaru the Unshaven was the archpriest to Khÿmäroreibätu, the Goat-that-bestrides-the-Mountain, and tedious work he found it.

"I spend my days and nights wearing this goatskin cap," he complained to his friend Gnörymu, as they sat drinking together in the roadhouse of the neutral village of Hoimëdmetheterön. "I have been an archpriest of this horrible little mountain for twenty years. Everyone is so faithful to the Goat that I can't get a single heresy going, even to develop some decent persecution, much less threaten the town god and earn a chance to join the Court of Heresiarchs. I'll die on the mountain, and my successor will feed my flesh to the Goat's avatars, even as I did with my predecessor."

His friend Gnörymu the Glabrous sympathized with him, none more so. Gnörymu was the archpriest of Öweioreibäto, the Sheep-that-bestrides-the-Mountain, and he had much the same set of problems. He was a little better off: he was physically unable to grow body hair, so he could go without shaving and not draw comment to himself (unlike bristly old Klÿgnaru). Also, he had already resigned himself to the thought that he would never join the Court of Heresiarchs. Still, at one time he had shared Klÿgnaru's wild dreams, and he knew how hard a dream dies.

He tilted a beaker of fermented sheep-milk and filled up Klÿgnaru's mug with the stinking intoxicating mess. "Content yourself, old friend!" he said. "Between us, we rule the Mountain. If anyone doesn't like it, they can lick our elbows and die rabid. Maybe it's not much, but there's no one I'd rather share it with."

But Klÿgnaru went on grumbling. "You think we can at least skip the war this year? I lost a lot of herdsman over the summer. The war will take more of them. A war is really stupid when we have other things to do, anyway."

Gnörymu smiled and did not look at his friend. In fact, Klÿgnaru had stumbled across a persuasive heresy that might find many adherents among people on both sides of the Mountain: a peace movement. But Gnörymu was confident that, if he waited, Klÿgnaru would talk himself out of the idea.

And he was right: he knew his friend. After a few tense moments Klÿgnaru sighed and said, "I suppose you're right. I just needed to complain a bit, old friend, to someone who could understand."

"I do understand," Gnörymu assured him sincerely.

"Well, where shall we send them to fight? The Crispy Field? No, we used that last year."

"Two years since, and two years before that. What about the Ringlake Shore?"

"No. Definitely not. That's my best winter grazing."

This was why Gnörymu had proposed it. He nodded thoughtfully and waited.

"I'll tell you what," Klÿgnaru suggested at last. "What about the Long Curve? They can kill each other there to their heart's content and it won't bother my goats or your sheep. Except when their herdfolk don't return, of course."

"All right," Gnörymu said, with feigned reluctance. The Long Curve was a mountain pass, partly artificial, which took a long path around the

Mountain, from its southeast corner to its northeast corner. If he could not convince Klÿgnaru to fight on the Ringlake Shore, his preferred option was the Long Curve. And here poor Klÿgnaru was suggesting it.

"Same day as usual all right with you?" Klÿgnaru asked.

"It's coming up fast," Gnörymu complained. In fact, his preparations had been almost complete for months.

"Tradition, old friend! What's the point of this silly war if we don't keep to tradition?"

Gnörymu had his own ideas about what the war was for, but he gracefully conceded the date, since it was what he preferred anyway.

"Now: who should think up the pretext for the war?" Klÿgnaru asked. "I think I did it last year."

"Do it again, if you don't mind," Gnörymu suggested. "You think up such good ones."

"Thanks," Klÿgnaru said, foolishly pleased. "Rather enjoy it."

In fact, whenever they used Klÿgnaru's rationalizations for the annual war between the Sheep and the Goat, his own people became discontented and Gnörymu's people became enraged. Most people know that Klÿgnaru was not sincerely devoted to the annual war, and he never fought in the line himself. So his own fighters were demoralized and Gnörymu's gained a touch of extra fervor. It was when Gnörymu had noticed this, a few years ago, that he began to reluctantly lay his plans for his friend's downfall.

Klÿgnaru was a bad priest to his god—neither loyally orthodox nor boldly heretical. The power of his town and god were waning. Most of the goatherds whom Klÿgnaru had lost the last few summers had died from the poisonous bites of a breed of deadly snake-sheep that Öweioreibäto had sent in response to Gnörymu's prayers. He had hopes that the war this year would decimate the herdsmen of the Goat and result in something like a final victory for Öweioreibäto.

And, of course, a victory for her archpriest. Gnörymu had not been lying when he'd said there was no one he would rather share the rule of the Mountain with than his old friend Klÿgnaru.

But if he could rule it by himself, that was obviously best of all.

So they laid their plans, together and separately, and the annual war began on the traditional date, the first of Bayring.

As Tekätestu had foreseen, this was the day after Aloê and Morlock entered the Long Curve on their ill-fated attempt to reach Thyläkotröx City.

Aloê and Morlock passed many-mouthed idols of Tekätestu all along the road for some considerable way outside of his city. Some were weathered, if well-maintained; some were brand-new, their edges sharp from the stonecutter. Often these newer images stood atop the ruins of older totems.

"The remains of Mädeio?" Aloê remarked to Morlock. He shrugged and nodded. That added up to *I guess so* from a normal person, or so Aloê guessed.

In the red dry hills above Tekästomädeien they finally stopped seeing idols of Tekästu. Others began to appear—at first sporadically, then more and more frequently. There were two that were most common: one showed a goat standing proudly atop a mountain peak; the other was a sheep doing the same.

"Khÿmäroreibätu," Morlock read, for Aloê's benefit. (She was still struggling a bit with written Kaenish, and there was a different set of characters used for inscriptions anyway.) "The other one is Öweioreibäto."

"The Goat That Forever Stands Upon the Mountain," she translated into Wardic. "And: The Ewe That Forever Stands Upon the Mountain."

"Ewe?" Morlock said doubtfully. "I thought it was 'sheep.'"

"An ewe is a female sheep, and that's a feminine ending."

"Oh."

"You wouldn't be much of a farmer, Morlock."

"Thank you."

Aloê wasn't sure at first whether this was ironic or not. But, glancing at the man, she decided he had really taken her mild slam as a compliment. Maybe it was a northern thing. She continued, "I wonder if the gods are friends to each other or enemies? Wherever the sheep-people put up an idol the goat-folk followed suit."

Morlock shrugged and said, "Friends?" in Kaenish. He seemed to be implying the word had another meaning hereabouts—as well it might.

She didn't feel like discussing it. They were a long way from the sea, and the air was getting dry and thin. She could deal with it, but she didn't like it.

The road they were walking was fairly well-maintained, but didn't seem much-used. Occasionally they met people hurrying the other way, most of whom passed without speaking. The only exception was a panicky neatherd who was driving four solemn cows downhill toward the city just as fast as they would go.

Which was none too fast, in fact. The neatherd was nervous and sweating, but his cattle were cool as icicles, treading the road at their self-chosen pace and calmly ignoring the man's heckling, shouts, and blows.

"It's that time of year," he said apologetically to Aloê and Morlock as he passed, to their complete mystification.

"Time to get them to market?" Aloê wondered after the man had gone by. "Time to get them to a butcher?"

Morlock shrugged. Not the man to go to with your farming questions, Aloê remembered.

"Or does something bad happen in the mountains this time of year?" she continued. "Maybe we should have asked him. Snowstorms?"

"No," Morlock said. "South winds keep Kaen warm all winter long."

"That's the first good thing I've heard you say about the place."

Morlock looked at her, mystified. For him, a warm winter was nothing to brag about, clearly.

"Rains, though," he continued. "Maybe floods. They can be dangerous in narrow places."

But water couldn't scare Aloê. "If that's the worst, we'll be fine, then."

The sandy road led steadily uphill to a cleft in the red rock of the dry mountains before them. It looked very narrow at first, but as they spent most of a day struggling toward it she realized how high the stone face of the cliff was. When they finally reached the entrance to the canyon they saw it was wide enough for a dozen men to walk down, side by side.

"If they don't mind holding hands, that is," she joked to Morlock, who nodded absently as he watched something off on the side of the road.

She followed his gaze and saw an idol of Öweioreibäto, that was the sheepy one, being beaten by a small boy in goatskins wielding a very large hammer. The idol finally fell to pieces, a large chunk of it landing on one of the boy's feet. He screamed and dropped the hammer. He hopped away into the peach-colored scrub along the road, holding his injured foot in both hands and hopping on the other, sobbing out curses against Öweioreibäto and prayers to Khÿmäroreibätu.

"So: they're not friends after all," Aloê remarked. Morlock nodded thoughtfully.

"I hope we're not walking into a religious war," Aloê said, and at that even Morlock smiled.

It grew dark very soon after they entered the cleft and began walking up the canyon beyond. But they carried on as long as the sliver of sky above showed blue. The surface of the canyon was a little rougher than the road, but it was smoother than Aloê had expected. Morlock said he thought it had been worked some—that, in effect, they were still on a road, headed from somewhere to somewhere. That made Aloê feel a little better.

She almost felt—whatever the opposite of seasick was. She was land-sick. She was tired of brownish red dirt under her aching feet, and irregular clumps of red rock banging against her toes didn't help. She felt like she was strangling as the steep walls of the canyon were pressed against her, and the thin air didn't help. She wanted something, anything, to distract her from her hellish surroundings, and Morlock's one-word replies to her conversational gambits didn't help.

But she kept her whining to the indispensable minimum and tried to crack the occasional joke, and didn't even shout in relief when Morlock decreed it was time to stop for the night.

Morlock dug their sleeping pit, made the fire, and pulled the provisions out of his knapsack while she sat and rubbed her feet. They ate dried sausage and passed a water bottle back and forth with a minimum of conversation.

"Wish it would rain," was one of Morlock's more surprising comments.

"What about floods?" Aloê asked, surprised.

Morlock shrugged. "Air's too dry."

She felt she could love this man.

"What did you find to make a fire with?" she said. "Do those scrub trees grow in the canyon?"

"Bones," he said.

"Bones?"

"Bones. I found a lot of them when I dug our sleeping pit. I think this was a battlefield, years ago."

In the course of digging their sleep pit, Morlock had come across enough dried bones to realize this was a battlefield. He'd finished digging the pit, and went on to use the bones as fuel for the campfire. And now he expected her to sleep in what was essentially an open grave. An open *used* grave.

She changed her mind about being able to love this man.

But she had to admit that the hole was quite comfortably free of bones, maggots and rats, lined with sand and leaves—better than some of the places they'd slept. They lay down together, and as usual he turned away from her without a word. Sometimes she slept back-to-back with him, but she had found she was actually warmer if she spooned up against his back and wrapped her blankets around them both. He didn't seem to mind—rarely moved the whole night through, though she had to admit several mornings it appeared he had not slept.

She wondered, idly, as they were nestled for sleep, what Naevros was doing and whether it would be better, or at least sexier, if he were here. No doubt he was hate-sexing the Honorable Ulvana or her moral equivalent at that very moment. Never mind: she loathed thinking about him this way— loathed herself when she thought like this.

"Morlock," she said sleepily, to distract herself. "Anyone waiting for you back home?"

"My *harven*-kin," he said. "Some friends."

"No girl?"

"No." The answer was harsh, unequivocal, interesting.

"A boy, then?" she hazarded.

"No. It's not like that. It's just . . ."

She thought of the terms she'd used, and smiled. "You prefer adults."

"Yes."

"Sound fellow," she said, still smiling, and went contentedly to sleep with her face pressed against his twisted spine.

Morning was a grayish reddish void, empty of sunlight. Aloê woke to find herself alone in the sleep pit. She crawled out of her sandy grave and found Morlock chewing dried meat with a marked lack of enthusiasm.

He saluted her with the water bottle and passed it to her as she sat beside him.

"Feel like an oily rag," she remarked after a drink. "I don't suppose we can spare any of this for washing."

Morlock shook his head regretfully. But he added, "Water cut this canyon, before people made it into a road. There's water here somewhere."

"Where?"

"Wells. Or streams dammed up to make lakes. We'll find it."

"Mmm." In her mind she was drifting under the surface of the mountain lake Morlock had created in her mind, shedding the filth from her skin like scales, renewing her life from the life-giving water.

She sighed, opened her eyes, and accepted the fibrous slab of dried meat that Morlock was offering her.

><

It was noon, by the gleam of gold in the blue sliver of sky over their heads, when they encountered the soldiers of the Goat.

They wore goatskin helmets and goatleather cuirasses shaped to fit their scrawny chests. Slats of pale varnished wood dangled from their belts, making a kind of protective skirt for their groins. They were armed with stone-tipped wooden spears, and rocks, and some had round wooden shields. There were about twenty of them.

"The enemy at last!" they screamed when they saw Morlock and Aloê. "Easy grazing for the Goat of War!"

"We are not your enemies," Aloê called. "We are not opposed to, um Khÿmäroreibätu."

There was some confusion at this, and then one goat-soldier cried, "All must die, so that their blood can slake the thirst of the Almighty Goat!"

"Yes!" cried another. "The Goat is great! Praise the Goat and kill the enemy!"

The others joined in with their own very similar opinions, and they smashed their weapons together and moved aggressively but not very rapidly forward.

There was obviously no reasoning with them, and they were pretty numerous. On the other hand, they were pretty undisciplined, and those spears were obviously not throwing weapons. Aloê met Morlock's cold gray eye, and he seemed to be thinking the same thing she was.

They turned together and ran away back up the canyon. Morlock drew his glassy sword as he ran, and Aloê spun her glass staff like a baton, gathering impulse energy as she ran alongside.

The goat soldiers shouted in triumph and began to pursue them, each as fast as he could.

The thing is, most people don't run at the same speed. As they all ran down the canyon, the goaty troop began to thin out—some running slower, some stumbling over rocks (or bones! Aloê thought), some running a little less enthusiastically.

"Now, I think," Aloê said quietly to Morlock, after a quick glance over her shoulder.

They turned back together to face their foes. The three or four in front were joyous at the prospect of battle, not realizing or caring that their line was much less numerous than it had been.

Aloê spun her crystal staff one last time, then gripped it firmly below the center and struck at the nearest spearman. The staff passed through the spear, shattering it to splinters, and proceeded to do the same thing to the spearman's arm. He fell screaming to his knees, screaming out curses in the name of his goaty god. She jumped over him and began laying into the next goat-soldier in the long straggling line.

Morlock's sword was a flash of glassy light at her side. She was worried at first he was a sword-waver—the kind of person it was dangerous to stand next to in a fight. But he used the edge of his bright blade only to block attacks; at every chance he thrust the point home with deadly efficiency. The sharp end of the sword was already red with enemy blood.

The front of the straggling line broke, and the terrified goat-soldiers ran back, stumbling into their fellows who were running up from behind. The panic and confusion spread, and soon dozens of soldiers were fleeing from the two glass-weaponed Guardians.

Eventually the mass of soldiers to the rear forced the frightened vanguard to slow down and regroup. They rallied each other, shouted a few slogans about cloven hooves of courage, and lumbered forward to attack again.

"Same same?" Aloê suggested to Morlock.

"Won't work again," Morlock said.

But it did, and twice more after that. They ran until their attackers spread out behind them, turned to counterattack, and drove the broken vanguard fleeing back up the canyon.

The last time, though, they heard a loud chorus of triumphant shouting farther up the pass: hundreds, thousands of voices re-echoing down the stones.

The two vocates looked at each other without speaking and took the better course of valor, running off in the other direction.

But they had not gone far before they heard sounds coming toward them up the canyon—not the sounds of an army, exactly, but many strange footfalls and a kind of muttering.

"Cavalry with muffled hooves?" Aloê whispered to Morlock.

He shrugged. "Camels, maybe."

"What's a camel?"

Morlock looked at her to make sure she was serious, and then briefly described a camel.

"You're making that up!" she accused him.

He didn't have time to respond, if he was going to, before they rounded the bend and saw what was making the noise.

Filling the canyon before them, down to the next turn, was a herd of sheep. They had to be sheep. They were about waist-high to Aloê or Morlock, had long floppy ears, and round bodies covered with closely crimped wool. But the wool gleamed like polished steel; the eyes of the beasts were red as blood; instead of bleating they seemed to be gasping or groaning; and each sheep had a pair of long curling horns, pointed at the ends, from which dark venomous fluid was dripping. The sheep had long pointed teeth as if they were meat-eaters.

As soon as the sheep saw Morlock and Aloê the flock rushed forward, gnashing teeth and thrusting with their horns.

"Don't get stuck by one of those horns," Aloê said, just to make conversation while they waited for the onslaught.

Morlock nodded seriously, and added, "Strike for the face. That wool looks to be armor."

They stood, in fighting stance, and waited. Aloê spun her staff a few times to build up impulse force. She wondered if she should say something mushy like *It's been nice knowing you* or *There's no one I'd rather die fighting beside.* But she decided that, even if the words were true, they might ring false . . . and they would probably be wasted on Morlock anyway.

Morlock stood like a stone until the beasts came within striking range. Then he stabbed and stabbed, the glass sword like lightning in his hand. Four bodies fell in a row, forming a low wall, and the beasts beyond milled about in confusion.

"A barrier! A barrier!" shouted Aloê joyously, and lashed out to smash two sheep-skulls, one with either end of her staff. "You beautiful son-of-a-brach's-bastard!"

He gave her a gray astonished glance even as he continued to strike sheep dead. She did the same, and soon they were surrounded by a wall of dead sheep at least two sheep in height.

But by now the army of venomous, steely, red-eyed sheep had filled the whole canyon, as far as they could see from bend to bend. It's true the army seemed mostly intent on marching past them now that they were hidden behind the army's dead flock-mates. But the pressure of the marching sheep was pushing the wall back toward them. Soon Aloê and Morlock might be killed by dead sheep, impaled by the horns of the beasts they'd slain.

"Do we wait it out?" she asked Morlock, hoping that he would not shrug or grunt or something. "I suppose they will pass by eventually."

"No," said Morlock. "Can you keep the wall? I'll get us out of here."

"Yes," Aloê said gratefully, and turned to keep wandering sheep from walking over the heap of dead ones.

Morlock said, "Noddegamra," and his glass sword fell into separate shining spikes. He gathered them up from the ground and slipped them into the many pockets he had sewn into his jacket and shirt and did something with one of them against the wall of rock behind them. Then he stepped two feet in the air, drove another crystal spike into the cliff, and put his foot on it. He drove a third spike into the wall and stepped up to it. Then he turned back to Aloê and motioned for her to follow.

He expects me to climb that cliff, Aloê realized. She almost refused, almost shouted for him to come back off the rocks and fight the sheep like a man. Then she thought about how crazy that would sound. The venomous sheep were there, and so was the army of goat-soldiers; she had to get away. And: she remembered Morlock rowing his seasick sodden self away to fight the dragon on the sea. *I'll need a boat. Or is it a ship?*

She groaned and sheathed her staff across her shoulders. One long step took her up to the first spike. His foot had left the second by then, and he was driving spikes up higher on the cliff and lifting himself up to them like a misshapen monkey.

"Have to go up straighter to reach the first shelf," he called back.

Shelf? What shelf? To Aloê's eye the cliff was a sheer mass rising up to the path of the sun.

"Shelf, schmelf, bite an elf," she muttered through clenched teeth as she followed somewhat slower. She hated heights. Hated them. Even when there weren't venomous sheep and clownish goat-warriors capering around at the height's base.

"What?" he called back.

"'S a boat. *Not* a ship."

He stopped what he was doing and looked down at her. She waved hurriedly at him to keep on going, clenched her teeth together, and kept going herself.

Presently she came to the thin irregularity in the cliff face that Morlock described so generously as a shelf. Morlock matter-of-factly pulled her up. She wedged her feet on the stone, with her back to the cliff, and tried to look down without obvious terror.

"Are you all right?" he asked.

It struck her as a very un-Morlocky sort of question. "Perfectly well," she said with quiet dignity. "Why wouldn't I be?"

If he shrugged she didn't see it, God Creator be praised. He bent over the venom-stinking sheep-filled abyss and shouted, "Armageddon!"

Aloê's vision was a little wavery, but she was pretty sure she saw the glassy shards of Morlock's sword flying up toward them from the cliff face. She resisted the impulse to duck; it would have sent her tumbling off the narrow ledge.

In the event, there was no danger. The shards reassembled themselves into a sword, whose grip landed in Morlock's outstretched hands.

"Nice trick," she said in a level voice she was rather proud of.

"Eh," he said, embarrassed and pleased. "Simple, really. Talic impulse woven into the shards holds them together, and makes them responsive to summoning. Got the idea from . . . from . . . from something I'm working on at home. I'll. I'll. I'll show it to you sometime."

"Love to see it," she said, lying politely through her clenched teeth.

"I have to refresh the talic charge," he said. He sat back and ascended into rapture: she saw the faint glow through his closed eyelids.

As she waited she looked down into the chasm below. The tide of sheep up the canyon had stopped for some reason. The sun, straight overhead now, painted a stripe of noon-light down the middle of the pass, making the steely wool of the deadly flock shine like gold. As she waited, the edge of light moved to the opposite side of the pass, climbed the red-black stones of the canyon wall, was gone.

Morlock awoke. Aloê smiled when he met her eye, and she repressed any light-hearted comments she may have thought of regarding noonday naps. She was very much afraid that, if she opened her mouth, vertigo would force her to vomit.

Morlock held a corner of his jacket under the pommel of the glass sword and said, conversationally, "Noddegamra." The glass sword fell to shards again, which Morlock deftly caught in his jacket and afterward stowed efficiently in his myriad pockets. He met her eye again.

"Onward and upward," she said gamely, managing not to puke, and he rose up with serpentine grace, using only his legs. She herself took three times as long to do the same thing, keeping one hand at all times on the stone wall behind her.

Morlock did not watch these ungraceful proceedings, but was occupied in driving spikes into the stone face of the cliff and climbing up them. He seemed to be doing nothing other than pushing them in with his fingers, as if the cliff wall were made of, say, a moist cheese. But when she came to them she found them as firmly placed as if they had been set in cement a week before. No doubt there were technical details involved that Morlock would be willing to share at great, if slightly incoherent detail, should she be able to call out a question.

But she didn't actually give a damn how they worked at the moment, as long as they did, and her stomach was bouncing around inside her midriff anyway and she was finding it hard to breathe. She'd risk speech only if it seemed necessary.

The cliff face began to throb as she climbed from spike to spike. At first she thought it was just a new sign of her own vertigo, but the shaking became worse, was obviously part of the world outside herself. She heard a great stomping sound, in rhythm with the shaking stones, and a roaring sound that was something between a trumpet call and a forest fire. And along with all of that: the triumphant chanting of the goat-soldiers. Khÿmäroreibätu's counterattack against the venom-sheep was coming.

When it hove into sight, Aloê began to wonder if she was dreaming all this, or lying mad in a dark room somewhere. The details were feverishly bright, dense, and impossible to believe.

She saw a goat as large as a house, with steel plates protecting its long agile legs. It had a long flexible nose like a tube. A man was riding on its neck, and he held a goad or something in his hand. And when he stabbed the goad into the back of the giant goat's head, the goat screamed in rage and fear, and fire sprayed out of its long nose.

The sheep were screaming, their steely wool red-hot with the monster-goat's flames. The goat danced forward among them, crushing some sheep under its metal-clad legs. Behind the goat came companies of plate-armored pikemen, stabbing the burning sheep as if they were venomous sausages to be served on sticks.

"What in the nightmares of God Avenger is *that?*" Aloê demanded.

"Looks like a cross between a goat and an elephant," Morlock remarked.

Aloê looked suspiciously at him, several spikes above her on the cliff face. "What's an elephant?" She remembered someone else using the word to her once.

Morlock explained what an elephant was.

"Stop making things up!" she screamed at him.

He rolled his eyes, shook his head, and continued to plant crystal spikes in the wall.

They were already well above the goat-elephant, perhaps even out of the range of its fiery blasts. But the real danger proved to be the heavy impact of the creature's iron-sheathed hooves. They shook the ground; they shook the stones of the cliff wall. More than once Aloê had to catch herself from falling off the glassy spike she was standing on—and one time she did not manage to catch herself. She fell a body length back down the cliff before she managed to grab on to one of the lower spikes.

Morlock, as soon as he saw, dove back down the cliff, swinging past the spikes without seeming to touch them until he reached Aloê.

"Are you all right?" he asked again.

"It's that elephant-goat thing," she said apologetically. "Threw me right off the cliff."

They waited while it moved onward past them. Aloê was tired, so tired. But she didn't want to risk another fall down the cliff due to a goat-quake. Morlock seemed to understand that without needing anything to be said.

She watched with weary interest as the goat-elephant's rider drove the beast on, pitilessly plying his goad. His screams had Kaenish words in them, she realized belatedly.

"I am coming for you Gnörymu!" he screamed. "The Goat will have his vengeance!"

The Goat mentioned must have been the god, Khÿmäroreibätu, Aloê realized. The elephant-goat was female, with very full teats, as a matter of fact, that leaked the same sort of heavy burning fluid the beast sprayed from her nose.

The elephant-goat swung around the next twist in the mountain pass. The goat-quakes receded, fell still. Now, among the smoking corpses of the venomous sheep, there were wool-clad soldiers fighting against the goatskin-clad pikemen. Aloê had no idea where the sheep-soldiers had come from and what that implied about the war between Khÿmäroreibätu and Öweioreibäto. Nor did she care. She figured it was safe to climb again, so she started back up the cliff. Morlock kept one spike ahead of her all the way, climbing up without taking his eyes off her. She had the impression he was going to reach out and catch her (or try to) if she fell again. This struck her as somewhat patronizing, but also comforting, so she said nothing about it.

At one point she simply had to stop climbing and rest. She hung onto a spike and leaned against the cliff with her eyes closed, breathing heavily but getting little life from the thin, smoky, venom-laden air.

Morlock's voice broke in on her awareness. "You're surrounded by water."

"What?" she said irritably, opening her eyes.

"You're surrounded by water," he suggested again. "You can't fall, really; the water is holding you up."

She was about to respond very severely indeed. He was obviously trying to reassure her because he thought she was paralyzed by the fear of falling. She was, of course, afraid of falling. Who wouldn't be? But she wasn't paralyzed by that fear or any other. She was afraid, weary, sick, and disgusted, but she could damn well do what was necessary.

She looked up to shout this in his face, but was stopped by his expression: open, concerned, patient, watchful—as if her state of mind was the most important thing in the world.

"I'm all right," she said at last. "Thanks."

He nodded and they climbed slowly, at her pace, up the cliff to the next ledge. Once Morlock was on it he reached down, lifted Aloê up, and set her down beside him. Then he summoned Armageddon to him by shouting down the cliff face again.

This ledge was wider than the last one, and deeper, too. Part of it receded into shadow, but she could hear the chuckling of water in those shadows, and the hard red rock was carpeted with green moss.

"I am not moving from here for a while," she announced after she had surveyed the area and caught her breath.

Morlock nodded solemnly and remarked, "A rough climb."

This might be more patronage, but she didn't think so. Even he couldn't have been used to climbing cliffs while venom-sheep and elephant-goats and goat-warriors and sheep-soldiers fought a chaotic battle below.

Thinking of the gigantic goat, she said, "You made up that elephant thing, didn't you? Admit it."

"No," he said seriously. "They really exist, in the jungles somewhere east of Anhi. I read about them when I was staying at New Moorhope."

"And they breathe fire?"

"Well. No. At least the books didn't mention it."

"I *knew* you were making them up."

He threw up his hands in exasperation. She laced her arms in between his and embraced him. She kissed his ugly bloodstained face and whispered, "We made it! We made it! You crazy bastard!"

She felt the violence of his reaction, and mistook it at first for repugnance. Then she noticed his hard-to-miss erection.

"I can't help it," he said miserably, noticing that she had noticed, and tried to pull away.

"Maybe I can," she said, feeling a little drunk, and kissed him on the mouth. He was in love with her, of course. It all made sense to her now, since that ridiculous *you're surrounded by water* comment. He had avoided her because he thought it was hopeless. Maybe it was hopeless, for reasons he didn't know, and maybe she was crazy for trying this. But it was a crazy world full of elephant-goats and death. Being crazy made her fit right in.

"I don't expect anything," he continued. "We're too different."

She bit his ear and whispered into it, "Fuck you. We're the same in every way that matters, different in every way that's good. And you love me. Tell me you don't and I'll call you a liar."

He was telling her that he did love her, but not with words. His mouth was all over her face, his clever fingers entangled in the fastenings of her clothing.

The world contracted to a warm nest that contained only the two of them. She laughed a little unsteadily and undid his buttons as he was undressing her, tearing a few of them loose when they wouldn't come free willingly.

The ugliness of his body (pale as a deep-ocean fish, hairy as a spider, that odd twist in his shoulders) did not distress her. It was so powerful, so strong, yet so skilled, patient, controlled. He didn't tear any of her fastenings. His long clever fingers and his luminous gray eyes (the only things about him that could really be called beautiful) . . . they cherished her, moved over her, celebrated her, hungered for her.

It was deranged. It was not how she had imagined it would be at all. That was why it was right; that was why it would work this time. It would work this time; it would work this time. She wanted him and she was ready to have him.

The world tumbled around and around, and she found herself spreadeagled on the moss with him poised above her. She wrapped her limbs around him, drawing him closer.

He mounted her. The wet lips of her vagina kissed the taut silken head of his penis. He penetrated her, or she engulfed him.

Triumph. Triumph. This was what it was like. This was how it should be. Nothing would go wrong this time.

God Creator, she was so wet. It was almost as if she were urinating. It felt exactly the same.

Oh, God. Oh, God. What if she were? If she were . . . The shame of it. The stink of it. The shame summoned back all the other shames, all the other stinks, the stench of his semen, no she did not have to think of that, she was not going to think of that, her mind was her own; she could think what she wanted.

She could think what she wanted. But she couldn't *feel* what she wanted. She felt the tightness in her vulva, the stretching feeling, the pain, the fear, the shame. The pain. The pain. The pain. She'd been stabbed. She'd been struck with staves. She'd been burned and clawed by a dragon. But it was nothing like this. Nothing should feel like this. She hated it. She hated herself. She hated the fear she couldn't control. It was a ring of red-hot metal in her cunt, contracting, growing brighter, tighter, more painful, sending out thornlike protrusions of fiery pain. It would not work this time. It was just like all the other times. It would never work for her.

"Stop!" she screamed in agony and despair. "Stop! Stop! Get out—get out—I'm sorry—God, I'm sorry. *Please get out.*"

He was out, his face a mask of shock and fear. She had seen that mask before, other faces wearing that mask. Not for a long while, though. She had hoped she would never see it again.

The contractions of her vagina subsided; the pain cooled, receded, disappeared, leaving only the greasy residue of shame and frustrated desire.

"Did I . . .? Did I . . .?" Morlock stuttered.

She knew that mask, too: the mask of shame and fear. She'd seen it and worn it. She could spare him that, at least.

"Not your fault," she said wearily. "It happens whenever . . . whenever I try to . . . to do that."

"Always?" he asked, with a curiosity she thought in extremely poor taste.

"Every time. Sorry. I should have let you know."

Now he wore the mask of pity. She'd seen that one, too, and hated it as much as all the others.

Now would come the long pointless conversation: *Have you tried this?* and *Have you tried that?* and all of the helpful suggestions that added up to: *What the hell is wrong with you anyway? Why did I get stuck with this piece of damaged goods? Where can I return it for my money back?*

Morlock, though, said nothing. She was shivering, and he picked her lightly up with one arm and drew her gown of leaves over them both with his free hand.

She lay atop him sullenly, silently, her back on his chest so that she would not have to look at him pitying her, being angry with her, despising her, shaming her. She could do all those things without his damn help.

His hands kept moving over her under the gown, and she almost snapped at him to stop. Didn't he understand that it was over, that it had failed, that she was broken and could never be fixed? Or was he one of *those* types: the smug sexual healers. *Oh, yes, my dear, I can cure your sad weeping vagina with my magic penis.*

But now he was scratching the hair at the nape of her neck, and she had to admit that it felt good. She did admit it by making a little *all right, do that some more* sound which to a less perceptive person might have sounded like a moan.

But he was still cherishing her, worshipping her with his powerful beautiful skilled hands. She felt almost as sorry for him as she did for herself. It was no good. She was no good. It was obviously hopeless. It was so stupid. But it did feel good. It gave her a sad glimpse of the beauty that could have been if she weren't so broken, so worthless.

His fingers touched her labia.

"Wait a moment," she said.

He waited. Time passed.

"Never mind," she said breathlessly at last. "Um. Go ahead and . . ."

He went ahead and.

And he gently stroked her labia with his cunning fingers till she began to be wet again.

And he spread her labia wide with two fingers. She gasped. The gown was still over them, but she felt utterly, gloriously exposed—had never felt so naked, so shamelessly open. He didn't need to see her to know everything about her. He was deeper inside her now than any man had ever been.

And he pulled back the hood of her clitoris with his thumb. She knew what was coming next, and she whimpered gently, not in protest, arching her back because she could not be still. He was taking so long; he was being so gentle; he was playing on her nerve-ends like harp strings.

And he reached around with his other hand and began to flick her clitoris with his fingers. She found herself giggling a little because somehow . . . somehow she didn't give a damn. If he didn't give a damn, she wasn't going to give a damn. If he wanted to bring her off with those glorious hands, who was she to argue?

When she herself masturbated she usually tugged at her nipples; the extra sensation was pleasing. She kept raising her hands to her nipples to do it now, but then dropped them, embarrassed. Then she realized how stupid that was. She had already embarrassed herself as much as she could; she might as well enjoy herself, too. Besides . . . she found herself pleased by the sense that she was exposed, known to him, that he was watching her, taking pleasure in her desire. Now he was biting her ear, and that was her gag, and she tried to tell him that, but all that came out of her mouth was a kind of cooing sound, and that sent a line of light straight down from her throat to her cunt, so she cooed louder and the line became brighter and hotter, and she arched her back higher and screamed as she rode a tide of shame and fear onto the hot golden shore of orgasm.

Orgasm. If the pain was like a red ring of iron tightening in her cunt, orgasm was like an explosion of golden light. It was the sun between her legs. It was freedom from every feeling except pleasure. It was pretty good. Pretty good. She wouldn't mind doing that again.

She rolled over and straddled Morlock. "You're breaking the rules," she said, feeling rather drunk. "Is not how you're supposed to act."

"Sorry," he said, smiling, not sorry at all.

Her mouth was all over his face. "Smug son-bitch," she murmured between kisses. "Two can play game."

"Eh?" he said wittily, a sound that apparently indicated alarm.

Now her hands were between his legs, stroking the shaft of his penis. His expression became transfixed, his eyes glazed. He looked a little bit like that when he was in the ecstasy of vision, but this was a very different ecstasy she was subjecting him to. She delighted in the sensation of power it gave her. She scooched down on his body and confronted the ugliness of his penis eye-to-eye, as it were. It was red and taut, like muscles that had been overworked, like flesh that was inflamed with infection. She wondered if it hurt, and if that's why men were jerks so much of the time, combining their pleasures with pain, their pains with pleasures.

She kissed the red velvety head of his penis with wet lips. He gasped, so she did it again a couple of times, licking it a little as she did so. God, how his crotch stank: of sweat and maleness. It was horrible, but she had a kind of hunger for it. She moved her wet mouth up along the top of his shaft as she trailed her fingers along the more sensitive underside. He groaned or said something in a language she didn't know and came, hot wet jism spraying on her throat and chest. It should have been one of the most disgusting things that had ever happened to her, and in a way it was. But she was so glad. It was strange. Sex was so strange.

"I'm sorry," he said, lifting her up. God Avenger, he was strong.

"*Thank you* is the correct expression, if you need to say anything, you savage and uncivilized mushroom."

"Thank you," he breathed in her ear, while wiping his ejaculate off her with a corner of his discarded jacket.

They lay for some time in each other's arms, wordless, basking in the moment, listening. There no longer any signs of battle from below, and the air was darker, much darker. How long had they been at it?

Not long enough, she decided.

"Sweetheart," she whispered in Morlock's ear. "Will you bring me off again?"

CHAPTER FOURTEEN

God in Exile

Aloê woke from a warm golden dream with a sudden steely shock. Her limbs were all entangled with an animal or . . . with an animal or something.

It took a moment or two for her to realize that the animal in question was Morlock. He was still blissfully asleep, his face unguarded and peaceful in a way that Aloê had never seen it. He was drooling slightly also.

Memory settled down on her, layer by layer, until she had remembered all of yesterday's bizarre events. Why she had ever thought Morlock was the solution to her peculiar problem, she could not imagine. . . .

No, that wasn't fair to her or to Morlock. The man was a problem solver, in many ways the most remarkable man she had ever met, even if he wasn't so much to look at. And he was crazy about her, in a good way. At the very least she'd found a way to deal with her trouble.

But the situation presented certain difficulties. They still had to work together—and, on this mission, live cheek-by-jowl. What if she decided she didn't want to . . . to be intimate again? Or what if his infatuation faded? Infatuations do. They had been crazy, reckless, and stupid, but one way out of the dilemma was to look each other in the eye this morning and say, *All right; it happened; we don't regret it. But it's not going to happen again.*

Morlock's beautiful gray eyes opened and looked straight into hers. "Praise the day, Vocate Aloê," he said, smiling but somehow serious.

"Bring me off again," she said: greedily, incoherently, as she kissed his face. And he did, stroking her body with his strong clever hands, kissing her face and neck, whispering words in her ear that she didn't understand. He carried her over the threshold of orgasm.

Afterward, as she lay there resting in his arms, she said, "Hey. I'm not the first woman you've done this with."

"It's true," he said. "I'm no Jordel. But I've been around the block a few times, as the saying is."

"Oh." A thought occurred to her. "Jordel has not been around *my* block, in case you were wondering."

He nodded gravely, accepting this, but saying nothing.

"So who are some of your women? Anyone I know? The Honorable Ulvana, I hope not?"

"Who?" Morlock asked, genuinely baffled.

She laughed aloud, and something inside her that had never stopped hurting . . . Suddenly, it didn't hurt anymore. Somehow she knew it would never hurt again.

"Never mind," she said. "What about breakfast? Aren't you usually up by this time?"

"I suppose so."

She waited for him to go on, but he didn't. She thought about all those nights when she was curled up around him for warmth, and he was turned resolutely away, still as a stone. . . .

"You've had blue balls for all this time?" she said wonderingly. "That's why you were always getting up and starting the fire and making things and stuff?"

"I'm not sure what you mean," he said, a little stiffly. "I often wake up early—get a lot of things done—this place may not be good for a fire, but—"

"Breakfast can wait a little longer."

"I—I don't think—"

"Your mouth is saying no, honey, but your penis is saying yes."

His mouth stopped talking. She climbed atop him and gently embraced his penis with her thighs. She slowly rotated her hips up and down, down and up. He made a sound like he'd been stabbed and sprayed semen all over the back of her legs and her ass.

"I bet there's more in there," she whispered tauntingly in his ear.

"Not at the moment," he whispered back. "Um. Thank you."

"Say what you want to say."

"Aloê," he said, like a prayer, like an incantation, like a confession. "Aloê. Aloê."

She kissed him three times, rolled off and went to wash.

The green recess, as she had suspected, concealed a stream from above that pooled a little before sinking down into the veins of the rock. The water was as clear and cold as mountain water could be. She scraped herself with it, scrubbed herself with it, immersed herself in it as much as the pool permitted.

The water carried the filth away like time carrying away the past. Something had ended and something had begun. She laughed and emerged clean from the pool, renewed, a part of her alive that hadn't been yesterday.

Morlock also scrubbed himself fastidiously in the cold mountain water, although he didn't look as refreshed by it as she'd been. They decided to eschew a fire and chew some flatbread and dried meat for breakfast. Then Morlock led the way uphill into a green mossy cleft between two rocky red slopes—a steep climb, she would have called it before yesterday's vertical ascent.

They came at last to some stairs carved into the mossy stone. The stairs led to a plateau, and a road across it, and on the other side of the plateau what looked like a perfectly horrible little mountain town.

"Well, we'll lunch in style at least," Aloê remarked.

Morlock shrugged. Falling in love had not made him more talkative, it seemed.

⋙⋘

According to the borderstone, the name of the town was Hoimëdmetheterön, which neither of them could make out as the name of any god. The borderstone was flanked by a wooden pillar bearing a strange symbol carved in stone. Aloê thought it was a hand covering up a statue: you could just see its feet below the hand and part of its head protruding on top. Whatever Morlock thought provoked him to grunt and shrug.

They stopped for lunch at the Brŷderwog Inn, the little town's finest (and only) house of entertainment. Aloê had the ordinary lunch (venison soup with a bowl of pickled cabbage), whereas Morlock indulged in the special lunch (the same with some yellow pepper ground into it). The server, without prompting, swore binding and valid oaths about the harmlessness of the meal, and asked them to swear that they were not missionaries.

"Won't swear," Morlock said, meeting Aloê's eye. "Merely affirm."

"That's all right," the waitress said, quite bored by it all. "This is an open town, that's all, so we don't like people preaching their gods in here."

"That's no kind of conversation," Aloê agreed. So that's what the fist-covering-the-statue sigil must have meant: keep your gods to yourself. She'd have said as much to Morlock, but he would have just grunted back at her.

"It occurs to me," Aloê said, when the server had made her lugubrious way back to the kitchen, "that all this treachery in Kaenish culture can work to our benefit. An innkeeper back in the—back home might feed us substandard or even poisonous food, if sufficiently reckless, but around here even the sausage vendors have to ensure their food is wholesome under oath."

Morlock nodded slowly, and Aloê was afraid he was about to grunt thoughtfully.

But he actually said something. "Unless the server makes the food," he remarked, "the oath might not be effective. Suppose the cook wants to harm the waitress?"

"You have a morbid imagination, partner," she said, not in a disapproving way. "I was going to bargain with the server for supplies. Maybe I'd better go back and talk to the cook."

Morlock nodded and began to extract Kaenish money from his multitude of pockets.

"Enough," she said, when it was enough, and swept the coins into her hand.

The cook was an almost pyramidal man—wide at the hips, standing wide with bowlegs, narrow shoulders, and pointed cap—lazily puttering about the cavernous kitchen. She bargained with him for some dried sausage, cheese, and bread, which he swore by specific and binding oaths were free from harm. "And none of it from sheep nor goat," he added with a certain satisfaction.

When she got back to the table with their bag of food, she found Morlock playing with fire. He was holding a fragment of burning wood on his palm. The flame was not rising but pointing at a crumbly gray cube of something lying on the table.

"What the hell," she said cheerfully, "are you doing?" She plonked herself next to him on the bench and plonked the food next to herself.

"It's a poison detector," he said. "Variant of the Pursuer instrumentality."

"Of course. One sees that at once."

"The flame should nod toward anything poisonous—even a drug strong enough to cause sleep, though I'm not sure about that."

"What's that, then?" She pointed at the cube that the flame was pointing at.

"Rat poison. It's all around the room. They must have a serious rat problem."

"And it's on our table? I'm going to invoke that waitress' oath—"

"Don't. I put it there." He picked up the cube with two fingers and tossed it into the darkest corner of the room—where, if Aloê was not mistaken, there was indeed a rat waiting for it. Then Morlock burned his fingers clean using the still-living flame of the poison detector.

The waitress brought their food and drink in on platters, started to say something, eyed the flame in Morlock's hand, and thought better of it. When the detector acquitted the meal of being poisonous, Morlock snuffed the flame and they dug in.

The only other people in the refectory were already eating, but not very determinedly. They seemed to be there mostly to talk. One was the hairiest man she had ever seen, the other the baldest (except, perhaps, for the Summoner Bleys).

". . . we'll call it a draw, of course," the bald man was saying ruefully.

"Don't we always, Gnörymu my friend?" the shaggy man replied, and laughed boisterously. "But you thought you had me this time: admit it."

"Klÿgnaru, stop. You're embarrassing me."

"No need to be embarrassed. We are friends, old friend, but our gods are not, and of course you serve your god. That is why we will die on that mountain, me serving Khÿmäroreibätu and you serving Öweioreibäto. We're too loyal to do anything else."

They continued their conversation, apparently settling a treaty of peace, and Aloê realized where she had heard the shaggy man's voice before: he was the elephant-goat rider. Wasn't Gnörymu the name he'd screamed out—*I'm coming for you Gnörymu*, or something like that? Yet here they were drinking bear-meat soup and sharing a loaf of bread. It was odd.

She glanced at Morlock to try and signal him somehow, but she saw he was already listening as he ate. He met her eye and lifted his bowlful of soup in salute. And that was odd, too—to have someone understand her without a spoken word. Someone besides Naevros.

They finished their soup and got up to leave. Something brushed by

Aloê's leg and scuttled along the floorboard to run out through a break in the swinging door that led to the street. Aloê would have said it was a rat, but it was wearing some sort of hooded robe.

As they passed the two archpriests, the shaggy one said, "And here we have the unwise pair who blundered through the middle of our battle. My god tells me they are Wardlanders."

Morlock stopped and looked calmly at the two priests, his hand not very near the glass pommel of his sword, nor very far away. Aloê tried to imitate his air of casual menace.

"Don't worry," said the bald one, Gnörymu. "My god told me to steer clear of you, and I expect Klÿgnaru was told the same."

"But they're not avoiding us," the shaggy one complained. "Look, youngsters, you were sent our way by that treacherous little godling Tekätestu the Many-Mouthed in the hope that we would kill you in our annual war. I'm glad you avoided that, because we're not here to do Tekätestu any favors, nor the Two Powers, either. Because he hates you, I'll do you this favor—a piece of advice. Avoid Thyläkotröx."

"We don't even know the way there from here," Aloê said.

"The way where?" the shaggy man said vacantly. "Never mind! I have spoken. Good luck to you, travellers."

Morlock seemed inclined to stay, so Aloê took him by the arm and led him away into the street.

"They can start a riot, at which we will be the guests of honor, just by saying more loudly what he said to us." So Aloê reminded Morlock when they were safely outdoors. He shrugged impassively and then nodded more meaningly up the red dusty street.

Coming toward them was a limping figure wrapped in a hooded robe— much like the rat (was it a rat?) that Aloê had seen. But this was man-high— perhaps woman-high. Hunched over, it moved awkwardly up the street. The few townspeople in sight looked on with scorn, maybe a little fear. Aloê could understand that: she was fairly sure that the feet she saw hobbling underneath that robe were no human feet at all.

The figure stopped in front of them, and drew back its hood.

The face revealed was human . . . and not human. It had downy fur and an upturned soft flexible nose like a dog or a rat. Underneath it were sprouting long whiskers. But the eyes and ears and chin—the rest of the face was human, and female.

"Do you know me?" she said to Morlock. "We met a time ago."

"Friend of yours?" Aloê murmured.

"I don't remember you," Morlock said to the rat-woman.

Her face and shoulders fell. "I was different then. I was happy and bright."

Morlock took a step back, his faced stretched with surprise. "Yes. I remember you now. I never knew your name."

"I had a name then, but even I don't remember what it was. The One burned within me, destroying that knowledge and much else. I am called Masösa now."

"I'm amazed that you survived. The One seemed to have—it seemed to have—"

"The One was in me and through me. I was an early apostate from Thyläkotrox, He Who Walks Beneath. I was not happy in Thyläkotrox. The One made me happy, and I gave myself to it. It was a happy green time. I saw you there, at the end of it."

"You infected me with the One."

"I wanted all the world to be happy and bright. You were so unhappy. Perhaps I did wrong. When you killed the One with fire, we all burned. Some burned to death. Some were burned but lived. Many of us were burned nearly to death; we lay dying in the streets. Then Thyläkotrox returned. In his mercy, he healed us and we did not die. In his wisdom, he punished us like . . . like this." She gestured vaguely at herself with a ratlike paw. "I am not happy and bright now. But I know a truth that I didn't before. The universe is not happy and bright. Only power matters. This is the lesson my god has taught me, and I am grateful for it. I hope someday to repay him. As lowly as I am, perhaps I could still repay him."

"What would you have of me?"

"I? Nothing. Nothing. Once I hated you for killing the One, but other hates have swallowed that hate. But my god wishes to speak to you. He has a message about the Powers who live in the north, the Masked Powers who hunt you through the world."

This was news to Aloê and to Morlock, too, by the bemused tone in his voice as he said, "They hunt me?"

"They hunt Ambrosius."

"No names," Aloê interrupted hurriedly. A small unfriendly crowd was gathering. Perhaps they suspected proselytizing. Maybe they were biased against rat-people. But they probably had no love for the Wardlands or Wardlanders. And Ambrosius was a famous name.

"My god wishes you to come with me," the rat-woman said. "Will you, or not? I must return to him."

"Why can't your god appear to us here?" Aloê asked.

The rat-woman drew her hood over her face and gave a rather Morlockian shrug. She turned and lurched back up the street the way she had come. The vocates met each other's eye and nodded.

They had to risk it, despite Klÿgnaru's warning.

⁓⧨⁓

Upslope from the town, the mountain split into a narrow ravine. Aloê had a nightmarish sense of repeating the past—a past unpleasantly thick with venomous sheep and fire-breathing elephant-goats. But they passed through the ravine without incident. Masösa stopped on the far side, unhooded herself, and turned her ratlike face back toward the ravine.

The slopes above them were riddled with holes. In each one stood a hooded rat-sized figure. And in a boulder nearby there was a wide dark recess, about ankle high, like the sewer hole in a street.

No face there, not yet, but it was to this hole that Masösa spoke: "Lord, I have brought the one you commanded me to bring."

"Plus one," Aloê snarled.

"There is also this woman, as you see, you who see all," Masösa added, with tautological subservience.

Something was taking shape in the sewer-hole: a hooded head, the face enveloped in shadow, only the ratlike tip of the nose and the red burning eyes visible.

"Thyläkotröx, you who walk below, we welcome your manifestation," said Masösa breathlessly, and bowed low. The hooded rats in the recesses of the cliff all chittered together.

Masösa bowed even lower. She sobbed in pain or religious ecstasy. She frantically pulled away the long robe she wore. She was nude underneath, crouching now, and Aloê looked with some horror on her body, with rat-haunches, and a long naked pink tail, and coarse gray hairs covering her distorted trunk. She had six nipples, like a female rat.

But that wasn't the worst of it. Her back was rippling, changing as they watched. A mouth with two enormous white lips appeared on her shoulder. It had long needle-teeth and a slender white tongue. The voice of the god spoke through it as Masösa hissed through her teeth.

"Welcome, young Ambrosius," said the god.

"Eh," said Morlock, delighting Aloê no end.

"You are discourteous," the god's mouth said, as Masösa grovelled in pain. "But no matter. You have done me a great kindness in the slaying of my enemy, the One, and it is my nature to reward my friends and punish my enemies. So it must be, for such as me. Thence comes the tal that sustains us and gives us our power."

"Gods, you mean," Morlock said.

"The gods of Kaen, and many another god. Whether the Two Powers (may they be damned to the emptiness of unworship) are the same, we do not know. But they are our enemy, and yours, too, and so we have a common enemy again."

"Are the Two Powers hostile to the Wardlands? Why?"

"I neither know, nor care. But you did not attend to my meaning, Ambrosius. The Two Powers hate you in particular. They seek you up and down the world. They send out the weaker gods like dogs to trail you and those who share your fiery blood. I could gain a great reward, and access of power and freedom you cannot conceive, simply by telling them where you are."

"Then," Morlock said.

The god's mouth on Masösa's back made a hissing sound of irritation. "I visualize that you mean, 'Why don't you tell them, then?' But I hate the Two Powers more than I hate you, or this traitorous follower of mine, or those rock-rats above that are my only remaining congregation.

"Once it was different with me. Long I reigned beneath the streets of Thyläkotröx City, and my people were not unhappy, I believe."

Aloê looked on Masösa, writhing in pain, and remembered what she had said when they first met. Aloê wondered how accurate the god's belief was.

The god continued, "Then the Two Powers began to send their emissaries, human and bestial, into our lands. They had come to establish a beachhead against your Wardlands. If they had wanted only the coastline, I would not have cared; no god of Kaen would have cared. We do not use the sea, or love it, or claim to rule it.

"But they wanted our people and our cities, too, and that we could not permit. I was one of the first to be attacked, but through the fear and love of my people and the power that was in me and my land, I resisted the onslaught. Below the streets of my city I waged a long war against the invasion of the Two Powers.

"The struggle did not weaken me. I was not weakened. But it distracted me and my priests, and we did not keep proper watch on the sea. That was when the One came, and began to infect my people with happiness and the freedom from fear. When at long last I felt the presence of the One among my congregation, it was too late. His worshippers were immune to my terrors, forgetful of my love. My images were destroyed and I was cast out. I found this colony of rock-rats who were just barely wise enough to worship me, and I waited for I knew not what; my visualization, future and past, was shaken by the combat of so many gods.

"Then you came out of the sea and killed the One with fire. I returned with my rats and fought with the emissaries of the Two Powers in the burning streets. But in the end, I could only recover the most deeply wounded of my former citizens, the ones discarded as hopeless by the Two Powers. I healed them and punished them. Most I sent out into the world as missionaries, to bring my faith to the world again. This one I speak through, whose guilt was the greatest, I have rewarded and punished most of all. The rats can barely see me, barely hear me, and only the wisest of them. So she has become my audible avatar, my visual voice. It is a great pain to her and, I believe, an almost equally great pleasure. Almost. Almost."

The avatar of the rat-god reached out its forepaws. They were skeletally thin. It lifted itself out of the sewer-like hole and crawled onto the ground on all fours. Its long tail hung behind: limp, gray, and nerveless.

"And now," said the white mouth on the weeping woman's shoulder, "how shall I reward you, Morlock Ambrosius? Yes, and punish you, too. You benefited me by slaying the One. But you shamed me, yes, shamed me, because

I could not do the same. Yes, I think I shall punish you now and reward you later. . . ."

Like the spectator at a quench-ball match, Aloê turned to see what sort of response Morlock would make. She saw with surprise that he was making no move at all. His eyes stared fixedly at the hole Thyläkotrök had emerged from. The god had spellbound him somehow; he didn't seem to be able to move.

Aloê drew her staff from its shoulder sheath and stepped between the crawling god and the spellbound man. She spun the staff to build up its freight of impulse energy and said, "No further, Thyläkotrök."

To her surprise, the rat-god's avatar stopped its crawl. It looked at her with its red burning eyes.

"I visualize that you are protected from binding spells," the gray mouth on Masösa's shoulder said. "How wise. And you believe in other gods; that is also a protection from my influence. You believe in the Creator, Sustainer, Avenger?"

"I suppose so. I haven't thought about it much."

"That is the safest way to be, in a world full of gods. Your friend has thought about it, thought about it too much. He can neither believe nor disbelieve, and through those doors of doubt I have many ways of entrance."

"You are lying, I think, rat-god. Otherwise you could control him as you do poor Masösa there."

"Poor Masösa here," said the pale mouth on Masösa's shoulder, and laughed as she writhed under the weight of her god's amusement and scorn. "But I do not control poor Masösa, here. She has chosen to pledge herself to me, in fear and hope, as you may soon do. After I punish your friend." And the rat-god's avatar began to creep forward again.

Aloê would never have chosen to fight a god, and she did think briefly about leaving Morlock to his fate. It might come to that, in fact. But she could not bring herself to flee without striking a single blow.

So she struck one, lashing out with her staff to release the impulse power.

The god's avatar rippled like a candle flame. The gray teeth of the god's mouth gnashed in anger, and Masösa screamed. The rats in their recesses chittered sadly and put their paws over their faces.

The god's avatar disappeared to re-form slowly on the other side of Morlock.

"Direction means nothing to the gods, reckless enemy," the gray mouth whispered. "I can come from any side, even below. Flee my wrath, as you have imagined doing, and my reward to you shall be your own life."

"Sleep and death are brothers," Aloê replied, spinning her glass staff again. "I stand beside my comrade. My intention protects him, in all directions and none. Chew on that, rat-god."

"I will slay you, and you will find the truth of death, which is other than you imagine."

The god's avatar leapt through the air at her. It changed direction in midflight to attack Morlock. If she had struck at its first leap, she could not have recovered in time, but this was not Aloê's first fight. She struck at the avatar's humped back, and now the white mouth screamed in harmony with Masösa as the avatar vanished again. The avatar reappeared beside the sewer hole—diminished in size, if Aloê was not mistaken.

"Flee like a rat, rat-god," Aloê sang out. "Live in accordance with your nature."

The white mouth extruded from Masösa's shoulder, riding the end of a long flexible snout. It turned and bit the rat-woman on her furry neck. She screamed, and the rats in their holes wailed in despair.

But the god's avatar grew. Now it towered over Masösa, its forearms bulging with muscle and bristling with black hair, its claws glittering like black glass. The mouth vanished and Masösa fell, shrunken like a burst bladder, to the rocky ground.

The avatar moved forward, its red eyes blazing, lighting up the interior of its hood to reveal its grinning rat skull of a head. It rose up on its hind legs, shuffling forward as it extruded the claws of its forelegs.

Aloê lashed out with her staff, striking the avatar on its bony snout. It shuddered but did not vanish. The skeletal grin did not change, and it moved forward. Aloê stepped back and felt her back against Morlock's still-frozen form. Maybe she had mocked the rat-god once too often: it seemed to have extracted enough tal from its lone semihuman worshipper to face down the worst her sole weapon could do.

But she would not flee. Maybe sleep and death were brothers, like the old song said. She hoped so.

Then Masösa screamed, "Thief! Thief! Give me my own back! Give me my life back or kill me!" And her emaciated form leapt onto the rat-god's avatar, tearing at it with her claws.

It shook her off and turned vengefully against her. Its claws caught her and slashed her deeply, belly to neck, and then the rat-snout sank deeply into the rat-woman's dying body. The avatar grew taller than ever as it drank the dying woman's last life and cast her aside.

"Traitor!" Aloê shouted. "Liar! False god!"

The words struck Thyläkotröx's avatar more deeply than her staff blows had done. "False god!" she shouted again. "You reward your enemies and punish your friends!"

At first Aloê thought the god was responding with a thousand anguished rat-voices. Then she saw that the rats were descending in a dark many-hooded wave from their holes in the cliff. Thyläkotröx's avatar turned to face them, raising its forelegs in aversion or threat.

The wave of rats swept over their god, screaming and snarling as they leapt up to bite him.

Thyläkotröx screamed, the first and last time Aloê heard him speak through his avatar, the last hopeless cry of a dying god. Then his avatar fell down to feed the members of his last congregation.

Morlock fell too, released at last from the god's spell.

The god died. Aloê felt the spiritual cataclysm; it almost struck her from full consciousness into the visionary state. She saw a wheel turning with a man (or something like a man) in the middle of it. . . . She fought to keep her eyes open, to see what was merely present, to reject the vision.

The hooded rats were feeding on their god, swarming over the vanishing avatar. They were growing, not in size but somehow in clarity, intensity, ferocity.

Regular rats were bad enough, in Aloê's biased view. What would god-fed rats be like? What were they feeding on, since gods were immaterial beings? She didn't want to know.

She turned to Morlock and shook him where he lay. "Come on, Morlock," she said. "We've got to get out of here. They'll be done with him soon, and maybe they'll come for us."

Morlock muttered something that made no sense, and did not otherwise move.

Aloê swore, briefly but sincerely, and sheathed her staff. She grabbed her fallen partner and hustled him to his feet. She half-dragged, half-carried him downslope. There was no reason to prefer it to upslope except that they could move a little faster.

Morlock was as heavy as a dead man. His eyes were glowing slightly, shining through the closed lids: he hadn't been able to refrain from being swept into visionary rapture by the cataclysm of Thyläkotröx's death. That meant he wouldn't be of much use any time soon: "The flight must take its course" was what seers said.

Aloê's course, with Morlock dragging her down, was uneven and slow. It was only midafternoon, but the dry high mountains to the east blocked out the light, and the slope downhill was rough, nothing like a road, or even a path.

A long arm reached out of the shadows and grabbed Morlock's shoulder from the other side.

Aloê reached for her staff, but a voice she instinctively trusted spoke from the shadows and said, "Let me help. It'll go faster this way."

"All right," Aloê said. "Thanks."

"No thanks needed. I act for my own reasons, and according to my own nature."

This caused the hairs on Aloê's neck to bristle a bit. But: help was help. She wanted to get away from those rats.

"You are wise," the voice said approvingly, after it was clear she was going to say nothing. "That pleases me."

"Who are you?" she asked.

"My name is Wisdom. I came here with some friends of mine, a pair of sisters: Death and Justice."

"'Death and Sleep are brothers,'" Aloê quoted, a little desperately.

"A different Death, perhaps; a different Sleep."

They travelled together for a while in silence.

"Death and Justice are two of the Strange Gods of the Coranians," Aloê observed eventually.

"Yes. There are many Deaths—there is so much death to go around, you see. But we found the Kaenish god of Death to be an inconvenience and had him disposed of."

"Oh. Did you?"

"Yes. You might ask your friends in the Graith—Illion and Noreê and

Jordel. They had something to do with it. Though perhaps they did not visualize it as we have done."

"No doubt." Aloê tried to see the shadowy figure across from Morlock, but the outlines would not resolve themselves. Even the hand lifting Morlock up from the other side seemed different from moment to moment: a shadow shifting among the shadows.

"I visualize it was when we destroyed the Kaenish god of Death that the Two Powers, whom I do not name, became aware that gods could die, and moved to invade other lands, slay other gods. That has been bad for us. I visualize it has been bad for you as well."

"It has. Do you . . . ?"

"No, we don't visualize their motives. It may be hate. They mostly hate each other, but at times they have shared a hate for something or someone else. It may be fear: they may fear that what happened to the Kaenish god of Death may happen to them. But I speculate there is a factor, hidden from our visualizations, which is the true cause of these events."

"What is it?"

"I have not come here to tell you that. I only speculate. I visualize that you will be in a position to learn. Perhaps one day you will tell me."

"If I can, without violating my loyalty, I will."

"Loyalty. How strong it is in you. It makes me sad."

"Why?" Aloê asked sharply.

"I have not come to tell you that."

"What have you come to tell me?"

"When your partner awakes, ask him about the Apotheosis Wheel. Remember the Wheel."

"Why should I do that?"

"Don't you want to know about it? I visualize that you do. And—yes—tell him about this."

The shadowy figure reached out a long misty arm and touched with one outstretched finger the twisting knotlike charm that hung from her neck.

"Why?"

"The knowledge will benefit you, and him. I am a god of Wisdom, Aloê Oaij, and I act in accordance with my nature. I help my friends and harm my enemies. Gods who do otherwise may end as Thyläkotröx did tonight."

"It's only afternoon."

"You are mistaken. It is night; we have come many miles; you are safe from the rats."

Aloê looked about and saw that it was night, deep night: the moons were visible in the sky, and the Hands blazed out in bright stars overhead. The mountains were merely shadows embroidered on the edge of the starry sky behind them. Morlock lay snoring on the grass, and Wisdom was nowhere to be seen.

"My turn to make camp, I guess," she remarked to the sleeping man, and set about the mundane tasks of evening.

CHAPTER FIFTEEN

The Golden Road

Morlock slept the night through and awoke blearily next morning a few moments after Aloê.

"Praise the day, Vocate," he said, yawning. He looked around vacantly at the camp and its environs, his expression soon changing to alarm. They were in an open field of peach-colored grass, the mountains many miles behind them.

"What happened?" he asked flatly.

It wasn't a rhetorical question—Morlock, thank God Avenger, did not waste time with those. So Aloê began, in order of importance, "We have been having sex—and you are not to stop bringing me off, by the way. We ran into an old friend of yours in the mountains. Do you remember that?"

"Masösa," he said. "Ah. Poor Masösa."

"Then you do remember?"

"I remember something. Did we reach Thyläkotröx?"

"The god-in-exile, not his city. It got a little tricky there."

"I remember. I remember. The god was going to . . . to kill me or something."

"Or something."

"And you fought the avatar and killed the god."

She waved a modest hand and said, "I did a little. Masösa and the rats did more."

"No. I was in rapport with the god. It was when you accused him of betraying his own nature, that was when he burst apart like an overheated sausage."

"Urm. Beautifully put."

"Then the rats ate what was left, but you struck the crucial blow."

"It was nothing really. You'd have done the same."

"If I could have. But . . ." He looked at her searchingly, and she thought he was going to say, *But I love you and you don't love me.* And what the hell was she going to say to that?

"But," he actually said, "then I felt his death. We were mind to mind when he died. I saw his life come apart, and when it did . . . when it did . . . I saw the arc of it."

"You saw the Wheel," she said flatly.

"The Wheel!" he shouted, seizing her arms with his hands. "The Wheel! Did you see it?"

"I glimpsed it," she said, a little short of breath. She hadn't often seen him like this. She was reminded, suddenly, that this was a man who could strike a dragon from the sky with lightning (if there was any lightning lying around waiting to be used). It was a little frightening, and very exhilarating.

"It was the Wheel that changed him into a god. He was born a man—like you or me!"

"Well. Not like me."

"It's a device. A mechanism to make a mortal into a god."

"If that's the right word."

Morlock's eyes focused on her. "Why do you doubt it?" he asked.

She shrugged. "It's just . . . You say 'god' and all sorts of things come into your mind with the word. What do we really know about these beings that come off the Apotheosis Wheel?"

"Hm. They can be killed."

"Right! And they must act in accordance with their nature. It's what gives them tal somehow, sustains their life."

"Yes. Yes, that's odd. I always thought they got it from prayer—feeding off their worshippers."

"I wonder if prayer is more for the worshippers' benefit—makes you more like your god."

"Eh."

"Yes. Whether it's really a benefit might depend on the god."

"You get to use the word, I see."

She'd have raised her hands if he didn't still have a grip on her arms. "Hard to avoid! But the rock-rats and Masösa seemed to become more like Thyläkotröx, so maybe . . ."

"I agree. And you're right about 'god.' It begs the question. We have to know what we don't know—see what we haven't seen. Not use words to cloak ignorance."

He frowned, deep in thought, and closed those glorious eyes. She didn't want to move, really—but she had to. Her side was sore from lying on the ground all night. She needed to wash and eat. She waited a while longer, though. The moment was precious to her: body to body, mind to mind they lay. It had never been like that for her, not with anyone.

When she had waited as long as she could stand she said gently, "Morlock. I need to move."

He opened his eyes wide in surprise, looked at his hands as if he had no idea how they got there, and released her. "I'm sorry. I—"

"Shut your stupid face," she said, and kissed him on the mouth before she rolled away and left him on the bed cloak.

⋑⋐

Much had changed in a single night. Morlock took a while to look around and orient himself. They were a very long way from the mountains, certainly. Behind them two streams converged to make a river, the biggest they had seen in rock-red rock-dry Kaen. It flowed between two highlands out to an open plain where the grass glowed a pale autumnal gold.

"I think this must be the Pöylma River," Morlock said, after gazing long at sky and ground.

"Oh," Aloê replied, clearly relieved. "Then you know where we are."

"Eh."

"Could you expand on that a little?"

"The Pöylma runs from Kaen into masterless lowlands and thence into the sea."

"Thence?"

"But if this is the Pöylma, we have crossed more than half of Kaen in a single night." He looked at her and waited.

She fidgeted but did not speak. He thought this unlike her.

"Something happened," he said after a time, "but you don't wish to speak of it."

"Yes," she admitted.

"It involves one of the gods of Kaen."

"A god. But not of Kaen. I think he meant to help us, for reasons of his own, no doubt."

"Did he place a geas on you?"

She shook her head slowly. "No. There's a specific reason I didn't want to mention it." She was absentmindedly fingering the talisman hanging from her necklace as she spoke.

Morlock nodded, waited.

"Is it all right if I think about it, and tell you later?"

"It is," he said, "if you think it is."

She seemed unsure, but did not say anything more.

The water from the rivers was a little murky; Morlock decided to boil it before using it to wash or drink or fill their bottles. While he was doing this Aloê went out and trapped two sinister toothy reptiles from the river, which she assured him would be good eating. After being cleaned, skinned, cut in pieces, and roasted, they weren't bad.

Morlock did not expect to find any guards blocking the way in or out of Kaen, and there seemed to be none. The Kaeniar were as insular in their way as the Wardlands were, but they did not guard their borders so much as ignore them and most things beyond them. The country had been invaded over the centuries, but the invaders either left or stayed behind to become Kaeniar themselves.

There was an odd open building on the banks of the Pöylma, between the two rocky red headlands that were the gates of Kaen. The building was floored with polished blue stone, and pillared with white marble columns. There was no roof at all, except for the lintels connecting the columns. They formed an oval, and in the center of the oval, in the middle of the blue floor, was a green stone bench.

As the vocates approached, Morlock saw four people sitting on the bench. When they got closer, he saw that three of them were clearly dead, and the fourth one was watching their approach with a bright hopeful gaze.

"Welcome, young Ambrosius!" the stranger said. "Welcome to Lophopöylmata, and well-met!"

"What is Lophopöylmata?" Morlock asked. "And who are you?"

"This is Lophopöylmata. When a priest has risen to the height of the Court of Heresiarchs and ruled there for a time over the peers, he or she is taken here, either to be slain or to walk the golden road of Talazh Rame, to ascend the Apotheosis Wheel and return to Kaen as a god."

"And are you leaving, or returning?"

"You shall know, in time. You shall know all, in time. Perhaps you, too, will walk the golden road of Talazh Rame, in time. But, for this moment, I think you will be the perfect messenger for my truth."

The stranger's smile was broad, too broad to be pleasant. In fact, it was not really a smile at all: the stranger's teeth were bare because he had no lips, no flesh covering the bare bone of his skull. He spoke without moving his mouth at all. His eyes lurked deep in the bare bony sockets.

"Morlock," Aloê broke in. "Who are you talking to?"

"Don't you see them?" Morlock said vaguely. "They must. They must."

Aloê swore by God Avenger and, unsheathing her staff, stepped between him and the skull-faced stranger.

Only then did Morlock realize what was happening: another god was taking him over. A deep, smoking fury woke within him. He summoned the visionary rapture so that he could fight against the god in its own sphere.

As he ascended into vision Morlock felt/saw the carnal shadow of his body fall to the ground. He stood, a pillar of monochrome flames, and faced the skull-faced god.

Aloê stood between them: her talic self a copper cloud of glory. She was speaking with her mouth, but he didn't hear it. But he heard her defiance, mind to mind.

There were long webby threads reaching from the skull-faced god's fingers, stretching around Aloê as if there was something pushing them aside. But they ran onward to Morlock, sinking hooked anchors deep in his talic self. He forced himself to attend to these: there was an anchor that stank like Khecür Tnevnepü, a tiny mouth with razor-teeth clenched tight (a memento of Tekätestu?), a crooked ratlike claw that reminded him of Thyläkotröx, other anchors, perhaps from other gods he didn't even recognize. He had walked through Kaen collecting devotions like ticks. And it was these anchors that the skull-faced god was using to try and master him.

One by one Morlock turned on the anchors in his spirit, focused his fury on them and dispelled them. The veins of influence broke when their anchor was destroyed. In the end, Morlock stood free, himself again.

He turned his awareness outward to see that Aloê had struck the skull-faced god with her weapon and (even more deadly) her intent to reject him. She was stepping forward to renew the attack.

But there were other gods advancing toward Lophopöylmata through the talic gloom. One carried a reaping sword, another an executioner's axe, the third a long glittering razor of argument and a deep cloudy shield of doubt.

Morlock reached out and impinged his awareness on Aloê's.

The contact was blistering. Her fury more than matched his own, and it was tangled up with skeins of guilt and desire. These, in turn, emanated from an ugly distorted image buried deep in her awareness: an image of himself.

He could not speak to her: the process of verbal thought was alien to the process of vision, hostile to it. But he tried to let her share his vision: the approaching gods, the cloud of their anger, the danger in this place.

She shook him loose, almost frightened, it seemed, and a long bright streak of physical pain shot through the coppery cloud of her talic self, like lightning in a sky lit by sunset.

He turned back to his body and lay down in it like a grave, rejecting the vision, pulling the mask of matter and energy over the true face of the world.

He opened his eyes and saw Aloê's dark face hovering over his. "If we need to go, let's go," she said.

He rolled to his feet and they ran, hand in hand, down along the banks of the Pöylma, through the unguarded gates of Kaen, into the golden fields where no writ ran.

"But we don't know where we're going," Aloê gasped.

"We do," Morlock said. "Skull-face told me. We'll take the road of Talazh Rame, the road that runs into the sea."

"The sea!" shouted Aloê, and seemed to draw fresh strength from the word itself. "The sea!" She ran ahead, releasing Morlock's hand, and danced down the banks of the Pöylma, plunging straight into the broad blue water and swimming across to the other side.

Morlock followed her: less swiftly, less joyously, but equally intent.

PART FOUR

THE SHADOWS OF OLD AZH

Marco Polo describes a bridge, stone by stone.

"But which one is the stone that holds the bridge up?" asks Kublai Khan.

"The bridge is not held up by this stone or that stone," replies Marco, "but by the arc that they form."

Kublai Khan remains silent, thinking. Then he continues, "Why do you speak to me of stones? It's only the arc that matters."

Polo responds, "Without stones, there is no arc."

—Calvino, *Invisible Cities*

CHAPTER SIXTEEN

The Way Forward

That night it rained. The storm came on suddenly, but it was the kind of long soaking rain that promised to last all night (if not longer)—cold rain with the first faint flavor of winter in it.

Morlock levelled several trees growing by the river: as narrow as saplings, as tall as oaks. He cut them up and rapidly built a shelter, roofing it with their cloaks and sleeping blankets.

Aloê helped as much as she could, but she could hardly keep from laughing at the grim determination on Morlock's face.

"We won't die, you know," she said at one point, "just because we get a little wet."

He shook his head and said something inaudible over the voice of the rain.

In the end they were inside, damp but not soaked, huddling together for warmth, and she had to admit it was better than being outside.

Noticing that Morlock was suffering from an erection, she said, "Hey! You know what we haven't done in a while?"

He brushed away her questing hand and said, "No."

"Your mouth says, no, but your penis says—"

"I saw something in you."

She stopped what she was doing and looked him in the eye. "What do you mean?"

"When I was in vision. I had to make you see . . . see those others."

"The Strange Gods. Yes."

He was silent for a while and said, "Is that who they were?"

"I think so."

"Interesting."

"But irrelevant, partner. You were talking about something much more interesting: me."

"I saw something in you. I'm sorry, but—"

"You said all that before. What did you see?"

"It was about me." He paused.

She smiled at him, and felt a little sad. Had he seen something of her feelings for him? Had he been offended? She couldn't help it if he wasn't Naevros syr Tol. She wished it was enough for him that he was what he was—that they had what they had.

"I didn't understand it," Morlock said. "But there was a halo of guilt, and fear, and pain. I don't. I don't want. I don't want you to *hurt* like that. Not for me. Not for anyone."

"You'd rather do without me than cause me any pain?" Aloê reflected wryly on her limited experience with men. This Morlock was an odd one, all right. "Don't worry, partner. It was all my fault. I should have told you something. Because I didn't, you came in danger from that god. I hated the thought of it."

She waited for him to ask, but he just lay there and looked at her with those damn eyes of his.

"It's like this," she began heavily, and told him everything about her conversation with Wisdom.

When she was done he said, "So that was Wisdom we saw."

"And Death and Justice, yes. They seem to have something against the Kaenish gods—maybe this was a new Kaenish god of Death."

He nodded.

"You don't seem surprised by any of this," she observed.

"Well. We had passed over much of the country in one night. I knew something had happened."

"But you didn't ask."

"I knew you would tell me when you thought the time right."

"But—" She glared at him. "How did you live so long, *trusting* people like that?"

Now he was surprised. "I know who to trust."

She looked away from his eyes, those luminous eyes. "So this," she said, touching the talisman around her neck, "is a charm against binding spells."

He nodded.

"I wear one because— Anyway, they seem to give some protection to me from the influence of these gods or whatever we are to call them."

"'Gods' will do."

"'Gods' with a hesitation. 'Gods' with a note in the margin."

He smiled and opened his hands, which apparently was supposed to mean something.

"Do you know how to make one?" she said, a little sullenly. "A charm against binding spells, I mean."

"No."

"I'll show you."

She used some of the long grass lying about and made the long winding symbol at the heart of the talisman. She explained that the material didn't matter, only the shape of the symbol and the intention woven into it. Teaching him how to weave the intention with the matter was the hardest thing, but it wasn't particularly hard to teach him that or anything else, except how to speak in something other than grunts.

"So," she said, putting it around his neck, "there you go. Don't say I never gave you anything."

He didn't say that, or anything else. Just smiled and touched her face.

"There's something Thyläkotröx said that's bothering me," she said.

He looked his question and waited.

"It's about you—not believing, or disbelieving, in any god. Apparently it's not safe."

"If he wasn't lying."

"Maybe. But maybe you should—decide, one way or the other."

His gray eyes looked at her now out of two dark wells of doubt. "I was raised to believe in Those-Who-Watch and in God the Creator, Sustainer, Avenger. I like to think that my *harven* father's ghost stands beyond the rim of the world in the west, watching and protecting me."

"But you can't."

"No. But, sometimes, in vision, I feel . . . a kind of immanence, a soul within the world. I don't know. Maybe it's just a reflection of my own mind; that's what some seers say."

It was her turn to say something, and she wasn't as comfortable as he was with silence, and anyway part of her wanted to tell him. She had always wanted to tell somebody, but she never had.

"God did a miracle for me once," she said.

"So that's why you believe in him?" he said, clearly surprised.

"Her. Yes. I was—I was—I was . . . God Avenger, I sound like you."

"Not that bad," he offered with a smile.

"Well, no one could be. All right. All right. Since you ask. I—there was this older man on my family's estate. Some rich cousin of my father's. This was when I was a little girl."

"Yes," he said, and there was iron in his voice.

"Don't get upset. It was a long time ago, and the good guys won. Nothos was this old bastard's name. Cousin Nothos. He was always bothering me. I hated his stupid face and everything about him, but he was always putting his face on me and bothering me when I was five. He even tried to sneak into my room sometimes at night. But no one would believe me except Fnarklo."

Morlock eased up a little. "Who is Fnarklo?"

"Fnarklo was my pet fish-hound. He slept in my room, and he would never let this old bastard in. When I was almost six, somebody killed him, killed Fnarklo, I mean—cut his throat right through to the bone. I tried to tell people it was Cousin Nothos, but no one would listen. How I hated them all. I hate them still. They let it happen."

She stopped speaking, and he didn't say anything.

"Well!" she said. "Do I have to paint you a picture? Do I have to go over every disgusting detail?"

He opened his hands, said nothing, and waited.

"He raped me most nights for about a. About a. For about a year, I guess. It started in summer and it ended in summer. I remember that part."

He nodded, watched, waited.

"When I realized no one was ever going to listen to me, I tried lots of different crazy things. I tried a few times to kill Cousin Nothos, but he just thought it was funny. I guess he'd been through it before, seen it all before. I could never outsmart him. So then I figured, maybe I'd kill myself. So I went to the island where old Fnarklo died. Hard to explain why. Thought maybe they'd believe me after I was dead, though I don't know now why I thought that. I was going to drown myself. Go under the water, breathe in through my mouth not my gills and just go down, down down in the dark, till I was dead."

Morlock nodded as if this was a very reasonable plan and said nothing.

"I was going to do it. I was, I swear I was. But"—she balled up her fists and pounded her knees—"but *it wasn't fair*. He was the one who should be dead. There was this philosopher who lived on the estate, and he said that it wasn't right to pray for harm to others and we had to put up with Cousin Nothos' little ways and someday I would grow up and understand things better. But I thought that old philosopher was a lying sack of snot. What about people who are doing bad things? Is God Avenger just supposed to sit by and do *nothing*?"

If Morlock had any solution to the Problem of Evil, he didn't offer it at that time. He didn't offer anything, but waited for Aloê to continue.

Eventually she did. "So I. So I said. I said to God. I said, '*You* do something about it. It's *your* job. *You* do something.' And that was when I found it. It was a book. It was half-buried in the mud. Most of the pages were destroyed. But it was a book of binding spells. It was Cousin Nothos' book: he put his name on the flyleaf. You know, 'Please return to; reward offered.' And I knew then how he fooled everybody, why everyone was so blind to what anyone ought to be able to see. It had to be magic; he was binding them with magic. People don't act that way. They don't turn away, and let someone get hurt, and do nothing when they could stop it. They just don't act that way without a reason. Anyway, I was sure of it then. Less so now."

Morlock didn't venture an opinion. He waited.

Aloê went on. "He must'a—He. Must. Have. Dropped. It. That night, when he was killing Fnarklo, he dropped it and lost it in the dark and the mud. And then a year later I found it. It was a kind of miracle, wasn't it?"

Morlock shrugged and waited.

"There wasn't a complete spell in the book. It was almost entirely ruined. But there were parts of spells I thought I could fit together. And I knew that people who use binding spells are subject to them in turn. So I. So I made a spell up out of the different spells I could read part of in the book. That was dangerous. Wasn't it?"

"Yes," said Morlock quietly. "It was."

"But it worked! Whenever he got aroused, his penis hurt. Like fire, he said. Kept on trying to dip it in cold liquid. My grandma found him dipping his erection in some cold soup in the pantry. That's when they decided that Cousin Nothos was crazy and his little ways couldn't be tolerated anymore. Ruin a granddaughter, so what. Ruin the evening soup, that's different. I hate that old woman. So anyway they locked him up until he died."

"He's dead then," said Morlock, with unmistakable satisfaction.

Somehow, after everything she'd said and remembered, *that* was what made her break down and start weeping like the little girl she'd had to give up being long ago. He held her and waited and waited. God Sustainer, how the man could wait.

"I was so glad when Nothos died," she said, when she could talk again through the tears and snot, though she was still weeping. "I knew I was all screwed up inside, broken, ruined. It was because of the magic. You have to use part of yourself to make it.

"And I never could . . . I never. Not once. It was like. Like with you, before, that first time. It hurt so bad whenever anyone was inside me, sometimes when I only thought maybe someone wanted to be.

"But when he died I figured. I figured. Well! He's dead; spell's gone; I'd be all right. But I'm not. It's always been the same. Always will be, I guess. Still. I can live with it. And maybe me finding that book was a coincidence. But I got what I needed when I prayed for it. I have to be loyal to that. I have to stand by that girl no one else would stand by. So I believe in the God she believed in, and screw anyone who doesn't like it."

She sat up and wiped the tears from her eyes. "So! That's the story of my religious conversion. I hope you enjoyed it."

Morlock had a thoughtful look on his face. "I saw the spell-anchor, I think."

She looked askance at him. "*You* saw it."

"In your talic self. During my vision. It was like the hooks the gods had set in me, at least a little."

"Well. Good for you."

"Aloê, I broke them."

"What?"

"I broke the anchors in introspection."

She thought about this through a silence that was nearly Morlockian in length. "Are you saying you can do the same for me?" she asked finally.

"No. Maybe you can."

⇒⇐

Visionary rapture was slow in coming; she was soaked through with words—words she remembered, words she had said, words she had thought of saying, words. Their logic was hostile to the visionary state.

Morlock fell asleep, but she stayed awake, and listened to the rain, and thought things without words. In the hour before dawn she ascended into vision without thinking about it, and found herself floating some distance above her own body.

Instead of turning her awareness outward to the living world, she turned it inward to her living self. She saw nothing like the anchor that Morlock had described . . . but then he hadn't said much. She summoned memories she normally suppressed: about Cousin Nothos, about the time she had tried to have sex with Navigator Stynsos (the first of many failures, until she learned to not even try, not even care).

The pain lanced through her talic self, and she saw its source, deep within her: like a fishhook, perhaps, but one stuck in an old trout who'd run away with the bait, the hook still in him, the flesh growing around the evil bitter thing until it seemed like part of the fish.

She inserted long fiery fingers of intention into herself, drew the hook from her, willed it out of herself, drove it into nothingness.

The pain was not gone, but it had changed, lost its focus, its bitter corrosive heat. She passed from vision to sleep without ever touching consciousness.

Aloê awoke in midmorning. There was a gray light filtering through the thoroughly damp walls of the shack, and the rain was still drumming its fingers on the roof. Morlock was peering through a break in the wall with a mopey expression on his face.

"Still raining," he said to her somberly. "Looks like it's not stopping soon."

"Well," she said, sitting up. "We may get a bit wet then."

Morlock's face became even more somber, even grim. He nodded.

"Morlock," she said, "you do realize we are going to an island? Islands are surrounded by water on nearly every side. It's sort of a tradition, I think."

He grunted and looked so sad that she had to laugh.

"It'll be all right," she said, patting his hand. "I suppose we should eat before we get started. Have we got any of that dried meat you're so fond of?"

Making

They had reclaimed their cloaks and rolled up their blankets and were leaving the shack semi-ruinous and bereft in the dim day.

"River over there," Morlock said, nodding southward.

"Maybe just runoff from the highlands," she said, listening over the roar of the rain. "Still . . ."

She didn't say it because she didn't have to say it: it might carry them faster than their feet to the Sea of Stones.

They followed the sound until they came to the river. Aloê judged it a magnificent piece of water: broad and pleasingly deep around the middle, with nice sharp banks and a delightful absence of the dimples and foam-streaks that mark underwater obstructions.

There was a stand of those odd thinly tall trees near the shore, and Morlock went to fell a lot of them with Armageddon. Aloê whittled pins for a while, then split the trees into rails and stripped off their bark. At last she started nailing them together into the frame for a canoe.

"What's that?" Morlock asked, as he came over with a load of trees in his arms.

"Frame for a canoe. Enough with the trees already; leave some for the next guy."

"Eh," said Morlock, and dropped the trees.

"Get me the bark off those trunks."

"Why?" said Morlock, sitting down.

"Cover the frame. Keeps the water out, you know."

"Will that work?" Morlock was wearing his skeptical face.

"Yes. Even better if you can do that waterproofy thing."

He could and did, although it took a significant chunk of daylight—longer than building the canoe itself. Maddeningly, he looked as if he were napping, at least until you noticed the slight glow from his closed eyes and the odd crinkling sound from the bark he was transforming.

Aloê borrowed Armageddon and used it to cut two decent slabs of wood for paddles out of a fallen pine tree. She was done, and the rain was done, and the sky in the east was bright and full of broken clouds when Morlock lifted his head, sneezed, and said, "How's that?"

That was brilliant. Not only was the bark resilient and waterproof, but the edges were sealed together somehow.

"Morlock," she said, looking up. "I am never going to travel without you again."

"See that you don't," he said almost smugly, then sneezed again.

They lugged the canoe to the river, loaded their gear and themselves into it, and pushed off from the bank.

The sky above was a broken field of golden clouds streaked with shadowy blue. On their right were the red highlands of Kaen; on their left the misty green mystery of the masterless lands; abruptly blue water all around them.

"Isn't this like heaven?" Aloê called forward to Morlock, sitting in the prow.

"Never been there," said that grumpy young man.

Aloê laughed and skillfully drove the canoe down the river westward through the suddenly glorious day.

❧

They were on the river enough days for Aloê to lose count. They rowed all day and slept in each other's arms at night, but they hadn't been messing around at all since they left Kaen. Aloê didn't want to, because she wanted to so much. If they tried to screw again and it didn't work, if nothing had changed—she didn't want to even think about it.

It hadn't escaped Aloê's notice that Morlock had taken to sleeping with his back to her. She knew that they could be doing other things besides coitus, and she waited for him to suggest it. But apparently he was waiting for her. He was good at waiting, but she was pretty sure she could win at that game.

She was never sure who won, but one night, anyway, the waiting stopped. She woke in the middle of the night from a heated sex-dream and lay panting against Morlock's misshapen spine wishing these things didn't just happen in dreams.

Then she heard herself whispering, "Hey: can you fuck me? Right now, I mean."

She wasn't sure he was even awake—but he was, and required no coaxing. He had her undressed much more quickly than she had him undressed, and faster than she could say *I don't think I need any foreplay this time* he was inside her.

It was always a shock to be entered, to feel herself surrounding something that wasn't herself. She had felt it before and remembered it vividly. The memory was shrouded with pain, though, and the fear of pain.

Even though it was what she had hoped for—maybe because she had hoped for it so long and so uselessly—she was surprised that this time there was no pain at all. In fact there was an odd sensation she had never felt before. As he thrust into her it blazed up: a pleasure as intense as pain, along the inner surface of her vagina, right at the top. It was like when you feel an itch between your shoulders or in the small of your back, and you can't scratch it, and you live with it so long you almost forget about it (but not quite), and then you reach back and scratch it. It was like that, that blazing moment of relief, but it went on and on, and was renewed with every thrust.

"Oh God, that's good," she whispered in his ear. She tried to say it again but only got as far as the first syllable. When she spoke the "oh" it tingled from her neck down to her cunt, so she opened her throat and kept saying it, one long indeterminate vowel, brightening the blaze within her.

Then, too suddenly, it was over.

"What's wrong?" she said, as he stopped moving.

"Um. Nothing. It's just—"

"Oh!" He had come inside her. Her insides were sticky with him; she could feel it oozing out of her. It was sort of disgusting and funny, the way lots of things about sex were disgusting and funny. That was all right. It was just that she had sort of expected to have an orgasm herself.

"That was nice," she said, though, and meant it.

He laughed and drew out of her. Then he reached between her legs and brought her off with his cunning fingers as he gently kissed her all over her face and neck, twisting one of her nipples with exactly the right level of rough gentleness. Soon she was screaming her way to orgasm again—all the way, this time.

"All right," she said gasping, when she could speak again. "That was a little better than nice."

They lay silent in each other's arms for a long time.

"I have a technical question," she said at last.

He made a sort of murmur that was probably intended as an acknowledgement.

"I sort of expected us to come at the same time," she said. "Does that not usually happen?"

"Not to me," he said. He shrugged. "If—"

"No, never mind. Shut up. You're taking it as a criticism, which is all wrong. This is the best thing that ever happened to me that didn't involve a boat somehow."

"Ship?"

"Or a ship. Or swimming."

"If—"

"No, I don't want to hear it. Take yes for an answer. You make love as well as you make other things. Higher my praise cannot go, so stop fishing for compliments, you conceited bastard."

He took her hand and put it on his penis. That startled her enough to change the direction of her thoughts.

"Are you kidding me with that thing?" she said.

"If," he said firmly, "you'd like to try again, we could try again."

Now she made a kind of murmur which was intended as acknowledgement, and they tried again.

This time he had her on her hands and knees, a position that seemed to her excessively undignified, except that it felt stunningly good when he entered her—even better when he reached around and began stroking her clitoris.

It was like the opposite of visionary rapture. Instead of fleeing from the constraints of matter it was like her mind was being pressed down into her body, being consumed by it, until she was one big nerve that throbbed with pleasure.

They didn't come at the same moment, but this time she came first and had the ecstatic sensation of him thrusting into her all the way through her orgasm.

Afterward they lay together, too spent for conversation, not willing to be parted by sleep, kissing each other occasionally, utterly entangled.

She did not say, *I love you*. But that was the first time she felt herself thinking it.

They screwed almost every night until they reached the Sea of Stones. The only exception was a day when they screwed twice during their noonday break.

That day she remarked to Morlock's shoulders, as they paddled downstream through the afternoon light, "Now I see why people are obsessed with sex."

He moved his head from side to side and said, "I guess so. Sex doesn't have to be good to make people crazy, though."

"The voice of experience speaks."

He did not shrug, thank God Avenger. It was a difficult thing to do while keeping a good stroke with a paddle, which was one reason she enjoyed talking to him in the canoe. Unable to shrug or use cryptic hand gestures, he was forced to fall back on words to express himself. Sometimes one could tease whole sentences out of the man.

"Some," he admitted. "Never as much as I wanted. Obviously."

"Why obviously?" she said. "Is it true about men, that they're insatiable about sex?"

"Everyone likes it. Not just men, anyway."

"So?"

"I've rarely had sex with a woman more than once."

"Why not? Fuck them and forget them, is that your motto?"

He looked back incredulously at her. "They find me ugly, Aloê. Once for curiosity, or because they want something. Rarely twice."

Ugly? She supposed he was. But God Avenger. The man was a force of nature.

"Stupid bitches," she opined, and he laughed.

In Morlock's memory, those were the happiest days of his life. Thoughts of them often returned to him later in dark moments of exile and loneliness and the presence of death. He never troubled to count them; he never forgot a single moment of them. But the golden days, whatever their number, ended, and one morning they smelled the clean sharp breeze from the sea biting their faces, and by noon they were rowing out of the mouth of the river into the wide bitter waters of the Sea of Stones.

"And now," Aloê confessed, after they drew their canoe up on the greenish sand of the shoreline, "I have no idea what to do."

Morlock said, "The Talazh Rame is north of here. The heresiarchs who go to the Apotheosis Wheel must have some way to reach it. Let's go and see what it is."

"That's what I was going to say next."

Anyway, that was what they did next.

The Talazh Rame was a ruined road on stone stilts that ran from the Narrow Sea in the west into the Sea of Stones in the east. They saw the tall supporting columns of stone from miles away as they walked northward on the beach. Black broken stones poked out of the green waves like fingers, for perhaps a mile or two into the sea itself.

At the base of a towering stone column on the beach was a relatively humble building of dark wood. Beached beside it was a bireme of ten oars on a side.

"Water taxi?" Aloê asked.

Morlock didn't know what that meant, but guessed it was some sort of ferry, and nodded.

But as they approached the building they came upon a stone marker, inscribed in Kaenish runes. There was a spiderish sort of image and the word *Hÿlohyphäntu*.

"The Woodweaver?" Aloê hazarded a translation.

Morlock nodded. "Looks like a Kaenish godstone." He gestured northward, where another finger of stone accused the sky.

"Something tells me we'll want to avoid this place," Aloê guessed.

Morlock pointed at something farther off: a bluish green cloud on the northern horizon. "Pine trees."

"We can make our own boat. With propellers!"

He nodded. "Not a ship?"

"Shut up!"

They walked around the border of godstones and legged it all the way to the distant stand of trees.

Not distant enough, though: the stand had clearly been visited recently, logs being dragged off in the direction of the Woodweaver's temple or ferry-service or whatever it was. So much was obvious from the stumps in the wood, the marks in the ground.

"We'll have to keep an eye out," Aloê said, following his gaze. "Still: if those dim fish can make boats out of this wood we certainly can."

He nodded.

"But where we're going to sail it: that's another question," she said, asking the question with her distressing beautiful eyes.

"Whatever the Wheel is," he said, "it will present a unique talic distortion."

"One of us will look for it in visionary flight, you mean."

"Yes."

"You talk about distortion. The Wheel might distort the identity of anyone who comes into contact with it. That seems to be what it's for. Finding it while in rapture might be pretty dangerous."

He shrugged. "The alternative?"

"I bet that Woodweaver, or his priest, has a way of finding the Wheel."

"Would they give it to us? Should we trust it if they do?"

"Gleh. All right, do you want to toss a coin for it? Being the lucky person who gets to risk his sanity looking for the Wheel, I mean."

"You're the shipwright. Make the ship. When I'm done looking around, I'll help."

He helped a lot before then, too. He felled pine trees with Armageddon while Aloê painstakingly redrew the sharklike design of her propeller-driven dream. Then he left her to split the trees into planks using her glass staff and some wedges. He returned a half a day later with wooden buckets of pitch he had harvested from fallen pines. Then he bent and cut the planks of pine to Aloê's specifications.

"All right," she said at last. "I can get started while you're in rapture. Maybe finish then, too."

"Hope not," he said. He left the sword with her and lay down to compose himself for vision.

It was a risky practice to send the spirit far from the body in the talic sphere. Distance means nothing to the spirit, but it means something to the body: the more the bond between them is stretched, the more apt it is to break.

Still: this was his choice, for reasons that seemed good. He let his body go and ascended into vision.

The temptation to lurk about Aloê was strong, but the thought of spying on her was repulsive. After all, he might not like what he found. . . .

His mind drifted away from his body and, as it did, became less his mind than a drifting eye, observing the talic world without clear purpose. The sea below/within him was luminous, dense with life of different levels of intention, different intensities of tal. A timeless time passed as he communed with this ocean of light.

Then he saw it. Like a pillar of light standing out from the ocean: an island that seemed made of tal rather than stone. He gazed on/in it with wonder, lost in its intricacy and complexity richer than any mere meaning. The significance of it came to rest slowly into the stretched-out web of his mind. If the Apotheosis Wheel was not here, something else worth knowing about was. With difficulty (intention and execution were so slow! he saw the sun cross the sky twice as he struggled with his thought), he marked the place in the shifting map of the sea, on his own mind, on the mind of the world.

Then he knew he must return to his physical self and his beloved waiting for him on the margin of the sea. He looked down/through the living sea one more time. Fascinatingly, the sea creatures there were arranging themselves in different levels and patterns. The ones with less tal implicit in them were sinking lower; the ones with more tal, brighter in his vision, were rising up, assembling themselves in rank, for all the world as if the sea were the page of a book, with words on it he could read.

And then he saw that it was.

And he saw that the words read, in Dwarvish runes, BROTHER BEWARE.

Suddenly he felt the presence of other eyes in the sky of the talic sphere— a pair of them, grinding on each other like gears, driven by hatred of each other . . . and of him. He felt their particular hatred like a word spelled out in fire, not water. *Ambrosius, we hate him. I hated him first. Liar, liar . . .*

He fell from vision like a stone falling from the sky. Or: the earth was the stone, falling upward to crush him with matter. His mind was lost, wandering among lightning-crowned atoms as big as fists, and his vision was over.

><=

He came to himself, inside himself, and knew something was wrong. His hands were bound and he was lying on a wooden floor. An oily voice was pouring oily words into his ears.

". . . even if your companion never recovers, you alone will make an excellent addition to the crew. As experienced a sailor as yourself must know how important it is to match rowers on a crew. Now I have an oarsman somewhat like you, smaller than average, perhaps, but feisty."

"Please do not tell me," Aloê's voice said, "that you think me feisty."

"But you so self-evidently are! And you won't lose that after you encounter the Weaver. Indeed you will not. Your will remains intact, but unable to affect your actions. It's what makes you a perfect sacrifice to the new god."

"What new god?"

"By the eight legs of Hÿlohyphäntu! I don't know. But there is always a new god. The ascending heresiarch comes down the Talazh Rame from Kaen. He goes to old Azh in the boat the Weaver makes. And, if he returns, he comes as a new god, and wends his way back up the Talazh Rame. That is the way it always has been, since Kaen first had gods, or so I suppose."

Morlock opened his eyes. Aloê was sitting, bound hand and foot, looking straight at him. Standing over her was a Kaenish priest. His velvet robe was covered with silver webwork, and his low-crowned priest-hat sprouted eight legs like a spider. His left hand held a knot of gray silken threads. There were seven threads altogether. Each thread went to the neck of a man standing nearby, staring emptily at nothing. The priest's other hand held a thorny staff topped with a unicorn horn, looking oddly like the tusk of some otherworldly sea-creature.

"Welcome back," Aloê said, smiling at him. "Sorry about this. They caught me sleeping."

"I was gone more than a day."

"You were gone a month, Morlock."

"I'm sorry."

"Was it worth it? Did you learn anything?"

"Yes."

"Don't be sorry, then. This gentleman, who does not give his name, is the sole priest of Hÿlohyphäntu, the Woodweaver."

"And should I give my name to the twain who have been wreaking havoc all across the wrinkled face of Kaen? I think not. Your names I know. My name you will never know."

"This cautious gentleman proposes to toss us to his god, who will enslave us by stinging us in the spine. Then we will be human sacrifices for someone who has ascended the Apotheosis Wheel. Do I have the gist of it, oh man-of-mystery?"

"Yes!" cried the shaven priest. "Although," he added, to Morlock, "I think you will not go to Hÿlohyphäntu. There is a rumor that the Ambrosii are much-sought-after by certain persons of power, and certain other persons may acquire certain powers by certain means which I'm afraid—"

The priest went on for a while without saying anything of content. Morlock glanced around the chamber. One wall was an iron screen painted with runic imprecations and containment spells. Beyond it lay the gleaming hulk of a gigantic spider: the avatar of Hÿlohyphäntu, clearly. Its eight eyes watched the priest without ceasing, while its legs worked incessantly on long unvarnished planks, fitting them together into the side of a half-built galley. The claws at the end of its legs were articulated and moved about their work as deftly as skilled fingers. The legs themselves were bound with chains that glittered with silver-inscribed talismanic symbols. They allowed the god some freedom of movement, but not overmuch.

A god Hÿlohyphäntu might technically be. But it was clearly a captive as well. Was the priest its chief worshipper, or its jailor? Perhaps there was no difference.

Also of interest: mounted on the wall were Morlock's glass sword and Aloê's glass staff.

"Got the picture?" Aloê said, when he looked back at her.

"Think so," Morlock said.

"I tried to do it, but apparently the thing is keyed to your voice."

"More a specific intention coded into the word. I'll show you."

"Thanks."

"It's nothing."

"It must be me you think is nothing," the priest raged at them. "I have been explaining certain things which certain people might—"

"Noddegamra," Morlock said conversationally, exercising a specific intent.

The glass sword fell from the wall, raining down in crystalline shards to the floor.

The priest turned to gape at it.

"Armageddon," said Morlock, and the shards flew to his hand, re-forming into a sword in midair.

Morlock leapt to his feet and, wielding the sword two-handed, slashed the bonds at Aloê's hands and feet.

She jumped up, and her nimble fingers undid his bonds in an instant. "Let's wreak some havoc!" she shouted in his face.

Now the spider-priest had recovered from his shock and stood back toward the iron screen and his captive god. The seven silk-bound men stood forward to attack. Their eyes were still empty, but they held their hammers and saws like weapons.

Aloê dodged behind him to grab her staff from the wall. She spun it to build up impulse in the well, and laughed as she saw the spider-priest cower away from her against the iron screen.

Hÿlohyphäntu had left off shipbuilding and was now hovering close to its side of the screen. It lifted a bristly leg . . . And there was something gray and silken across the clawed hand that served the spider-god as a foot.

But the bristly hair of the spidery leg brushed through the screen and warned the priest of his god's motions. Now the priest scuttled away from the screen, and three of the captive men moved to stand between the priest and the screen. The caged god hissed in frustrated rage.

"Aloê!" Morlock began.

"Already there," she said, and struck the corner of the iron screen with the glass staff.

The iron didn't break but it bent, distorting several of the symbols.

"You fool!" the priest screamed. "He'll eat all our souls!"

"As long as he starts with yours, Smÿlgondru," Aloê sang back.

Aghast the priest groaned, "How did you know my secret name?"

"It's embroidered on the underbrim of your hat, you cunning beast."

Hÿlohyphäntu was tearing at the corner of the iron screen with five of his clawed hand-feet. Aloê recklessly inserted her staff into the small gap and forced it to open wider.

She was rewarded by the spider-god extruding a clawed finger-toe and striking at her.

She easily dodged the claw, but leapt back.

Hÿlohyphäntu screamed and threw the iron screen across the long room.

The freed god leapt at the closest person, who was still Aloê, coolly spinning her staff to build an impulse charge. Morlock ran to stand beside her.

"Door's over there, honey," she remarked.

"Wasn't sure *you* knew."

The spider-god reached out at them with a clawed hand-foot each.

"Your jailor, Smÿlgondru, is over there, Hÿlohyphäntu," Morlock remarked conversationally.

The spider-god hesitated, stood motionless for a moment, its talismanic chains clanking.

Morlock and Aloê began to edge away.

Hÿlohyphäntu noticed and lumbered forward.

The vocates turned and fled toward the temple-prison door. The spider-god, weighted down with talismans, was too slow to catch them, and his avatar was too big to pass through the doorway.

As they fled into the thin frosty moonlight of a late autumn evening, the spider-god had turned back into the temple-prison and was advancing on his sobbing priest.

"They'll be after us soon," Aloê said as they ran. "Where to?"

"How near being done is the boat?"

"It *was* done," Aloê cried in despair. "But they burnt it when they captured us. The priest had his bound men tossing torches right into it!"

Morlock wasn't sure what she was driving at and said, "Let's go there."

"I guess you're right. Maybe there's something we can salvage."

They ran on steadily, not frantically, a pace they could maintain all the way to the boat site.

The boat was resting on the beach, bright and unbroken in the moons' blue light.

"It looks all right," Aloê gasped, as they drew to a halt on the sand. "But I saw them throwing torches in it." She turned to Morlock and said suspiciously, "Did you do something to it?"

"I don't understand," Morlock said. "Why would anyone make a boat that could be burned?"

"It's made of wood! It's sealed with pitch! They burn, Morlock."

"That's why I dephlogistonated them."

"Dephlog— What does that mean?"

"They won't burn."

"Champion Morlock!"

Morlock couldn't tell if Aloê was being sarcastic or not. Sarcasm or enthusiasm seemed equally misplaced, but it was clear that he had much to learn about the art of shipmaking.

"Are there provisions onboard?"

"Only water, unless they drained it. Why—? Oh."

The drumming of feet in the night behind them was the answer to Aloê's unfinished question.

"Let's push her off and get out of here," Aloê said.

They forced the light craft off the sand, and then Aloê hopped lightly from the water to the deck. She turned noncommittally to help Morlock up after her.

"What's her name?" Morlock asked. He'd heard it was bad luck to travel at sea in an unnamed craft. His sea voyages had been unfortunate enough that he wanted every protection possible.

"She's the *Fnarklo*," Aloê said, a little defiantly.

"Good. Good."

"You really think so?"

"Yes."

Morlock knew little about ships, but it was easy enough to spot the two sets of pedals for working the propeller drive.

Aloê said, "I attached impulse wells to the pedals and charged them up. I based the wells on the ones you put in my staff."

"Good. Let's go."

Each took a bench—Aloê the one by the steering arc—and they began to pedal. The *Fnarklo* was more than a bowshot from shore before the hulking spider-god and his crew of minions appeared behind them.

Aloê laughed, looking back over her shoulder. "Did you see?" she shouted to Morlock.

Morlock had seen that there were now eight naked minions on strings, one of them plump and hairless, and that the spider-god now held the strings.

"Yes," he said. "Poor old Smÿlgondru."

"To hell with poor old Smÿlgondru."

"Yes. Exactly."

"Do you know which way we're supposed to be going, by the way? A sea is a very large piece of water."

"Yes." Morlock closed his eyes. "Over in that direction."

"What? Port or starboard? How many points?"

"What?"

"Oh, God Sustainer save us. I suppose you should steer, Morlock. Don't run us into any submerged rocks, please."

"If they're submerged, how will I know where they are?"

"Look at the surface of the water. Right? Are we speaking the same language?"

Morlock shrugged.

"I can hear you shrugging, there."

"You steer. It is east some considerable way. We can be more precise, and you can teach me to steer, in the morning light."

"Fine. As long as you know where the Apotheosis Wheel is."

"If that is not the thing I saw, what I saw was at least equally interesting."

"God Avenger look away from us. What a disaster this is going to be. Why didn't I grab some of those map-thingies from the temple when I grabbed my staff? They were right by me on a shelf!"

"Why didn't you?"

"I was in a hurry. The spider-god was after me."

CHAPTER EIGHTEEN

Old Azh Above

The days were cold and bright, and the breeze was delightfully irrelevant to where they were going. Aloê loved the salt spray of the Sea of Stones, indefinably different from the world-ocean she knew so well. They had only uncooked fish to eat, caught from over the side, but she didn't mind raw fish. She loved the wooden *Fnarklo* almost as much as she had loved the canine original, but was always thinking of ways to improve the cunningly made little boat. She occasionally discussed them with Morlock, when he wasn't puking over the side.

That was the only fly in her ointment, but it was a pretty damn big fly. Morlock was sicker than he had been on *Flayer*. That made sense: the motion was choppier in the smaller craft. They devised a sea-anchor that absorbed wave impulses—powering the impulse wells and also keeping the ship steadier at night. But she was appalled by how horrible this wonderful experience was for Morlock—shocked by how it never seemed to get better.

He never complained, though. She compared his patience and endurance to every man she had known, even every woman, and couldn't think of anyone who could match him. Somehow he was the best even when he was at his worst.

One night the wind got a little lively and started throwing the waves and the boat around, and Morlock was especially miserable. The next morning he looked like a drowned man, only not so peaceful: his red eyes ringed by dark circles.

"I love you, you know," she said to him then, because she could not refrain from saying it any longer.

"I didn't know." He looked at her, as if worried she was mocking him, was apparently reassured by what he saw. *"That passed, and so may this,"* he quoted, apparently trying to give her some kind of hope, as if she'd confessed to him that she had some fatal disease.

"Don't think so," she said, brisker than the wind. "It seems to be permanent."

"Love you too."

"I know, partner. I've known since you were saying dumb things to me on that cliffside."

"Eh."

"And every time you say that."

Despite its name, the sea was wonderfully free from navigational hazards, also, so Morlock took the steering arc. Aloê felt pretty confident they weren't going to hit anything that would put a hole in *Fnarklo*. And on the fifth day, they saw the island that Morlock had seen in his visionary journey: a tall spiralled black tooth on the eastern horizon.

"You were right," she said soberly, watching the sun set behind it. "Whether it's the place we're looking for or not, it's worth a visit."

"I thought it would be farther east," Morlock said doubtfully.

"Telling distances at sea is a tricky business," Aloê assured him, "even when you're inside your own skull."

They didn't approach any closer that night: Aloê was worried there might be shoals near the island.

In the morning, the island was nearer than ever . . . and farther to the north. The island had at least three distinct points, and it stood at a dramatically different angle to the sun's path than it had last night.

Morlock looked at the island, the boat, the sky, the sea. Then he looked at Aloê.

She was drawing the sunline with her eye: from dawnpoint in the west to setpoint in the east.

"No, you're not crazy," she said. "I think the island moved more than we did."

"Odd."

"You are a master of all the arts, Morlock, but especially understatement."

They made toward the island and circumnavigated it. The high cliff wall was open at only one point, and they landed there, on a beach of black sand and stones.

And bones. The beach was littered with dark decaying human bones.

WELCOME TO OLD AZH was scraped in wedgelike Kaenish letters on the sheer face of the cliff nearby.

"Well, the natives are friendly," said Aloê, gesturing at the grinning skulls.

"Don't think they're natives," Morlock said. "Kaeniar, maybe."

"You can tell that from the bones—? Oh. You're thinking of the boat crews from Hÿlohyphäntu's temple. That makes sense. What happens to the boats?"

Morlock waved at the wet horizon.

"Oh. The island drifts and leaves the empty boats behind it."

"Yes."

"Or the gods can handle a boat without human help."

"Perhaps."

"I feel like I do all the work in our conversations, Morlock."

"Work is good for you."

"Then—no, never mind right now. But we're not done with this. Shall we go on into the island?"

Morlock nodded. They went side by side, past the bones into the high narrow notch on the cliff wall. They came upon some stairs and climbed them to the top of the island.

There they found a citadel of black stone: narrow streets, with narrow high buildings clustering around a central plaza of unwalled red-pillared temples or assembly halls.

There were no people—not even any bodies, not even a mummy or a statue. There was nothing to indicate anyone had ever lived in the high empty city atop the island. If so, it was so long ago that even their ghosts were dead.

"I feel," Aloê said, after they had been walking through the cold empty shadows for hours, "that we're going to come into a room where the only thing is a bell on a wire and a sign that says, 'Don't ring the bell.' But we won't be able to read it, so we'll ring the bell and some giant stone walrus will come out and eat us the way it ate everyone else. And then it'll go back to sleep and wait for the next interloper. Is that how you feel?"

Morlock thought it over and said. "Not the walrus."

"What, then?"

Morlock led her back to the stairway. He went down on one knee and tapped the topmost stair. "This is worn by weather, not feet. Have hundreds, have thousands of heresiarchs trod these stones over the ages?"

"You obviously don't think so. This entire city is a distraction?"

"Maybe people lived here once. But what we seek is not here."

She looked at him, his ragged dark clothes stained by sweat and sea salt, the twist in his torso emphasized by the angle he was holding himself at, the careless grace with which he moved that powerful misshapen body, his pale unbeautiful face beautifully lit with intelligence, his clever fingers gently touching the dry stone of the stair as if it were his lover's skin.

She was his lover. Why wasn't he touching her skin like that?

She took him down like a lioness taking a deer.

"Um," he said as they went tumbling around the empty stone walkway.

"Enough of your fancy talk. You realize I was alone for a month, working on that boat, never having sex at all?" This was not strictly true, since she had masturbated herself to sleep every night, but it was true enough for argument's sake. "I let you off the hook while we were aboard *Fnarklo*; you were so obviously unwell. But you're obviously feeling better now. So: service me, champion. Fill me with your burning seed. Put your hands on me at least, damn it!"

He already was, disentangling her from her clothes with eager reverent skill, like a priest unwrapping some brand-new holy relic fresh from the relic-maker. She almost always tore some of his when they undressed each other, but she was as frantic to see and feel his body as he was hers.

"This is your religion, you know," she whispered in his ear.

He drew back his face to look at her. "Sex? Like the Purple Patriarchy?"

"No, you lout. Love."

"Oh." He thought about it. "A god that suffers like love, heals like love, forgives like love, becomes angry and jealous like love? Maybe—"

"Oh, shut up for once!" she shouted, and greedily covered his open mouth with hers.

They coupled twice in the lifeless fraud of the empty city, and he brought her off twice more with his hands. They lay together on the stones for a time, basking in each other. On impulse, Aloê pushed herself into the visionary state, and Morlock (sensing this) ascended with her. Then for a timeless time their talic selves were as entangled as their limbs: coppery fire transfixed with black-and-white crystalline flames, black-and-white branches blazing with burning veins of reddish gold.

The vision faded, but the sense of closeness, of contact, did not.

"In some places we'd be married now," she said sleepily.

"Um. Words for witnesses." In his taciturn way, Morlock was reminding her of the binding feature of a marriage ceremony, in most parts of the Wardlands: someone to witness the commitment, whatever form it took.

"Yes," she agreed. "Yes, I suppose so. We should look to that when we get back home."

He writhed like someone in physical pain. "If you want to," he said at last. "Mention it to me again when we get there."

"Not if you don't want to, of course."

"Of course I want to," he whispered. "But you will have . . ."

". . . options? So will you, champion. No, listen, I've ridden your beast many times now, and you can't tell me you never got a request for seconds."

"Not never. Rarely."

"The rare ones are the good ones. Or am I wrong about that?"

"No." He touched her hair reverently, reverently. "No."

"The idea of being with anyone other than you makes me sick. Didn't you see that in me?"

"Wasn't looking for it."

"Look for it next time we're in rapport. Or the time after that; we'll have many times together. Our whole lives. I feel it. Do you want to cast some sort of mantia to see if I'm right?"

"No. I never look at the future about something that matters to me."

"Why not?"

"Looking at the future changes it. I have you now. I have you now. That's what matters to me. It will always matter to me that I had you now."

"Then!" she whispered, and (because he was obviously ready) she threw her leg over him, and straddled him, and mounted him. "Who has who?" she asked, gasping. It was a perfectly reasonable question to which he did not respond, at least not with words.

Afterward, she was cold among the stones and the long shadows of the afternoon, and they put their clothes back on.

Speaking no words and needing none, they went back down to the narrow bone-thick beach, where a set of unpleasant surprises awaited them.

There was a new set of bodies on the beach: ten fresh ones, newly slaughtered with a single slice each across the neck. They were naked, and they seemed to have done the deed themselves. Anyway, there was a bloody razor-sharp clamshell in the right hand of each corpse.

One of the corpses was plump and hairless as a baby bathed in its own blood: Smÿlgondru, paying the penalty for angering his spidery god.

Near the narrow beach, half-sunk in the bitter green-gray water, was the wreckage of the galley that had brought the crew (and, presumably, their would-be god) to Old Azh. They had wrecked the ship before killing themselves at his command, it seemed.

But that wasn't the worst of it. The worst was this: they had wrecked the *Fnarklo*, too: smashed it to bits on the rocky beach.

"Damn it!" Aloê said, fighting back tears. All those days of work wasted, and now they were stranded here if they couldn't repair the boat. But that wasn't really it. She had loved that crazy little boat, and now they had killed *Fnarklo*—again.

Morlock was looking all about. She followed his wandering gaze, and then she said aloud what they both were thinking, "Where did he go? Is there a door in the cliff wall we didn't see?"

"Maybe." Morlock shrugged.

While he looked at the stone, she looked at the sea and she shouted, "No! It's below the water! It must be."

"A cave below the water?" Morlock said doubtfully.

"Or one whose entrance is. It makes sense, Morlock. You saw an island alive with life and talic force. It's not because of that empty citadel up there: it must be underneath. I'd better go have a look."

Morlock's expression grew even more doubtful, and she continued, "No arguments, Morlock. If some aged heresiarch made the swim, no doubt you could, too. But he knew where he was going, and we don't."

Morlock acknowledged the force of reason by opening both his hands. "I'll fish wood out of the water," he said. "No matter what happens, we'll need a boat to leave the isle."

"Right!" she said, although he was half-wrong about that. He needed a boat. In a pinch, she could swim, but it would be a very unpleasant pinch to swim all the way to shore.

She plunged into the water without further consultation, and without disrobing or disarming. She did not propose to meet this heresiarch (or a god fresh from the Apotheosis Wheel), half-naked and weaponless.

In the event, the cave was obvious as soon as her head was under the water: a bright mouth opening in the sheer side of the under-island. She swam straight into it, and before she knew it she was surfacing in bright breathable air.

As her eyes adjusted to the light she considered swimming back to fetch Morlock. But she decided not to, in the end: she would at least look around a bit first.

It was a decision with significant consequences, and her mind often returned to it later. But she never could decide if she'd made a good choice or a bad one.

CHAPTER NINETEEN

Old Azh Below

There was a bright bland beach of yellow sand edging the dry interior of the undersea cave. Aloê lifted herself onto it and immediately found herself facing a solemn-faced denizen of the place. He sat, naked but clothed with an enormous sense of dignity, with his hand upon his chin. His silken hair, as white as snow, lay in loose curls across his scalp. His eyes were very strange: a white pupil, inside a white iris, inside a white cornea. The colorless eyes looked out of a colorless face—whiter even than Morlock's fish-belly whiteness. His skin was almost translucent in its paleness, but apart from that he was extremely handsome, almost inhumanly handsome.

She was not feeling especially dignified herself, standing there dripping seawater (and, she abruptly realized, semen: she could feel a strand of it crawling jellylike down her thigh).

"I'm sorry if I am intruding," she said in Kaenish. Her thought was that if Kaenish heresiarchs came this way to become gods, the locals might speak some Kaenish. Or, of course, the heresiarchs might learn a little of the local tongue—enough to get by.

Apparently that was the case, because the man just looked at her and said nothing. The inhuman dignity of his face never changed, even to acknowledge her presence. If he had not moved his head slightly to follow her movement, she wouldn't have been sure he even saw her: his white-in-white-in-white eyes were hard to follow—empty of emotion, but seeming full of ageless wisdom.

They stood, golden eyes clashing against ivory, for a long moment. Then a kind of joyous barking and howling rose up in the cave beyond.

The ivory man's face finally changed, expressing a transcendent wonder and joy. He said something like, "Ooof!" or maybe even, "Woof!" and tumbled over on the sand. He ran off on all fours, eagerly wailing in answer to the voices beyond, his sandy genitalia flopping in the air between his widespread legs.

"I seem to have misread the situation," Aloê remarked to the empty beach, and followed the tracks of the beast she had mistaken for a person.

She walked up the beach into a kind of city. The buildings were built of bright translucent stone and the cave roof far above was gently, pleasingly luminous. Most of the inhabitants, pale people-like beasts like the one she had met on the beach, seemed to be in the street, yipping and howling with excitement. They were following a kind of domed vehicle or car, moving without an animal to draw it. Periodically the vehicle would pause and excrete, from several pipes in its side, a long gleaming chunk of wobbly red jelly. The people-beasts fell on them with great joy, pressing their faces into the gleaming red surface to gobble it up.

They were very polite, though. There was room for three or four people-beasts to eat at every rope of jelly, and they always shared. There was no fighting. Anyone who didn't get a chance at the currently extruded jelly followed the vehicle, yapping and howling happily, as it moved on and excreted more jelly farther down the street. Aloê briefly wondered whether another vehicle came along later to spray down the streets, as in A Thousand Towers. But then she saw there was no need to clean up the leavings. There were no leavings. The people-beasts licked the very stones of the street clean of the jelly, and then carried on cleaning the jelly off each other with their tongues. The licking frequently became sexual, and many people-beasts were coupling in the streets still gleaming with their saliva.

Aloê was in no position to sneer, since she had recently been screwing in the street herself. But she did wonder whether sex always looked as absurd to an impartial observer as these wildly coupling beasts did to her.

Others, who were not having sex or had finished having sex, lay around in the street making grunts at each other that might have been conversation.

Only one figure, she saw as she carefully picked her way across the beast-crowded paving stones, stood apart from the others. He sat on a stone, wearing a short shirtlike robe, watching her approach with a lively interest in his warm gray eyes. Those eyes reminded her of Morlock, as did his dark unruly hair and long clever fingers. Otherwise he looked something like Naevros—without Naevros' smiling catlike smugness.

"Welcome," he said to her in Wardic. "Are you not terrified by the Keepers of the Wheel?"

"Is that who they are?"

"Once. Long ago."

"What happened to them?"

"Some of them ascended to the Apotheosis Wheel and became gods or were destroyed. The rest, less ambitious, and more restful in their nature, gave themselves up to physical pleasure. Gods can't know that, you know—to eat, to drink, to swim, to fuck—all these are alien to their nature. They are not sustained by matter and can take no pleasure in it."

"Then why be a god?"

"Immortality. Many of those who come here feel their bodies failing. They fear death, and prefer to be gods. The Wheel kills most of those."

"Oh? The Wheel is not reliable, then?"

"It is perfectly reliable. It never lets someone be a god who is unworthy of godhood, and it assigns each aspirant a godhood worthy of his nature—or her nature."

"Who's to judge all that?"

"The Wheel."

"Do all gods come from the Wheel?"

"I don't know."

"Did Torlan and Zahkaar come from the Wheel?"

"I don't know who they are."

"You may know them as the Masked Powers—the Two Powers—as Fate and Chaos?"

"I don't know who they are."

She almost asked about God Creator, Sustainer and Avenger, but thought better of it. It wasn't relevant to her current business, and she had no reason to believe this fellow anyway. The fact that she felt she could trust him she discounted: it was another reason to suspect him, really.

The stranger smiled with Naevros' lips. "You are wise," he said.

"Thanks."

"Too wise to consign yourself to the Wheel. Consider the considerable loss, and the dubious gain. If you want power, you can rule here with me, or even over me, if you prefer. You could raise these sad beasts back to the level of people by your example and teaching. And I could give you pleasure. Somehow I know we would be right for each other."

She looked at him coldly. "Yes, you seem especially designed to please me. Of course, you must tailor yourself to the wishes of every aspirant. What do you really look like?"

"You would not wish to see it."

"But I do wish to see it."

The stranger gave a very Morlockian shrug and vanished. In its place was a bulbous, vaguely manlike thing formed from a transparent jelly. It looked like the food jelly, except it was colorless and glowed slightly. There was a hollow foggy place in the middle of its head, and from that a voice came forth—no longer much like Morlock's or Naevros'. "This is as much of my true self as can be seen with your eyes."

"Then there is more of you."

"Much more, in the talic realm. I pervade the island."

"Do many people take you up on your offer of sex and power?"

"Some."

"What happens to them?"

"They join with these." The gleaming arm with no hand gestured carelessly at the people-beasts.

"Then you are the true Keeper of the Wheel."

"The truth is as I told you. But the Keepers made me so that they might give themselves over to pleasure, and become what you have seen, or ascend to the Wheel and become gods, in which case they left this place to meet their destiny."

"Then you are the true Keeper of the Wheel."

It bowed its gleaming, fog-holed head. "It is not part of my instructions to argue with you."

"Why do you answer my questions? Are you bored here?"

It paused before answering. "I answer your questions, because I am instructed to do so: to ward off those who can be tempted from godhood, and lead those who cannot be tempted to the Wheel. I perceive that you will go there now."

"In a moment. I am curious. Why do you obey these things who are no longer people? Why not leave this place?"

It paused again and said, "I *am* this place. I cannot leave it. And there is another thing."

"Yes?"

"I abide by my instructions in addressing all who come in their own language. The problem here is in your language. I do not see that it has the ability to refer to such as me. It constrains me to refer to myself as a *self*. But in truth, I am not a being who carries out instructions. I am, in fact, merely the instructions of the Keepers, woven into the weft of a talic structure."

"You don't choose. You don't think."

"I don't think so, no."

"All right, then. Take me to the Wheel."

The jelly-thing stood and walked straight through the crowd of beast-people as if they weren't there. They made way for it without fear, without even seeming to notice it or Aloê.

"Do you keep them alive?" Aloê asked. "Do you run the food-cars, or whatever they are?"

"Yes, and provide fresh water, and healing, and all that they need."

"Why?"

"I am instructed to do so. Also, their tal is necessary to the maintenance of this place."

"This place. That's you."

"Yes."

"So you do it for yourself."

"I might, if I were a self."

"Maybe you are and you don't know it. Maybe selfhood can grow from the circumstances you find yourself in."

"Or maybe I am *not* a self, and *you* do not know it. I was instructed to act as a self, to deceive those who could be deceived."

"What if you yourself were deceived? That would prove there was someone there inside you, a self who could be tricked."

"My instructions tell me to avoid such paradoxes. We are here."

The jelly-thing stood still and gestured at a pit in the icelike stone of the street. There was a stair descending in a long spiral down the hole into darkness.

"Descend to ascend," it said. "Good-bye."

Aloê thought for a moment. It might be she had learned as much as she could, that there was no point in descending. She had no thought of actually ascending the Apotheosis Wheel, but it might be dangerous even to be near it.

Still! There was knowledge here about how gods were made. Perhaps there was some way to use that knowledge to ward off angry gods, or even unmake them. Perhaps Torlan and Zahkaar had come from this god-factory; perhaps not. That didn't matter. What mattered was the knowledge, and she wouldn't get it here contemplating her navel.

"Good-bye," she said to her guide, and took the long spiralling stair downward.

The stones darkened as she descended, from the crystalline clear of the street paving to ebony black at the stair's end.

At the bottom of the stair was an empty room. Opposite the stair was an arch, and through the arch was the Apotheosis Wheel.

It was in use.

As she stepped through the archway she was struck by a wave of sound and heat and stench and something else—a nonphysical shuddering like flame rippling through her: talic distortions, strong enough to echo in her flesh.

The sensations were strong enough to knock her down, but she struggled to her feet again and strove to keep order in her mind and body so that she could observe what was happening.

The Wheel was enormous, almost filling the great graystone chamber that contained it. It was golden, with many spokes, bright and, it seemed, hot. In the center, where the axis was, lay a bound form that screamed and screamed as the Wheel spun. The heat of the Wheel seemed to be cooking or burning the figure like a webwork griddle cooking a sausage. The figure was hard to see clearly, shrinking to mouselike smallness, billowing out under its own smoke like a storm cloud of indefinite shape.

Here was the former heresiarch, aspirant god, who had killed his oarsmen as a first sacrifice to himself. Was the Wheel killing him or making him into a god? Maybe the processes included each other, or at least overlapped.

She walked around the Wheel, fascinated in all its blurry details. There was a long basketlike object along the wall in the back of the chamber. She was tempted to investigate it, but didn't want to interrupt the process of the Wheel—or be drawn into it, either. She might be able to ask the newborn god after it descended from the Wheel, if it ever did, and if it wasn't so hungry for worship that she didn't have to fight it to retain her selfhood.

The Wheel began to slow. She turned from the basket thing to look at the wheel. The being at the center was still indefinite, cloudlike, but somehow still within the blinding golden motion of the Wheel. She thought about arming herself, but decided not to: she would have a better chance at friendly contact without her staff in her hand, she thought.

There was a sniffling sound behind her.

She turned back to the basket thing.

It had raised up from its wickerwork body a tympanum of wet gleaming flesh. A mouthlike opening appeared in the tympanum as she watched and drew air through it: that was the sniffing sound.

The tympanum was facing her—looking at her, it seemed, or at least sniffing at her.

She reached over her shoulder for her staff.

The basket-thing unfolded arms and legs and leapt to its feet.

She got in one strike on the creature's outstretched right arm. But its left arm struck her on the side of the head and she fell to the ground. As she lost consciousness, she saw the basket-thing's chest open up like a mouth. Inside it was a body-shaped cavity. Darkness swept over her before she saw more.

><<

Morlock was gathering bones on the beach in the red light of evening. He didn't think there was enough undamaged wood to make a two-person boat, and so his thinking had turned along different lines. In his mind he had sketched out a design for a boat with a small hull, and bony rails or skis on which the craft would ride, skimming along the surface of the water like a skipped stone. (Swimming Morlock avoided whenever he could, but he had skipped many a stone in his time.)

Of course, the speed of the craft would have to be very high for the skis to work, but Morlock had some ideas about that.

At the moment he was chiefly seeking shoulder blades from the bleached bones on the sacrificial beach. Many of these had moldered away over the ages, but some were still in usable condition, and Morlock had a fair pile of them before him when his world was completely overturned.

A beast made of wickerwork vaulted like a porpoise from the sea in front of him. At the top of its arc, it unfolded wings from beneath it and began to fly away.

As it went, he saw through the basket-surface that it held a prisoner within: Aloê, her dark face slack in unconsciousness, but her arms bound by wickery bonds. Her hand still held the glass staff he had made for her.

The wicker-beast flew eastward, straight into the red eye of the setting sun.

Fear, and the rage born of fear, threatened to toppled Morlock's mind: for a time his rage was redder than the sun. He clenched his shaking hands, unclenched them, clenched them again.

He fought the rage like an enemy, threw it from him like a slug or a parasite trying to drain his blood.

There was no time for this. He must go after her. Either she was alive, in which case he could help her, or she was dead, in which case he would have his vengeance. In either case, he must go after her.

The shaking in his hands receded. He went back to his task. And, bone by grim bone, the boat began to take shape as the sun set and the stars wheeled above.

PART FIVE

A MASQUE OF POWERS

What is man, that thou art mindful of him?
or the son of man, that thou visitest him?

—Psalm 8

CHAPTER TWENTY

The Sisters

Aloê woke to an aching head and the blissful knowledge that she was at sea again. She could hear creaking (like ropes, sort of); she felt and smelt the salt breeze of the Sea of Stones.

Blissful enough simply to be alive, she realized, retracing the steps of her memory. She was captive of the wicker-beast, or whatever it was: she could feel the bonds on her limbs. But she could also feel the comforting smoothness of her glass staff in her right hand. She was alive and at sea, and still armed. How bad could it be?

She opened her eyes and found out.

Far, far, below her, moonlight glittered on the rough surface of the waves. She was not exactly *at* sea. She was many hundred feet above it.

"Ugh," she said, feeling vertigo. A stinging, stinking fluid worked its way up her gullet and tried to force its way out of her.

She spat and cursed and kept herself from vomiting. Not that vomiting was so bad. But this was a bit of control she could have when almost everything happening to her was out of her power.

To distract herself, she tried to think about what she knew. She did not know if Morlock knew she had been taken, so she could not count on some crazed Ambrosian rescue mission. No doubt he would try to find her, but it wouldn't be easy for him. She was on her own.

The rough water below her told her they were not far from shore. The fact that she was not dead told her that the wicker-beast (or whoever had sent it) didn't want her killed, at least yet. She would have preferred to do something, but sometimes effective action requires one to wait. She waited, and watched.

The sun rose abruptly, transforming the world with light. She gasped at the green-blue gilded water below, as she had never seen it. There were shadows deep within it: sea creatures. How enormous they must be if she could see them from this distance. Or maybe it was just their shadows she saw, distorted by the angle of the sun. How she longed to dive into those waters and find out the truth of it.

But she was bound just as firmly as before. If she fell from this height, it wouldn't matter whether it was water or stones awaiting her below; she would die either way.

She waited, and watched.

They came to the long muddy margin of the sea; the green lips of the land bristled with reeds and wetland trees, hardly a beach to be seen.

The basket-beast was descending a little; they were closer to the green-brown land than they had been to the sea. Aloê realized anew how terribly fast the basket-beast was flying. If it continued its descent (and it *was* continuing its descent) and if they crashed into the ground, she would be killed without question in a most horrible way. That was stupid, of course. Whoever had sent the basket-beast had not done so to kill her in such an elaborate way. Unless they were mad. Or the basket-beast was mad . . .

She fought against the fear creeping through her. There was no point to it, even if everything she feared was true. If these were the last few moments of her life she would use them like a person, not blubbering or wailing. She waited and watched.

The land below was strangely empty. It didn't seem infertile; there were the marks of roads, and they passed over at least two cities. But the roads were broken by wild greenery and unused; the cities were smokeless and lifeless. If people could live here, and had lived here, why didn't they still live here?

She thought the wickerwork beast was slowing at last, straining the wickery cables it used as muscles to turn its wings as brakes against the air. Aloê watched as well as she could, from her bound perspective: she had designed many a ship, but not for the air; it would be an interesting challenge to fashion an airship, and she used thoughts of this as a distraction from the fear that she was about to be smashed into the ground. The sense of foreboding could not be escaped, but increasingly it didn't seem to be in her but around her—part of the air they were flying through or the land they were passing over.

The basket-beast began a long spiral downward. Aloê had the opportunity to see their destination long before they actually arrived. It was like the barn or outbuilding of a farm, but there was no farm nearby; the building was in the middle of a clearing deep in a forest.

The wicker-beast landed, a little roughly but not hard enough to kill anyone. It wrapped its wings around its midsection again, effectively blinding Aloê. It lumbered for a few moments—evidently into the building, from the change in light—and plonked itself down against a wall. The bonds restricting Aloê loosened and slid away into the wickerwork, and the basket confining her stretched out enough for her to lie down, but the roof was just high enough to allow her to sit up, not stand.

Aloê couldn't watch anymore, so she just waited.

Eventually a girl's voice said in Wardic, "So you're here at last."

"Are you talking to me," Aloê asked, in the same language, "or this motile basket here?"

A long pause. The girl said, "Who or what are you?"

"I am Aloê Oaij, Vocate to the Graith of Guardians. And you?"

"I don't get it," the girl complained. "I don't get this at all. Do you mind giving me a little more detail?"

"Not if you tell me who you are."

"Because I really expected you to be Morlock Ambrosius, if you know who that is."

"Slightly. Who are you, again?"

"As far as I know, I don't have any sister named Aloê. He is a randy dog; we all know that. But until my mother got pregnant he was under a self-set infertility spell. I wonder if—"

"Who are you?"

"Who do you think?"

"Do you always answer a question with a question?"

"What do you mean, 'Do I always answer a question with a question?'?"

"Look, girl, if you want to talk to yourself, that's fine with me. If you want to talk to me and have me answer, you'd better tell me who you are."

Silence. Then, grudgingly, the girl said, "My name is Ambrosia Viviana."

"Oh. Any relation to Merlin Ambrosius and, um—"

"The Lady Nimue Viviana? Yes. I'm their daughters."

"Their daughter, you mean. Singular."

"Oh, so you know all about it, then? Why are you asking me, if you know so much?"

"No, but the way grammar works—"

"Listen, I don't need grammar lessons from you, Santra."

"Who's Santra?"

The girl sighed a lonely sigh. "This guy who liked grammar. Never mind about him."

"You must be Morlock's sister, anyway."

"A remarkable deduction. Yes, a woman born from the same parents as a man is usually considered that man's sister. Likewise, the aforesaid man may be considered the woman's brother. At last we make some progress! Let us continue our search for truth!"

"Sister, singular? Not 'sisters'?"

"Listen," screamed the girl, "you don't know anything about it, so just shut up! When I speak, I speak for myself, and that's it! Got it?"

Aloê rolled her eyes, and then closed them. It felt wonderful. She leaned against the wickery bonds of her captor's innards and went to sleep. She heard the girl Ambrosia railing at her a few times, but ignored her. Sleep was good and didn't shout at you. Sleep good. So tired. Sleep.

When she awoke considerable time had passed—the ambient light was red, as if it were evening. She wished she could sleep some more. She wasn't hungry yet but was likely to be soon. And there seemed little to look forward to but more conversation with the bratty Ambrosia.

Unless she could get out of there.

The wicker cage she sat in was long, but not wide. She placed her back against one side, her feet against the other. Then, gently, testingly, but firmly, she began to push.

Green reeds like tentacles extruded from the walls, binding her feet, arms and head.

She stopped pushing and went limp. After a moment, the reeds withdrew and left her free.

"All right, you bastard," she said to the wickerwork beast. "But that's not the end of this."

"Who's there?" asked a woman's voice. "Do we have a new arrival?"

Aloê thought for a second before answering. But it really didn't sound as if it could be Ambrosia's voice. It was deeper, indefinably older.

"Yes," she replied. "I am Aloê Oaij, Vocate to the Graith of Guardians. I guess you didn't hear me come in earlier."

"No, I was . . . sleeping, I suppose. I'm Elpis. Or you might call me Hope—Hope Nimuelle."

"Oh? Another daughter of the Lady Nimue?"

"And the Summoner Merlin Ambrosius. Mother isn't strictly speaking a lady, as I understand the term."

"Nor is Merlin any longer a summoner. Strictly speaking."

Hope laughed. "True enough. I don't think he makes the claim himself— anyway, I've never heard him do so."

Aloê was intrigued. Hope seemed much more conversable than her bratty sister. "Then why do you make it for him, if you don't mind my asking?"

There was a long pause, and Aloê was beginning to worry that she'd pushed her new acquaintance too far, when Hope answered, "A kind of nostalgia, I suppose, for a life that I never had. Exiles dream about the Wardlands, you know, and so do their descendants, to the last generation, it seems. Some portion of the Coranian religion is based on it. I've often walked in dreams from Tower Ambrose down to the ruined wall at the edge of A Thousand Towers, where the Station Chamber of the Graith stands over the River Ruleijn. We live the life we are given, of course, but I think I would have preferred that other life, the one I was not given, to live in the peace and music and learning of the Wardlands."

Aloê felt a pang of guilt. She, after all, and her comrades on the Graith of Guardians, were the reason why this apparently gentle and reasonable woman could not go to the place where she felt she belonged. "Well, if it's music you want . . . I can sing a bit," she offered.

Hope laughed a warm generous laugh. "We may have time to put that to the test."

Aloê didn't like the sound of that. "Oh? How long have you been prisoner here?" Or *was* Hope a prisoner? Until she spoke her question, Aloê had never even doubted it.

Hope sighed. "My affliction makes it hard to trace the passage of time. Some months, at least, though."

Months? This did not sound good. "God Avenger! Are you trapped in a sort of basket, too?"

"Yes. It has been tedious."

"At least you have your sister for company."

"Not really."

Aloê smiled ruefully, sure that she knew what Hope meant (although it turned out she was wrong about this).

"But how do you . . . ? How do you . . . ?"

"Don't seem to hear what. Hear what you're saying," Hope said thickly, in a voice unlike herself somehow.

"It's just . . ."

"Sorry. Still not hearing. Ask Ambrosia. Likes to explain things."

"Are you ill? What's wrong with you?" Aloê was wondering if this affliction might affect her in the months (months!) to come. But she was also surprisingly worried about the well-being of this woman whom she had only just met, and had never in fact seen.

"My sister," whispered Hope, and said no more.

There was a kind of thrashing sound, then silence. Ambrosia gave a long sigh. "I wonder what day it is?" she said aloud.

"The same day as when we first talked, I think," Aloê said. "Although it seems to be night now."

"Hey!" Ambrosia yelped. "Are you still there? Mallowy, or whatever your name is?"

"Aloê," the vocate responded icily.

"Yes, exactly. Look, I'm sorry if I was rude, earlier. I didn't grow up around people, and I guess I'm still learning how to act."

"Your sister doesn't seem to have that problem," Aloê pointed out.

"Just because she's my sister doesn't mean she's lived the same life as me. Have you got any sisters?"

"Yes." Aloê thought about her smug vicious siblings, male and female— the ones who had known all about Cousin Nothos and did nothing to stop him, nothing to help her. "All right. I see your point. Maybe I'll just try to clue you, as they say, from time to time."

"Thanks. I enjoy learning stuff. It's one of the things I'm really good at. I'm going to have to learn a lot more about people if I'm going to rule the world."

"Oh. Um. Are you going to rule the world?"

"Well, at least the interesting parts."

Aloê scuttled her half-formed plan to educate Ambrosia in civility. If the only thing that protected the future from Ambrosia I, Ruler of the Interesting Parts of the World, was the girl's abrasive manner, Aloê wasn't going to tamper with it.

"Are you feeling all right?" Aloê asked.

"Am I crazy, do you mean?"

"No," said Aloê honestly. She didn't think there was any point in asking a crazy person if she was crazy. "Your sister seems to be suffering from some sort of affliction, and I thought you—"

"My sister *is* my affliction," Ambrosia said curtly. After a pause she added with painful honesty, "And I'm hers, I guess."

"Fair enough," said Aloê, who could imagine the horror of being confined with one of her sisters for months on end. "It's just that she seemed to pass out when I was trying to ask her an urgent question."

"Oh, always ask me the questions. I'm good at questions."

"Well, you've been here a long time."

"Months at least. It's hard to track the time. I was in Withdrawal for a while, but Hope kept sneaking out and using the life. And that's not fair, don't you agree? She's already had so much more than me."

"I can't really tell what's fair in that sort of situation," Aloê said carefully.

"I suppose not. But that can't be your urgent question, is it? About how long we've been here?"

"No, but it's related. How do you piss?"

"Well, I usually— Wait a moment."

Aloê had waited many a moment already, so she said, "I'm waiting."

"Are you saying you haven't urinated since you've been here?"

"I haven't."

"So when was the last time?"

"Sometime yesterday morning."

"Yesterday morning. Not the morning of the day now ending, but a day before that?"

"Yes. Although the wickerwork beast knocked me out when it captured me yesterday. I might have relieved myself when I was unconscious, I suppose. But I see no signs of it."

"And you would, I guess."

"Well, at some point we would have passed through the sea, so . . ."

"But you couldn't have been underwater for very long, or you would have drowned."

"No."

"No?"

"No."

"Are you fully human, do you think?" Ambrosia said curiously.

"Yes."

"I don't know if I agree. This is really wonderful. I mean, your *sphincter urethrae* must be made of steel!"

"What's the sphinxy youthy-thing?"

"Muscle. Keeps you from urinating. I read about it in a book. Of course I read another book that said it was a yellow elf in your schmedge that kept you from urinating. But I think that was satire, or a metaphor, or something. The book about the muscles was more convincing."

"So when you have to do it, you . . ."

"The usual way. I may be odd in some respects, but my plumbing is quite ordinary. Oh! You're asking *where* I do it?"

"Yes."

"I just sort of squat down and do it through the wickerwork."

"And you've been doing this for months?"

"I know it sounds disgusting, but, you know, the thing is actually a plant. It uses the urine—absorbs it and takes it away."

"Yeccch."

"Look, you do what you have to do in this sad life."

"You're wise for one so young."

"I bet I'm as old as you! Older, even!"

"How about . . . how shall I put this—?"

"Dung? There won't be any."

"I don't see how that can be."

"Periodically, the basket-plant will extrude bubbles of water. You can wash with it or drink it; it's perfectly clean. But you're not going to be fed. Your life is sustained directly by tal."

"What?"

"It's brilliant, in its way. You have to give him credit. There are traps around this place, which was a kind of herbarium in the old days when people used to live around here. The traps catch animals, and kill them by extracting their tal. Then the tal is directed by a shielded channel toward us, sustaining our physical life without the need of ingesting physical sustenance. Like it?"

"Sounds cruel."

"I know, and I can't figure out why. It's no worse than killing animals and eating them—they're dead all the same. Still, this seems worse somehow. Ingenious but cruel. That's him all over. He let me inspect the traps the last time he was here and was letting us walk around a little bit."

"He?"

"Our captor. Merlin Ambrosius. My father and your former colleague in the Graith."

"Weird. Do you know *why* he's kidnapped us?"

"I know why he kidnapped me and Hope. I don't know about you. I kind of expected you to be Morlock."

"Morlock?"

"That's my brother," Ambrosia said smugly.

"Yes, I know."

"Merlin hates him so much— Wait a moment, do you mean you know Morlock? Know him personally, not just about him? I guess he's kind of famous back in the Wardlands."

"Well. He's known to some."

"Does he ever talk about me?" Ambrosia asked eagerly.

Gingerly, suspecting that the answer would sting the volatile girl, Aloê said, "Not to me."

"Hmph," Ambrosia said sulkily. "I don't suppose you know him very well, then."

Aloê bit back a sharp reply. For one thing, she didn't want to hurt the girl. For another, she was coming to realize that what Ambrosia had said was true. There was much she didn't know about this man she had recently decided she loved.

"Ambrosia, would you do me a favor?"

"Guess so. Anything to keep the peace. What is it?"

"Will you pretend you're not there for a while? I absolutely have to empty my bladder, and I can't do it while we're having a conversation."

Ambrosia laughed. "Sure, why not? I have to think about something anyway."

It took a very long silence and many relaxing thoughts of rushing waters, but Aloê finally succeeded in voiding her bladder in a corner of her wicker cage. After she did so, bubbles of water began to extrude from the wicker walls, and she used them to rinse the cage and herself, and also quench her not-inconsiderable thirst. It must have been trained not to supply water until someone made water, Aloê reflected.

She, too, had something to think on. No matter why she had been kidnapped, she was not spending months in this cage. She was already itching for more space and light; she would be crazier than Ambrosia in a few days.

But she didn't think she would have to. After all, she had her staff.

The binding reeds that prevented escape took time to react. It could be that, if she charged the impulse wells in her staff, she could strike a couple of blows harsh enough to blow a hole or two through this thing.

She would take her time. There would probably be only one chance; she didn't doubt that the wickerwork beast would take the staff from her once it knew what it was capable of. And she wanted a maximum impulse charge in the staff. She formed the habit of shaking the staff back and forth more or less continuously, switching hands when she grew tired. It wasn't as good as spinning the staff, she suspected, but she didn't have space for that. Eventually, the impulses would add up. As long as she didn't accidentally release their energy by bumping the sides of her cage with the staff; she was increasingly careful not to.

It was boring. But she had little else to do, other than sit and think, which she could do at the same time, doubling her meager entertainment.

"Hey, Aloê," Ambrosia called over.

"She's out at the moment, sailing on the Broken Sea. Would you like to leave a message, or wait?"

"I guess that's funny. Listen, I had an idea."

"I'm listening."

"Was Morlock with you when you were kidnapped?"

"Not with me. Not so very far off."

"It must be. It *must* be. Only I can't quite . . ."

"This is where you tell me your idea, Ambrosia."

"Oh. Yes. Look, if you talk to Hope you might get a different story—"

"Where is she, by the way?"

"Shut up!" Ambrosia shouted shrilly. "You're talking to me now, see? Talk to her later if you want."

"Well, almost anything beats talking to you."

Silence for a moment. Then Ambrosia said, "Lots of people say that. I'm sorry. I guess maybe you don't understand what it's like."

"That's true. Don't let it worry you. What was your idea, honey?"

"Merlin wants all his children in one place, this place, is the thing. The Two Powers are after him, see."

"Oh. Are they?"

"They're after Ambrosius, anyway. Who else can it be?"

"Hm."

"This region is safe from them, for a couple of reasons."

"Name them."

"Look, let me tell you this in my own way."

"Why? I have a reason for asking about the Two Powers, Ambrosia."

"Ah. All right, all right. There's some kind of talic wave over this whole area. It makes human life difficult, godlife impossible. It's like a god repellant. The Two Powers may run rampant over the rest of the world, but they can't come here."

"Interesting! Who made it? Merlin? Or is it natural?"

"I asked him, last time he was here, but he didn't say anything. So I figure he didn't make it, or he would've been boasting all over the place—that's the kind of shnakbart he is."

Aloê didn't know what a shnakbart was, but the broader point was fairly clear. "I've heard stories," she said.

"I could tell you some. Anyway, if the Two Powers catch someone of his blood, they can use the blood to find Merlin pretty reliably."

"Useful to know."

"I can teach you the spell; it's pretty easy. Blood of the person you're trying to find works best. Next best is the blood of their life-mate, because mate changes mate as two become one."

"Oh?" Aloê started to have a glimmer of where this was going.

"Sure. But not so bad is the blood of a descendant, parent, or sibling. So Merlin wanted himself and his blood under protection somewhere. Mama isn't here—she's technically crazy, and this talic force might kill her."

"Why?"

"She's always drifting off into rapture, her mind a thousand miles from her body. But if she did that here, the talic force would drag her mind so far from her body that they could never be reunited."

"Unpleasant."

"The technical description for the state is 'death.'"

"I know. Ambrosia, I studied seeing with Zuluê at New Moorhope in the Wardlands."

"Oh. Oh. I'd like to go there sometime."

"I wish you could," Aloê said. There was that stab of guilt again. How different would the brilliant and embittered young Ambrosia be if she could have studied with the great seers of New Moorhope, the great makers of Thrymhaiam? And she could be enriching the Wardlands instead of being permanently shut off from them.

"Anyway, he put Mama in a jar and hid it, I think. He's always doing that, and she just lets him. They have this very sick relationship, let me tell you. Me and Hope am here—"

"Are here."

"Shut your face!" screamed Ambrosia. "Oh God, I'm sorry," she said almost immediately. "I'm trying to be better about that. Really I am."

"It's all right, honey," said Aloê soothingly. She didn't like being screamed at, but she was beginning to pity this bitterly unhappy girl.

"Ah. Anyway. So it just makes more sense to assume that Merlin was intent on grabbing Morlock, and got you by accident. Otherwise we would have to posit another motive on Merlin's part. And 'it's vain to do with more what can be done with less,' you know."

"Vain, but fun sometimes."

"We're too busy for fun, here. So, what I'm wondering is—had you been travelling with Morlock for a long time? Had he like, bled on you or something that morning?"

"Or something."

"Huh? Hey! How long had you been travelling together?"

"A while."

"Oh, gross. Oh, I don't want to hear this."

"So don't ask questions if you don't want the answers."

"This is my brother we're talking about. You can't be screwing my brother."

"Why not?"

"Oh, all right. Why not, I guess. I don't know why I should care. How recently had you, um—"

"Less than an hour before I was captured."

"Yeccch. Look, now we know, anyway. The cage-beast must have smelled Morlock's, er—"

"Semen," Aloê supplied helpfully.

"Gross. Anyway. It must have smelled it on you. And it grabbed you instead. Simple! I guess you're mad."

"Not really. I think I can do something here that maybe Morlock couldn't."

"What?"

"Get out."

"Really? I have a plan for getting out, too. I can't tell you mine, but you can tell me yours."

Aloê considered it. But she wasn't sure that the wickerwork beasts couldn't hear; they could certainly smell, after all. Also, she didn't think it was smart to let Ambrosia have anything she wanted on such unfair terms; it might get to be a habit with her. "No," she said at last.

"Oh, come on!"

"Absolutely no."

"I'd tell you. Really I would. But I'm afraid you'll tell Hope and she won't like it. She's got no imagination."

"She seems much more mature."

"Like I said."

Aloê didn't respond to this at all. She sat and spun the ends of the staff back and forth in tight circles that just failed to graze the walls of the cage she sat in. Ambrosia made various discontented sounds that didn't rise to the level of words, finally muttering her way to silence.

Conversation ended there for a while. The ambient light of evening had long ago faded into darkness, and Aloê felt the urge to sleep. But she didn't.

There was a fair charge built up in the impulse-wells of her staff; she didn't want to release it accidentally by laying it down or jostling it in her sleep.

A dark ocean of time passed by, unmarked by islands of word or thought.

Eventually Ambrosia said, "Hey, Aloê."

"Yes?"

"So. You've had sex. What's it like?"

"With your brother?"

"Ugh. No, that's sick; I don't care about that. Why would I? I mean in general."

That was a little tricky for Aloê to answer. Eventually she said, "Good when it's good. Bad when it's bad. Like most things. I'm not sure what to tell you, honey."

"Is it like in books and poetry and things? Like music and sugar and thunder and stars in your eyes and junk? Or is that all lies? I can't believe it's such a big deal, you know? But part of me wants to believe it, and I guess you know which part *that* is."

Aloê had never been in a position to have sentimental ideas about sex, but she thought she knew what Ambrosia meant.

"It's not exactly like they say—," Aloê began.

"I *knew* it!"

"—but it is very intense. I guess that's what all the poetry is about. It's messier and more ridiculous than most books will tell you. But it's very important—whether it's going well, or going wrong, or not going at all."

"Oh," said Ambrosia gloomily.

Gingerly, because she really had no idea how old the girl was, Aloê said, "I take it you never . . ."

"Not likely. Your father trying to kill you all the time cuts into your social schedule."

"What? Isn't Merlin putting you here to keep you safe?"

"To keep *him* safe. If my spilt blood was lying around in the world somewhere, the Two Powers might use it to find him. The only alternative to the present situation would be to completely obliterate my blood physically from the world, which would be a nuisance. So here we sit."

"He can't be that bad," Aloê replied, fully aware she was expressing a hope rather than a fact.

"I'm just telling you like he told me. He says I'm old enough to face facts, that I'm a very smart girl. When I'm a little older, I'll make him face a few facts. I will!"

"The rat-bastard. I'm sorry, honey."

Ambrosia seemed to be sniffling a bit, but she replied with great dignity, "That's all right. Not your fault."

Another ocean of silence passed—longer than a lifetime, but shorter than a night.

"Listen, Aloê!" Ambrosia said urgently.

"What is it?"

"Oh! I'm sorry! You weren't asleep, were you?"

"I wasn't asleep. What is it, honey?"

"I'll tell you my plan for getting out of here, and you don't even have to tell me yours."

"Don't tell me anything you don't want Hope to know—"

"I know you like her better than me; everyone does. But it's me that's going to get us out of here. And I've got to tell you now because it's going to happen now. I've been repressing Hope so that I can finish it."

"Repressing?"

"Yes. I'll explain that later, if you really want. But I've got to tell you this other thing now. Aloê, I got to!"

"All right. What is it?"

"The problem is how to get out of here, right? Because every time we try to bust out of the cage somehow the cage itself stops us. Am I right?"

"You are right."

Ambrosia laughed, a little crazily, and said, "So I applied the Nemean principle, is what I did."

"What's the Nemean principle?"

"There's this old story about this big guy running around the world fighting monsters. One of them is this lion, the Nemean Lion; its skin is so hard that arrows and swords and stuff just bounce off it. So he kills it by clubbing it to death—"

"Subtle."

"Listen, you're fighting a monster, you have to do what works. Am I right, or not?"

Aloê had the odd feeling that Ambrosia was speaking from personal experience. From her own, Aloê acknowledged, "You are right."

"Anyway, he'd like to use the lionskin as armor, because he might be fighting someone else someday. But how does he skin it?"

"You tell me."

"He uses the lion's own claws. They're the only thing hard enough to cut the lionskin. You see where I'm going with this?"

"Not really."

"We've got two cages here. What if we can get one of them to rip open the other? The cage's defenses are directed toward an inward threat, not an outward threat. You see? All we have to do is bait one of the cages to attack the other!"

"I don't know if I like the sound of that. Anyway, how could we do it?"

"In principle, it's very easy. The wickerwork beasts, as you call them, are triggered by the blood of Ambrose. But they also absorb the blood shed within the cage."

"How do you know that?"

"We've been in here for months. Or maybe you don't menstruate?"

"Oh. Right."

"So the trick is to get the blood out of the cage somehow."

"Well—"

"And the obvious solution was to unweave part of my fireproof cloak, imbue the threads with my blood, craft a particular physical impulse into each thread that would draw them to re-form into a kerchief-sized piece of cloth on the exterior of the cage beast, and feed them through the wickerwork thread by thread."

"Fairly obvious, I suppose."

"Figured it out forever ago. Crafting the impulses was tricky, but kind of a fun puzzle. There hasn't been much else to do around here. Anyway, except for a few details, I've mostly been waiting for another cage-beast to show up."

"Ambrosia, I think you should talk to Hope before you try this—"

"That's not possible, for a couple reasons you don't seem to understand, and one that anyone could. I'm not *going to try this*. I *have done it*. I've been feeding the threads through the cage-beast all night. And I think it's working. Listen!"

In the silence that followed, Ambrosia heard a distinct sniffing sound. The nose of the wickerwork beast that held her had smelt a fresh source of Ambrosian blood.

The cage abruptly changed shape, rising in height and narrowing drastically. Aloê leapt to her feet and narrowly avoided striking anything with her glass staff.

She was worried that the reeds would emerge to bind her again, but they didn't.

There was a creaking sound, and Aloê found that she could see in front of her. Part of the wickerwork beast had unfolded itself to make arms, ending in long sticklike fingers, which were reaching for a dark-stained rag on the exterior of another dormant wickerwork beast.

Aloê hoped that the chest-cavity was about to open and she could just leap out, and perhaps that would have happened.

But it turned out that Ambrosia was wrong about the wickerwork beast having no exterior defenses. As the one beast extended sticklike fingers to grab the bloodstained cloth, the other beast raised up a basketweave arm to ward them off.

The beast that contained Aloê formed its fingers into a solid blocklike mass and punched the other wicker-beast savagely.

Any fears that the blow had injured Ambrosia were dispelled by the girl's shriek of triumphant (and slightly hysterical) laughter.

The wicker-beast containing Ambrosia now flowed into a different, more manlike form. The wickerwork around the chest cavity grew thin enough that Ambrosia could see the shadow, at least, of the girl's form there. Ambrosia's wicker-beast grew two arms with blocklike fists.

"Enough of this, gentlemen," said Aloê. She would have preferred to strike at the wickerwork in front of her; it was thin enough to see through. But she didn't have room for a full swing of her staff. So she planted her feet as firmly as she could on the wickery stomach-floor of the beast, gripped her glass staff with both hands, and drove it upward into the wicker-beast's head, releasing the impulse charge.

The upper half of the beast exploded in a shower of green sticks and reeds. The body fell down to the ground, carrying Aloê with it.

"What happened? What happened?" Ambrosia was calling out.

"Mmmph," said Aloê, half-stunned, and crawled on her hands and knees out of the hole she had made in her living cage.

She stood up and breathed in a grateful gust of free air. The light where she stood was dim and gray: it was dawning behind the clouds outside, she guessed.

The other wickerwork beast had not resumed its dormant cage form. It stood on two widely planted feet like tree trunks. It held its blocklike fists before it like a boxer. And its flat moist tympanum of a face was pointed directly at Aloê, shifting to follow her as she moved. Could it see as well as smell? Or was smelling enough to locate her precisely?

She spun her staff like a baton, recharging its impulse wells. It was glorious to be able to move. And she would celebrate by smashing that thing holding Ambrosia, and the one holding Hope as well—she didn't see that one, but it must be close at hand.

The standing cage-beast lurched forward to strike at her. She stood her ground and struck a two-handed blow with the glass staff on one of the blocklike fists. The fist smashed apart into splinters. Aloê swung the staff back around and, stepping forward, struck the framework holding the flat tympanum face. It broke, and the tympanum ripped with a hideous wet fleshy sound. Aloê clenched her teeth and, dodging the beast's remaining fist, continued to land blows at the top of the beast until it fell over and split.

Gasping with laughter, Ambrosia emerged from the breach in the wicker cage. Her limbs were trembling and she stood uncertainly, blinking at the dim gray doorway as if it were a blazing light.

Her hair was ragged, filthy, a dark red. Her long-nosed, strong-jawed face expressed determination and intelligence in spite of her present physical weakness, but she looked to be about fifteen. She turned luminous gray eyes, painfully similar to Morlock's, toward Aloê.

"Hm," she said. "You're pretty." Her voice was dry with disapproval.

The wickerwork beasts were still moving. They were sinking shafts into the earth, and Aloê remembered what Ambrosia had said about them being plants.

"Quick," she said to the girl. "Where's Hope? We have to rescue her and get out of here before those things regroup."

"Hope?" said Ambrosia vaguely, as if she was having trouble remembering who that was. "Hope." Her pale face split in a wild mad grin. "Hope is in here," the girl said, tapping her thin chest.

It was a crazy thing to say. And yet: there was no other cage beast at hand. And Hope's voice had come from the same direction and distance as Ambrosia's had . . . but never at the same time.

What had the girl said? *I am repressing Hope.* What could that mean?

As she stood in doubt, struggling to formulate a question, her question was answered.

"Hope," said Ambrosia vaguely. "Hope. I'm not." She fell over on her side and began to writhe.

Aloê ran over, thinking the girl was having some sort of fit.

The body grew still before Aloê reached it. But it wasn't Ambrosia anymore. Instead of a girl, it was a woman: taller, heavier, blonder, older, with eyes of dark blue looking out of a face with smaller sharper features than Ambrosia's.

The dark blue eyes blinked a couple times, looking up at Aloê.

"Vocate Aloê Oaij, I guess?" said Hope's voice out of this stranger's mouth. "Thank you for getting us out of there. I presume it was you who did."

"Yes," Aloê said unsteadily. "Hope Nimuelle—what are you?"

"I am the daughters of Nimue and Merlin. We are twins, you see, of a special sort. When one is aware, the other recedes into non-being. We are never together, never apart."

"God Creator."

"Yes, or somebody. Help me up, dear: we need to get away before we are recaptured."

"I'm not in danger of being recaptured," Aloê pointed out, as she helped Hope up to her feet. The ragged red clothes that had been too long and baggy on Ambrosia were a tad short and a tad tight on her sister.

"Oh. Well, I wouldn't be too sure about that, Aloê; I've been doing some thinking about it."

"A family habit, I see."

"But you must suit yourself, of course."

"Well, I'd like to stick together for the time being," Aloê said, "if it's all right with you—with the both of you. But there is somewhere I have got to go, and if you won't join me we'll have to part ways."

"Where are you going, then?"

"Deeper into the dead lands. I have to find this thing powerful enough to threaten the Masked Powers."

CHAPTER TWENTY-ONE

Voyage of the *Boneglider*

B y the light of the major moons, both hovering over the eastern horizon,
Morlock was busy polishing the skis of his odd standing boat when the
island gave birth to a god.

Morlock became aware of this when he saw the shadow of his mortal body
lying on the ground beside his unfinished work. He looked up with the flesh-
less eyes of vision to see the luminous face of a god rising out of the island—a
hump of undistinguished matter, turretted and spiralled with blazing talic
force.

The god rose higher and higher—more distant from the material plane.
But he saw Morlock. He reached down with one of his many unformed arms
toward Morlock.

Rage uncoiled within Morlock like a snake. Another god trying to take
him over, land hooks in him. Morlock clung to the knowledge that his body
bore a talisman, that his psyche was protected. And he cried out to the god
of love he had half-imagined with Aloê, in whom he could not quite believe.
Aloê was gone; he had to find her. He had a life that mattered to him and
others; it was more important than being the first acolyte of some former
Kaenish heresiarch now calling himself a god.

The god continued to rise upward and reach down—but, suddenly, was
gone. Some wave of talic force, high above the material plain, had driven him
westward, like a wind driving a butterfly.

Morlock watched him go with fierce satisfaction, then turned to contemplate that wave of talic force. His maker's mind decided it was artificial,
the product of some inconceivably powerful immaterial artifact. More to the
point, it would affect his immediate plans to travel eastward.

Eastward. Where Aloê had gone. The thought anchored him, dragged him back down into the entanglements of matter. He opened his eyes to find himself lying in the midst of a cloud of disassembled skeletons. He rolled to his feet and got back to it.

It took him a day and a half more work to finish the thing, working without rest. A good deal of the time was spent moving a forge, piece by piece, from the empty city at the top of the island down to the beach, so that he could use the sparse beach sand as a sealant and cement on his odd craft. He needed small but significant amounts of glass as well to anchor a web of talic mirrors and manifolds that would amplify the impulse-force applied to the propellers.

He supposed he should go down to the Apotheosis Wheel and continue Aloê's interrupted investigation. He should continue on his mission to discover more about the Two Powers. He should do a great number of things. But he never wavered in his intention: he would go after his beloved; he would find her; if she had been hurt, he would have vengeance.

In the end, his work was done. It was an ugly thing: a narrow coffinlike hull mounted on a pair of bone-bright gleaming skis. A pair of propellers deep beneath the water would drive the craft. There was almost no room within the hull to move, and none for provisions or water. That was just by design: he had no provisions and would not need them for this trip. He would make it in visionary withdrawal. If it worked at all, it would get him to the eastern shore of the Sea of Stones relatively swiftly. If it did not work, he would think of something else.

He said no good-byes to Old Azh, but he did feel he should name his boat. He wasn't superstitious, but he always had terrible luck at sea, and riding an unnamed boat was supposed to make bad luck worse.

"I'm calling you *Boneglider*," he told the craft as it lay on the beach of broken bones and burned sand.

Morlock half pushed, half carried the *Boneglider* into the deep water just off the floating island. He climbed aboard, unsheathed his blade and laid it in the hull, and then laid himself down beside it. He elbowed the hatch shut and closed his eyes in the sudden darkness of the coffinlike shell.

Vision came on him swiftly, and with it a sense of menace from the east: the wave of talic force striking him, even as it had struck the god. But there were two differences. One was that the god was not anchored in matter, as

Morlock's talic self was. The other: Morlock did not ascend to the higher levels of vision but hovered low above the plane of matter and energy. He could resist the talic wave from the east for a while, but he feared it would get worse as he moved eastward, nearer the source (whatever it was).

Well, each trouble had its hour. That trouble was not yet; he'd worry about it when he had to.

He applied talic force to the impulse-multipliers at the base of the propellers. They began to spin, and the *Boneglider* lurched away from the island, slowly at first. Morlock touched the steering arc with his mind, and the boat's course was now directly east.

The *Boneglider* was still lumbering through the waves slowly, very slowly, too slowly to use her skis. Morlock spread his talic awareness a little farther, mingling it with the waters around him. He funnelled the impulse energy of their motion into the impulse-multipliers driving the *Boneglider*'s propellers.

Faster now.

Morlock experimented with different geometries of thought-funnel, finally settling on a fifth-dimensional shape that drew in a maximum of impulse energy with a minimum of talic extension. He wove his talic self into a crown of such funnels wound about each talic multiplier.

Now the *Boneglider* was running through the water faster. Soon she was standing on top of the waves, running along the surface of the water with her skis, holding the narrow hull away from the water. Only the propellers and the steering oar were actually in the water.

Morlock coldly estimated that the boat was moving five or six times as fast as a horse might trot. Speed was hard to gauge, as he could not exactly see the water with his talic vision, only the talic presence of living things and motive impulses in it.

Time was hard to gauge as well. Once he felt the presence of the sun over him, and a moment later (it seemed) two moons were peering at him: Trumpeter rising in the west, Chariot lowering into the east.

But time did pass, and soon he could trace its passage in pain, a pain that must be intense indeed in his body if he felt echoes of it in his vision. The pain increased as he went eastward. The talic wave, the force in the east, became like a wedge, prying his overextended talic awareness away from its anchor in his material body. If it succeeded in doing that, he would die. The thought of death carried no terrors in the visionary state. But if he died, he could not help Aloê, could never see her again. That was a terror worse than the fear of death.

Reluctantly, he veered his course northward, to ride the edge of the zone of hostile talic force. He would beach the *Boneglider* on the shore as near as he could to the eastern shore and then search out Aloê by foot from there.

For a while, he was running almost due north. Then the sense of dread, of threat and pain, subsided in the east. He turned the steering arc with his mind to a northeast course.

For all the pain, and dread, and sense of loss, this was the least unpleasant sea voyage Morlock had ever experienced. His body was seasick, as usual, but those sensations hardly echoed in Morlock's talic self. He saw, for the first time, something of the wonder of the sea: its power and depth, the intensity of its life, the beauty no longer masked by nausea.

A shark passed nearby, its talic presence like a single musical note: hunger. He steered around a set of submerged rocks—the rocks themselves invisible to him, but for the sessile fish whose souls like single eyes looked out at the *Boneglider* as it passed above them. The plants too had a slow slumbrous talic life: one rope of sea-ivy as broad as an oak tree, rooted deep under the sea, throbbed with life that was almost at the level of awareness. What thoughts would it think if it ever woke?

But he became aware that there were other talic presences in the sea—as alien as himself. Two voices, their incomprehensible words edged with hate like gusts of winter wind laden with ice crystals, spoke to each other, answering hate with hate, but bound with common purpose. They were heading past him. Toward Old Azh?

He had sensed their presence before, through his own vision and from memories he had accidentally acquired from his *ruthen* father. They were the Two Powers, Torlan and Zahkaar, Fate and Chaos. Morlock kept his motion steady, on the premise that they might notice any change.

Possibly he should follow them. That would be more in line with his mission: to find out what he could about the hostile Powers. Or maybe he should have stayed in Old Azh to investigate the Apotheosis Wheel. If the Two Powers were interested in it, maybe it was a threat to them.

But that would mean abandoning the task of finding Aloê. He would not do that: not for the Wardlands, or his oath to the Graith, or any other reason.

When the chill inhuman presence of the Two Powers had long passed, he felt others. A choir of demons, wearing stolen bodies, rowing a galley with inhuman speed, trailing after the Two Powers.

Who in this world or any other would recruit a crew of demons and follow the Two Powers across the Sea of Stones?

But that was not his trouble, at least not in this hour. The menace in the east was receding again, and he shifted his course again.

Everything was going as well as it could. His body was growing weak, its connection to life more tenuous through prolonged absence of his talic awareness. But the journey was nearing its end.

He was just about to congratulate himself when he saw that he was steering into a storm.

The storm strode out of the south on crooked fiery legs of lightning. Morlock felt the surge of waters long before the thunderbolts came within striking range. Their force, passed on to the *Boneglider*'s propellers, drove the boat faster than ever through the water. He drove eastward as fast as he could. In his talic eye he could see the edge of the sea, the dense gold-green of sea-life fading into the colder sparser tal of land-life.

But the storm caught him before he came to shore. Lightning began to fall like hail around him. He couldn't direct it away from himself and also drive the propellers with his mind.

With sluggish, half-aware hands, his picked up his blade Armageddon and held it over himself. If thunder was going to fall on him, or the *Boneglider*, perhaps he could absorb it into the talic matrices of the glass blade.

A bolt fell, straight on him. It shattered the lid of the *Boneglider*'s coffinlike hull, but the aether of the bolt was drawn into Armageddon before it could do any further damage. Three more bolts fell toward the boat, and Morlock drew them with his mind into the blade he now held straight out into the open air.

The waves were now high and steep, with narrow deep troughs between them. He had to choose between driving on eastward as fast as he could, or turning into the wind.

Inexperience betrayed him. He thought that, with the speed he had gained from the storm's own power, he could ride through the troughs between the waves all the way to shore, or at least to calmer waters.

Soon he was driving the *Boneglider* along the side of a wave that was rising, rising, rising, and curling at the top as it rose. He realized his mistake by then, that there was no stable course through the waves with the storm-wind on the shoulder of his craft. But it was too late. The wave curled over, and the water like the fist of a giant crushed the *Boneglider*.

Morlock shook loose from his vision and found himself floating, deep in dark water, amid the fragments of his dead craft. He kept his grip on Armageddon: it still blazed with implicit thunder and the hot aether would be more buoyant than wood or waterlogged flesh.

He drove his body upward through the bitterly cold surge of waters. When he came to the surface he was nearly deafened with the roar of the wind, the crash of the waters, the high hissing shriek of the rain.

He had no notion of west or east or north or south. He had no plan, other than to stay afloat as long as he could.

How he hated the water, so inimical to the fire in his blood! But that fire sustained him, when many another would have died. In time the wind grew less; the surge subsided; the rain and lightning passed northward. Morlock was left, dog-paddling grimly, toward the black border of the land.

In the end he crawled onto a long muddy beach, exhausted, waterlogged, and bone-chilled, but with his sword still in hand.

Awaiting him was a group of tall gray people. They also had swords. He thought they were armored, too . . . but when he looked up at them in the dim gray light, he saw that the flat gray plates on their faces and arms, the row of spikes running down their spines—these were growing directly out of their skins.

"Mandrakes," he whispered.

"We don't call ourselves that," said one of them, in the language shared by dragons and dwarves. He swung the mace in his hand, and Morlock fell down into darkness.

CHAPTER TWENTY-TWO

The Waste Lands

Hope's shadow strode behind her all afternoon—but it was not Hope's shadow at all. It took a while for Aloê to be sure of this: the dark shadow dancing on the red-gray ground. But Hope's fair hair was bound in a long braid. Ambrosia's dark red hair fell in wild tangles past her shoulders. The shadow outlined in golden light on the gray ground behind Hope had hair like Ambrosia's, not Hope's.

Aloê lifted her eyes from the ground to comment on this to Hope, but the other was looking at her, smiling wryly, and said, "Yes, that's Ambrosia's shadow, and she has mine. We see each other in mirrors sometimes, as well. It can be inconvenient."

"No doubt."

"I don't suppose you like her much."

"Ambrosia? She can be difficult."

"She is difficult, and brilliant. I am not difficult, but not brilliant."

"That's a harsh assessment."

"It's my father's. He had some plan of using us a secret weapon against the Graith."

"Oh?" As a vocate, Aloê was interested in the details.

"Since given up, I believe. He found me teachable, but not talented enough. Ambrosia is wildly talented, but she will not be led."

"She says he is always trying to kill her."

"That's an exaggeration, I think."

It had never occurred to Aloê to be grateful for her family, but she was, belatedly and begrudgingly, coming to see that they had their points. A lack of any tendency to child murder (exaggerated or not).

They were walking fairly, but not directly, toward the setting sun. Ambrosia, in one of her intervals of awareness, had insisted she could sense the direction of the talic wave, and added that she was sure anyone with the senses of week-dead beef or better could do the same. Aloê and Hope, after walking due south and then due north again, did agree that the locus of dread did seem to shift a little along the eastern face of the world as they moved at right angles to it. They sketched a map on some bark torn from a dead tree, and drew angled lines that represented fairly well their imprecise sense of where the dread was emanating from, projected back on their northernmost and southernmost positions. In the end, they decided Ambrosia was right. It's true that it took them most of the day to see something Ambrosia had sensed right away, but they reached their conclusion more amicably, which was not nothing.

Dead trees were handy whenever they needed them: for shelter, or fires, or anything else. It was live ones that were rare, and even those (when they found them) were oddly gray. The grass of the plain they walked over was an odd mix of dead brown and living gray. They saw few birds, and no land animals.

"Aloê," said Hope in some distress. "I'm sorry."

"Ambrosia waking up?"

"Yes. Give her my love, won't you?" Hope often said that.

"Yes." Aloê usually said that, too, but she rarely carried through on it. Conversation with Ambrosia didn't leave much room for expressions of affection.

Hope sat down in the dust among the sparse gray grass. She closed her eyes and sighed. Her face clenched in pain. It twisted and twisted until the features themselves shifted like clay being shaped by invisible fingers. Her pale hair burst, dark-red, from its braid. She spoke a wordlike sound of pain, but by the time the word was finished it was spoken in Ambrosia's voice. Hope was gone.

"How are you?" Aloê asked.

"I am," Ambrosia said, shrugging her crooked shoulders in a gesture that reminded Aloê painfully of Morlock. "It's better than not-being. Even if it stings a bit."

"Is it hurting you worse when you change over? It looks like it does."

"Yes. This talic wave—we are especially vulnerable to it then, I think."

"Do you want to stay here? I can go on alone."

"No. Listen, Aloê, you're not immune to it. Everything that thinks and feels suffers from this thing."

"I know," Aloê said curtly. The feeling of dread and impending doom was heavier than ever now, growing with every step westward. She carried it like a dead body across her shoulders. She needed no reminder of it.

She offered Ambrosia a hand up from the ground. The girl took it and they walked on in silence through a landscape empty of any life but their own.

Until they came to a little town, a cluster of plowed lands rising from the dead fields. There were posts like Kaenish godstones set up at intervals, marking the edge of the town. But they mentioned no god; they just said the name of the place was the Colony of Truth, in Kaenish runes and several other languages. (So said Ambrosia confidently: it was one of her waking times.)

The Colonists surrounded their town with a halo of small farms, but everyone seemed to live in a cluster of buildings in the center of the settlement. They arrived at sunset, and the first townsperson welcomed them with an eager, almost frantic, warmth. She had carroty hair and wore a farmer's smock. She carried a basket of root vegetables under her arm as she walked in from the fields. She caught sight of them and ran up eagerly, her pale speckled face split in a scarlet smile.

"Good even, new-friends!" she cried in Kaenish. "Or is this tongue unsuiting to ye-twain? I—"

"The both and all of us like this tongue right well," replied Ambrosia, falling in with the woman's odd dialect with breezy confidence. Aloê was prepared to admire her for it, until Ambrosia gave her companion a smug side-glance as if to say, *See how bright I am!*

"I hope I can make myself clear to you," Aloê said. "The Kaenish I know is a little different from what you are using."

"Gnaw ye-one not for it," said the woman, laughing. "'Tis not native tongue-song to me neither. There was a eldern unpriest who taught this babblement to new-friends for a long lifetime. I-among-others was one such, a time and a time ago. The name of me-in-particular is Farna, by the gate."

"What manner of lip-melodies dost ye-one-self prefer, o Farna?" Ambrosia asked eagerly. "I-speaking-for-myself would wager I ken of them."

"This tongue will do," Farna said, a little less warmly, and Aloê guessed she was nettled somehow. Maybe Farna didn't want anyone knowing where she hailed from; the place had the look of a refuge somehow—the buildings were in radically different styles, suggesting builders from different cultures.

"We are passing through," Aloê said, before Ambrosia pressed the point and alienated Farna even more. "But if there is a place to stay the night, we would gladly pay in the coin we have."

"'Passing through,'" Farna repeated. "Then ye-twain intend not to stay, to teach and learn and live among the Colonists of Truth?"

"Sadly, no. We have other business in these lands. Does that never come up?"

"In truth, where we-universal all are whether we see it or no, I have never seen a new-friend merely passing through. We-in-particular come to stay here, and there are no others at all. Except for ye-twain."

"If it's inconvenient—"

"No, no, I-for-myself-and-others beg you not to misunderstand. This has not happened before, but whatever is, is right, and we-universal must apprehend it and adapt. All of us-in-particular would wish it."

"I'm not sure I follow you."

"I think," Ambrosia said in a subdued tone, "she's saying they can find a place for us; the locals are just not used to the idea of passersby."

"Ye-one hast grasped it well, and I welcome ye-twain to the Colony of Truth for as long as you would stay, for part of your day or the rest of your lives. Stay ye-twain as guests for nowness: we use not the coin of king or priest here."

"Thank you," Aloê said. "Perhaps we can pay you in work, if our stay becomes longer. We don't wish to be a burden."

"Everything that can be, will be," Farna said composedly. "And nothing that cannot be, will be."

"I'm not sure about the first part," Ambrosia said, "but the second part is all right."

Aloê was pondering ways to unobtrusively tell Ambrosia to shut her pie hole, but Farna turned to the girl eagerly and said, "Then ye-one will wish to speak with Jeuter, our phenomenologist. He has a great interest in what is and is not, what can and cannot be."

"Death and Justice," Ambrosia said. "I am going to love this place!" Aloê was thinking the opposite, but refrained from saying so.

"I-among-others am pleased," Farna said, smiling with a pained expression. "But I must ask you to leave all talk of gods behind ye-twain while staying with us."

"Is it because you do not believe in them?" Ambrosia asked.

"No. We-in-particular came thither to escape them."

"Excellent," Aloê said, understanding at last. "The perfect place for it."

"And for no other thing," Farna said, nodding ruefully. "The land, you have seen it: void of beasts, losing its grass and trees. The living it is hard. But we-in-particular live here free, and wish that we-universal could be the same."

Ambrosia's lively face displayed her interest and skepticism. But she held her lively tongue for the moment, which relieved Aloê very much, and they followed Farna to a biggish building in the center of the little town.

In a torchlit room that ran the length of the building, there were long tables and benches at which many of the townspeople were already sitting and conversing. Mostly the male townspeople were sitting, Aloê noticed, after a moment. The women seemed to be flitting about the room, bringing them things: dishes of food, mugs of drink.

One group of men turned toward them with surprise and delight on their faces. "New-friends from the wider world!" one with a gray explosion of a beard called out. "Is that what you bring us, Farna?"

"I am, I am indeed, Old Gnourn," Farna said. "They-twain would stay only a night or so, however."

"Oh!" said Old Gnourn, somewhat baffled behind his barrier of beard. "Well, for a while or forever, new-friends are always welcome."

"Thanks," Aloê said, strangely moved. They were more than a sea's distance from Kaen and its religion of cruelty. "I am Aloê Oaij, by the way, and this is my friend Ambrosia Viviana."

"There was no need to introduce yourselves, you know," Old Gnourn said. "You can be any name you like in the Colony of Truth. All names are true, or none." There was a general humphing and pumping of agreement from the row of beards.

"You-several might get an argument from our new-friend here," remarked Farna slyly. "But I must get these thurkle-roots to the kitchen."

"Yes, thank you, Farna," said Old Gnourn dismissively. He turned to Aloê and said, "So you are a logician! Yet as brown as a Qajqapciar! The truth tells us that brown skin and logical abilities are a rare match."

"Oh. Does it?" Aloê said frostily.

"Please don't be offended. We only deal with things as they are here, not fantasies and poesies and dreams, and it is our experience that—"

"Do you really know that many people with brown skin? I don't see anyone like that here."

"Well. No. But it's common knowledge that—"

"Have you not found common knowledge to be as frequently in error as poetry, if not more so?"

The beards murmured thoughtfully. "We don't think much of poetry," one of the grayer beards remarked. "It is imprecise and rarely yields falsifiable statements."

"But she's got you there on common knowledge, Old Gnourn," a grizzled but not utterly gray beard observed. "If I went by the common knowledge back in Screevale I would be on my hands and knees and barking at the behest of an entity I will not name. Truth, not familiarity, is the standard for knowledge."

"What should we do about it?" asked Old Gnourn grumpily.

"Well, truth tells us that bad decisions are taken on Fuffnardays and Thebnardays, so suggest we table the question until tomorrow when we can discuss it with the agricultural accounting reports."

The beards all agreed with this. But now Farna had returned with a steaming tureen of dark fluid, in which knobbly objects bobbed up and down. "Who would have some affer-nut soup?" she asked.

All the beards were interested in affer-nut soup, it turned out, and they served themselves from the tureen as Farna carried it around the table.

Aloê would not have objected to some affer-nut soup herself, but, not having been asked, she waited until Farna said, "If you-several are done charming these young ladies, perhaps I should take them off to the kitchen."

"Yes," said Old Gnourn, through a mouthful of partially chewed affer-nut, "but don't make them work until they've decided to stay. That's fair according to the dictates of truth, I think we can all agree."

There was general agreement, although one beard started to make noises about the universal obligation to contribute to communities, whether one benefited from it or not. But everyone ignored him, apparently from long practice. The beards went on eating the soup, and the three women went to the kitchen.

The kitchen was an equally large room, warmer (because of the ovens), with benches where many women were already seated, eating with urgency from full steaming plates.

"We-distinctive serve ourselves back here, if ye-twain don't mind it,"
Farna said apologetically.

"Of course not," Aloê said, going with their hostess to a table where, following Farna's lead, she collected a platter and a spoon and then filled the
platter with food from troughs. There was no meat. What looked like bread
was a baked crust formed from the paste of some root vegetable. There were
some green and yellow vegetables that Aloê didn't recognize, and what seemed
to be a mushroom gravy.

It all tasted well enough, but it was hard to enjoy anything under the
dreadful feeling of impending doom that pervaded the place. But it had been
long since their last meal, and anything was better than nothing.

"Why do you let them treat you like servants?" Aloê asked. "Not that it's
any of my business."

Farna sighed as she settled herself on a bench, and some of the women
nearby nodded and laughed at Aloê's question. Others looked outraged.
"They-exclusive say it is nature's law, a dictate of truth, that woman serves
man. It is true that many cities are run that way. But it is easier to give them-
exclusive what they expect, and, by any gate, this way—"

"I would not sit down beside those schmeckle-faced knepps," Ambrosia
remarked, as she seated herself, "if they were sharing out the last chunk of food
in the world."

The women within hearing distance roared with laughter, and the
laughter spread generally along the benches as Ambrosia's line was passed
from group to group.

Farna smiled a weary smile and nodded agreeably at Ambrosia.

There were many introductions. Aloê toasted with a spoonful of gravy
everyone who was pointed out to her, but didn't trouble to memorize the
names. Tomorrow morning they would be leaving here.

There was some general discussion of the dictates of truth during the
dinner, and whether it was permissible to hum or even sing while one was
working. Some said that music had no truth-value since it contained no
testable statements and that lyrics were merely a form of poetry, which was
incompatible with truth. Ambrosia stood it as long as she could, and then
leapt into the fray, pointing out that the mathematical nature of music made
the presence or absence of notes as testable as a proposition in geometry. She

said a good deal, too, about the metaphorical nature of language and the limits of testability as a standard for truth. The discussion grew quite lively, and Aloê watched with amusement and not a little wonder at Ambrosia's energy. Personally, with her belly full for the first time in many a day, she wanted principally to find a safe warm place to sleep.

The dinner ended and the seminar eventually broke up, with knots of women eagerly discussing matters musicological, mathematical, and semantic while others hauled the dirty dishes away to be washed in crocks.

Farna grabbed Ambrosia and Aloê each by an elbow as they rose from the table, "If ye-twain would be kind enough to come with me-alone, there is a thing that I would show you. And then I will take ye-twain to your room, for I see that ye are tired."

"Thanks," Aloê said, and Ambrosia nodded tensely, ready for another argument and self-evidently not tired at all.

Farna led them out of the kitchen into the night, and on through the small settlement to the fields in the back of town, on the opposite side where Aloê and Ambrosia had arrived.

"Ye-twain-or-singular have not asked, and I thank ye for not asking, a question many ask when they come hither. But ye may ask it now."

"All right," Aloê said. "Where are the children?"

Ambrosia jumped a little at this. Evidently she hadn't noticed that the colonists they had seen were all adults—more on the elder than the younger side.

"They-entire are there," said Farna, and pointed out into the dark field.

Aloê solemnly looked at what she thought was a graveyard, full of images of children of various size. He feelings changed to alarm when she realized that the overgrown shaggy shapes were not representations of children. They *were* children. Or at least the bodies of children.

Ambrosia stepped curiously up to the nearest figure. It was smooth and hairless like a baby, but twice the size any baby ought to be. It was buried up to its waist. Its fingers extended like branches or roots and grew straight into the ground.

"They're like mandrakes," Ambrosia called over to them. "It's breathing!"

"Yet it is not alive," Farna said flatly. "The colony lives on because of immigrants: those who choose to come here so that they can live free. But there are costs, and this is one. The children die, and all the babies are born like this."

"Why do you do this with them?" Aloê said. "This looks like . . . a field that is tended."

"Yes," Farna said evenly. "The children do not live, but something in their unlife shields us-inclusive from the full weight of the shadow to the east. Life here is nearly unbearable. Nearly. In the shadow of this field it is . . . bearable."

Aloê wondered if she would feel the same, in Farna's place.

"If ye are thinking of staying," Farna said evenly, "ye should know about this place. I came here pregnant. I did not know. They-inclusive told me only after it was too late. I think I would have made the same choice, knowing everything. But I always thought . . . It was my-alone choice, not theirs. And they took that from me."

"Thanks," Aloê said. "Ambrosia. For—my sake, come away."

The girl was on her knees, poking with gentle curiosity at the empty breathing face of the infant-plant.

"Aristotle," Ambrosia said, "speaks of a rational, an animal, and a vegetable soul. I wonder if the talic wave destroys or drives away the first two *in utero*, leaving only the vegetable soul to sustain physical life."

"Ambrosia. Please."

"But it's so interesting! It suggests there are types of tal not subject to the force of the talic wave. And that suggests methods of protection from it."

"Who is Aristotle?" asked Farna.

Ambrosia sighed. "This guy I used to know," she muttered scornfully, and rose resentfully to her feet.

Farna led them away to a smaller building, some distance away from the great kitchen where they had eaten. "This is New House," she said. "It is ready for dwelling. Ye-each-or-twain may stay here as long as it likes ye. If ye wish to stay, it will be your house and we will make up another New House."

"Farna, I thank you," Aloê said sincerely. "But I have to tell you we are not here to stay. We will be gone in the morning."

"There will be other mornings," Farna said. "Remember the colony, and know ye can return when ye long for its freedom." She put her hand affectionately on the side of Aloê's face, kissed Ambrosia's startled forehead and walked away into the night.

Aloê never saw her again.

≥€

In the sleeproom were bedrolls on ropework frames—a little like sea-hammocks. Aloê fell into hers with glee and muttered a quick good night to Ambrosia, even as she was falling asleep.

She awoke some hours later with chilly feet. Someone—Ambrosia no doubt—had taken off her shoes and covered her with a blanket woven from straw. But the blanket had slid off her toes and the chill woke her.

"Y're a g'd k'd, 'mbrosia," she muttered, and snuggled back into her hammock.

She didn't expect a response and didn't hear one. What drew her back from the threshold of sleep was, she didn't hear anything: no snoring, breathing, no muttering about obscure and improbably named philosophers, nothing to indicate Ambrosia was in the room.

Aloê opened her eyes and looked around. By the light of the moons perco-lating through the thin shutters, she could see she was alone.

"Of course, you silly fish," she muttered to herself. The girl didn't sleep. Her rest came when her sister Hope took up the task of living.

So where was she, in the middle of the night? Engaging in philosophical disputes about music and mathematics back at the colony kitchen?

Or, more probably, had she gone to face the danger of the talic wave by herself?

Aloê groaned. Someday. Someday she was going to get a full night of sleep.

But that day was not today.

Aloê tossed off her straw blanket, pulled on her shoes, and ran out into the frosty night full of dread.

It was not hard to know which way she must go. It was the way she hated most to turn. She could not bring herself to walk straight through the grove of undead babies, but apart from that she made no detours, running south and east as the feeling of doom grew on her to become a physical ache in her heart. Every step she took seemed like a dreadful mistake. That was why she knew it was right.

She saw the end of her journey by the bitter blue moonlight of Trumpeter high overhead and lowering Horsemen. It was a kind of mirror, darkly glit-tering. Before it sat as if spellbound or asleep a human shape. Ambrosia, by the wild dark hair.

Spellbound, perhaps, but not asleep. As Aloê forced herself to go nearer, she heard Ambrosia muttering words. When she got closer she saw who she was muttering to. The reflection in the dark mirror was Hope.

"I finally have it figured out," Ambrosia was saying sleepily, in a gentle voice that sounded surprisingly like Hope's. "The mirror drives back any talic imprint with its own force. The minds kill themselves if they can't turn away. Minds anchored in bodies can live for a time. Am I . . . Am I still anchored in a body?"

"Turn away," said Hope's image, in a shrill voice that sounded more like Ambrosia. "You're killing us both. Personally, I'm not ready to die."

"I die every day," Ambrosia whispered. "Close my eyes and I'm gone. Wake up in a new world; everything is different. I die every day. So tired of dying. Maybe the mirror could heal us—make us one person—not split down the middle anymore—"

"We are *not* one person," Hope said, in her oddly Ambrosian voice. "The fact that you've forgotten it and I remember it is a bad sign."

Aloê was perplexed as to what she should do for the sisters, but she could not, she simply could not, stand in the path of that dreadful talic mirror any longer. She closed her eyes to keep from looking at it. That helped, but not much. She stepped aside, felt more relief, felt the sense of dread and imminent doom subside slightly, and stepped again. The emotional burden was now definitely lighter, and the physical pain receded entirely. She sighed.

"You interfere with my visualization," whispered a voice near at hand.

She opened her eyes and saw *something* behind the talic mirror.

In fact, she saw suddenly, there were two mirrors, one facing east with its back to the west. The presence, whatever it was, stood between them. Or anyway: was between them; she couldn't tell if it was standing.

It was a kind of hump of nothing that glistened in the moonlight. It was a surface of matter—dusty, greasy, translucent or transparent. But the stuff was just suspended there in midair; it wasn't on anything.

In the middle of it, the dust and grease formed a human mouth that whispered, "You do not belong here. Your presence was of so low an order of probability that it was safely ignored."

"Long odds pay off big," said Aloê, and drew her staff. Spinning it to build an impulse charge she said, to gain time, "Who are you?"

"I," said the unbeing before her with whispered disgust. "I. I. I. I. I. I. I. I. I. I."

"Yes, you. Who are you? I, for instance, am Aloê Oaij, Vocate to the Graith of Guardians."

"The Graith!" said the unbeing bitterly. "How what-you-would-call-I hate it. How it balks what-you-would-call-me."

"Glad to hear it. And you are?"

"What-you-call-I should never have been," whispered the unbeing. "There was a plan, this world that had to be cleansed. An entity had to be dispatched to tend the plan. But it took so long. There were so many failures. In time the entity-that-was-not-I became contaminated with selfhood, with matter, with feeling. It became what-you-would-call-I."

"Cleansed of what?" said Aloê, still spinning her staff. In fact, she thought she knew.

"Of you, and all like you. Of life that breeds in material filth. Of life infected with selfhood."

"Then you, and those like you, are immaterial beings? You exist only in the tal realm, like the gods of Kaen?"

"They are filth of a different flavor, but still filth. They carry their puling selfhood across the threshold of should-be-cleansing death. The-ones-you-would-call-us are not like that."

"And you come from elsewhere?"

"In the deep north, at the edge of this world, stands the Soul Bridge, spanning the leap to the sunless world," whispered the unbeing. "The ones-you-would-call-us fled there when the sun was born, poisoning this world with life, and fertility, and selfhood. Someday the sun will die and those-you-would-call-us will return."

"Here's hoping that day never comes." The turn of phrase reminded her of her companion(s) and she called out, "Ambrosia! Hope! Are you hearing this?"

"Can't hear," said Ambrosia/Hope dreamily. "Too busy listening."

"No, snap out of it," shrilled Hope/Ambrosia. "This is important!"

"Not soon enough the unday comes," agreed the unbeing. "So the plan. The cleansing. The scraping away. Someone had to go. Some entity. Those-you-would-call-us were all the same. So the one-not-yet-I was sent across the Soul Bridge and became the one-you-would-call-me."

"And how you hate it, hm?"

"Hate," hissed the unbeing with gleaming greasy lips. "Hate. It is not for the one-you-would-call-me. Yet it is for all the ones-you-would-call-us. Those ones, the forever strangers, they hate the sun and the life it seeded through the world. They/we will kill it/him/her! This is not hate! It is merely the thing that must be, the thing we intend."

"Only an entity with selfhood can *intend*," Aloê said. "Either those ones you talk about are selves, or you are not one of them any longer."

The greasy lips issued a whistling sort of wail, as if Aloê had uttered something the unbeing had long feared.

Aloê struck with her staff then, driving a blow straight at the unbeing's midsection.

It hissed its pain and anger through the greasy lips and moved to attack.

Aloê was fascinated to see shockwaves moving through the unbeing's self. It was not as immaterial as it seemed. Ages of matter had percolated into it, become one with it, in a jellylike suspension. It reminded her a bit of the Keeper of the Wheel, except that she didn't like it. Also: it could feel pain; it could be angry.

Aloê dodged away from the unbeing's attack, leaping into the zone of dread with a suddenness that shocked her into stillness.

The unbeing turned toward her—and hesitated.

Of course. Of course. Aloê forced herself to think through the despair induced by the talic mirror, the pain of the mind fighting itself. It stood between the mirrors because it had cause to fear them. And they protected it from something else it had cause to fear.

She spun the glass staff and stood back farther into the zone of despair. "This way, you-who-I-do-call-you! Or are you afraid? You fear and you hate, like a fish wriggling on a hook."

It hissed, but didn't move.

On impulse, Aloê lashed out with the staff at the edge of the talic mirror. It spun as if it were on gimbals. The zone of dread passed over her; she felt as if she were being slashed in two. Then it passed from her and fell on the unbeing.

It screamed, "No! Death! Failure! Shame! Death!" Then it whispered, "Death. Nothing. Nothing, anymore . . ." and it walked straight into the talic mirror.

The world abruptly changed shape. Ambrosia/Hope was screaming, and Aloê was rolling over moonlit frosty fields, laughing, laughing. The weight of the world and hell had been lifted from her. The zone of despair was gone.

She looked up and saw this: no talic mirror, no unbeing intent on the world's death, nothing but Ambrosia on her knees, weeping for the lost image of her sister.

CHAPTER TWENTY-THREE

The Temptation of St. Danadhar

Morlock awoke in a locked room on a heap of straw. The mandrakes had taken his sword from him, but they had wrapped him in a blanket. A fair trade, as he was shaking like a wet dog, even with the blanket; without it he might be dead.

His hands and feet were bound. That was bad. He did what he could, which was mostly think and wait.

Just once, he would have liked to travel by water without a shipwreck or some other disaster. Well, he had travelled with Aloê by sea . . . but then he had lost her, the worst disaster of all.

Presently the cell door was unlocked and a group of mandrakes walked in on their sly almost soundless serpent feet. There were seven of them: six wielding spears and the seventh carrying a mace that looked ceremonial as well as functional. They wore only kilts, but the mace-wearer's was belted with gold.

"Then?" he said to the mandrakes, who were staring at him with their fiery red eyes, threatening him with their spears.

The mandrakes looked at each other. "We don't understand you," the mace-bearer said.

Morlock waved his hands at the spears. "Nor I you. What do you want with me?"

"Us? Nothing," replied the mace-bearer. "But God wants to talk to you."

"Eh."

"None of that!" the chief mandrake said fiercely. "You will respect the God."

That depended on the god's behavior, as far as Morlock was concerned, but there was no point in saying so. He nodded toward his feet instead.

The mace-bearer was in doubt, but one of the spear-bearer's said, "I am not carrying him," and stepped forward to cut the bonds on Morlock's feet.

"Thanks," Morlock said, standing. "I am named Morlock."

"We know it," said the mace-bearer. "Come with us."

The mace-bearer led the way out of the cell and out of the little stone building that housed it.

Outside was a fair-sized fishing town. All the inhabitants seemed to be mandrakes. There were also female mandrakes, if he was not mistaken.

Morlock was interested, but tried not to show it.

This was what he knew about mandrakes. When a dragon died, mandrakes were hatched from the dead worm's teeth and planted themselves in the ground. When they grew large enough, they pulled themselves loose and walked free for a while. Eventually they transformed into dragons, as caterpillars change into butterflies.

But here was a whole town full of mandrakes who had not undergone the dragon-change. He passed by an elderly female, her dugs sagging down to her kilt's belt, being helped along the street by three solicitous mandrakelings. Children? Grandchildren? If mandrakes were but the larval stage of dragons, how could they have children?

Was it possible that the dragon-change was no more inevitable in mandrake than it was in his *harven*-kin, the dwarves?

Under Thrymhaiam, dwarves learned and abided by a strict moral code that repressed cruelty and selfishness. Those who kept the code kept themselves and avoided the dragon-change. Could mandrakes do the same? If so, who had taught them to do so?

Now Morlock also wanted to have a conversation with God.

But he hoped in vain. They came to the largest building in town, set on a stand of pillars high above the sandy earth, and the mace-bearer climbed the freestanding white stone steps to enter the building—clearly the temple of the God. But when he came back down again his shoulders were slumped, and he said to the spear-carriers, "Take him back to the jail."

"What's wrong?" said Morlock. "I'd like to talk to your god."

"It doesn't matter what you want," the mace-bearer snapped. But, when he saw the spear-carriers gazing at him with curious looks he added, "We'll have to come back later. God is asleep."

Morlock shrugged and walked with his captors back to his cell.

But he had something to think about. For one thing, he knew that the local god needed sleep. And he thought he had recognized a claw-mark on the white stone steps. And the center of the temple floor had recently been reinforced with fresh pillars—elegant in form, but highly functional and cut from a different stone from the rest of the temple. It was interesting.

He waited a good part of the day, long enough to be bored with his own guesses. He looked out of the small barred window in the door and saw that there was a guard set outside. He'd expected that. The guard, if he wasn't mistaken, was the same one who had cut his feet loose. There was a scar or something on the left side of his snout.

"Hey, guard," he said. "What's your name?"

The guard looked at him sideways through a serpentine red eye.

"Eh," said Morlock, and turned away.

He waited a while, thinking about what he knew and what he guessed was true, and how he could turn it to his own advantage. It did not look promising. He wished Aloê were here to talk for him.

He was so deep in thought that he didn't realize at first that someone was talking to him. "Hey, Morlock," the guard had said through the cell window.

"Yes?"

"My name is Danadhar," the guard said.

"Thank you," Morlock said. "The one who struck me when I first arrived, the mace-bearer—"

"Skellar."

"—he said you do not call yourselves mandrakes."

"We do not," the guard said coldly, and started to turn away.

"Wait, if you would," Morlock said. "I don't mean to offend. What do you call yourselves?"

"Oh. We call us the Gray People, or simply the Grays."

"If I were back home among my people," Morlock said, "we might exchange family names and family news. But I will not offer to do that, as it might place you under some obligation." Under Thrymhaiam, hospitality was a powerful force, and he was curious if it was here.

"It is better not," Danadhar admitted shamefacedly, and Morlock knew his guess was close to the target. The Gray People had bound themselves to a code of virtue like his *harven*-kin.

"Let's talk of other things," Morlock said.

"Like what?" the guard asked emptily.

If the Gray Man was looking to Morlock for guidance in conversation, he really must be in a sad way. Morlock suggested, "Tell me about your god."

The guard began to turn away again. "Mocker!" he hissed.

"Wait!" Morlock said. "Why are you angry? Your god asked to speak with me. Don't you think that, eh, that my curiosity is natural?"

"I suppose so," Danadhar said reluctantly. "Yes, I suppose so. But it was the way you put it."

"How?"

"You say 'your god' as if there were many. But there is one true god, and his truth is for everybody."

"Understood." Morlock pondered his next statement carefully. "Danadhar," he said at last, "my own tradition, as taught me by my *harven*-kin in the western mountains, forbids me to self-bind in casual oaths. But I assure you that I will not mock you or your faith."

"Well. The God-speaker says our faith is true everywhere, true for everyone. It seems strange if we are not to tell others of it."

"Then."

"I don't know where to start. The God teaches us not to steal, not to withhold good things from those who need them, to honor our blood—"

"*Harven ruthenye*," Morlock said. "Chosen and given."

"Yes," Danadhar said. "Yes."

"My *harven*-kin taught me much the same," Morlock said.

"Then the words are true. They are true everywhere."

"Eh," Morlock said. "They are good rules. That is true. And your—the God taught you all these things?"

"Yes. Yes. Yes, he did!"

Morlock measured the urgency of this statement against any need for such urgency.

"But," he ventured.

Danadhar was silent.

"Did the God appear only recently?" Morlock guessed.

"Yes," Danadhar sobbed.

"Does he look like he was supposed to?"

"He looks more like the Ovinar."

"What's that?" Morlock didn't recognize the word.

"The Ovinar. The Enemy. The one responsible for all the evil in the world."

"Eh."

"The God-speaker says it is a test of our faith. He says. If we can see the God even in the Anti-God . . . then our faith is strong. I'm not sure—I'm not sure if my faith is that strong. I shouldn't have said that. I shouldn't talk anymore." But he didn't go away. It was as if he was waiting for something.

"Danadhar," said Morlock thoughtfully, "after the God began to dwell in the temple, did the dragon-plague begin to spread among the Grays?"

"Shut up!" the guarded roared through the window. "Shut up or I'll kill you!"

Morlock shut up. He had pushed the Gray One as far as he could.

Danadhar's snout disappeared from the cell window.

Morlock sat silent among his thoughts as the sunlight faded outside.

Presently, the troop of spear-carriers returned and told Danadhar that God was awake again. They opened the cell door and led him to the temple again.

They went again in procession through the town. It was dusk and there were snout-nosed children playing hide-and-seek in the village streets. The spear-carriers gently nudged them out of the way when they ran up to stare at Morlock with wide red eyes.

Skellar, bearing his gilded mace, was waiting for them at the temple steps. He curtly told the guards to wait there, then had Morlock precede him up the white stone steps to the temple.

"God, I have brought him," Skellar said as they entered.

The interior of the temple was a single great room, but it had not always been. Morlock saw ragged scars running down the length of the load-bearing walls in various spots: the traces of interior walls that had been cut out.

The center of the temple was a sort of well or waterless pool. Filling it with his serpentine coils was Rulgân the Outlier.

He had changed much since Morlock last saw him. His green-black scales had dulled to a leaden sheen. His right foreleg, in contrast, was a cage of intricate silver wires. Within the cage were the withered black bones of the dragon's lightning-ruined leg. And also, glowing like an eye in rapture, the Banestone of Saijok Mahr.

There was very little fire evident about the dragon at all, only a little smoke trailing from his jaws. The only light in the chamber came from the Banestone and from a peculiar crystalline device. Luminous cables extended from it into the narrow apertures of Rulgân's ears, and into the empty holes where his eyes had been.

What was that thing? Was it intended to heal Rulgân, or imprison him, or something else entirely? Morlock's fingers itched to examine it, but he doubted he would ever have the chance.

In spite of the state of his body, the dragon's voice still rumbled, deep as the canyon at the world's dark heart, when he said to Skellar, *It is well. Leave us.*

Morlock could not read expression on the plated faces of the Gray Folk, or even tell if their faces were meant to communicate emotion. But Skellar's stiff bow practically shouted his reluctance to leave. Still, he left.

You are surprised by my appearance, I see, Rulgân rumbled. *Or perhaps you thought me dead.*

"I hoped you were," Morlock admitted. "But you seem to be dying now."

No. This is a— This is temporary.

Morlock shrugged.

I wanted to see you, said the dragon, *to let you know I won. I am the person who did it to you. Let there be no doubt.*

"Then?"

If you are asking what I have done, the dragon said with some irritation, *I wish you would say so. However. What you would ask is of no moment. What I say is: I have defeated you, Morlock. When the Two Powers find you, remember it was I who gave them you.*

Morlock grunted skeptically. "And then you expect their reward to heal you from this . . . state?"

The dragon's leaden frame rippled, and the mutilated face bent in lines of surprise.

This is their reward, the dragon said. *They found me, floating where you left me in the ocean. They learned what I had to tell them. It fed their visualizations, and they knew when and where they would encompass you. So they brought me here and installed me as the god of the mandrakes.*

"Eh."

You don't understand, I see. This device was invented by the mandrake priests of old to draw new citizens to this town—new converts to the simple mandrake faith of virtue and fairness. They hoped to build a civilization of mandrakes on this bleak coast.

"They've made a good start."

The dragon laughed derisively. *The town is very old, and as large now as it has ever been. Someday a conquering king will notice it and sponge it off the map.*

"In the long run, we're all dead."

I don't know what you mean by that. But this device allows me to see through the eyes of every mandrake in the world. I cannot speak to them yet, persuade them yet, control them yet. That is what the device is for, and the skills may come in time. But the wealth of knowledge I have gained in this short time! I have begun to visualize as the gods do, constructing scenarios of the world, past/present/future.

Morlock looked with interest on his enemy. He was hoarding knowledge now, not gold. And feeling the impulse to share it, if only through boasting.

"I congratulate you," he said, without irony.

The dragon laughed derisively and said, *And I saw how you were teasing Danadhar. Go easy on him, please. I have plans for that one. Skellar is old and corrupt, commanding little respect among the mandrakes.*

"They don't like to be called that."

I, their god, am above such concerns. You, their prisoner, are not. Morlock: farewell forever.

"Until next time," Morlock said, and turned away.

➢◄

Danadhar was waiting at the foot of the temple stairs among the other spear-carriers.

"Come," he said impatiently to Morlock.

Morlock walked among his captors to a round house faced with black granite, standing not far from the temple.

"Go in," Danadhar told him.

Morlock opened the door and went in.

The interior of the house, like the temple, was one single room. But, unlike the temple, it had been built that way.

The floor of the house was heaped with gold and silver and a scattering of gems. On the heap, facedown, lay a Gray Man. He was bereft of kilt or mace, but Morlock thought he recognized him as the God-speaker, Skellar.

Skellar was not just lying atop the treasure; he was grovelling in it. His snout was buried deep in gold coins: kissing or nuzzling them.

"I am here," Morlock said, to cut short this embarrassing display.

Skellar rolled over on his side to face Morlock, but did not rise. There were gems and coins adhering to his genitals, apparently stuck there by some sort of oil or smegma.

"What did God say to you?" Skellar demanded.

"Why didn't you stay and eavesdrop?" Morlock asked.

"He has a way of knowing," Skellar said. "Well?"

"Then he has a way of knowing that you asked me this, and what I say to you," Morlock said.

"Insolence," Skellar observed coolly. "There was a time when no one in town would have spoken to me thus."

"Eh. That must have been some time before my arrival."

"Obviously. But things really got bad when God showed up."

"Didn't you ever expect him to? Aren't you his priest?"

"Please. Don't pretend to be naive. Danadhar told me enough about your conversation to let me realize you know what we are about, here."

"I'm not sure I do."

"There is no God, really. The God-speakers of old made up the faith simply to keep the Gray Folk from suffering the dragon-change. I understand the dwarven-kings of old had some similar method. When the God showed up a few months ago and worked the various miracles in the Open Books, I had to accept him or lose my congregation. But I know an opportunist when I see him. I own a mirror after all."

"Gods exist. Why didn't you invite one into your temple?"

"The God-speakers of old tried that, but they wouldn't have us," Skellar said. "Most were former men and women. They wanted to be worshipped by their kindred. Besides . . ."

"Yes?"

"Gods-as-they-are reign through power, not by example. We need our people to follow a strict moral code, or we will lose them to the dragon-change. We are really better off without a god in the temple. Then people can fill the empty space with their dreams, and things work better for us."

"What keeps you from the dragon-change?" Morlock asked, nodding at the hoard.

"The greatest discovery of the ancient God-speakers, greater even than morality."

"Yes?"

"Hypocrisy!" cried the mandrake, his red eyes alight with enthusiasm and something else. "The tension between pretended morality and its genuine opposite protects the hypocrite from the dragon-change."

"Eh." The air was very smoky in the vast treasure-cluttered room, and Morlock thought he detected the tang of venom in it.

"It doesn't matter if you accept the truth on which our civilization is based," Skellar said stiffly. "But there is a reward for you, perhaps as much as fif—as much as ten gold coins if you will help us to preserve it."

"How?"

The priest asked, "Will you please kill God? Then everything can go back as it was."

Morlock laughed. "No. Your god, your problem."

"To hell with you then."

"And also with you."

"I was not speaking metaphorically." The God-speaker raised his voice. "Danadhar!"

Slowly, reluctantly, the spear-carrier came through the dark door. He did not look at Skellar or at Morlock. "Yes, God-speaker."

"This stranger is an enemy of the God. He must be destroyed. I want you to take him outside of town and kill him."

Now Danadhar turned to stare at the priest. "But . . . the faith tells us we must never stain our weapons with unoffending stranger's blood!"

"He *has* offended. Exactly how need not concern you at the moment. But perhaps you are right. Yes, I'm sure you are right."

The spear-carrier sighed in relief. "Thank you, God-speaker."

"So take his own sword. It is on the hoard, here, let me give—let me loan it to you. Take his sword, and kill him with that. Well out of town, mind you. Then hide the body and bring the sword back to me. I will perform certain rites which will cleanse the sword and you of any accidental blood guilt. Then everything will be all right again, as it was before the stranger came."

Danadhar accepted Armageddon from Skellar with obvious reluctance. "God-speaker, please—"

"Yes?"

"I am tired and hungry. I have watched all day. Can someone else do this important task?"

"I am surprised at you, Danadhar, shirking your responsibilities this way. No, someone else may *not* do it. You are my best lad, Danadhar. The God and I were talking just today about how good you are. You are the only temple-guard I can trust with this."

"Yes, God-speaker," Danadhar said glumly. "Thank you, God-speaker." He gestured wearily at Morlock with Armageddon and herded him out the door of the God-speaker's house.

"Walk before me," the Gray snarled at Morlock. "Run and I'll skewer you."

Morlock didn't run. He waited while Danadhar dismissed the other guards, and then walked ahead of him down the street.

"Where to?" he asked the Gray.

"What difference does it make?" groaned Danadhar.

Morlock didn't answer. He walked along the street until it was no street any more. They went into the country until the Gray Folk's town was hidden by the dark shoulder of a hill.

By then it was full night. Chariot glared redly in the eastern sky; Trumpeter peered through broken clouds high above the western horizon.

"Stop," said Danadhar harshly.

Morlock turned to face his captor.

There was an oil or water seeping through the plates on Danadhar's face. (Tears? Sweat? Something else?) The Gray's right hand trembled as he raised Armageddon to strike at Morlock.

"It is dangerous for you to do what you know to be wrong," Morlock observed.

"But *is* it wrong?" Danadhar said. "The God-speaker told me to do it! The God makes the faith and the God-speaker teaches it!"

"You know it is wrong, and you know what the God-speaker is. You have seen how he lives."

"He says . . . Some are called to take on the burden of evil so that others can be good. And he has not changed, somehow . . ."

"Eh," Morlock said. "The air in his den reeks of smoke and poison. Already, when alone with his hoard, he crawls through it on his belly like a worm."

"He said," Danadhar said sadly. "He told me to."

The Gray stabbed halfheartedly at Morlock. Morlock, who had been waiting for the moment, dodged the blade but didn't avoid it entirely—nor did he intend to. The point slashed his left shoulder deep enough to draw blood; it fell, bright in the shadows, from the glass sword to the dry winter grass, where it began to smolder.

Danadhar reeled back. "Your blood burns!" he gasped.

"It does," said Morlock, holding his bound wrists up to his wounded shoulder. The burning Ambrosial blood began to gnaw through the hempen knots.

"So does mine," said Danadhar. He used Armageddon to slash his left forearm. Blood bright as Morlock's fell from it and infected the earth with fire.

"You are my *ruthen* kin," whispered the Gray. "I have shed your blood. And I would have killed you. I am as guilty as that pig in his golden wallow and that dying monster in the temple." He raised the glass sword, now with the point toward his own neck.

Morlock's hands were free. "Noddegamra," he said.

The glass sword fell to fragments as the Gray's lower jaw gaped with surprise.

"Armageddon," said Morlock.

The pieces flew toward Morlock's right hand, reassembling themselves in the air as they flew.

Danadhar fell to his knees. "Is it a miracle?" he said. "Have you come to teach us the truth?"

"Eh," Morlock said, backing away slowly.

"What does that mean?"

"You figure it out," said Morlock, and fled into the night, leaving behind the blood burning on the ground and his bestial blood-kin kneeling beside it.

CHAPTER TWENTY-FOUR

Sleigh Ride

That night a winter storm fell on the dead lands like an avalanche.

Aloê had spent one memorable winter in the Northhold; she was not the proverbial Southholder gaping in amazement at her first flake of snow. But she was sure she would have died that night if she had been on her own.

It was Ambrosia who saved them.

They were walking westward toward the Sea of Stones when Ambrosia arbitrarily stopped the march.

"Snow coming," she said curtly. "Got to get ready."

"Maybe we should try to reach the Colony of Truth?" suggested Aloê.

"No time. Smell the snow on that wind! Besides, they won't be glad to see us. They'll be finding gods under every mushroom in the fields before too long."

Ambrosia brusquely set Aloê to collecting deadwood, and then turned to weaving a sort of hut out of the dry field grass.

"At least the wood's dry," was the girl's only comment after Aloê had brought a third armload. "I wonder how long it's been dead?"

"How much more wood do you think we need?" Aloê asked.

"Depends," Ambrosia replied. "How badly do you want to live?"

"That's no answer."

"Just keep bringing it until the snow is getting too deep to walk in."

Aloê stolidly returned to collecting wood. Ambrosia lit a fire and went back to weaving her hut.

Aloê watched the hut grow in installments, catching a glimpse whenever she brought in a load of wood. It was looking like a dome or bubble of dry grass at one point. Then Ambrosia started covering the outside of the dome with clay she had excavated from the ground nearby.

The wind by now was pretty fierce, and edged with stinging ice crystals. Aloê was collecting wood at a run, now, piling it on the north side of the hut so as to form a windbreak for their shelter.

"Good," said Ambrosia tersely when she saw what Aloê was doing.

Then the snow fell on them like a wall of white. Aloê barely made it back to the hut with a last armload of wood, guiding her way by the last guttering light of the fire.

Ambrosia was standing by the tunnel-like entrance of the hut. "Come on!" she shouted. "Bring it in here!"

Aloê ducked down and entered the shelter on her knees, still cradling the firewood in her arms.

Ambrosia came crawling in behind her, and fastened the door when she was in.

The inside of the shelter was also lined with clay. The bare ground was lined with grass, except in the center where Ambrosia had built a clay-lined fire pit, complete with fire. There were cunningly placed breeze-holes to bring in a maximum of fresh air and let out the smoke while losing the minimum of heat.

"Amazing!" Aloê said, dropping the firewood on a heap already bolstering the northern wall.

"Thanks," said Ambrosia. "Where would you be without me, eh?"

"Dead."

"Maybe. Maybe. You're no creampuff, though. I'd'a stayed looking at that mirror till it ripped my soul in half if it weren't for you."

"Well, I enjoy hitting things. It's nice to put the habit to some productive use."

Ambrosia laughed sleepily. Her eyes closed for a moment, then jerked open again. "I'm a. I'm snoozy. I."

She fell over on the hut floor, her face and hair rippling like water. Presently she was gone, and it was Hope who opened her eyes, nodded amiably at Aloê, and glanced around her bemusedly.

"I take it we are narrowly escaping death again," she said presently.

"Thanks to Ambrosia, yes."

"I'm glad you're warming up to her," Hope said.

Aloê wasn't sure this was entirely true. "Well," she temporized, "the girl's had an odd life."

"Yes. Yes. Although I'm always annoyed by people who want special consideration because of their sad life-stories. The thing is, Ambrosia *doesn't* want special consideration. She simply wants to rule the world."

"Or the interesting parts, at least," Aloê offered.

Hope smiled quietly and nodded. "This would be almost cozy," she said, looking around the hut. "If only we had some food. And blankets."

"While you're wishing, don't forget a bottle of wine and mead. And a storybook and a handsome fellow to read it to us. Well, failing any of that, I'm going to sleep."

Hope said something in response, but Aloê's world was already getting dim and fuzzy. She crawled into a heap of dead grass and escaped from the world for a while.

Her dreams were luminous and mostly untroubled: she seemed to be swimming through warm waters alongside someone she trusted. The dreams ended as a shockingly bright cold current dragged her and that shadowy other apart.

She opened her eyes with a sense of loss and relief. Ambrosia was crawling through the tunnel-like entrance to the hut, pushing a bundle of wood ahead of her.

"Ah!" said Ambrosia. "You're up again."

"Urm."

"If that means, 'What's for breakfast?' I don't have anything for you. Otherwise this setup would be rather cozy."

"Your sister was saying the same thing last night."

"Oh. Well, I tell you what."

"What?"

"Storm's over. We're several feet deep in snow. Not much chance at digging for roots, or whatever could grow around here before you destroyed that god-shield. Let's hit the road and find a town or a farm or something to buy some food and a place out of the cold."

"It might be a long walk," Aloê reflected.

"Right!"

"Ah. I see what you mean," said Aloê, and crawled shivering out from her grassy blanket.

"It's not too bad out there—a little breezy, maybe," Ambrosia said. "Hope wove us some grass cloaks last night. At least I assume it was her."

"It wasn't me."

"Then. Let's leave the shelter here with the fire burning. If travel is too difficult, we can come back here."

"To starve."

"It might take months to starve. Cold can kill you in hours or less."

Aloê shuddered, and accepted the grass cloak from the imperious girl. She led the way out of the hut.

The tunnel-like entrance now opened into a trench of snow. Aloê stood up and surveyed a blinding white wilderness of hellish cold. The shelter was almost entirely buried in snow: only the crown of the roof was clear, due to the fire within, no doubt: the surface of the snow about it was splayed with a glittering crown of ice.

The sky above was a clear glorious blue, like warm seawater on a summer day, not too far from shore. But there was nothing warm about the air, with its cruel wind toothed like a saw-edge with crystals of blowing snow.

"Like I said," Ambrosia said, standing up beside her. "Not too bad."

"God Avenger," Aloê said, through chattering teeth. "What could be worse?"

"Freezing rain," Ambrosia said. "Or—hey, you're serious? Is it too cold for you to travel?"

"We can't wait for spring. Let's go."

"I grew up in the northern foothills of the Blackthorn Range," Ambrosia said, like an old woman reflecting on her long and varied life, "so this isn't so bad."

"I grew up in the Southhold of the Wardlands. I was twenty years old before I first saw snow."

"No! Really?" Ambrosia looked at Aloê with wild surmise. "What's that like?"

"I'll tell you on the way. Let's go."

"Take these, first," said Ambrosia, reaching into a nearby trench, containing their (almost depleted) stock of firewood. What Ambrosia handed her was a pair of screens made of sticks and grass on light wooden frames. "Snowshoes. Ever used them?"

"A couple of times, when I was fighting dragons in Northhold."

"Oh. Oh, yes?" Ambrosia pondered this while Aloê tied the snowshoes to her feet with twine wound from dry grass. When Aloê was about half-done, Ambrosia reached into the trench and drew out a pair of snowshoes for herself and was done securing them on her feet before Aloê took her first tentative steps.

"Where to, do you think?" Aloê asked the unwontedly quiet girl. "Should we scout for a town in visionary flight?"

"Maybe not," Ambrosia said. "With that god-shield down, whatever the whatever-it-was was worried about might be snooping around." She shrugged crooked shoulders and said, "I say south. Somewhere along the coast there should be something."

"If nothing else, we can fish."

They turned south and started slogging along the wind-packed surface of the snowdrifts.

They had not been walking long before the heard the merry sound of sleigh bells.

"Death and Justice," muttered Ambrosia.

"What is it?" Aloê asked.

"Worse. Who is it?" the girl said glumly.

Presently the sleigh came into sight over a ridge of snow. It was drawn by a team of eight fat men, wearing furry coats that made them look like bears. In the driver's bench of the sleigh was a tall man wearing a heavy white mantle and a warm red hood against the bitter wind. Instead of a whip he held a carillon of bells, and he played on it to drive the team forward.

The sleigh came up alongside them, and the old man sang a long sleepy word in a tongue Aloê did not know. The team drew to a halt and stood in the snow without shivering. The fur-lined hoods of their coats were so deep that their faces could hardly be seen, but Aloê caught sight of a few empty or malevolent expressions.

"Io, Saturnalia, father!" said Ambrosia. "Did you bring me any presents?"

"Life," said the old man, "or death. Get into the sleigh or I'll have to dispose of you."

"You'll face my brother if you do!" shouted the girl furiously. "His *harven*-father taught him what to do with a kinslayer!"

"Your brother, who knows so very little, will not even know the location of your exsanguinated corpse. There is danger for us on every side, Ambrosia, and I will take what risks I must. Choose now, Ambrosia: life or death."

"What about my friend?" demanded the girl. "Can you at least give her a ride to the coast?"

"Your friend," said the horrible kindly looking old man, and turned his bright blue eyes on Aloê. "Is this the young woman who sprang my trap under Old Azh?"

"I am Aloê Oaij, Vocate to the Graith of Guardians."

"I take that for a yes. You must get in, too, my dear. You are in this as deeply as we are, I'm afraid. I am Merlin Ambrosius, by the way, if you have not guessed."

"I have. What happens if we don't go along with you?"

"I will set my team upon you both. They are other than they seem. Your death will be dreadful and its aftermath more unpleasant still, possibly. On the other hand, I have food and blankets and hot tea in my sleigh."

"You might have mentioned that to start with," Aloê said, and climbed into the sleigh. Ambrosia followed, grumbling.

"Excellent," said the old man. He gave the bells a shake and shouted at the team, "Now, Legio! Now, Carnifex! Now Illspell and Malice! On, Zavuv! On, Ornias! On, Ephippas! On, Andhrakar!"

The furry figures leapt forward and began to run through the snow, dragging the sleigh after them.

Aloê was not unhappy with the turn of events. The sides of the sleigh protected them from the worst of the wind; the blankets were warmer than the grass cloaks. She shucked off both her snowshoes and her shoes proper and tucked her frozen feet into the relative warmth of her kneepits.

"There was some talk of food and tea," she pointed out.

Merlin laughed. "You really adapt yourself to circumstances, don't you?"

"What else should I adapt myself to? Is the food in this basket here?"

"Yes, help yourself. You might hand me a mug of tea when you have a moment."

In the wicker basket on the floor of the sleigh was a clay jar of hot tea and three mugs. The food was a dish of spicy sausages and a packet of crisp dried vegetables. Aloê shared the food and drink with the glum-faced girl beside her, then handed the old man a mug of tea.

"Thanks," he said. "Seriously, how could it happen between you and Morlock? I don't understand it."

"Is it necessary that you do?"

"I am the boy's father, after all. I have a natural interest."

"Natural!" Ambrosia laughed bitterly.

"Don't talk with your mouth full, girl. You'll choke."

"Save you the trouble."

"I don't mind taking the trouble, if it proves absolutely necessary," Merlin said, with a smile frostier than the bitter wind.

"Are you going to kill me, too, if I don't answer you?" Aloê said, matching his coldness.

He looked at her with some surprise. "I think you're misreading our family banter, my dear. But don't let it worry you. In our way, Ambrosia and I are very fond of each other."

"Stupid old fool!"

"Ambrosia, behave. We don't want Vocate Aloê to get the wrong impression of the family she's become attached to."

"Attached to?" Aloê said with some dismay. She had no desire to be attached to any family, particularly not this one. "How's that?"

"Because you have attached yourself to my son, my dear. A reckless choice, and one I'd have tried to talk you out of, had I been present for you to consult. But the thing is as it is."

"You're wrong about that, Merlin," Ambrosia said crossly. "Your cage caught her because they'd just been copulating."

"Don't be vulgar, Ambrosia."

"I said 'copulating,' didn't I? Is there a more polite word?"

"In any case, you're quite mistaken. Your brother is this woman's life-mate, and vice versa. I've seen couples married for centuries who weren't as talically intertwined as those two."

"Oh." Ambrosia looked dubiously at Aloê. "Really?"

"Really. Hence my *natural* curiosity, but that's all it is."

"Where are we headed, if you don't mind satisfying my natural curiosity?" Aloê intervened, to change the subject.

"A town not too far from here, on the edge of the dead zone that once prevailed over these parts. We should be safe there, for the time being, until

I come up with a new plan to protect myself from the Two Powers. I confess that you, my dear, fatally wounded my original plan, once and twice."

"Nothing personal."

"I don't agree at all. Anything that affects my safety, I consider very personal indeed. But I recognize that your blundering intrusion in Old Azh was quite accidental, and I am willing to recognize your defeat of the Balancer and his god-mirror as something heroic."

"Thanks."

"Don't be too flattered. I tend to find heroes a nuisance."

"Then I'm even more flattered."

"All right. Repay my kind words by telling me the tale. How were you captured? What happened after?"

Whatever his vices as a father, Merlin was a good listener. He heard Aloê through and then said, "I had planned to visit the Balancer after my blood was secured. The site may still be worth a visit, though it will be a tad more dangerous now."

"More dangerous?"

"Of course. The god-mirror was a defense against the Two Powers. That much is clear. Why the Balancer needed one is an interesting question, though perhaps less than urgent. How the mirror was constructed and how I can use its principles most effectively for our defense: those are the pressing issues."

"It's a defense that might be dangerous to those in its path, though," Aloê observed.

Merlin laughed as if she'd made a joke.

"You think he cares?" Ambrosia called out. "Hey, Merlin, where'd you get your sleigh team? Was the harthrang-dealer having a sale—buy seven and get the eighth for free?"

"What nonsense!" the genial old man said. "One never does business with a demonolater. They simply can't be relied on. One makes one's own harthrangs, or one does without."

"What's a harthrang?" asked Aloê.

"A demon inhabiting a human body," Ambrosia answered, before Merlin could speak. "These corpses seem surprisingly undecayed, Father."

"Thank you, my dear. The cold may have a preservative effect."

"Or maybe it's due to the fact that those bodies are still alive. You fed living people to those sceathes so that you could have your little team of reindeer."

"It was necessary," the necromancer said patiently, as if he were teaching his daughter the spelling of a difficult word that was very important to know. "The flaring and extrusive talic imprint of the harthrangs will successfully mask our own presence from the Two Powers. I have put this to the test, Ambrosia; I know that it works."

"And the people who died for your experiment?"

"They would have died sooner or later anyway," said the kindly looking old man.

"You old fool! If you can't trust a demonolater, how can you trust a half-dozen demons? Where do you think demonolaters learn their dishonesty?"

"I don't trust the demons; I master them." Merlin shook the carillon of bells, and the furry team of dybbuks frantically redoubled their efforts to draw the sleigh forward. "They obey me because they fear me. I am the master of the arts of all makers and seers in all the worlds we know, Ambrosia. You should fear me, too."

"Old fool," the girl muttered stubbornly.

"You said you tested them," Aloê observed, to distract the old man.

"Yes, indeed," Merlin said, ready to be distracted. "I have been trailing the Two Powers for a month or so. Or their avatars, anyway."

"What's the difference between the god and the avatar?"

"Sometimes not much," Merlin said. "The god's being has at least two anchors: one in the border of the talic and material planes, the other in the border between talic and spirit realms. Or so the old seers say. The avatar is the material echo of the god's nearer anchor. Its appearance is a function of the god's intentions as complicated by his identity."

"Or her identity."

"If you insist. I followed the avatars of Torlan and Zahkaar through the wreck of Old Azh. There was something they wanted to destroy there—"

"The Apotheosis Wheel, I think."

"Possibly. There was once much in Old Azh to learn, but there is not now. The Two Powers went through the island like fire through a prairie."

"Did they kill the last Watcher?"

"Eh? The mechanism, you mean? Kill is not the correct nomenclature, my dear. You can only kill something that is alive. But certainly the talic mechanism that once ran the island was inactive when I arrived, after the departure of the Powers (or their avatars). Most of those empty dog-people are dead; the rest will not survive long."

"Probably they did not pay attention to their daughters."

"Oh, do be quiet, Ambrosia; the grownups are talking." Merlin looked sideways at Aloê. "A strange ship passed my galley while I was on the Sea of Stones. It moved very fast, and not with the wind, but it had no oars. It strode across the waves on a pair of long legs—"

Aloê laughed. "That crazy bastard. Yes, yes. I can see it. The reduced friction would make very high speeds possible. But it might be a very fragile craft. I hope he didn't run into a storm."

"If you are referring to my son—"

"Isn't it obvious?"

"I confess I suspected it even at the time, even though I thought Morlock was safely in the bag." He looked darkly upon her. "Is that the attraction? You design ships together? Because otherwise I can't see it."

"Have you ever met your son?"

"Not since the day he was born. But we do have nonphysical communication from time to time. And I have seen pictures of him."

"Hm." Aloê found this remark distressing, but tried not to show it. Even such tenuous contact with an exile might be held against Morlock as a violation of the First Decree. But there was always the possibility that Merlin was lying.

"You don't intend to enlighten me, I see," Merlin remarked. "Possibly the explanation would involve unsavory details—"

"Or savory ones."

"Gross!"

"Ambrosia, enough."

Abruptly tumbling about their heads was a flock of chellnor birds, their gray wings flecked with white winter-feathers. The flock ran squawking westward.

Merlin and Aloê laughed in surprise.

"Where did they come from?" Aloê wondered.

"They nest in snow sometimes," Merlin observed. "I wonder if the team kicked up their nest. Life is returning to these dead lands, certainly. What you did was extremely inconvenient for me, my dear, but no doubt—"

Ambrosia leapt up from the back of the sleigh and snatched Aloê's glass staff. As Merlin and Aloê gaped, Ambrosia spun the staff, glittering in the sun, and smashed the skull of a harthrang who was climbing up the side of the sleigh. The skull shed its brains in the bitter white breeze, but the hands tried to hold on to the side of the sleigh. Ambrosia methodically pounded on the fingers until they could grip no longer, and the headless harthrang fell by the wayside as the sleigh ran on.

"The bells!" shouted Ambrosia at the gaping Merlin.

Aloê turned to see that the seven remaining harthrangs pulling the sleigh were looking backward, and three were fumbling at their harnesses. She seized the carillon from Merlin's nerveless fingers and shook it fiercely.

The harthrangs quailed at the shrill steely voices of the bells and turned away again, intent on the road ahead.

"Thank you, my dear," said Merlin frostily to Aloê, as if he were offering to cut her throat, and seized the carillon back. "And thank you, Ambrosia," he said as his daughter silently handed the staff back to Aloê. "I can't think of what drove the harthrang to it. It will have to abandon that body, and when I get around to activating its oath, it will begin a very unpleasant spiral to the final death."

"Maybe it was desperate," Ambrosia suggested.

"What does it have to fear more than me? I ask you."

"I'm telling and telling you. But you never listen." The girl sat down again in the back of the sleigh.

They rode on in silence, except for when Merlin gave the carillon an occasional imperious shake, to keep the harthrangs at their task.

Finally they came to a small town. The sea was near enough that Aloê could smell it, and the air was milder there than any she had felt all day; the snow was melting in the town's single street.

The snow was unmarked by footprints. There was one chimney in the middle of town that was issuing a dim thread of smoke from its black mouth; the houses were reasonably well-kept. But there was no other sign that the town was still occupied.

"Who lives here?" Aloê asked.

"For the time being," Merlin said, "we do. I will ask you ladies to unharness my team and draw the sleigh into yonder barn. Then I will stake the harthrangs to their posts as a perimeter guard, and we can rest from our travels."

Aloê and Ambrosia dismounted and approached the harthrangs gingerly. The harthrangs watched, enigmatic in their furred hoods, but did not otherwise move as the women unhooked them from the bar of the sleigh.

"Ambrosia," Aloê whispered.

"Hm?"

"I think this body is dead."

"This one, too. How recently is yours gone?"

"Sometime today, I think."

"This one, too."

"What does it mean?"

"Tell you later."

"Is it good or bad?"

"Really bad."

They finished releasing the harthrangs without incident. Merlin dismounted the sleigh and began speaking to the harthrangs in a language Aloê did not know. It sounded like a mudshark crunching bear-bones.

The two women unpacked the sleigh and dragged it into the barn Merlin had pointed out. It was next door to the one building that seemed to be occupied.

Inside the barn were several horses, about five cows, and a large number of chickens. The chickens were all dead, but the larger animals were alive.

They wouldn't be much longer without help, though. They had plenty of fodder, but their water troughs were bone dry.

"What happened here?" Aloê asked Ambrosia. "Did the people just walk away?"

"Hope so," Ambrosia said. "Don't think so, though," she added, after a moment. She was reminding Aloê more of her brother all the time, and not in a good way.

Once they had the sleigh in the middle of the barn and the great doors closed, Aloê dragged one of the water troughs out of a side door and started filling it with wet snow and slush.

She dragged it back into the barn with rather more difficulty. By then

Ambrosia had disappeared somewhere. Aloê found a pair of water buckets and used them to carry snow into the barn until all the water-troughs were full to the brim with slush.

She did all this with a sense of mingled obligation and futility. "Don't know who's going to take care of you when we're gone," she told a horse who was taking tentative licks at a pool of melting snow. "But maybe we can let you loose to fend for yourselves." The horse made no reply.

She looked up to see Ambrosia standing nearby. The girl was looking more alarmed than ever.

"What is it, honey?" Aloê asked.

"Come see."

Ambrosia led her out of the back of the barn. Not too far away was the town graveyard. One of the crypts was standing open, mysteriously free of the melting snow. There was room inside for two or three bodies, but there were none within. Many a runic imprecation and trap had been freshly carved into the weathered stone.

"This is for us, I think," Ambrosia said. "Me, and Morlock, and maybe you, now, too. The spells would bar anyone from detecting what was inside, even something as acrid as the blood of Ambrose."

"How could we live in there?"

"I don't think we are meant to."

"How did you find it?"

"I was looking for it. Come on; there's something else."

Ambrosia led Aloê into a house next to the graveyard. Inside the sole room were the bodies of an old man, and old woman, and a young man.

"So they didn't walk away," Aloê mused. "They were killed. No, wait!"

She knelt down by the side of the old man. His chest was rising and falling; the whites of his eyes were still clear, not darkened by the brown shadow of death. "They're still alive!" she said. "At least some of them."

"No," Ambrosia said, with unusual somberness. "Some of the bodies may still live, but only their vegetative souls. The people aren't here anymore. They have been killed, eaten."

"By the harthrangs."

"That's what demons live on: the tal of living rational souls."

"I take it you're telling me we should get out of here."

"Not yet," Ambrosia said thoughtfully. "He'll be expecting something like that, and will have prepared against it. But something is obviously going to happen that he doesn't seem to expect. Maybe we can make a break then. Be sure to follow my lead," said the imperious girl.

"What if you are Hope at the time? Should I follow her lead?"

Ambrosia thought in silence for a while. "Almost certainly not," she said. "Hope's first thought will be to help Merlin. There's no way you can stop her from being a fool. Be sure to get away yourself; there won't be anything you can do for us."

"We'll see."

"Uh. Was I—?"

"Don't worry about it."

They returned to the front of the barn, where Merlin was waiting for them.

"All eight harthrangs have been anchored about the village," he said, with a sly smile. "Their talic imprint should shield us from any unwanted attention from the Two Powers."

Ambrosia nodded indifferently. "Eight, eh? So you gave one of the townspeople's bodies to one of the demons. One of the harthrangs is a double. Is that it?"

"Yes," said Merlin irritably. He had obviously wanted to explain this himself.

"Which one is it?" Ambrosia asked.

Merlin thought a while before answering, but finally admitted, "It is Andhrakar."

"He's the strongest, then?"

"Not necessarily. Perhaps he is merely the most reckless. Occupying two bodies at once puts him at a certain risk."

"Only from you. And you can't afford to harm him."

"You're talking nonsense, daughter. I will do what I must. Andhrakar knows that. So should you."

"But others will do what *they* must. And that's something you don't really understand, father, not the way I do. That's why I will be the greatest ruler in the history of this world, and you are a man whose home was burgled by a rogue godlet."

He looked at her quizzically. "Trying to goad me into a rage? It won't work, you know."

"Only into thinking. That probably won't work either."

"Either way, we'll be more comfortable inside." He gestured for them to precede him, and they did.

The building was the smithy, and the smoke was coming from the big central furnace.

"We should set up some beds in here, my dears," the old man said. "It may be inconvenient, but we should sleep in the same room for the time being." He gestured with the carillon.

"In case his tame demons attack in the middle of the night, he means," Ambrosia observed.

"I heard him," Aloê said curtly.

They raided rooms in the rest of the house for beds, and then scavenged up food in the rest of the town to last them for a day or so.

"And now," Merlin said, like a kindly schoolmaster dismissing his students to play, "you may amuse yourselves, my dears. I strongly suggest that you do not leave town; the harthrangs have been instructed to stop you. For myself, I must give some thought on how to lure my son into this zone of protection, and then what my next steps will be."

Ambrosia muttered inaudibly and drew Aloê to the side. "He's not telling you, so I'll tell you. There are things you have to be aware of around demons, bound or not. Try not to pay too much attention to any voices you hear in your head. Certainly don't accept any offers they make. If they won't leave you alone, just scream for a while."

"Seriously?"

"Yes. It has a dispersing impact on ghosts and demons generally. That's why the first thing a specter will do is paralyze your larynx. And don't ascend into vision unless you absolutely have to. He probably doesn't care if you get possessed by demons; it'd change your talic pattern, which is the only thing entangling you with the blood of Ambrose—i.e., *him*."

Aloê smiled at the odd, intense, hatchet-faced girl. "But you would care, honey?"

"Sort of. Don't get mushy on me. I have to go write a letter to my sister."

It was a meditative afternoon all around. Aloê, too, gave a lot of thought to what would happen next. Because she was pretty sure something would happen that the other two (or three) weren't counting on.

The long afternoon passed; they gathered to eat around sunset. Ambrosia had become Hope, by then. There was very little conversation through the meal, and afterward they settled down to sleep.

Merlin's bed was next to the forge, with Aloê's and Hope's beds on either side, closer to the doors.

"Wait a moment," Aloê said to Hope, after they said good night, "*do* you sleep?"

Hope laughed. "I used to. In fact, I've lived more of our life than Ambrosia has. But once she figured that out, she started fighting back, and now when I sleep she usually takes over. Tonight I think I will not sleep."

"Happy waking, then," Aloê said, and dragged herself to her bed. It wasn't such a great bed, apart from the fact that it *was a bed*. She'd almost forgotten what it was like to sleep in one, but she caught the knack of it again pretty rapidly.

In a dark hour full of whispering, Aloê heard a voice call out, "Aloê. Merlin. Wake up. Wake up. They're here."

Aloê's eyes gaped open. The great room was lit by the red light of the forge. All around the room, like sentinels, stood the harthrangs. They were not wearing their hooded jackets; symbols had been cut or clawed into many of their faces; and all their dead eyes stared at Merlin.

"Get back to your posts," croaked Merlin furiously. He reached over by the furnace to grab the carillon of bells and gave it a vigorous shake.

Silence. In the dim light, Aloê saw the steel bells misshapen like wax, dripping molten metal that set Merlin's bedding alight.

The harthrangs stepped forward.

Merlin's throat issued more croaking sounds, but they didn't rise to the level of words.

The dead faces of the harthrangs smiled. Their teeth had been filed needle-sharp.

Aloê jumped as someone touched her arm. It was Ambrosia. "Let's get out of here," she said. "This is it."

"What about your father?"

"What about him? He killed everyone in this town to feed that demon. Now it's turning on him. He made his own bed; let him burn in it."

The two women turned away, but there were harthrangs behind them too, and they were seized and held. Aloê kicked and elbowed her captors as much as she could, but it was useless. She could smell their rotting flesh. They weren't alive: if the bodies felt pain, it didn't matter to the beings that controlled them.

"Look, Andhrakar," Ambrosia said. "You're making a mistake. We aren't parties to your filthy bargain and we have unlimited capacity to harm you. This is your last warning."

The harthrangs did not respond in any way. They continued to smile their needle-toothed smiles at Merlin and stepped toward him again as the others did the same.

"How do you know which one it is?" Aloê asked.

"They're all the same now," Ambrosia said impatiently. "One of the demons ate all the others. Listen, you remember what I told you to do in a certain context."

"Yes, I think so."

"Do it with me. Loud. Now."

Ambrosia screamed and Aloê followed suit.

The girl's scream was high-pitched, ululating, angry rather than frightened—a war-cry. Aloê matched it and bettered its volume.

It hit the harthrangs harder than a sledgehammer. They staggered and their hands slackened; the women dropped to the floor and ran.

Aloê was headed for an outer door, but Ambrosia grabbed her and led her to an inner room of the house—a guesting room, by the looks of it, with ornamental chairs of polished dark wood that looked relatively unused.

"This door looks solid enough to keep them out," Ambrosia said. "And no windows or other doors. It's perfect!"

"What if that fire spreads—the one Merlin started?"

"Even better! Demons hate fire, as a rule, and it'll damage the corpses to uselessness. We can sit comfortably in the burning house until they're all driven off. I wonder if he started the fire on purpose? He is pretty clever sometimes."

"Um. Ambrosia. *I* can't sit comfortably in a burning house."

"What? Oh. Oh. Of course not. Sorry, Aloê; I was forgetting you're not one of us."

"Thanks."

"Listen, I said I was sorry!"

"And I said, 'Thanks' and I meant it. Calm down, honey; we'll think of something."

They listened for sounds from the next room. There was a kind of wet crack, and Merlin made a kind of clucking sound.

"It got him," Ambrosia said glumly. "I guess the fire didn't work."

"One bone, Ambrosius," the dead throats chanted in the other room. "One bone I will break for every time your bells made me cower."

Aloê speculated on how many times that had happened, over the months Merlin had been travelling with his bodyguard of demons. From the look in Ambrosia's wide worried eyes, she was making the same calculation. Hundreds of times? How many bones were there in the human body? Would the demon double up when it ran out of bones to break?

Another crack, and a gargling sound from the old man's throat.

Ambrosia's expression was now getting frantic. As for Aloê, she was sickened . . . but she remembered the crypt in the graveyard, and the empty faces of the townfolk whose souls had fed the demons, and she was disinclined to risk her safety for the sake of Merlin's.

Still, their turn might come next.

A door slammed open in the next room, and the winter wind howled through it.

Someone took a long single stride into the smithy.

"Put the old man down," said the newcomer. "I would have words with him."

"The old man has spoken his last words," the eight dead throats of Andhrakar replied. "Leave him to the pain he has earned, and you will earn no pain for yourself."

"Eh," said the newcomer, and drew his sword.

Ambrosia was staring at Aloê in wild surmise. Aloê said, "Let's go meet your brother, honey. He'll need us in half a hot second, or I'm very much mistaken."

"Right!" shouted Ambrosia.

Aloê seized the door handle and pushed on it.

It rattled but did not move. The harthrangs had barred it from the other side.

"We thought we locked them out," Aloê observed wryly. "But we really locked ourselves in."

CHAPTER TWENTY-FIVE

The Binding of Andhrakar

Morlock had been running for days before he caught sight of the burning building. At first he passed through settled lands, where he could acquire food and gear for the road for some scattered hours of work. As he came closer to the source of the talic wave, settlements were scarcer, and then vanished entirely. He sometimes saw fragments of walls and houses, but no people, no animals or birds. The trees were all dead. He noted all this, and thought about it as he ran. When he could not run any longer, he walked. He slept as little as he could.

His course, after all, was clear. He would run toward this thing that he hated and dreaded, in the hope that it masked the person he loved.

Then: the eucatastrophe. He awoke one night to a soaring feeling that everything would be all right, that the world had been healed of a terrible wound. The absence of dread and terror was exhilarating, disorienting—like drunkenness.

Finally he realized: the talic wave was gone. And that was a disaster. He had been assuming that Aloê had been carried eastward because the source of the talic wave was there. Now he had no guide, no way to find her.

Still, he smiled to himself. "They got more than they bargained for, I guess," he remarked to the dead land, the moonless night.

He risked ascending into vision, hoping to see something to give him guidance.

And he did. To the west and north—far away, but too near for comfort, were the grinding, hate-filled avatars of the Two Powers.

And there was something nearer at hand that he had seen/felt before: the flaring convulsed talic imprint of a choir of demons. It was due west of him, but moving south rapidly.

He returned to himself to find his body half buried in snow. He shook loose from the deadly white cocoon and slogged through the storm. Not toward the thing he had seen, but south of that, tracing a line in his mind on an imaginary map of the world. Somewhere on that line, he would meet someone he knew, or so he guessed. It was all he had to go on.

When day came, so did a sign of hope: a shelter made of wood and clay, with a fire burning in its heart.

No one was there. But he could sense Aloê's presence. She had been here; he was sure of it. He slept a couple hours in a heap of dried grass, and dreamed they were wrapped in each other's arms.

When he awoke he broke up the shelter into sticks, wove twine from the dried grass, and made snowshoes for himself. He went faster after that. He was heartened to see snowshoe-tracks leading away from the shelter, and followed them.

He was not surprised to see two sets of them. The snow shelter had been cunningly made by experienced hands. He had all the respect in the world for Aloê's cunning, but making snow shelters was not a skill she would have acquired in the Southhold.

He saw the snowshoe tracks joined by sleigh tracks and then disappear.

A tracker he was not. But the imprints clearly told him the sleigh was drawn not by animals, but by things wearing snowshoes. Men.

"Or harthrangs," he remarked to the brilliant blue-and-white day, and ran on.

His guess was confirmed when he came across a corpse lying beside the sleigh tracks. Its skull had been shattered, and the brains were scattered in a pinkish gray splash along the nearby snow. The corpse was void of any kind of life, but it bore the talic stress of recent occupation by a demon.

He ran on grimly in the sleigh's wake.

At last he came to a dead town, not too far from the warm embrace of the sea. He unbound his feet from the snowshoes and approached cautiously, loosening Armageddon in its sheath.

In the center of town was a building with a fire in it. But he went first into one of the dark houses.

Lying prone on the floor were a man, a woman, and three children. Two of the children were dead as stones. The other bodies were still breathing, but they bore the talic imprint of lettuce: their rational souls had been eaten from within.

Morlock left the house with its door open behind him and crept closer to the occupied building in the dead town's heart. A smithy, almost certainly: that great central chimney was for some kind of furnace or forge, anyway.

There was not only a fire in the building, he saw. It was on fire. There was smoke leaking from the roof away from the chimney.

He had a dreadful feeling he had come too late. He kicked open the door and stepped in.

Eight harthrangs stood in various places about the room. There were three beds, one of which was on fire. And one of the harthrangs was holding an old man by the neck and carefully, deliberately, breaking his arm.

Morlock had never seen the old man before, in a way, but he knew his features well. It was his *ruthen* father, Merlin Ambrosius.

"Put the old man down," said Morlock. "I would have words with him."

"The old man has spoken his last words," the eight dead throats replied in chorus. "Leave him to the pain he has earned, and you will earn no pain for yourself."

"Eh," said Morlock, and drew his sword.

"I will kill the old man, and you will have no words with him," the eight dead throats spoke in chorus.

"I was never that fond of him," Morlock said. Partly he was bluffing. But he also felt the shape of his world changing when he noticed that the door to an inner room had been barred shut and someone was rattling it from the other side. There might be many people with the reckless courage it would take to force their way into a roomful of demon-possessed corpses. There might be many, yes. But he knew only of one.

The harthrangs rushed at him, their hands weaponless, hoping to bear him down with their numbers.

He took a long leap back across the threshold so that they would have to come at him singly. He stood in the dark wintry wind, facing the light and warmth filled with demons, and waited through the long seconds he must wait.

The bodies of the harthrangs were well-matched in size and strength (the better to pull a sleigh or row a galley together, he supposed). But they were coming from different parts of the room, and they arrived at different moments. When the first harthrang stood framed in the doorway, Morlock kicked him with one foot high on the chest. The harthrang tumbled backward, its hands flailing for purchase that was not to be found. Morlock leapt atop it, landing with both feet atop the harthrang's head. It crunched under his heels like a gigantic bug.

The corpse began to convulse desperately. Harthrangs did not feel pain, so Lernaion and the sages of New Moorhope had taught him. But they hated to lose the cruel pleasures of a stolen body. He stabbed the corpse in the neck. The dead heart of a corpse did not make fresh blood, as a living one does, and without blood not even the pseudolife of the second death can be maintained. This, too, was wisdom from New Moorhope.

But the convulsing corpse threw him to the floor, sprawling in the middle of a cluster of harthrangs. He leaned into the roll and tumbled past them on the cluttered floor of the smithy. He jumped to his feet and ran to the other side of the room, where he saw another door open to the chill white night.

He ran through it and took his stand outside the second door, waiting again for the harthrangs to form up and attack. There would be one less, now. And they were armed. He saw five grabbing up iron implements from the smithy: tongs, shovels, a string of horseshoes. The sixth stood in the center of the room, watching the fight, holding Merlin (whose face marked him as unconscious or dead). There was something there worth thinking about, but a more urgent matter suddenly occurred to him.

There had been at least eight harthrangs in the room when he arrived. There were now seven. Where was the other one?

And this door had been standing open.

Morlock turned left, not quite in the nick of time, to confront the missing harthrang. Before he was set to strike with Armageddon, it had gripped his sword arm with one dead hand and his throat with the other. The dark world began to get darker.

Morlock took a wrestler's stance, gripped the harthrang under the right armpit with his left hand, and threw it with all his strength rightward, toward the open door.

It lost its footing and its grip on his throat, but not its hold on his arm. The body fell across the threshold of the open door.

With one eye on the approaching crowd of corpses, Morlock dragged the fallen harthrang partly back over the threshold and, using his free hand, slammed the door shut against its neck. It began the flail and kick at him. He put his left and lower shoulder against the door, set his feet in the hard snow-covered ground, and began to force the door shut against the harthrang's neck.

Letting go of his arm, the trapped harthrang kicked and punched and threw itself about. It wasn't giving up easily. Plus, its fellow corpses were now pounding and pushing at the door from the other side.

The door vibrated with a solid *chunk*, and the shining edge of an axe-blade was protruding through its surface, about a thumb's width from Morlock's straining shoulder. It disappeared. Morlock knew it would be back soon.

Morlock pondered various unpleasant alternatives when suddenly came a sound he had been dreading: splintering wood.

But it wasn't *his* door that was splintering. Two new pair of footfalls stormed into the room inside.

"Hey, Morlock!" joyously shouted a voice he seemed to know, but didn't quite recognize. "Save some for us— Hey, where is he?"

"Door," said the most glorious voice in any world.

As if it had heard, the door suddenly ceased to press on Morlock's shoulder as hard as it had been. Most of the harthrangs had turned away: toward *her*.

He stabbed Armageddon into the heart of the fallen harthrang and twisted the point once it was set, so that the corpse would bleed out faster. Then he threw the door open.

One harthrang remained on the threshold within, the axe-bearer. Morlock thrust instantly at its neck, but it was ware of him and parried with the axe. It tried to trap Armageddon between the axe and the doorpost. Morlock slashed down and cut at the axe-wielder's right knee. By the time the harthrang realized what he was doing and desperately slashed at him with the axe, it was falling aslant in the doorway; the axe buried itself in the hinges of the door.

Over the slumping harthrang, Morlock saw Aloê and a young woman (or older girl) in fierce combat with a crowd of demon-haunted corpses. Aloê was dealing her glass staff with deadly efficiency—or it would have been, if her opponents weren't already dead. The crowd of them didn't give her time to spin it and build up an impulse charge. The younger woman had a two-pronged hay-fork in her hands and was using it with enthusiastic skill as a spear.

Then the maiden unleashed the most dangerous weapon in the conflict: her voice. She screamed, in a prolonged and precisely ululating wail, *"AN-DHRA-KA-A-A-AR!"*

The harthrangs were disoriented—one could almost say dismayed. Morlock was fascinated. He risked ascending to the lowest level of vision. It lost him considerable mobility, but he thought it was worth it to understand what was happening.

And it was. The girl's intention, woven into the pitch of her scream, set up a kind of ripple at the border between matter and tal. It distressed the demon inhabiting the corpses.

The girl ran out of breath and the scream ended, but the memory of it lingered in Morlock's mind. If he could project the same effect, using the talic lattice of his sword as a focus . . .

Morlock began to sing—a single vowel, sliding up and down the scale until he found the perfect painful pitch. As important was the intention— a specific stutter of tal-cloaked rage . . . or maybe it was more like laughter. Morlock sang the note and projected the intention through Armageddon.

The slumping harthrang in the door ceased its vain struggle to release the axe from the doorpost and fell backward, struggling to escape the deadly song.

Now Aloê and the maiden had joined in. All the harthrangs were retreating toward the one holding Merlin.

Even in his light trance, Morlock could see the flaring webwork of demonic tal spreading out from that one harthrang to all the others. That corpse, the one holding Merlin, was the material anchor of the demon controlling all these undead.

The harthrangs fell, all but the one at the center of the talic web. That one lifted Merlin high in both hands. It seemed to be about to break Merlin's back. Then, no doubt, it would flee—to eat other souls, ruin other lives elsewhere.

On impulse, Morlock threw Armageddon like a spear. It passed just under Merlin's slack body, through the harthrang's chest.

"Noddegamra!" shouted Morlock, and the sword burst into fragments, slaying the undead body.

"Armageddon!" he shouted.

Spattered with thick cold blood but glowing with demonic life, the sword flew back to Morlock's hand.

"Got you," Morlock snarled, and drove the blade deep into the earthen floor of the smithy.

He looked up, and in the next instant Aloê was in his arms. All the pain and grief and loneliness in the world ended then forever, at least for a little while.

≥≤

"If you guys are done," the girl said tentatively, after the first flurry of kissing had subsided and Aloê and Morlock were gazing at each other in great and incredulous content.

"Oh!" Aloê said. "I forgot! Your sisters is here."

Morlock looked more closely at her. Was she disoriented? It was unlike Aloê to make so odd a mistake.

But the girl was looking at him with a kind of hurt yearning, and he said, "You would be Ambrosia Viviana, I expect. It's good to meet you at last. Is Hope here?"

"Everybody asks me about Hope!" the girl shouted, in sudden inexplicable fury. "What am I, her housekeeper? 'Oh, you, here's a message for Hope.' 'Thanks person-who-doesn't-give-a-fractional-damn-about-me! I'll deliver it first thing!' Like that! Only *all the time*!"

"What," asked Morlock, "are you talking about?"

"It's a touchy subject," Aloê said, glancing at him with an odd look— both concern and relief. "Hope is . . . is safe at the moment. Will you accept that?"

Morlock nodded. Aloê said it; of course he would accept it.

The girl was standing closer now, tears in her eyes. "Look. I'm sorry. I'm a—"

He put a hand on her right shoulder. Like his, it was higher than the left. Her face looked a little like his, too. That was no good luck for her, he was afraid. "It's all right," he said.

Then she was hanging on to him desperately. "I've missed you so long!" she sobbed, this girl he had never met before. "Ever since I knew you existed. I said, I said, 'Someday, we'll meet. And there will be someone else. Someone who understands. And everything will be all right. And now. And now. Here you are. And everything is all right. You say it is, and it is. It is! It is!"

Morlock looked over her crooked shoulders at the burning room, littered with corpses, centered on the broken body of their *ruthen* father.

Aloê hugged her from the other side. "That's right, honey," she said, meeting Morlock's eyes with a sad smile. "Everything's all right now."

Every storm subsides in time, and the violent ones pass soonest. After a while, Ambrosia was snorking back snot and wiping the tears off her face with her sleeve.

"Hey, we'd better do something about that demon," she said, pointing at Armageddon.

The glowing glass blade was showing cracks that widened, narrowed, widened again. It was oddly like teeth champing.

"Eh," said Morlock. "I hoped that had ended the matter."

"Nope. It was a good idea, though. The angularity of the crystal lattices has a confining effect on the demonic tal, but the bonds need to be strengthened, more lattices added. Maybe they should be Moebius-ed together, if we can work out the geometry."

Aloê was smiling significantly at Morlock, as if to say, *Now it's your turn, friend.*

"We might be able to craft a suitable ur-shape in a higher dimension," he said to Ambrosia, and Aloê's face fell a little.

"Uh. Yeah. Run the demon around and around on a narrow little path until he's back where he started before he started. I like it!"

"I wish we had some lightning, though."

"Right! Put the demon straight out of our misery! But I wouldn't bet on any good thunderstorms until spring around here."

Morlock nodded, and began to think about ur-shapes that might meet their particular needs.

"I'll tend to Merlin," Aloê said resignedly, "while you two work it out."

"Merlin," said Ambrosia. "Gah."

In the end they superheated the forge by redirecting its heat back toward it. Morlock placed Armageddon, still containing the demon, into the hottest part. Then, as Ambrosia contained the demon by walking around the forge and singing his name at the pitch of most pain, Morlock went into deep vision and imposed new sets of lattices in the molten glass, folding and refolding it as it became denser and darker, swallowing the forge's heat along with most of Armageddon's matter, until there was only a single cold piece of glasslike metal in the heart of the frost-covered forge.

"That," Ambrosia said, tentatively tapping the piece of singing metal, "is stable. Old Andhrakar's not going anywhere!"

Her face was slick with sweat. Morlock, arising from his trance, pounded her higher shoulder. "That was good work," he said.

"You too," said the girl. "You too. Boy, I don't want to ever have to do something like that again!"

She picked up the piece of metal binding the demon, and it began to sing in exquisite hungry pain. "Wow," she said. "This thing really wants to kill someone."

"We should bury it, or something."

"Or something. The crypt!"

"What crypt?"

"Our father's plan to put us out of action while he ran like a rabbit from the Two Powers. Come on; I'll show you."

Morlock inspected the crypt in the graveyard, added a few refinements to the traps, carved a warning on the door, then placed the bitter dark blade in the crypt. He and Ambrosia closed the door and activated the sealing runes.

"And that," said Ambrosia with satisfaction, "is the end of Andhrakar!"

"Hope so." Morlock looked at the odd angry girl in the gray light of dawn. They had been working all night, but she didn't seem weary. There was a fire in his blood. "I wish we had met before."

"In person, you mean? Death and Justice, so do I. Life hasn't been easy sometimes."

"Eh."

They went back into the smithy as Ambrosia bent his ear about many a thing, most of which he did not understand.

In the smithy, Merlin (with his left arm and both legs bound up in splints) was talking as intently to Aloê, who was listening with a look of cool skepticism in her golden eyes.

The old man turned from her in mid-sentence as his son and daughter approached.

"So you are here at last," the old man said sourly, "and we can finally begin the business at hand."

"Is he ready to travel?" said Morlock over Merlin's head to Aloê.

She had spent enough time in the Northhold to know how discourteous Morlock's action was. Her eyes widened slightly, but she smiled and said, "There's a sleigh. He could travel in that, if he's of a mind to."

"I am not!" said the old man furiously.

"Then," Morlock said laconically, and turned to the women. "I think we should leave as soon as possible. The Two Powers took note of me when I was in the visionary state, and they may be here soon."

"You young fool!"

"We know enough, I think, to justify a return to the Wardlands," Morlock continued.

"Has it escaped your notice," Merlin said querulously, "that I and my daughters are exiles and may not return there?"

"You can," Aloê said, "under our protection. Not to stay, perhaps—sorry, honey! But to take refuge from the Two Powers and help in the struggle to maintain the guard. Worst come to worst, you can set sail on the Sea of Worlds until the Graith deals with the Powers."

"The Graith!" Merlin said and spat, as if it were a foul taste in his mouth. "No, my dears, I have a better plan, one much more likely to succeed, now that we are gathered together. Consequently, that is the one we will follow. I have discovered a method of totally obscuring our presence from the Powers' scope of visualization. A cloak of invisibility, as it were. But it could be penetrated by a Pursuer spell based on our shared blood."

"Or other fluids!" Ambrosia said, looking wryly at Aloê.

"Shut up, daughter. This has not worked out quite as I hoped, but all may be well."

"No," said Morlock.

"You have to listen to me."

"No," Morlock said. "You may come with us in the sleigh, and join us on the road to the Wardlands. Or you may stay here in this charnel village that you sacrificed to feed your demons. But we will not listen to you."

"You're an idiot, you know. You defeated and bound one demon—the three of you. I alone bound eight of them and drove them like draft animals for months, trying to save your sorry skins—"

"Our blood, father, our blood," interrupted Ambrosia gleefully. "Let's not pretend you care about anything else. We saw the crypt you made for us."

"I intended you to see it, to understand what the penalties for disobedience were. I never expected it to be used."

"But now it *has* been used, as a final resting place for your pet demon— you know, the draft animal we had to save you from."

"This is all beside the point," Morlock said. "Merlin, will you come with us, or stay here?"

"Stay here," said the old man sullenly with tears on his face. "Marginally better chance. Two Powers will be on you before you know it."

"If they are," said Morlock in the pride of his youth, "so much the worse for them," and turned away from the wounded weeping old man.

CHAPTER TWENTY-SIX

Between Two Thrones

They left the sleigh in the barn and saddled the horses for riding. The beasts were burly and underexercised, eager for a run. They were also a little restless with their reins in the hands of such inexperienced riders. (It turned out that none of them were great equestrians. Aloê had the most experience riding of the three, and she hated it.) But persuasion and firmness had their effect, and the horses in fact seemed eager to leave the town, as if they understood some of the evil that had taken place in it.

They rode toward the sea, west as straight as they could through the pathless snows.

But as they rode, the snow grew thinner and the sun seemed to creep across the sky. It kept swinging to the left, however they turned.

The air got colder, thinner, drier.

"We're not headed toward the sea, are we?" Aloê said to Ambrosia, and found with surprise she was talking to Hope instead.

"Which sea?" Hope asked.

"The Sea of Stones," Aloê replied.

"I don't think we're headed there anymore," said Ambrosia, suddenly sitting in the saddle where her sister had been a moment before. "I don't know where we're headed."

Aloê turned toward Morlock, riding glumly on the other side of her. "What's happening?" she asked.

"We are going north and east, no matter where we try to go," he said. "A kind of ur-path."

"Can you figure out how to get away from it?" she asked.

"The geometry is complicated," he said. "I've been thinking about it for many days."

"Morlock: we only left Merlin behind this morning."

"Time is part of it. I'm not even sure we are on the same path. Sometimes you seem so far away."

His voice sounded so desolate that she reached out to touch him. But when her hand came to where he had been, he wasn't there anymore. She dimly saw him riding alone, far ahead of her, his head bowed as if weary or discouraged. It was a cloudy afternoon where she was, but he was already wrapped in midnight, divided from her by more than a stretch of road. By the time night swept over her, she could see him no longer.

And it was a bitter bright morning now. The grass below her horse's hooves was dark blue, the individual stalks crunchy with a pale coating of frost. Ahead was a grim forest: the trees were a type she had never seen, with black twisting trunks and glossy blue leaves. The last thing in the world she wanted to do was enter the place. But that was where the ur-path, as Morlock called it, was leading her.

She dismounted when she reached the eaves on the forest. She turned right in the forlorn hope that she could choose her own path. He steps took her straight on into the blue shadows of the dim wintry wood.

Her horse died before she was very far in. (So it seemed. In the dense blue shadows of the wood, the passage of time was harder to track than ever.) The horse began to shudder and convulse, falling to its side and spewing up greenish froth dense with the stalks of blue grass. It died screaming in agony, its eyes extruding from their sockets, ringed with greenish foam.

Aloê was no Westholder, making a kind of religion out of horses and horse-craft, but even she was shocked and horrified by the beast's cruel death. But she told herself it was not a pointless death. The horse had clearly been poisoned by the blue grass; she would trust no food or water in this cruel wood. Not that she had felt hunger or thirst since she had started this long lonely road.

Presently she heard voices she thought she knew, filtering through the dense thickets of black branches and blue leaves. Sometimes they seemed to be ahead of her, sometimes behind her or on either side. She tried to reach them, but the path took her always in the direction that it would, never the one she wanted.

But in the end she came into a frosty blue clearing lit by the searing cold light of Trumpeter hovering on the eastern fringe of leaves. Arguing in the clearing were Morlock and Ambrosia.

"There is no point going forward," Morlock was saying. "We will just end up back here again."

"But we can't just stay here forever!" shouted the girl.

"Wherever you go," Aloê said, "don't go without me."

Morlock spun about, saw her, ran toward her, and seized her with his powerful arms. Through all this he did not say anything, nor needed to.

"You guys spend a lot of time on that," Ambrosia said, her voice about as chilly as the wintry air.

"Never enough," said Aloê breathlessly as Morlock reluctantly loosened his embrace. She hung on for a few moments after he relaxed, and did not let him go entirely. She could not escape the dread of that feeling when she reached out her hand and he was gone, already out of reach, lost in some private night of loneliness and despair. That must never happen again. It must never be like that between them. Never again.

"Something has changed, hasn't it?" she said, as they walked back to stand with Ambrosia in the middle of the clearing. "We are on the same path again."

"At the end of it," Morlock speculated. "Or near the end."

In the silence that followed they heard someone approaching through the frosted blue bracken with long confident strides.

It was Merlin. His white mantle was ragged and stained from long travel. His face fell as he saw them standing in the clearing.

"So you are still alive," he said. "I had hoped you would be dead by now."

"Sorry to disappoint you," snarled Ambrosia.

"It's nothing personal, my dear. But I calculated that, after a certain point in death, your blood will be useless as the basis of a locator spell for me, and I might use the concealment I have devised from the Two Powers. Since you were obviously set on a self-destructive course, I at least hoped to benefit from your deaths if I could not prevent them. You see that, don't you?"

"Gross," said his daughter.

"We are all four here," Aloê said. "You think it is possible we can move forward now?"

"What?" said the old wizard. "Are you trapped here? How many years has it been for you since we parted?"

"Nothing so long as a year," Morlock said.

"Hm. I thought I was going my own way, but obviously the Two Powers are waiting for us down every possible road."

"Yes," said his son. "Do you know how they do it?"

"Oh, now you are interested in what I have to say? Young fool. This is all your fault. No, I have no idea. If I did, I would not tell you. Knowledge is precious and rare and must be shared only with those worthy of it."

"Eh."

"Scintillating as always," the irritable old necromancer remarked. "Shall we put Aloê's suggestion to the test?"

Aloê tightened her arm around Morlock, and the four walked together into the bitter wintry wood.

The sun was waiting for them as they left the clearing, dappling the forest floor thinly between the dense clouds of dark blue leaves overhead. The day was scarcely warmer than the night had been.

"What is this place?" Aloê asked. "Are we even in the world anymore?"

"This is Tychar," Merlin said, "where the Two Powers have dwelt since the beginning of time, according to the Anhikh sorcerer-priests. If it seems unpleasant to you, let me assure you that it could be worse. The path we are on seems to be clear of the local wildlife, which is menacing beyond belief."

A cold glimmering mist was rising on either side of the path they walked. It rose high overhead, obscuring even the winter sun. Ambrosia reached out to touch it, curiously, and withdrew her hand with a cry of pain. For a moment, just one moment as the hand was in the glimmering fog, it seemed to be three or four hands.

"Don't do that," Merlin said curtly, and no one did thereafter.

The ground underfoot became rocky, dry, lacking even the venomous undergrowth of the blue wood.

A slope of dark rock appeared before them. Their path led around it, and around it again. It seemed to be changing shape as they moved.

Finally the slope disappeared and the mist sank away.

They were standing on a dark stone island surrounded by a lake of faintly glowing but utterly opaque fog.

On one side of the lake stood a throne of black and luminous white, and on it hovered rather than sat a presence of white and black lines in continuous motion.

Facing this, across the lake, was a matching throne—white for the first one's black, black for the first one's white. It, too, bore the weight of a presence: a spectral being of luminous white and black patches that faded in and out and shifted continually.

"Oh dear," said Merlin drily. "I think we've arrived."

You were always here/now since time/space began, thundered one of the presences. There was sound accompanying the meaning, but the symbols seemed to impose themselves directly on Aloê's mind.

Natural law, the conflict of our wills, required it, thundered the other.

Also, I preferred it this way, signified the first god, rather snidely Aloê thought.

Liar! I preferred it first, shouted the other.

At least you admit you are a liar. I therefore deduce your following statement a lie. Ha, ha, ha. You are rebuked.

You cannot rebuke me! Neither of us can rebuke the other. Further, I rebuked you first!

They went on and on like that, their angry bolts of meaning passing back and forth over the glowing lake, the dark island.

"Why are we here, I wonder?" Aloê asked.

Ambrosius is here because we hate him, one of the presences thundered. *I hated him first,* it added hastily.

But I hate him with greater efficiency and truth, the other Power thundered smugly.

It is our equal and opposite intent to understand Ambrose until he is destroyed, thundered a Power.

In fact, disputed the other, *we will destroy him until he is understood.*

That is in practice the same thing, and you are now being jejune, said the one Power.

No, said the other Power. *You are the jejune one. I have often remarked on it.*

And they hated each other back and forth for a long while.

Aloê thought glumly about the dream omens Jordel had told her about before she left the Wardlands: being sifted into different color sands, being dissected with a two-bladed knife. And: in a prison with no walls. That seemed to sum up her current position with ominous accuracy.

"How can such stupid beasts understand anything?" cried Ambrosia in torment, as the bolts of hate passed overhead.

We are not beasts, pointed out one of the Powers. *We are the Two Powers.*

Further, said the other Power, *we are not stupid. Zahkaar is stupid. I am wise with all the events that have been fated, are fated, and will be fated.*

Since no event is fated, Torlan is stupid and therefore Zahkaar is wise. Ha ha ha.

"So which is which?" Ambrosia asked, turning from one to the other.

"Stripes is Torlan; Patches is Zahkaar," Aloê murmured. "That's what it looks like, anyway."

I had patches before Zahkaar, thundered the striped Power with great dignity. *But they were unfitting to the Supreme Power of All.*

Supreme Power of all liars, thundered Zahkaar, and they were off again, casting talic bolts of fury back and forth, as the mortals between them were shaken by their hatred and their power.

And their stupidity. Aloê more and more realized that Ambrosia was right. They were powerful beyond belief, far mightier than any god she had encountered in her travels. But they were stupid as stones.

Time passed. Ambrosia fell into unconsciousness and awoke as Hope. Morlock was appalled at first, thinking that his sister was dying. Aloê explained the business as well as she could, with Merlin throwing in a few sullen words of correction.

She was aware of a certain sense of peace and balance as she spoke but didn't realize what it was at first. Then she knew: the Two Powers were no longer throwing hatred at each other. It was possible they were listening.

Merlin caught her eye and nodded. "Yes, there is some danger there," he said. "Whatever we say to each other becomes part of their knowledge."

This was disturbing and comforting. The Two Powers could not really be the cosmic entities they pretended to be, perhaps even thought they were, if they needed to eavesdrop on mortals. But they could not share knowledge and plans with each other without the Two Powers knowing of it.

Morlock and Hope were talking, tentatively, to each other. It was oddly moving, this first meeting of a brother and sister.

Time passed.

There was a stream of water on the island that ran down into the fog. The water was clear and free from poison. Their bodies were kept alive by the same sort of tal-infusion that Merlin had used in his cage-beasts. Aloê increasingly felt light and empty as a dried leaf, but not hungry nor any nearer death.

Time passed.

And they talked. They had to talk. There was nothing else to do, for one thing. For another, the Two Powers would often cease hurling their bolts of hate at each other and fall silent to listen. That silence of the gods was a great relief to the mortals. The worry that they were feeding information to the Powers was trivial by comparison. But Aloê began to wonder if the Two Powers were not very subtle, in fact. If they wanted to know something from the mortals they had captured, they had set up the perfect trap to get those mortals talking. But they never seemed to act on what they heard.

And the flow of information was not only one way. Once, when Morlock and Hope were discussing the Balancer, Morlock lifted his head and said, "Do the Two Powers know the Balancer?"

We know all, thundered Torlan. *Or at least I do.*

Zahkaar intoned, *All that is, or was, or ever shall be is but the shower of sparks from our blades locked in eternal combat.*

That, said Torlan, *is a stupid metaphor. Blades do not act like that.*

You're stupid. Blades acted like that in the endless un-time that preceded your intrusion into my being. They will act like that again in the un-begun un-time that awaits your dissolution.

You're the intruder!

"Then you do not know the Balancer?" Morlock asked. "He is but one spark among others in your conflict through time?"

We know the Balancer, Torlan thundered. *He is our servant in the world made by the conflict of our wills.*

I knew him first. I know him better.

Lies!

"Did he suggest you capture Ambrose?" asked Aloê. She thought she guessed what Morlock was getting at.

The idea was an artifact of natural law—

—the conflict of our wills.

It does not matter who had the idea.

Aloê translated that as a "yes," and so did Morlock (or so she guessed from the thoughtful look on his face).

Time passed. They engaged in various plans of attack or escape; at least, Aloê, Morlock, Hope, and Ambrosia did. Merlin sat aloof, almost as scornful as the Two Powers, speaking rarely and almost never of their situation.

Perhaps his scorn was justified. All of their attempts failed. The one weapon they had was Aloê's glass staff, but it's impulse wells were void of charge and could not be filled. They daydreamed catapults to hurl . . . something at the Two Powers, or extendable bridges to take them over the lake of burning fog. They daydreamed many things, but the dreams always sank on the rocks of reality. "If only we had this . . . If only we had that . . ." They had nothing but themselves. And it was not enough.

Merlin was particularly amused by the bridge plan. "Yes!" he said mockingly to Morlock. "If you could run across the top of the fog, perhaps you could punch one of the Two Powers. Perhaps even both of them. That would solve everything. Man of action!"

Morlock's gray eyes grew a bit wild. Aloê could not remember ever seeing him like that. He turned away without speaking.

Time passed.

A time came when Morlock said in a dry unemphatic tone of voice utterly at odds with the madness in his face, "I am going to walk through the fog."

"Young fool," Merlin muttered.

"If I get across, I may be able to—"

"If you get across, you may be able to leap to the paths of the three moons, or juggle the sun with your bare hands. You don't understand what the fog is. It is a talic zone projected by the Two Powers. Passing through it will strip the potentiality from your actuality until you are nothing. Then, my son, my proud man of action, you will be dead."

"I believe I can maintain the integrity of my identity indefinitely under the talic pressure of the fog. I will follow the path of the stream: it must come to some outlet below. If I can reach the other side of the fog—"

"You believe this because you want to believe it. Your *harven* father probably taught you that suicide is wrong, and this is the feeble pretext you give to your self-destruction."

"Old man," shouted Morlock furiously, "shut up!"

"No use in my talking, certainly. There would be some point in that only if there were someone to hear me."

Morlock turned away. He hugged his sister, who was Ambrosia at the moment, and kissed Aloê fiercely.

"I am sorry you were brought here," he whispered, "because of me."

"Get as far as you can," she said, "and then come back. The first try may not succeed. The last step, not the first, completes the journey."

He looked at her with those wild gray eyes and said, "Aloê, good-bye."

His father's suicide theory seemed more likely all the time, so she didn't say good-bye. She said, "Morlock, come back to me. Like some stupid fisher-man's stupid wife, I say it: come back to me."

He shrugged unhappily with his crooked shoulders, turned away, and walked downhill into the mist. Presently he was gone.

"We will all go that way, eventually, I suppose," Merlin remarked. "Just as boredom and frustration made us talk, boredom and frustration will send us into the mist. It is the only escape, the only refuge for us. But I have lived with death as a familiar enemy for many years, now; I am not so eager to rush into her arms."

Aloê and Ambrosia made no reply, but stood next to the stream and watched the spot where Morlock had vanished. Even the gods were silent. They waited.

>=<

As Morlock walked he summoned the lowest level of vision—not enough to prevent him from walking, but enough to exert some control over his talic self.

He was startled by the pain that emanated from the fog, like cold fiery claws or burning veins of poison. The ascent to vision usually precluded any feeling of physical pain.

But perhaps this was not physical pain. He felt himself to be less himself, and even less with each step he took. But he clenched the monochrome flames of his talic identity like fingers and struggled onward.

He followed the course of the stream through the glowing fog. It grew wider, deeper, stronger, louder. The thunder of its waters rang in his ears. He hoped that meant this pain he was in would end someday. He no longer remembered what was causing the pain, but hoped if he could pass through it he would leave all shame and fear behind.

A woman with many faces but one single mouth approached him, looked at him curiously with an improbable number of eyes, and passed onward in the mist.

Pain. Time. Mist. Long slow footfalls.

The river ran downhill into a valley. On each side of the river were level meadows. And on one side of the river he saw a flock of white sheep, and on the other a flock of black sheep. And whenever one of the white sheep bleated, one of the black sheep would cross over and become white; and when one of the black sheep bleated, one of the white sheep would cross over and become black. And he saw a tall tree by the side of the river, one half of which was in flames bright as wrath from the root to the top, and the other half was green and in full leaf. Nearby he saw a young man sitting upon a mound, and two hounds (long and thin like knife blades) in leashes lying by his side.

The young man was playing a lute in a piece of sunlight that somehow fell through the mist. His shoulders were crooked as Morlock's own. The youth's face was long and snouted, and covered with gray scales like metallic plates, and his eyes were red.

"Who are you?" Morlock asked. "Why are you here? Will the pain end soon?"

"I am here because you are here," said the youth, putting down his lute and giving Morlock a sharp red glance. "I am Ambrose the Ancient, the founder of your house . . . or as much of him as remains in you. You may not be here much longer yourself, though, if you are seeing me. You are in some zone of dispersal that is separating what you are from what you might be. When that process is complete, you will be no more."

"Will the pain stop then?"

"I don't know. In time I must have died, I suppose, but your life meets mine at an earlier point, when I would have scorned the release of death. Go back, Ambrosius. Escape the fog and live. You never know what may happen, eh?"

"Sometimes you know."

"Then you are wiser than I, and don't need my advice." The gray youth took up the lute and began to play again.

Morlock turned away from the music and struggled uphill alongside the river. He could no longer remember what he was doing or why. But he remembered that someone had said something to him about footsteps, so he kept on taking them.

They did not make the pain stop, though. Nothing did. Soon there was no memory of words, no footsteps, nothing but the fog, and the pain, and the sound of someone screaming far away.

⇒⇐

When they heard Morlock screaming, Ambrosia leaped forward to go after him, but Aloê grabbed her. "Wait!" she said.

"One of us has to go!" Ambrosia shouted. "And he's my brother! You're just his bimbo!"

"Shut your foul mouth and listen. Hook my belt to your belt. Maybe I can pull you back if—"

"Right! Right! I'm sorry, I just—"

"Shut up and go."

Merlin was there also. As his daughter passed into the mist he hooked his belt onto Aloê's, then shed his white (well, whitish) cloak and tied it to the end of the belt.

Now Ambrosia started to scream also—and, horribly, Hope's voice could also be heard. Aloê and Merlin pulled on the white robe like sailors hauling up an anchor. Through the mist two monstrous figures could be discerned: a two-headed screaming woman and something manlike, bristling with arms and legs like a troll.

But as they emerged from the mist they were merely Morlock and Ambrosia, their eyes wild and mindless. Merlin tended to Ambrosia (who fell to the ground like a stone), while Aloê led Morlock's staggering steps to the other side of the island.

><

There came a time when Morlock was himself again, and the pain of life receded a bit. He hoped he was on the other side of the mist, but when he opened his eyes he saw that Aloê was sitting beside him.

"Didn't make it," he croaked. His throat was sore for some reason.

"No, sweetheart."

"How far'd I get?"

"Hard to say. Not far. Ten or fifteen steps."

"Oh."

He had failed. They were doomed. And, however it had happened to him, he was the one who had done this to her. Aloê would be alive and facing the future back in the Wardlands if it were not for him. That dark thought accompanied him all the way down the long slope to unconsciousness.

CHAPTER TWENTY-SEVEN

Supple Confusions

Morlock was not eager to return to awareness, but when he did it was not so bad. Aloê and Merlin were talking in quiet voices of some place in the southern islands that they both knew. Ambrosia was playing a board game against herself, using scratches on a flat rock for a board and pebbles for pieces. He went and sat down across from her and they played the game for a while, speaking rarely, absorbed in the game.

Later he walked with Aloê around the island's edge. They spoke in hushed voices of the last time they had made love, and the island of Old Azh. She told him of the strange dog people who lived under the island and the strange not-living thing that tended to them . . . or had done so, before the Two Powers destroyed all that. Evidently Merlin had witnessed the devastation, but Morlock did not wish to speak to the old man.

The gods were mostly silent, perhaps because they were listening. That was Aloê's and Merlin's thought, but Morlock was not so sure. It was more as if they were running down. . . .

In the quiet calm that comes from accepting failure, Morlock suddenly saw something he had not before. He took things he knew and fitted them together like the parts of a puzzle, of a machine, of a broken statue. The face was lost in splinters and atoms but still, it was there, if he could find the right pattern. And when he found it, he saw the solution smiling at him.

"I know what to do," he said, loud enough so that the others could hear him.

They all looked at him: his father, his sister (who was Hope at the moment), and his beloved.

"What is it, honey?" said Aloê, her glorious golden eyes wet with pity.

He examined his solution and it was sound.

"I can't tell you," he said, and turned away from them all with some satisfaction. He had work to do. At last, he had work to do.

In Merlin's often-expressed opinion, Morlock had gone mad. The younger maker used Aloê's glass staff to break off pieces of rock from the island surface, and then he spent endless time using the rock to work on other pieces of rock.

"Madness and suicide are the two common afflictions of long-term prisoners," Merlin remarked, and proceeded to tell stories of jails he had known.

Aloê was not sure he was wrong. But when she looked at Morlock, she saw none of the wild-eyed recklessness that had driven him into the lake of mist. He worked calmly, carefully, swiftly (given his materials).

What he made, in the end, was nothing extraordinary, although he displayed it to the others with a considerable amount of satisfaction. It was simply a perpetual motion machine—a small hand-sized version of the ones attached to impulse wheels all over the Wardlands.

There were two wheels of intermeshing gears on armatures. The one wheel drove the other, and the other drove the first. Given the materials he had to work with, the transfer of momentum was not perfect, and he occasionally had to tap one wheel or the other to keep the gears meshing.

"And this is your great solution?" Merlin burst out at last. "This is your weapon against the mightiest beings in Laent? Shall we make an army of these little things and send them on wheels to topple the two thrones—is that what you propose?"

"This is not a weapon, no," Morlock said. "It is really a statement of the problem." He tapped one of the gears and remarked, "Torlan is greater than Zahkaar. This much is clear."

This doomful truth even Ambrosius sees, thundered Torlan, the symbols freighted with hate for Zahkaar.

A god who grovels for the opinion of mortals is no god, replied Zahkaar. *It is because I am greater that they do not see it.*

There is one thing to see in you: an inferior god.

You are inferior, as I shall prove at Time's end.

The talic bolts of hate flew back and forth over the mortals' heads for some time, and eventually stopped.

Morlock had ceased to tap the gears of his little machine, and they also ground to a halt.

The cold light of an unsuspected idea flooded Aloê's mind.

Merlin stepped toward his son and faced him over the motionless stone toy. The old man's hands were trembling. He flicked one of the gears and shouted, "Only Zahkaar is real! Fate and its idiot-child time are but the dreams of Chaos! Soon he will awake and sweep all away in his fury!"

Zahkaar roared on his throne. *Vile Torlan, even Ambrosius sees my glory! Surrender your futile struggle and forget your useless hate! In the end as in the beginning, I must triumph!*

You, raged Torlan, *are inconsistent and inept! When Ambrosius spoke for me you were void of belief. Now you deign to sniff after the opinions of a mortal. No true god would do thus, and you have done it, therefore you are no true god. You are rebuked.*

Zahkaar thundered snidely, *You did it first, therefore you rebuke yourself by your own logic. Ha ha ha.*

You did it first! You always do everything first!

Thank you. I accept your praise and surrender. I am First, and you are Nothing.

I am First and you are Nothing! I hate you! I hate you!

I hated you before you existed.

My hatred called your being into existence.

Meanwhile, Merlin was staring at Morlock, who bore it calmly. The younger maker looked at Aloê and Ambrosia.

It was clear that Morlock could not speak his idea aloud, lest it become part of the Powers' knowledge. But Aloê was sure that she understood. Morlock was proposing that the Two Powers were not gods at all . . . or at least not living beings. There were machines—or, better, two gears of a single machine that drove each other into motion.

Who had made them? Why? The first was easy enough to guess: the Balancer. The why was harder to figure out. Perhaps it mattered less, just now.

She met Morlock's eye and nodded pointedly. Ambrosia's sudden laughter was also an obvious acknowledgement.

Merlin snapped his fingers under Morlock's nose to get his attention. Then he took a corner of his ragged weather-stained cloak and dropped it down between the gears. They slowed, stopped.

Merlin glared at his son. Morlock shrugged and nodded.

The cloak, Aloê mused. What was the cloak?

Merlin's cloak was . . . *Merlin's cloak*. He had always claimed he had a method to hide from the Two Powers. Could it be used as a method to conceal the Two Powers from each other? And if it did would they simply . . . stop?

Aloê met Ambrosia's eye. The girl was laughing so hard she was crying.

"And that is all?" Merlin was saying to his son. "No word of apology? No sign of respect for the old man you despise?"

"I am sorry," said the younger man calmly, "and I do not despise you."

Aloê looked at the father and son, so similar and so different. In this foggy hell, Merlin was concerned about his own ego. And Morlock—he never was. She almost wished he were. But she had to admit, in this deadly moment, his calm and self-control were a strength greater than the ability to throw a lightning bolt or two.

Merlin was staring at him, breathing heavily. "No," he said theatrically. "No, that is not good enough. You, and your god of Fate, and all the world will be swept away when I give Zahkaar the victory!"

He sprang at Morlock, wrapping his long fingers around his son's neck, screaming incoherent abuse. The two men fell struggling to the ground.

Ambrosia and Aloê ran over to separate them. Ambrosia was rolling her eyes as she did so, a cue Aloê hoped was opaque to the Two Powers. She herself thought Merlin was pretending too hard, but guessed that the Two Powers weren't subtle enough to notice it.

Aloê dragged Morlock to one side of the island while Merlin and Ambrosia went to the other.

Aloê glared a question, asking him as hard as she could without speaking, *Did you get it?*

Morlock shrugged, a gesture that Aloê translated as, *Eh*. That was the best clue she could hope for, probably.

"Great Torlan!" she shouted. "We bring you a message from the Balancer. It is urgent that it comes to you alone. Bring us over to your throne, if you would."

Abruptly, Morlock and Aloê were standing beside the black-and-white presence on the white-and-black throne.

"I was with the Balancer at the time he died," Aloê said hurriedly, not allowing herself to be disoriented. "He told us that time would soon end and his purpose was gone. But he gave us a secret that will ensure your victory over the Other Power."

Tell me, thundered the god.

"If I tell you, I tell him," pointed out Aloê. "We must conceal ourselves from the Enemy Power. My colleague must weave a magic called the, uh, the—"

"Final Shroud," suggested Morlock.

"—the Final Shroud about you. And then we can tell you what we have come to tell you."

Do so, said Torlan, and emitted talic gusts of amusement at Zahkaar's expense.

Morlock went into deep vision, and Aloê followed. As her coppery talic avatar stood beside his monochrome one, she watched him weave a talic pattern of reflection about the self-styled Power of Fate. It was like a talic mirror, where the Power could see nothing but itself. The Power's own talic force was used to blind the Power to anything else.

Once Aloê caught the mental knack of what Morlock was doing, she joined in and helped him. Soon they had Torlan completely cocooned in the talic mirror.

So this is victory, mused Torlan, in talic symbols that reverberated and re-echoed like thunder in a narrow canyon. *I see nothing but myself . . . except for you two.*

Morlock dropped out of vision and was gone. Aloê found it more difficult to find her way back to her body, but the sense that Torlan's entire malefic attention had focused on her was a great encouragement. Eventually, she opened her eyes to see Morlock's concerned face hovering over her.

"Did we do it?" she asked.

For answer, he waved at the black-and-white throne. It was empty. Across a great gulf, she saw Ambrosia and Merlin dancing around a white-and-black throne that was equally empty.

It was true, then. The Two Powers were merely two parts of a talic machine. Without the driving hate of the other part, each became void.

And the glowing fog was gone.

Hand in hand, Morlock and Aloê ran down the black-and-white steps into the wide dead space where the killing mist had been. They met Merlin and Ambrosia at the stream and embraced, laughing.

"Well, Guardians," said Merlin wryly. "When you tell this tale to the Graith, don't forget to remind them that the Two Powers were defeated by old exiled Ambrosius."

Aloê nearly replied furiously—she didn't know what, exactly. But the old man's amused look stopped her. If he said these things to be annoying, perhaps it was better to not be annoyed.

"They were right to fear us," said Morlock, looking at the empty thrones.

The old man clapped him on the lower of his shoulders and didn't speak.

"I guess you'll be going back to the Wardlands, then," Ambrosia said glumly.

They *would* be going back to the Wardlands, then . . . a fact that Aloê had only just begun to accept in her heart. They would not die, on that dark rock, in that prison without walls, while idiot-gods clamored above them. They could go home.

"Yes, honey," Aloê said. "Right away, in fact."

"I suppose it's against the rules to hear from your exiled sisters sometimes," Ambrosia went on, giving Morlock a sidelong look.

Aloê was trying to figure out a diplomatic way of saying yes when Morlock surprised her by saying, "No. There are no rules, except what maintains the Guard. Let me hear from you. From you both," he added hesitantly. She gave him a brief glare, a longer grin.

"Well, good fortune to you, Guardians," Merlin said. "I say it to you and no others of your Graith. For myself, I think I will see if I can take apart one or both of those talic devices we thought were gods. The remains should be instructive." He nodded and turned away.

"I'd better stick around for that," Ambrosia said. "If *he* knows something, *we* should know it."

"Agreed," said Morlock, and hugged her good-bye.

The angry girl, blinking back tears, waved at Aloê and ran to catch up with her father. They were quarrelling about something before the Guardians were out of earshot.

Aloê took Morlock's hand, and they walked away together under the dark blue eaves of Tychar. They were alone, and weaponless, entering the deadliest place in the world in the jaws of winter.

But they were happy there, and all through the long bitter road home.

APPENDICES

THE LANDS OF LAENT DURING THE ONTILIAN INTERREGNUM

Laent is a flat or shield-shaped land-mass bordered by ocean to the west and south and empty space to the east; north of Laent is a region of uninhabitable cold; south of Laent is a large and largely unexplored continent, Qajqapca. Beyond that is believed to be an impassable zone of fire.

Along the western edge of Laent lies the Wardlands, a highly developed but secretive culture. It has no government, as such, but its borders are protected by a small band of seers and warriors called the Graith of Guardians.

Dividing Laent into two unequal halves, north and south, are a pair of mountain ranges: the Whitethorn Range (running from the Western Ocean eastward) and the Blackthorn Range (running from the Eastern Edge westward). There is a pass between the two mountain ranges, the Dolich Kund (later the Kirach Kund). North of the Dolich Kund there are only two human cities of any note, Narkunden and Aflraun. The rest of the north is a heavily wooded and mountainous region, inhabited by humans and others of a more or less fabulous nature (e.g., the werewolf city of Wuruyaaria).

The Whitethorn Range, by custom, forms the northern border of the Wardlands. The Blackthorn Range is divided between the untamed dragons and the Heidhhaiar (Deep Kingdoms) of the dwarves.

Immediately south of the Whitethorn Range was the wreckage of the old Empire of Ontil, ruined by its rulers' ambitions, ineptitude and misused powers. A period of general chaos and more-or-less continuous warfare obtained in these lands until the advent of the Vraidish tribes and the rise of the Second Empire of Ontil (some generations after the present story).

South of the former Empire of Ontil lay the so-called Kingdom of Kaen. The ancient cities of the Kaeniar considered themselves at perpetual war with the Wardlands, which lay just across the Narrow Sea. The Wardlands, however, took little notice of the Kaeniar, or any other domain of the unguarded lands.

The region between the Grartan Mountains and the Whitethorns was called the Gap of Lone by inhabitants of the unguarded lands. Inhabitants of (and exiles from) the Wardlands called it "the Maze," because of the magical protections placed on it.

Immediately south of the Blackthorns was a wooded region of extremely poor repute, Tychar. Farther south was the Anhikh Kômos of Cities, Ontil's great rival who unaccountably failed to take advantage of Ontil's fall to extend its domains. The largest Anhikh city, where the Kômarkh lives, is Vakhnhal, along the southern coast of Laent. Anhi may or may not extend its domain to the Eastern Edge of the world—accounts differ.

THE GODS OF LAENT

There was no universally accepted religious belief, except in Anhi, where the government enforces the worship of Torlan and Zahkaar (Fate and Chaos).

In Ontil an eclectic set of gods are worshipped or not worshipped, especially (under the influence of Coranian exiles from the Wardlands) the Strange Gods, including Death, Justice, Peace, Misery, Love, and Memory.

In Kaen, each city and many places in the country have at least one local god, whose priesthood serves as one of the two branches of government (the other being the military and civil power of the tirgans). There is, at least in theory, a higher rank of national gods, and an upper echelon of universal gods, although their actual existence has been disputed by a significant minority of Kaenish heresiarchs.

In the Wardlands at least three gods, or three aspects of one god, are worshipped: the Creator, the Sustainer, and the Avenger ("Creator, Keeper, and King").

The dwarves of the Wardlands evidently assent to these beliefs. (At any rate, they have been known to swear by these deities.) But they have another, perhaps an older, belief in immortal ancestor spirits who watch the world and judge it beyond the western edge of the world. The spirits of the virtuous dead collect in the west through the day and night, and pass through at the moment of dawn, when the sun enters the world and the gate in the west is opened. Spirits of the evil dead, or spirits that have been bound in some way, may not pass through the gate in the west. Hence, dwarves each day (at sunrise, or when they awake) praise the rising of the sun and the passage of the good ghosts to Those-Who-Watch in the west.

APPENDIX C

CALENDAR AND ASTRONOMY

1. *Astronomical Remarks*

The sky of Laent has three moons: Chariot, Horseman, and Trumpeter (in descending order of size).

The year has 375 days. The months are marked by the rising or setting of the second moon, Horseman. So that, if Horseman sets on the first day of Bayring, the penultimate month, it rises again on the first of Borderer, the last month. It sets after sunset on the first day of Cymbals, the first month of the new year. All three moons set simultaneously on this occasion. The number of months are uneven—15—so that Horseman rises or sets on the first morning of the year in alternating years. Years where Horseman sets on the first day of the Cymbals are, idiomatically, "bright years"; those where Horseman sets with Trumpeter and Chariot on 1 Cymbals are known as "dark years."

The period of Chariot (the largest moon, whose rising and setting marks the seasons) is 187.5 days. (So: a season is 93.75 days.)

The period of Horseman is 50 days.

The period of Trumpeter is 15 days. A half-cycle of Trumpeter is a "call." Calls are either "bright" or "dark" depending on whether Trumpeter is aloft or not. (Usage: "He doesn't expect to be back until next bright call.")

The seasons are not irregular, as on Earth. But the moons' motion is not uniform through the sky: motion is faster near the horizons, slowest at zenith. Astronomical objects are brighter in the west, dimmer in the east.

The three moons and the sun rise in the west and set in the east. The stars have a different motion entirely, rotating NWSE around a celestial pole. The pole points at a different constellation among a group of seven (the polar constellations) each year. (Hence, a different group of nonpolar constellations is visible near the horizons each year.) This seven-year cycle (the Ring) is the basis for dating, with individual years within it named for their particular polar constellations.

The polar constellations are the Reaper, the Ship, the Hunter, the Door, the Kneeling Man, the River, the Wolf.

There is an intrapolar constellation, the Hands, within the space inscribed by the motion of the pole.

≫⋘

In the Wardlands, years are dated from the founding of New Moorhope, the center of learning. According to Professor Gabriel McNally, the "year of fire," when the Guile of Masters invaded the Wardlands, was New Moorhope 2748, Year of the Hunter, in Ring 394—a "bright year." The year following was N.M. 2749, Year of the Door, Ring 394, a "dark year." The conflict between the Two Powers and the Ambrosii are harder to date specifically, but Dr. McNally tentatively concludes it was a "dark" year, late in Ring 394.

The reader should know that Dr. McNally's views have been disputed, especially by Julian Emrys, grandson of the eminent Ambrosian scholar H. N. Emrys. Julian Emrys' own early reputation as a scholar was gradually obliterated by his bizarre claims to be one of "those-who-know" and (in his own words) "the last descendant of the ancient Ambrosian kings on Earth." But, as Dr. McNally conceded, in his fair-minded if blistering review of Emrys' *New Evidence of the Old Ambrosians*, "the fact that Mr. Emrys is crazy does not necessarily imply he is in error."

In any case, settling on a definite date for these events is a little like trying to decide in what year young Sigurd slew his dragon or old Beowulf faced his.

≫⋘

2. A *"bright year"* and a *"dark year"*

Bright:

1. *Cymbals.*

> New Year. Winter begins.
> 1st: Chariot & Trumpeter set. Horseman rises.
> 8th & 23rd: Trumpeter rises.

2. *Jaric.*

> 1st: Horseman sets. 13th: Trumpeter rises.

3. *Brenting.*

> 1st: Horseman rises. 3rd & 18th: Trumpeter rises.

4. *Drums.*

> 1st: Horseman sets. 8th & 23rd: Trumpeter rises.
> Midnight of 94th day of the year (19 Drums):
> Chariot rises. Spring begins.

5. *Rain.*

> 1st: Horseman rises. 13th: Trumpeter rises.

6. *Marrying.*

> 1st: Horseman sets. 3rd & 18th: Trumpeter rises.

7. *Ambrose.*

> 1st: Horseman rises. 8th and 23rd: Trumpeter rises.

8. *Harps.*

> 1st: Horseman sets.13th: Trumpeter rises.
> Evening of the 188th day of year (19 Harps):
> Chariot sets; Midyear—Summer begins.

9. *Tohrt.*

> 1st: Horseman rises. 3rd & 18th: Trumpeter rises.

10. *Remembering.*

> 1st: Horseman sets. 8th & 23rd: Trumpeter rises.

11. *Victory.*

> 1st: Horseman rises.13th: Trumpeter rises.

12. *Harvesting.*

> 1st: Horseman sets. 3rd & 18th: Trumpeter rises.
> 6th: Chariot rises, noon of 281st day of year. Fall begins.

13. *Mother and Maiden.*

> 1st: Horseman rises. 8th & 23rd: Trumpeter rises.

14. *Bayring.*

> 1st: Horseman sets. 13th: Trumpeter rises.

15. *Borderer.*

> 1st: Horseman rises. 3rd & 18th: Trumpeter rises.

Dark:

1. *Cymbals.*

> New Year. Winter begins.
> 1st: Chariot, Horseman, & Trumpeter all set.
> 8th & 23rd: Trumpeter rises.

2. *Jaric.*

> 1st: Horseman rises. 13th: Trumpeter rises.

3. *Brenting.*

> 1st: Horseman sets. 3rd & 18th: Trumpeter rises.

4. *Drums.*

> 1st: Horseman rises. 8th & 23rd: Trumpeter rises.
> Midnight of 94th day of the year (19 Drums):
> Chariot rises. Spring begins.

5. *Rain.*

> 1st: Horseman sets. 13th: Trumpeter rises.

6. *Marrying.*

> 1st: Horseman rises. 3rd & 18th: Trumpeter rises.

7. *Ambrose.*

> 1st: Horseman sets. 8th and 23rd: Trumpeter rises.

8. *Harps.*

   1st: Horseman rises.13th: Trumpeter rises.
   Evening of the 188th day of year (19 Harps):
   Chariot sets; Midyear—Summer begins.

9. *Tohrt.*

   1st: Horseman sets. 3rd & 18th: Trumpeter rises.

10. *Remembering.*

   1st: Horseman rises. 8th & 23rd: Trumpeter rises.

11. *Victory.*

   1st: Horseman sets.13th: Trumpeter rises.

12. *Harvesting.*

   1st: Horseman rises. 3rd & 18th: Trumpeter rises.
   6th: Chariot rises, noon of 281st day of year. Fall begins.

13. *Mother and Maiden.*

   1st: Horseman sets. 8th & 23rd: Trumpeter rises.

14. *Bayring.*

   1st: Horseman rises. 13th: Trumpeter rises.

15. *Borderer.*

   1st: Horseman sets. 3rd & 18th: Trumpeter rises.

THE WARDLANDS AND THE GRAITH OF GUARDIANS

According to Gabriel McNally's reconstruction (generally accepted by scholars of Ambrosian legend, always excepting Julian Emrys), the Wardlands were an anarchy with no formal government at all. According to legend, the Wardlands had not been a kingdom since the golden age at the beginning of time, when the King (usually identified with the divine aspect known as God Avenger) ruled in person in Laent and elsewhere. Since then it has been considered blasphemous, or at least irrationally presumptuous, for any person to assert a claim to rule the Wardlands. Those who try to do so are exiled or (in extreme cases) killed.

What in other cultures would have been state functions (national defense, dispute resolution, even road-building and repair, etc.) were carried on by voluntary cooperatives: the Arbiters of the Peace, the Guild of Silent Men, the League of Rhetors, etc. Most famous in the unguarded lands was the Graith of Guardians, sworn to maintain the guard.

The Graith had three ranks of Guardian: the lowest and most numerous were the thains, wearing a gray cape of office. They were hardly more than candidates to the Graith proper, and they undertook to obey their seniors in the Graith, even more senior thains.

Vocates, in contrast, were full members of the Graith, privileged to stand and speak at the Graith's councils (known as Stations). Their only obligation was to defend the Guard, and the Guarded, as they saw fit. Their cloak of office was bloodred.

Most senior in the Graith were the Three Summoners. They had no power to command but were generally conceded the authority to lead the vocates of the Graith proper. The Summoner of the City convened and presided over Stations of the Graith. The Summoner of the Outer Lands was charged with watching for threats to the Guard from the unguarded lands. The Summoner of the Inner Lands was charged with watching for internal threats: those who would try to disrupt the fertile anarchy of the Wardlands and establish the sterility of political order.

The greatest danger to the anarchy of the Wardlands was obviously the Graith itself. Members of the Graith were pledged to abide by the First Decree, which forbade any acquisition of power or authority over those under the Guard. Nevertheless, Guardians were exiled more often than the Guarded for political aspirations to government (euphemistically referred to as "impairment of the Guard"). Power corrupts, and the Guardians wielded power more often than their peers among the Guarded.

NOTE ON AMBROSIAN LEGENDS

Dorothy L. Sayers subtitled *Busman's Honeymoon* "A love story with detective interruptions," and I was almost inclined to follow her lead and call this book "a love story with sword-and-sorcery interruptions." But there are only so many subtitles a book or a reader can stand, so I thought better of it in the end.

The subtitle was the least of my worries. Accounts of the ill-fated love business between Morlock and Aloê are among the most diverse and problematic source-material in the Ambrosian legends. There are scraps of Khroic *ekshal* concerning it. They have a certain entertainment value, as the Khroic poet-seers tried to wrap their pyramidal heads around a love story involving a very different biology from their own. Von Brauch devotes a portion of the *Gray Book* to a tediously Arthurian rendition of it: here we see Morlock as a crooked knight errant clanking about in plate armor while Aloê is a pink-skinned wimpled nonentity who is always getting kidnapped by giants, for reasons never made entirely clear. The Dwarvish hero-songs, when they depict Aloê, make her into a wingless harpy, a vicious and insensate monster comparable to the Signy of the *Volsunga Saga*. Anti-Ambrosian satire from the late Ontilian Empire makes Aloê a tragic figure—heroic in some respects, but fatally influenced by the fell shadow of the Ambrosii.

There were probably always at least two versions of the story, Morlock's and Aloê's. I have tried to do them both justice here, piecing together a plot from stories which, candidly, are completely incompatible with each other.

My task was made easier by Julian Emrys' translation of *The Life of Blĵdhwocax*, a Kaenish hagiography about the heresiarch who unified the

Kaenish local religions, a crusade that began in or about the 395th Ring (as counted in the Wardlands).

Some readers may be interested in consulting this work for Blÿdhwocax's groundbreaking theory that orthodoxy is the ultimate heresy in a society that values religious dissent. Others may prefer reading about the religious persecutions his theory enabled (though they have a bloody sameness about them, after the first two or three). My own interest was strictly in the backstory: frequently Blÿdhwocax's mission took him to cities that were still in turmoil from Morlock and Aloê's passage, and the local accounts provided some useful material for my plot.

The dubious document known in the field as "Danadhar's credo of the unfaith" also yielded some key details. It's true that Dr. Gabriel McNally considers the work a forgery written (in McNally's acid phrase) "in entirely peccable Dwarvish." But I'm hoping that someone who knows enough about Laent to forge an entire document in Dwarvish (however peccably) might also know something about Morlock and his kith. And I confess I'm convinced by the argument of Danadhar (or pseudo-Danadhar) that the Gray Folk and the Ambrosians must have a common ancestry.

About the Author

James Enge lives with his wife in northwest Ohio, where he teaches classical languages and literature at a medium-sized public university. His first novel for Pyr, *Blood of Ambrose*, was nominated for the World Fantasy Award in 2010. He is also the author of *This Crooked Way*, *The Wolf Age*, and *A Guile of Dragons*, as well as a number of shorter fictions (most, but not all, focusing on Morlock Ambrosius). He appears infrequently on Twitter (as "jamesenge") and more frequently on Facebook (as "james.enge"). His website is cunningly named jamesenge.com.